Photo credit Karla Zens

Matt Stewart made headlines worldwide when he released *The French Revolution* via Twitter on Bastille Day 2009. (Rest assured, the version in your hand is significantly easier to read.) His short stories have appeared in *Instant City*, *McSweeney's*, and *Opium Magazine*, among other venues, and, when the moonlight strikes just right across the alpine lake in his mind, he's been known to blog for *The Huffington Post*. *The French Revolution* is his first novel. For more on Matt's adventures, visit www.matt-stewart.com.

THE
FRENCH
REVOLUTION

THE FRENCH REVOLUTION

MATT STEWART

SOFT SKULL PRESS
NEW YORK

Library of Congress Cataloging-in-Publication Data
Stewart, Matt.
    The French revolution : a novel / Matt Stewart
        p.cm.
    ISBN 978-1-59376-283-4 (alk. paper)
    1. Dysfuntional families—Fiction. 2. San Francisco (Calif.)—Fiction. I. Title.
    PS3619.T4968F74 2010
    813'.6—dc22

                                    2010004018

Cover design by Goodloe Byron
Interior design by Neuwirth Associates
Printed in the United States of America

Soft Skull Press
An Imprint of Counterpoint LLC
2117 Fourth Street
Suite D
Berkeley, CA 94710

www.softskull.com
www.counterpointpress.com

Distributed by Publishers Group West

10 9 8 7 6 5 4 3 2 1

For Karla

REVOLUTIONIZE
YOUR iPHONE

DEAR READER:

You hold in your hands the enhanced electronic edition of

• THE FRENCH REVOLUTION •

Seriously.

While this may seem like a standard-issue book format, much more chortles beneath the surface.

Via the French Rev iPhone app, zapping any page in the book with your iPhone's camera will whisk you away to a magical wonderland of bonus videos, secret chapters, author interviews, mouthwatering recipes, and oodles more.

Where any single zap will take you is ever-changing and anyone's guess, but if you were partial to a good Choose Your Own Adventure book as a kid, you're gonna love this.

If you decide to take the bait, go to www.matt-stewart.com or search for the French Rev app in the App Store—then zap this page to get started.

If you decide to continue reading, turn to page 1.

THE FRENCH REVOLUTION

BASTILLE DAY

The troops with few exceptions abandoned the King; and when, with scarcely any serious resistance, the Bastille was captured on the 14th, and the head of its murdered governor carried by a triumphant procession through the streets, the Revolution may be said to have definitely triumphed. Power had now passed both from the King and from the Assembly into the hands of a mob.

—WILLIAM LECKEY,
A History of England in the Eighteenth Century

Vanity made the Revolution; liberty was only a pretext.
—NAPOLEON BONAPARTE

On any given day in 1989, Esmerelda Van Twinkle was far and away the heaviest person to pass through the doors of the Copy-Smart flagship store on Market Street. Her arrival was announced to fellow CopySmart personnel by caustic electronic beeps generated by the special services van that ferried Esmerelda to work, followed by crunches from the van's hydraulic lift and Esmerelda's squeezed-up voice cursing at the driver, complaining that she was descending too fast, or too slow, or too unevenly, until the lift smacked against the curb with a screeching *thomp*. Esmerelda was on her own for the hike across the sidewalk, and she advanced in an uneasy shamble, the permanent bun containing her once-silky chestnut hair bobbing like a buoy in a tsunami, her balance disrupted by a quarter ton of flesh and thirty pounds of clothing and a cavernous wool bag over her shoulder stocked with emergency ham, distilled water, beef jerky, hard candy, cheese, ginger cookies, leftover pasta, pizza crusts, chocolate bars, a six-pack of apple juice, jewel-encrusted scissors, newspaper clippings, disposable handiwipes, an icing knife, breath mints, flip-flops, an industrial-strength hairbrush, deodorizing spray, herbal antinausea pills, coupons, and other assorted goodies that might be required at a moment's notice. Her double-shafted walker lurched forward in gulps as she plowed through the morning urban bustle, her gumdrop-shaped body quivering like a landed bass.

Any sign of weakness was an illusion, however, for years on the walker had built up considerable muscle tissue closer to the bone, a lining which would remain unseen until revolutionary weight-loss forces stormed her ramparts in the decades to come. In the meantime, Esmerelda considered the slog to and from the special services van to be her daily workout regimen, and she maximized her exercise quotient by performing dips on her walker: letting her mass fall perilously close to the sidewalk, then clenching her triceps, halting her body, tucking up her legs, and swinging forward in a herky-jerk motion that was marginally under control. Back when the City of San Francisco had been willing to provide her only a single-shafted walker, this makeshift exercise routine had resulted in several slow-mo tumbles, torn muumuus, bruised body parts, and shattered walkers, which Esmerelda had documented through driver affidavits and studio photography and statistical analysis and presented to the director of special services and his immediate superior in bound biweekly reports. These strongly worded digests cultivated rabid support among the City Hall rank and file and swiftly goaded the department into providing Esmerelda the pricier yet sturdier double-shafted walker she was using in the fall of 1989.

Esmerelda's self-propelled voyage ended twelve feet, or eight dips, later, at the CopySmart entrance, an automatic double-doored gateway installed back when Esmerelda pole-vaulted over the 350-pound mark and threatened Slippy Sanders with a strike unless he put in doors she could fit through without catching on the frame. But even with room to operate, as well as four high-friction rubber leg cappers that were replaced on a monthly basis, Esmerelda never took her walker into the store, as she was convinced that slipping on the freshly waxed tile floor was only a matter of time. Her face, seven chinned and shaped like a lima bean, reset; her minute eyeballs, pinprick nose, and paperclip mouth contorted for her first words of the working day.

"Chair!" she called, ringing the bell affixed to her walker with gusto. "Chair! Chair!"

Lakshmi appeared with the Gargantuan. A bandana was tied around her face, but it was doing a poor job of muffling her labored breathing.

"Turning!" Esmerelda announced. She shuffled clockwise, swiveling the walker across the entrance as Lakshmi wheeled the Gargantuan into position. When Lakshmi grunted her readiness, Esmerelda thrust out her pumpkin-shaped hindquarters and slowly bent at the knees. It was a real balancing act: gravity demanded a rapid descent, but if she let her rear down without careful aim she could very well miss the seat and crash to the floor, absorbing multiple injuries and adding another millimeter of give to the building's sagging foundation. Yet drawing out the sitting process dropped a veil of fatigue that disrupted operations in her pachyderm legs, causing her to miss the Gargantuan entirely, with similar unpleasant floor-smacking and structural consequences, or to hit the seat spot-on at a force capable of slamming the motorized wheelchair into Lakshmi's kneecaps and doling out a nasty case of whiplash. Compounding problems, the stench of her muumuu, rarely washed and thoroughly soiled by perspiration, spilled sauces, creams, and a variety of unknown secretions, was enough to knock Lakshmi out cold without some kind of respiratory filter.

But most of the time things went off without a hitch, and in a matter of minutes Esmerelda was settling into the Gargantuan while Lakshmi dry-heaved in the restroom. The Gargantuan was an impressive machine, with automated steering and a mechanical lift for moving up and down, a hard plastic tray that could be folded and stowed in a hollow arm support, a collapsible cup holder, a footrest, and a brass hook for her wool bag. The seat was double wide and triple reinforced, topped with a quartet of paisley cushions from which Esmerelda's mother could not eradicate the smell of boiled turnip using any commercially available cleaning solution. Lakshmi never understood why Esmerelda's hide was so sensitive to the tiniest poke or prod, but she knew that even one pillow short of four would result in haranguing of professional caliber, so she kept her mouth shut and made sure the cushions were there.

While successfully designed for comfort, the Gargantuan did not facilitate the task of urination. For a woman of Esmerelda's girth, using the facilities was not a minor task and required at least an hour for disrobement and manipulations, with a shower to clean off afterward, a towel-intensive dry-down, and a repeat of the morning's torturous dressing process. Slippy had put his foot down on her demand for an industrial-sized bathtub, and even Esmerelda had to admit that in an establishment the size of a three-bedroom apartment, her request might not have been feasible. This left her limited options for her personal toilet, none of them attractive. The first, the attachment of a bedpan to the Gargantuan's seat, had been nixed after a day of use; not only was the smell rancid and inescapable, the sound of Esmerelda's urine dribbling against the tin bedpan, followed by a string of stomach gurgles and a pronounced flushing of the face, never failed to bring commerce to a halt. The second option was much more extreme, requiring coaches, hypnotists, and a severe decrease in hydration. But in the end it proved effective, and an initial glut of accidents and hefty laundry bills was forgotten after a year of training, when Esmerelda became the master of her bladder and trained herself to pee only once a day, before bed, after which she hosed herself down and rolled into her double-king bed for ice cream and Letterman. This meant that when she got into the Gargantuan, she was there for the rest of the working day, which was fine with her, as she was fully acclimated to her own smell and volume and vicious sense of humor and much preferred staying parked in her mobile command center to tracking down Lakshmi and repeating the up-and-down rigmarole five or six times a day.

Once seated, Esmerelda drove the short distance to the cash register, put on her headset, and plugged into the telephone system. Next she counted and tabulated Slippy's money from the bank, filed the bills in the cash register, reviewed inventory, and consumed a small snack: a half-dozen donuts. She often used her last minutes of quiet to take care of some company bookkeeping, calculating tax withholdings and overtime pay and looking for suspiciously long lunch breaks and late punch-outs that didn't jibe with her dead-on memory of who was working when.

Seven o'clock. Lakshmi sprayed air freshener over Esmerelda's station, plugged in the buzzing neon OPEN sign, and turned over the lock. There was usually a burst of door-busters first thing: rip-snorting executives dropping off financial reports to be copied ASAP, teachers running off the day's worksheets, haggard college students putting the finishing touches on term papers, insomniacs of all stripes. A number of early-morning regulars combined their trip to CopySmart with a workout at the gym next door, depositing their projects with Esmerelda in shorts and T-shirts and returning to pick up the finished products in suits and wet hair, their sweet-smelling body products papering over Esmerelda's rising odor just as the air freshener started to fade.

But even with the executive, academic, student, and gym traffic, Esmerelda's fingers didn't really start dancing until after nine, when the secretaries arrived. Even after five years, the sheer volume of secretarial traffic continued to astound her, flooding the store with shoulder-padded blouses and the aroma of cheap coffee. Esmerelda's question: where did they come from? If one took a stroll around the neighborhood, even a long one—as Jasper did every day and reported back on in detail—

stumbling upon any sort of obvious office that employed secretaries was close to impossible. On her own commute through the area in the special services van, Esmerelda noted only typical San Francisco restaurants, bars, gyms, newsstands, laundromats, fashion boutiques, head shops, and many traditional Victorian-style homes—some of which, Esmerelda realized, may have been converted into commercial operations that required administrative support, but nothing resembling the façade of an assistant-intensive office building. Still, from the ornately painted Edwardian woodwork they came, smiling politely and enduring the inevitable copy machine meltdowns with deep patience, because at least someone else was dealing with the technical problems for once.

On a Tuesday morning in the fall of George Bush the First's inaugural year in office, Jasper Winslow walked into the CopySmart flagship store as the initial tide of secretaries began to ebb, whistling a butt-kicking rock song he'd just heard on the radio and twirling a box wrapped in tissue paper and knotted with twine. He waited by the greeting card rack as Esmerelda finished up with a customer, then trotted over and set the box on the counter.

"Happy Birthday, Ezzie!" he cried. As usual, Jasper's radio-whine voice projected too far, attracting fearful glances from a band of beggars edging into the store.

"Quiet, Jasper! This is a business."

"Nonsense, Ezzie, it's your big day. Loud and proud, I'll let the whole world know!" Jasper ran out to the sidewalk and delivered the squeaky observation that it was the birthday of his greatest friend in the world and everybody better celebrate hard if they knew what was good for them. He jogged back to the counter with the ruddy remnants of thrill on his face.

"Are you done?"

"Open your present."

"Not now, dummy. I'm working." Esmerelda took her work very seriously, Jasper knew, and her slit-eyed glare indicated she had reclassified their conversation at a few pegs below friendly.

He lowered his voice to a breathy fizz: "Come on, it's from Zoogman's. Now open it quick and see for yourself."

Zoogman's was firmly at the top in the pantheon of San Francisco bakeries, with an unmatched tradition of lights-out delicious baked goods and pastries that still outweighed Esmerelda's largely repressed bad memories concerning the institution. Seeing as it *was* her birthday after all, Ezzie dug out her sapphire-encrusted scissors from the giant wool bag and snipped the twine and tissue paper and scotch tape locking down the lid to find her favorite dessert in the whole wide universe inside: triple chocolate truffle swirl cheesecake, with Heath bar crumbs and caramel roses on top.

"Holy heck!" She drew a quick anxious breath; her pulse sprinted and stopped; her eyes dilated a quarter inch; a coat of perspiration gelled to her face like bubble wrap. She'd never told Jasper of her lust for Zoogman's masterpiece, a recipe so dangerously addictive it was kept under lock and key and unavailable to the public unless you could talk a chef out of retirement and had five hundred bucks to pay for ingredients.

"Where did you get this?"

"Why, I bought it at Bruce Zoogman's bakery. I know a guy, and I saved up some money. It's not every day that my babycakes turns twenty-nine." Jasper lifted a slice from the box and placed it on her tray. "Here, have some."

"Oh . . . what about the customers?"

"Don't worry bout that, Ezzie. There's nobody here."

Esmerelda consulted her surveillance cameras. Aside from the team of filthy street dwellers copying food stamps and cash on the self-service machine by the door, the store was empty.

"Just a taste. It looks real, real good."

"I hope so. Bruce told me it was one of his best ever."

Esmerelda reacted instantly, scooping huge handfuls of cake with her bare hands and shoveling it into her mouth, swallowing without chewing, sucking frosting off her fingertips, ten fingers crammed in at once. Her blood shot off on a roller-coaster ride through her coronary system, loop-de-looping through her legs and corkscrewing through her heart while the outside world turned colorless, her heart beat in her pupils. After another three bites, her blood was pumping so hard that even the cobwebbed capillaries of Esmerelda's pelvis were penetrated, her super-charged plasma shooting through mounds of fat and over-developed muscle tissue, snaking around fragile tendons and between aching bones and down into a dime-sized spot in a bodily zone she was professionally conditioned to ignore until just before bedtime: BOOM—it was ambushed, floored, decapi-tated. Esmerelda dropped her fork and her training, urinating on the Gargantuan and collapsing into glorious postorgasmic sleep.

She awoke covered in chlorinated water, propped up against a concrete step.

"Hello, Ezzie."

Jasper stood next to her in a large municipal pool. Esmerelda had never seen him naked before, and even drowsy and discom-bobulated she found a way to laugh at his penis.

"Forget pencil dick—you've got eraser dick, Jasper."

"Just wait," he said. "Even eraser-sized, I can shoot lead."

He parted her underwater legs, shimmied between them, and began to convulse like a bad salsa dancer. Esmerelda was cack-ling too hard to react at first, but after a time she recognized the lengths Jasper had gone to acquire the cake and hijack her out of work and transport her over and into the pool, not to mention his consistently friendly disposition and thoughtfulness, his smi-ley profile waving both hands at her through the CopySmart plateglass window, his daily observation that she was looking better than a pecan pie at Thanksgiving dinner; hardly the worst man in the world and not bad looking either. Also it was her birthday, and she hadn't gotten a piece in years. Gently she led him out of the flab fold he'd been screwing and down into her rarely seen nether regions.

Even in the right hole, the lovemaking didn't do much for Esmerelda, as she had difficulty distinguishing between Jasper's pelvic thrusts, stabbing fingers, knee bumps, and kicks. Instead she focused on dislodging a chunk of Zoog she discovered jammed between her teeth, which turned the encounter into more of a race, for her at least—her tongue versus Jasper's palsied spasms. As Jasper churned a frothy whirlpool in the shallow end, Esmerelda's oral swashbuckling grew more furious in parallel, her wide tongue lashing and digging at dental crevasses to free the stuck cake. They were both sweating freely when loudspeakers announced they had five minutes left on the private pool party, with Jasper issuing louder and more profanity-intensive exclamations, Esmerelda rumbling her assent, the slip-slap of colliding wet limbs, Jasper's face puckering, his back straight as a flagpole, the hard splash of pool water onto the deck, rolling motion beneath Esmerelda's cheeks, her teeth clicking, steam rising off the water and turning the air hot and dangerous, until a tortured shriek burst from Jasper's lungs and he collapsed into Esmerelda's pillowy chest. In the same instant, Esmerelda's tongue ripped the Zoogman's debris from her molars and cast it down her pulsating throat, bringing back that heavenly, urination-inducing feeling— not all the way to incontinence, but enough to turn her face the color of a radish, send a series of long gleeful shivers across her titanic figure, and reorganize her mouth into the faintest hint of a smile. This sudden decompression was so closely synchronized with Jasper's ejaculation, in terms of timing, that afterward they both released earnest, melodious sighs in appreciation of their seemingly perfect pool fuck.

After hitting four hundred pounds, Esmerelda had pretty much written off sex for the rest of her life, so, when she foundered halfway up the concrete pool steps—leaving Jasper to raise her up in the portable winch borrowed from his longshoreman roommate, Sven—she ran her fingers between her legs to check for evidence, to make sure this was real and not some Zoog-induced fantasy. The chlorinated water had washed her clean, and she couldn't find any physical residue to speak of, but when she looked at Jasper standing next to her in a worn cotton robe, she detected a soft pheromonal glow over his skin, which combined with his shining brown eyes and giddy lip licking for overwhelming evidence of virginity lost.

"Jasper, you devil," Esmerelda drawled, stepping into the sail-sized tunic he held open for her. "I never knew you had it in you." She settled into the Gargantuan with a series of heavy squishes.

"There's a lot to me you don't know about."

This was true. Although she'd known Jasper for nearly four years, the first three and a half of those had been indirect, more knowing of than actually knowing. For a long while Jasper had simply been the freaky black guy pushing a wheelbarrow full of coupons who kindly halted his march up and down Market Street to let Esmerelda palpitate across the sidewalk. Even by San Francisco–weirdo standards he was an unforgettable sight, what with the clown shoes, the soda jerk cap, the extra-extra-large overalls, and the everpresent doofus smile. Music crackled steadily from the transistor radio in his front pocket, mostly rock and soul, sometimes classical early in the morning. Many of Esmerelda's customers were put off by Jasper's dippy uniform and grin; nobody who looked so goofy could be trusted, they groused inside the copy shop, and he was probably on drugs to boot. But Esmerelda appreciated his gentlemanly patience— most people never waited for her, just walked on by as though large people didn't deserve eye contact—and after two years of crossing the sidewalk in front of him, she began acknowledging his deferential pause with a slight flick of her fingers. A major breakthrough occurred in the spring of 1988, when he offered, and she accepted, one of the heart-shaped balloons he attached to his wheelbarrow on Fridays. Jasper, a slow learner at best, eventually witnessed enough of Esmerelda's hourly feeding frenzies to recognize that a woman of her dimensions enjoyed a solid meal for a good price. He started funneling her the best of his dining coupons: two plain pizza slices for the price of one, value meal upgrades, three dollars off any entrée (with pickup), free dessert with purchase of a main course. These were much appreciated by Esmerelda, who drafted Lakshmi into buzzing up and down the Market Street corridor on her behalf, retrieving free sodas and upgraded value meals and three-dollars-off entrées, often burning through several loads of Jasper's coupons in a week. The discounts shaved hundreds off Esmerelda's meal budget and freed up funds for makeup and trips to the hairdresser and new muumuus for each season—little feminine touches that Jasper always noticed and commented on, thus endearing himself to Esmerelda even more.

Jasper largely did this out of his kind disposition, and there was an obvious courtship aspect as well—yet an important financial incentive was also at play: Jasper's salary was contingent upon the number of coupons actually used, not distributed. He was hauling it in if 3 percent of his coupons were redeemed, the scanned UPC barcodes transmitted to the payroll database, tacking associated incentives on to his paycheck. With Esmerelda hitting a personal redemption rate of 82 percent, Jasper's overall numbers jolted into the low double digits, a shift that sent his income soaring, roused the attention of his supervisors, and made him the odds-on favorite for Employee of the Year honors.

Yet despite the modest accoutrements he came to enjoy with his salary jump—a longer antenna for his radio, an assortment of rock band insignias sewn onto his overalls, heavy-duty tires for his wheelbarrow—Jasper mentioned none of this to Ezzie. Throughout their friendship and low-level flirtation, even after Jasper presented the Gargantuan to her as a gift—his sister was disabled and he had access to the mechanized wheelchair parts, cushions, and reinforced metals which his mother had used to build the thing—they had never discussed deep personal questions, relationship builders: how Esmerelda had grown so large, why Jasper had fallen into such an inane profession, their respective salary structures. Emboldened by their sexual union, Jasper strolled over to initiate this conversation as Esmerelda piloted the Gargantuan through the pool parking lot. But before he could squeeze out two words, Esmerelda swiped the cake box from his grip and flash-gobbled another slice of Zoog, staying sober just long enough for Jasper to load the Gargantuan into his mother's minivan and coax her onto the middle-row bench seat.

She woke up seated behind her cash register at work, her midday milkshake waiting on the counter. After a quick taste from the pink bendy straw, she caught sight of the wall clock, the hour hand onto early afternoon, impossible. Probably a dying battery, she reassured herself, Lakshmi letting things slide as usual.

"Slippy's mad at you, Ezzie."

"Haronk!" Milkshake shooting from Esmerelda's nose was a common Tuesday afternoon occurrence, and Lakshmi had prepared for the likelihood by standing well out of range. "What for?"

"You just took off this morning. He had to mind the register. Missed a lunch appointment. And"—Lakshmi's voice turned nasal—"you peed all over the floor."

"Shucks. It's my birthday, you know." Esmerelda turned to busy herself with the reorganization of papers or pencils, but found none on the counter. She slurped boisterously on her milkshake instead.

"Yeah, well, happy birthday. But you can't go running off like that, Ezzie. This is a business. Sometimes you have to work."

Esmerelda slammed down her cup as purple tinted her face. "Have to work? Hello! Little miss booty girl, I've been working here for five years and have never once taken a vacation. I don't take lunch breaks. I don't run out for tea and crumpets, or whatever you do all afternoon with those freakazoid friends I see you fooling around with on the sidewalk. Haronk! Now a sandwich please! This discussion is over."

Lakshmi sucked in her lips and retreated to the workroom. Esmerelda's invective was technically accurate but had conveniently overlooked Lakshmi's unofficial duties as comestible gatherer that frequently took her out to the sidewalk, where she paid off her freakazoid friend delivery persons with wadded cash from Esmerelda's great wool bag. The vacation claim was a slippery one too, for while Esmerelda had not officially taken any vacation leave from the CopySmart flagship store, she had used up more than one hundred sick days in her five years on the job, often in sequential order, supported by flimsy excuses of unpinpointable cramps and general anxiety and long-out-of-vogue mental health problems authenticated with obviously forged doctor's notes and counselor's reports. But Lakshmi knew better than to confront Esmerelda with facts when she was all riled up, and resolved instead to give her incorrect change on food orders for the remainder of her CopySmart career.

Slippy arrived ten minutes later, fresh off his afternoon tour of the CopySmart satellite outlets. "Ezzie!" he shouted from the entrance. "You've gotta stop the pissing!" The secretary Esmerelda was servicing bunched an eyebrow. "I haven't the mops or the time to clean up after you. Get some diapers or a grip, I don't care which—but if you ruin my floor again, you're out on the street."

"Slippy," Esmerelda said with ominous calm, "today's my birthday."

"I don't care if it's your wedding day, Christmas, or Chinese New Year—your bladder never gets a holiday so long as you work for me. Control yourself, for Christ's sake. Just because you're fat doesn't mean you have to be gross."

Slippy's wrinkly bald head approached the Gargantuan, and Esmerelda hoped with all her heart he'd bumble into milkshake range.

"Happy birthday, Esmerelda," he said softly. Her throwing arm relaxed. "I gave you the morning off retroactively. How did everything go?"

"Oh—swimmingly," she coughed. "Just swimmingly."

"Good!" Slippy slapped his ring-riddled hand against the counter. "Now, let's make some money. And remember: no accidents."

That wasn't an issue, as Esmerelda's conditioning was fully reinstated and she was holding it in like the time-tested urine vault that she was. And soon everything else seemed to be back on track too: her milkshake demolished, her hot-dog fingers bounding precisely over her oversized cash register buttons, her interaction with Jasper back to limited friendly banter. But amid the apparent return of normality, the day's critical turn went undetected: Jasper's aged semen secretly navigating the billowed folds of Esmerelda's uterus and slipping inside two of her ripened ova. Weeks dripped by, and the pair of eggs quietly developed into dizygotic embryos and later fetuses that kicked and squirmed anonymously, inflicting daily bouts of indigestion and internal discomfort. But these classic pregnancy tip-offs were missed, as Esmerelda chalked up the tummy trouble and bodily unease to her steady consumption of fiery tamales, greasy hamburgers, and cheap pizza that Lakshmi delivered to her counter at reduced price. The absence of menstruation went unnoticed too, for Esmerelda had stopped worrying about her cycle and the insertion of absorbent devices years ago, seeing that the leakage didn't get very far before crusting off against her leg to be hosed off at the end of the day, and all the aerobics required to manage the process just weren't worth it. The most obvious clue to her condition—major weight gain—was cancelled out by Esmerelda's prolific profile, as whatever change in stomach diameter wrought by her unborn children could not be isolated from Esmerelda's normal rate of fat increase.

Jasper cared for her throughout her stealthy enlargement, offering coupons for heartburn tablets and gas-reducing pills, a buck off the latest belly calmer from Johnson & Johnson, a free Alka-Seltzer package with the purchase of two others. He gave her shiny foil balloons to lift her spirits and stopped by during his lunch break to massage her gelatinous back with his long needle fingers. Esmerelda appreciated the back rubs—she was often tender from her eight dips across the sidewalk—and while the most penetrating of deep-tissue kneading could not directly prod the sore muscles buried beneath, the manipulation of her skin was still quite soothing. Jasper smiled and hummed along with the radio in his pocket, and Esmerelda, more often than not, joined in. Their off-key, raggedy duet filled the store until complaints came in, sometimes as long as five minutes.

Occasionally, after Jasper had given Ezzie a lengthy rubdown or presented her with a particularly large balloon, he asked if he could see her after work. Maybe, he posited, they could go for a dip. Hunger edged into his eyes, hinting at something furtive and unsettled, but it faded into his gentle smile as he waited for her response. Not that it was long in coming; he had only to wait for the laughter to die down, the haronking snorts to quit, the jiggling belly and bobbling of all seven chins to settle and stop.

"Are you crazy, Jasper? The last thing I need is another round with that eraser dick of yours. I'd rather watch bowling reruns, or even eat fruit." She looked up to see his face collapse, his posture melt to mush. "Aw, come on there, fella. Don't be so grim. You had your shot, and a good one too. You shouldn't be messing with ogres like me anyway. Go on, find yourself some fresh meat."

"I like you, Ezzie," he invariably responded.

"Sorry, bud. Not gonna happen. But thanks for the massage." His hands had stopped. "Felt nice."

An hour or so later, after Lakshmi reported that Jasper was stumbling through traffic, or ramming his head against a telephone pole, or lying prostrate on the median strip, his wheelbarrow uncovered and his coupons shimmering in the downdraft like ticker tape, she gave in. Jasper was summoned, a halfhearted apology was delivered, a date was suggested and greedily accepted. After closing time on the appointed day, they rode through the city together in a minivan piloted by Jasper's mother, Karen Winslow, a small, white-haired secretary at the machinists' union who listened to gospel at high volume. The dates weren't going very far, sexwise, even if they hadn't been chaperoned by Jasper's half-deaf mother, as Esmerelda kept her mouth shut and her eyes out the window, radiating misery and bristling at Jasper's touch. Undeterred, Jasper stroked her gritty hair and rubbed her tree-trunk neck and tried to pry her gloopy hands

from their death grip on her great wool bag, all the while informing her of the best tidbits he'd learned from the radio: the day's
most popular songs, leading news items, traffic patterns and
street closures, weather forecasts, celebrity birthdays. Together
they gazed upon the fractured streets and the wild people and
the eucalyptus trees and later on at the ocean twisting beneath
the Golden Gate Bridge, until they arrived at Esmerelda's mother's house at nine o'clock sharp and Esmerelda concluded the
evening with a handshake and a curt good-night.

In the summer of 1990, they were on an evening tour out
where Golden Gate Park meets the sea when Esmerelda felt a
punch in the stomach. She tried to pinch it, then stalled for time
by impressing the heel of her palm against her belly and chewing a fistful of herbal antinausea pills from her wool bag, but all
the tea in China couldn't hold back a gastrointestinal surge of
this magnitude for long.

"Jasper, I need to use the facilities. Tell your mom to pull over."

"But it's not bedtime yet. What's going on?"

"Look, I don't have details. But unless you want a mess in the
car, we better find a bathroom, pronto."

Jasper notified his mother with a series of piercing screeches,
and inside of thirty seconds they were stopped at a gas station.
With both hands he spotted Esmerelda as she pushed out of the
minivan and wobbled across the parking lot, spitting gooey
strings like an angry third-base coach. As soon as she was
installed in a semistable position leaning against a braced stucco
wall, Jasper ran down to the snack shop, bought a bag of sunflower seeds, and hopped back with a scuffed silver hubcap
chained to a key. Esmerelda grabbed the snack, pried open the
lavatory door, and speed-waddled to the commode, where she
hiked up her muumuu, slid onto the seat, and relaxed her sphinc-
ter in a single, surprisingly limber motion. To her dismay her
innards offered no immediate relief, but on the plus side she
observed that the restroom had been recently cleaned and was
handicapped accessible, such that the toilet was reinforced,

there were grab bars for gripping and stabilizing, and on the whole Esmerelda couldn't have been more comfortable except perhaps with a recent feature film.

Or several. The wait turned out to be six hours long, a bathroom visit of historic proportions, marking a momentous shift in Esmerelda's personal geopolitics.

"Everything OK? Need some water?" Jasper asked through the door after the first hour had passed.

"Of course not, Jasper. There's water in here."

"How bout some supper? I have coupons for the deli across the street."

A pastrami sandwich was tempting, Esmerelda had to admit, and would keep up her strength better than a measly bag of sunflower seeds. She was on the verge of authorizing the purchase when a steel-toed-boot-kicking competition broke out in her breadbasket and she realized the addition of processed meats was sure to end in digestive pandemonium.

"Thanks, buckaroo," she sighed, "but I'd better get back to concentrating."

She made progress with ensuing sets of abdominal squeezing—splashes, periods of moderate gushing—but the obstruction's bulk remained lodged in her midsection. Bolts of pain seared the rolling hills of her gut and trembled between her legs, shooting in white streaks from her statuesque brow to the lonely corners of her rarely seen feet. It got worse as the hours rolled by, splitting her insides from an unusual epicenter for a bowel movement, not the intestines or the anus or even the gut but somewhere more front and center, recognizable but noticeably different, like a lavatory in a foreign country. It dawned on Esmerelda that maybe whatever it was wasn't coming out the traditional number two hole, but for whatever reason, due to a plumbing mix-up or some very garbled directions, out of number one. She remembered reading an article that described kidney stones as having similar symptoms and was reaching into her wool bag to search for the clipping when an incredible spike broke through her eyelids and she knew it was far too late for a shred of newsprint to do any good.

This was it; it was happening.

Land mines and firebombs, rips and tears, six-legged kicks, teeth-piercing lips, self-imposed scratches and backhanded wall slaps, flagellation and mutilation, hand-to-hand field combat, daggers gouging out gallbladders. Remotely she felt barbed motion, inertia carpet-bombed and shattered. Fire streaked from her birth canal to her decomposing hair bun; her groans rang at such volume that even Jasper's mother heard it over her gospel tunes. As the hullabaloo grew louder and louder, the gas station attendant realized this was no ordinary six-hour excretion and called the police.

"What's going on? Ezzie!" Jasper's voice was so kooky when he screamed, akin to that of a female dwarf, and Esmerelda almost found a way to laugh despite the earthquake in her loins. "Open this door or I'll bust it down!"

It was silly to hear him say that, and not just because of his voice—even if Esmerelda hadn't been experiencing the most belly-busting pain of her life, hauling her big butt over to let him in was a physical impossibility after her hours of exertion. But his energy was infectious, his resolve admirable, his conviction inspiring, if mildly frightening. As she listened to his puny shoulder thump feebly against the door, Esmerelda was moved to action: she forced her dipping muscles inward, compressed her stomach, strained her hidden abs, and bobbed up and down on the toilet to loosen things up. Jasper heard her travails and took on a fresh determination in his ramming just as the police arrived with weapons drawn and ordered him to freeze: his assault on the bathroom not only constituted the destruction of private property but also was a textbook sign of an abusive relationship what with the hysterical woman inside. Seconds later the gas station attendant dredged up the backup restroom key from under a pile of invoices and yelled over for everybody to cool down, he'd let them in, when the mother of all hollers rangout from inside like agony incarnate, a dead dog on a doorstep. Jasper skidded to a stop and examined the door, assessing its breadth, its material construction, its hinges, possible weak spots. Another second tocked by and his head was down, he was charging, wild-man frenzy starring his eyes, snot foaming in his nostrils, legs churning smoke, glottal Hungarian consonants pouring from his throat, inducing the cops to panic and open fire. With a stiff crunch the restroom door gave way and Jasper barreled inside, falling at a fortunate angle that eluded the two bullets slicing after him and landing on the floor to get the first look of his daughter's head peeking out from between Esmerelda's legs, slick with blood and wailing like a walloped cat.

"Goodness," Jasper said as he wrapped the girl in toilet paper. "Is this my doing?"

"That's not all," Esmerelda said, reaching for the grab bars. "Kid's got company."

A minute later a boy was out too, dispensing train-whistle shrieks and spraying scum water from his eyes. Alerted by the racket, Karen Winslow climbed down from the minivan to find Esmerelda hyperventilating in a lump on the floor, Jasper rubbing her back, the cops wiping clean two writhing brown bodies with handiwipes from Esmerelda's bag, and the gas station attendant fingering a pair of bullet holes chest-high in the wall.

"Babies! That's wonderful, dear. I thought you were taking your time for a number two."

"They're mine, Ma."

"What?"

Esmerelda's desolate silence confirmed it.

"Jasper! I didn't even think you could, you know, were capable of—"

"This eraser can shoot lead, isn't that right Ezzie?"

"Apparently."

"So," asked the gas station attendant, "whatcha gonna name them?"

"At midnight, the radio says it's Bastille Day," Karen noted.

"July 14," Esmerelda said. "Yes."

"What's that?" Jasper asked.

"It's the day in 1789 that French regular folks took up arms and busted some prisoners out of jail," his mother said. "Radio said it started the French Revolution."

"Guess you could call this a jailbreak," Jasper said. "How about French names then?"

"Shoot, honey, I can't remember those names on the radio."

"Marat," Esmerelda said.

"Yes, yes, that's one of them."

"Heck, I'm out," said Jasper. "Pierre's the only French name I know."

"That's it, dear. Robespierre's another revolutionary."

"It's settled," Esmerelda blurted. "Marat and Robespierre."

"Which one's the boy and which is the girl?" posited the gas station attendant.

"Who cares?" Jasper's face drew thin and skeletal, ghoulishly framed by his patchy day-old beard. "What matters is will they have to spell out their names over the phone their whole lives. We can't call them Matt and Robeswear. They'll be cursed."

"My children are named Marat and Robespierre. And that's that." Esmerelda fell asleep decisively as emergency vehicles screeched into the parking lot and a team of paramedics hustled to remove her from the toilet. She looked so peaceful amid the EMTs' buckling knees, Jasper observed—her lips and eyes arranged in a slack, nonangry state of rest that implied some level of contentment—and he realized that in some way he'd given her this. With fingers crossed he willed her from falling off her stretcher, creating invisible guardian angels and well-padded cloud safety barriers with his mind, so intent on protecting her from harm or discomfort or accidental contact with anybody who wasn't him that it took a few seconds to realize the gas station attendant was speaking in his direction. "Take this for your wife," the guy was saying, pressing a carton of chocolate bars into his hands. "She'll need the energy later."

Jasper grabbed the candy instinctively as he hopped aboard the ambulance, trying hard not to betray the daffy mental disposition the attendant's mislabeling had cast upon him. Mistaking Esmerelda Van Twinkle for his wife! And him, a husband! Provider, man of the house, coming home to a peck on the cheek and a homemade dinner—or, in Esmerelda's case, he realized, a coupon-ordered smorgasbord, but still, warm food—then tucking in the kids and conversing about the events of the day and maybe dipping into her honeypot before nodding off on their king-sized bed. He expanded the scenario into greater detail over the course of the ambulance ride, with assorted lingerie and tubs of Crisco, until his knees began shivering and his mouth filled with slobber. Upon arrival at the hospital, he gamboled after Esmerelda's stretcher with the full vim of matrimony, energetically introducing himself to medical staff as Esmerelda's husband.

"What beautiful children you have, Mr. Van Twinkle," a nurse told him as he watched his boy and girl wriggle on the other side of the nursery window.

"Well, they're our first ones," said Jasper, who was trying his best to find beauty in their alien mahogany skin but wasn't having much success.

"They're darling. Listen, your wife gave me their names, but I'm not clear on which is which. Marat and Robespierre, right?"

"Sure," Jasper said uncertainly.

"Well?" The nurse pointed to the bassinets, one blue and one pink.

"Uh, boy's the first one, Matt."

"Marat?"

"Yeah, Marat. And then, Robeswear's the girl."

"Robespierre Van Twinkle. That's a superstar name if I've ever heard one."

"Hey," exclaimed Jasper, who was far more intrigued by the boy himself, a possible rapscallion apprentice, future defender of the Winslow name. "What about Matt?"

"Wasn't Marat the one they killed in the bathtub?"

Jasper nodded politely.

"Keep your eye on that one. He's got some kind of karma on him."

Jasper wasn't sure what karma meant, but, judging from the nurse's somber delivery, guessed it was some sort of waterborne illness that afflicted infants. He broke off in a wailing canter down the hall, flapping his arms like an ostrich attempting flight.

"Ezzie!" he exclaimed, rushing into her room. "Nurse told me the boy's got karma! What are we gonna do?"

"Oh, for heaven's sakes," Esmerelda said sleepily. "We've all got karma, Jasper. Settle down."

Jasper realized that karma might be one of those tricky medical terms for hair or toes or something standard. "Uh, just wanted to let you know, Ezzie. He's got karma, just like everybody else. Normal boy. That's good, having karma."

"As long as it's the right kind, the kid's gonna be OK. Now make yourself useful and run down to the mess. I've got a hankering for steak, and jelly rolls if they've got 'em."

"Sure thing, babe," he said, and kissed her molten forehead. Entrusted with errands, a family under his care. Music flooded his head; he started whistling one of those festive French songs, a cancan, driving accordions and feathery hats and ladies kicking up ruffled drawers. *Duh duh, duh-duh-duh-duh duh duh, duh-duh-duh-duh duh duh.* The breathy skip-beats grew louder as he rode the elevator down seven flights and hopped over to the cafeteria, and turned sweeter and more vibrato-heavy as he reviewed the laminated menu stuck to the wall. He was working his way through the side dish offerings and puffing blue notes when little slips of cognizance daisy-chained in his head.

Battered onion rings. Sounds pretty good. Battered. What is that anyway? Beer-battered? Funny, beer in a hospital. Or just batter, like floury watery shit?

Here, batter batter batter.

Batter up.

Bastard.

The tooting trailed off. He bolted from the cafeteria and leapt up the emergency stairs two at a time, sped past his children snoozing in their bassinet showroom, dodged a docked gurney, whipped around a corner, and, after knocking over a cart of cleaning supplies, slid into Esmerelda's room, took a knee, let it fly.

"Ezzie, would you, uh, do me the honor of, you know—"

"Haronk! What are you doing down there, Jasper? Get up where I can see you. You freak me out with stuff like that."

"Look, Esmerelda."

"Unh?"

Her eyelids creaked open, revealing bloodshot eyes, interminably tired eyes, heavy and hazel and growing increasingly more peeved at Jasper's inability to string a sentence together.

"Let's get hitched."

"Not funny, Jasper. I'm going back to bed."

"I'm serious. Married, you and me."

"Forget it. We'll have some legal wrangling for the kids, but marriage is out of the question. Anyhow, there's no wedding dress around that can hold me."

"Well, we can make one. Mama's a whiz with the sewing machine. Besides, I know you're a lot to love—and here I am, first in line."

"I told you, kiddo, no." She rolled onto her side. "Now let me catch some z's, would you? Giving birth takes a lot out of a girl."

He massaged her neck until she fell asleep, then trudged to the nearest bathroom and locked himself in. An hour later he stumbled out, destroyed. His clown shoes were scuffed up, the soles flapping off; his gummy shoelaces were chewed through in several places; his overalls were torn and stained red and yellow, a button missing and a snapped strap drooping like a limp pickle. His paper cap: well, forget about the cap, as torn up as it was, the top shredded, the white paper turned the color of deep-sea mud, the thin plastic cord under his chin long gone, the cap staying on his head only because after twelve years of distributing coupons his hair fit inside it perfectly, grew into it actually, tucked in tight as sheets on an army cot.

When the nursing staff saw the wreck of a father emerge from the bathroom, his face ripped with melancholy, his uniform in tatters, his feathery blue eyes strafed with woe, they looked away, toward the wall, at their watches, into their computers and waiting room magazines. Slowly they began to cry.

The karma-mentioning nurse started it because she was a crier, always had been. At weddings, funerals, baby showers, going-away parties, she cried, and she cried a lot at work from the joy of seeing newborns every day, with the occasional stillborn or mother dead from complications drawing fierce tears of horror from the dew of happiness. Seeing Jasper's face kicked it off, associating him with Marat and Robespierre, recalling his entry to fatherhood, weeping happy tears.

Then she got a good look at him. Absorbed his mutilated garments, his vibrating throat, his thin, failed lips, his pallid skin. His smile jarringly absent.

She cried harder, reached for him.

Her best friend on the shift, Stacy, while not a crier, couldn't help being moved by Jasper's mournful appearance, because not only was his hangdog face pitiful, but also, before nursing school, she'd worked as a legal secretary in a law office in a converted Victorian on Noe Street and had seen him around all the time, the Coupon Man, smiling and handing out coupons and sometimes balloons on Market Street, often opening the nonmechanical, narrowish metal door at the local print shop for her when she had to run off some copies. His defeated face was tragic and wrong, and she too felt tears wetting her cheeks.

Soon the other nurses on duty were whimpering by the nurse's station—they weren't sure why and didn't much care, just went with the flow and let their troubles pour out—and then the secretaries and administrators were sniffling too, stuck in the muck of collective gloom. It jumped to the patients next, picking them off one by one: tough old men with the end in sight finally breaking down, cancer patients purging pain from their bodies, depressed teenagers terrified by life's apparent meaninglessness. Sorrow trickled down the hall alongside Jasper's slump to Esmerelda's room, his presence instilling heartache in every lifeform he passed. Even the visiting dog from the SPCA got glum, as glum as dogs can get.

Esmerelda Van Twinkle, tough as burned bones, a hellcat, a coldhearted bitch and proud of it—and still the peals of lamentation got to her. She was wiping her nose and trying to read a day-old newspaper when Jasper slinked into the room.

"Jeez! Did you get hit by a bus?"

Jasper closed his eyes and sighed with such flourish that anyone who didn't know him would have assumed he was being theatrical. Esmerelda, however, was aware of his gigantic lung capacity and knew that his exhalations were honest and troubled. Her nose widened into a mushroom as she succumbed to the tearfest, the hot saline drops cascading down her puffed cheeks and over her seven chins until absorbing into her hospital gown.

"Ezzie, look."

"You're in a bad place, man. Taking me with you. Hand me my bag." He carried it over from a chair along the wall and stood beside the bed as Esmerelda fished out her sapphire-encrusted scissors.

"Come here."

He sat down on the mattress while she fiddled with her remote control and moved the bed upright. After a couple of power failures and a system reboot provided by a sniveling nurse, Esmerelda was able to reach him. Sliding the scissors beneath his paper cap, she wove the blades around his coiled gray-black hair, slicing a jagged line from his ear to the crown of his head. She peeled off the aged headpiece with uncharacteristic caution, unveiling his plateau-shaped hair formation in slow, sticky chunks, as if removing an old bumper sticker.

"There. Now you can breathe at least." Slurps and drips; she hadn't stopped crying throughout the operation.

Jasper pulled at his earlobes and blew out breath like an industrial air conditioner. "Ezzie, what's not to like about marrying me? I got a job, I'm a good man. And I'm crazy in love with you too. Bottom of my heart up to the top. All the way."

The wounded noises down the hall softened, replaced by honks of nose-blowing.

"Not now, Jasper. Let's get used to the kids first, OK?" Esmerelda turned a bleary eye to him and tried to nod, an already difficult procedure with the seven chins made impossible by the rain-swept conditions. Jasper got the point, though, and sat quietly stroking her hair while patients all around them called out for more tissues.

Shit if she wasn't a tough nut to crack.

When Esmerelda tried to slip into the house with her children, her key no longer fit in the lock. She hammered the anchor-shaped knocker until lights came on upstairs.

"Yes?" The door cracked open four links on the chain. Fanny Van Twinkle peered out in a zebra-striped bathrobe, a triple martini in hand. She was of average height, a few extra pounds in the trunk but certainly not fat, with wavy gray hair recuperating from a lifetime of homemade perms. Her onion-shaped face contained even brown eyes flecked pink from gin, a drooping nose, medium-sized ears like apple slices, vampire lipstick wound sloppily around her mouth. Her fine lips parted and she started to cough, a broken carburetor firing up.

"Hey, Ma," Esmerelda said. "Door's busted."

"I changed the locks. An unbalanced African American man recently assaulted me in the living room. He tried to hug me and called me Ma. It was very upsetting." Fanny pointed to the two blanketed lumps under Esmerelda's forearm, alternately crying and snoring. "What have you got there?"

"Babies. My kids, technically. Just bringing them on home."

"Your kids. Technically." Fanny knocked back half her martini in a soundless pour. "Thank you for the update. Heaven forbid I was not still your landlord—I never would have been informed."

"It's not that, Ma. They were a surprise, to me even."

"And the father?"

Esmerelda sighed. "Can I come in first?"

"No." Fanny pulled her bathrobe tight and smiled.

"What the hell's wrong with you? These are your grand-children."

Fanny wrinkled her heavy nose at this, her daughter's endless entitlement, the ache that never ceased. "I gave birth to one child already, and you are still here. I have paid my dues, and for what? Ignorance, disdain, all of the above. If your father were here to see this—humph! You may stay, but those mystery children are not welcome in my home."

"You're kidding, right?"

"Have I ever kidded you once in my life?"

There was no one to call but Jasper. "Here," Esmerelda said, "you started this mess. Take 'em off my hands until I can figure something out."

"But Ezzie, they need their mama."

"Lots of kids go a day or two without their mom. They'll live."

"Girl," he whispered, "they gotta suck on your titties to eat!"

"Dang it," Esmerelda admitted. "You've got a point."

Jasper telephoned his mother, and an hour later all three generations were strapped in the minivan and speeding north along the Great Highway, past the gas station birthplace and the pounding Pacific and up the fog-snuffed hills into the Presidio, Jasper's apartment on Stillwell Road.

They pulled into a cramped parking lot and parked next to a stairwell. A hard buzz ran through Esmerelda, and she began rapaciously picking a zit on her forearm. "There an elevator?" she asked.

"Nope. But it's just the second floor."

Esmerelda shook her head rapidly and forced a few beats of laughter. "Been half a decade since I've gone up that many steps. Not gonna work, toots; sorry."

Jasper touched her shoulder and angled his head like he'd seen successful football coaches do in the movies. "Babe, give it a shot. I'm gonna be here with you, no problem. We'll find a way."

"No problem? You try walking up a staircase with this kind of luggage and we'll see how you do."

"Do the man a favor and at least try. He wants to help you." Karen Winslow nodded from the driver's seat.

"Ya, and I am here too." Sven Johanssen, longshoreman and Jasper's roommate, skipped down the stairs. He was svelte, with an angular Nordic face and shaggy white-blond hair, and spoke with a heavy Swedish accent. He stank of pickled seafood. "We help you up."

"Forget it, it's not happening. Mechanically, can't be done."

"What else are we gonna do?" Jasper asked.

Esmerelda's face flushed, and she swung her arms like battle-axes. "I don't know, but you better think of something!"

Karen turned off the radio and Jasper sat down on the staircase, watching as Esmerelda calmed, brushed perspiration off her cheeks, and sucked down a bottle of water. She licked her thumb and rubbed out stains on her muumuu, swatted microscopic insects, helped herself to ginger cookies from her great wool bag. Jasper, Sven, and Karen exchanged incredulous glances as she killed ten minutes wiping clean the magnetic strips on her credit cards before taking a short nap. The evening turned chilly; the babies rustled in their car seats. Unaccustomed to such prolonged silence, they started to cry.

"Well, you went and upset my grandkids. No surprise really. Heck, I'd cry if I were them." Karen Winslow lowered herself from the driver's seat, appearing somewhat shorter on foot than in previous encounters, Esmerelda observed, just a little. "Their mom's a wimp."

"Their mom has a weight problem," Esmerelda clarified. "It's a long story."

"Wimp, coward, whatever. Esmerelda, you don't even try."

A terrible rumble rose within Esmerelda's muumuu, somewhere between her stomach and her larynx and her butt, a sound Jasper had heard only once before, at the CopySmart flagship store when Esmerelda threw a shit-fit over a bounced check. He grabbed Sven by his rugby jersey and dragged him behind a support pillar.

"Don't even try? I'm tired, for Chrissakes! Flattened! With these kids I never asked for!" The growl transmuted from potential to kinetic energy: her blubbery arms pushing her out of the van, slippered feet crunching gravel, tugboat body steaming forward. "What the hell do I have to prove?"

"Go for it, girl!" Karen Winslow called.

She didn't feel the first five stairs. With momentum on her side, the next five weren't bad either. Eleven and twelve were doable; she plowed through thirteen; fourteen was a real bitch. Fifteen: asphyxiation at hand, vision blurring, hundreds of pounds caving in on her lungs. She didn't remember sixteen at all, and woke up drenched in sweat and leaning against the wall on a landing from heaven.

"Halfway there, sugar." Jasper's Miss Piggy voice oinked in her ear. "I'm with you all the way."

"Need a snack," she gulped. "Something to get my blood moving. Check my bag."

Jasper fetched two chocolate bars, several pizza crusts, and a six-pack of apple juice. "OK," she said a minute later, dropping the last juice box over the railing. "Let's get this crap over with."

Two hours and eleven minutes later, Esmerelda collapsed on the apartment floor.

"Yeah! Yeah!" Jasper tried to execute a celebratory multistage handshake, but Esmerelda was unresponsive.

"I really didn't tink dat would work," Sven acknowledged. "But she did it. Good for you, gurl."

Esmerelda coughed feebly. A line of saliva flew across her face and landed on her eyelash.

"Don't die yet, hon. These guys want some dinner." Karen Winslow knelt beside her and passed over the children.

Away from the hospital's flickering fluorescent panels, the shadows of the Winslow minivan, the honest light of incandescence fell on them. It was Esmerelda's first good look, and she found everything about them disturbingly fragile. The girl was sleeping, soundless, a cool caramel customer, diaphanous cotton candy hair, milk chocolate pieces for fingers and toes. Beside her the boy yowled in a half dream, delivering sobbing diatribes to legions of infant Jacobin comrades.

"Marat, Marat," Esmerelda cooed. "Settle down, love. Two days in and the world's rattled you already." Her index finger wiped the rugged splotch of black hair over his brow, glanced his nose, raked up his drool. Suddenly he chomped down on her pinky.

"Hot damn!" Esmerelda exclaimed, pulling her digit from his slimy toothless hole. "What was that for?"

"He's hungry, dear," Karen said. "Give him a boob and he'll calm."

"Give him a boob? I can't even move." But before she could muster up the energy to complain about the throbbing in her temples and the dryness of her throat, Jasper and Sven were hauling her across the apartment and shouldering her up onto the mustard-colored couch. Karen arranged the newborns on Esmerelda's tummy and seconds later the boy was inside her muumuu, nuzzling her nipple. She fell back against the sofa, her body unplugged and eyes rolled shut, Marat's suckling sounds bleeding to white in her cumulus mounds of unconsciousness.

SANS-CULOTTES

In the late French revolution, we observed the extremes indulged by both parties chiefly concerned in revolution— the wealthy and the poor! The rich, who, in derision, called their humble fellow-citizens by the contemptuous term of *sans-culottes*, provoked a reacting injustice from the populace, who, as a dreadful return for only a slight, rendered the innocent term of *aristocrate* a signal for plunder or slaughter!

—ISAAC DISRAELI,
Curiosities of Literature, 1835

You hear them talking of nothing but cutting, chopping off heads, not enough blood is flowing.

—Parisian lemonade vendor, speaking of the sans-culottes

Nineteen ninety-one was a war year, yellow ribbons tied to trees, flags lashed to freeway overpasses and framed in bedroom windows. Bombs and planes preempted sitcoms, followed by press conferences with stern generals in shabby briefing rooms, fireworks over the desert. A television camera fell into an Iraqi ventilation chute and went blank. Elementary school students mailed packets of Kool-Aid to soldiers stationed in Saudi Arabia; troops received standing ovations in airports.

As Operation Desert Sabre commenced, a husbandless woman went into labor at the George Washington University Medical Center, in Washington DC. Twelve hours later, as mine plows cleared a passageway between the Umm Qudayr and Al Wafrah oil fields, Marisa Taylor was still at it but screaming and pushing optimistically. Her elaborate cursing saturated the maternity ward, demanding morphine, a lawyer, experimental medical procedures, a fucking table saw, but none of it could right the hemorrhaging, tangled umbilical cord, exhausted nurses falling asleep on the job, undercooked meals, and burned-out light bulbs that were the hallmarks of her four-and-change-day disaster. She was unfortunate to hang on as long as she did—all the way to the hundredth hour, when President Bush announced a cease-fire across the Persian Gulf—establishing a bona fide delivery record that would never be broken, obstetrics' DiMaggio streak. It ended with somnambulant acceptance, a small shudder, the boy's lumpy head riding down a canal of blood. Turned out there was no next of kin, Taylor was a Metrobus driver from Alabama who lived alone, fifty bucks in her retirement fund, an aunt in Birmingham who wanted no part of it, her one-night stand with a prissy Parisian diplomat wholly off the books. Weeks later, when faced with a blank line above "First Name" in the baby's Social Security registration form, an administrator with a morbid sense of humor dubbed the boy Murphy in honor of the only law that mattered in his life so far.

Esmerelda and Jasper fell under a monsoon of changings, feedings, and cleanings, plus double forty-hour workweeks on Market Street, in clown shoes and Gargantuan, tired smiles and sluggish fingers entering data at mere mortal speeds. After dinner they slept like steel weights, Esmerelda snoozing upright on the sofa with the kids nestled on her belly, Jasper snoring like an unmufflered Harley on his single bed. Amid the decentralized family foursome, Sven Johanssen rose each morning at four o'clock, slipped into his overalls, and drank a cup of black coffee before riding his ten-speed to the wharves in Bayview. Those crystalline ten minutes in the morning were the quietest of the day: infants slumbering silently, Esmerelda completely incapacitated from her nightly staircase ascent, Jasper's thunderous snores waning to occasional snorts after four hours under. Oftentimes the foghorns broke the stillness when he stepped outside, though after years of the routine he no longer noticed how the alternating bass notes created the sensation of floating, the way the soft, steady moans set him at ease. He slid to work on this serene carpet, a peaceful pedal through the Presidio's buzzing forest and past the Marina's shuttered bistros and boutiques, gloomy downtown monoliths, a lonely strip of warehouses and gang warfare, until he arrived at the wharves and found his hungover mates cursing the weather and listening to news radio.

At five o'clock, the children's stereo wailing began. Esmerelda pulled up her shirt and let the kids hook in, while Jasper dressed in the dark and got started on Esmerelda's morning hotcakes. After breakfast came burping and diaper replacement, the onerous dressing process, pained pleas to the infants for silence which proved successful only on the rare mornings that Jasper dug up the wherewithal to sing lullabies in his simple Spartan voice. At six the team moved downstairs, Esmerelda more confident heading down the juggernaut than up it, the children pausing their noisemaking to observe the spectacle, Jasper spotting her all the way. They piled into the special services van, wheeled across the city, and were spat out, with walker, at their respective places of business on Market Street at ten minutes to seven.

While Esmerelda Gargantuaned into position, Jasper slung the kids onto the sidewalk and knelt beside them, his eyes dancing mischievously. "Here's the deal," he said. "We got half an hour before I gotta get to work. You guys got any ideas on how to kill thirty minutes?"

"BA-WAH!" Marat cried as Robespierre applauded rowdily.

"That again?" Jasper asked coyly. "Well, I'll see what I can do." But there was only one activity in which Jasper ever indulged his children during the father-children bonding period from 6:50 to 7:20 AM, and a wild ride up and down the sidewalk in his wheelbarrow was it.

He fastened a pair of pillows to the wheelbarrow with duct tape and strapped the kids onto the pillows with bungee cords. With a weary yell he pushed off, slowly shoving the maroon hauler up Market Street's gentle grade. After a quarter block, he took a turn around a fire hydrant, swerved back onto the sidewalk, spun in three tight circles, jogged backward ten steps, took a corner fast through packs of pedestrians, wove a few figure eights around manhole covers, then gently rolled six stairs down into the Muni station and suddenly yanked back up, whooping like a tickled horse. He picked up speed as he got warmed up, pinning the kids on their backs, turning them sideways, on occasion flipping them upside down. Even with the homemade baby straps it looked really dicey, and the posse of street people encamped by the Muni station's steam grate clucked their disapproval.

But the children's faces ran pink in the wind, the urban slalom confirming Jasper's position as the all-time leader in pointless glee and coolness.

Esmerelda monitored the gyroscopic revelry through Copy-Smart's storefront window, fixated on the dearth of legitimate safety devices and hollering at Jasper to slow down. Her nervousness prevented her from eating, and the unusual sight of Esmerelda forgoing a prework snack put the rest of the office on edge too. Everyone loosened up after business began, preoccupied by customers and reassured by the babies' return to their mother's belly and a fresh breakfast burrito on the Gargantuan's foldable tray, though Esmerelda's relief soon turned to resignation as she remembered how she had to deal with these annoying kids all day, and for many years thereafter. But so long as they kept out of elbow range, Esmerelda could get through her shift, and while she didn't particularly enjoy their presence, Slippy Sanders was in love.

"See that?" her boss told her just after the twins' second birthday, pointing at the long but quickly moving queue. Swarming secretaries conversed with Robespierre and Marat in various baby languages; snapped photos; inquired about their haircut preferences, immunization records, bowel movements, and reading proficiency; and distributed candy and toys from their purses. Many reminisced over the days when their own children were small enough to fit in their laps, and though their stories were usually murderously boring, those teary-eyed administrative assistants left the best tips and made sure to come back to the CopySmart flagship store for all their paper-based needs.

"These kids are a gold mine," Slippy added. "Gonna get any more?"

"I'd rather cover myself in honey and wrestle a bear," Esmerelda snarled.

"I'm buying a playpen for the shop," he countered. "They're not babies anymore, and besides, you've earned it."

"Oh no you don't—my kids aren't going to be your puppies in the window. This is no zoo; they stay here with me."

"Suit yourself. But they're getting bigger, and you're getting smaller. The math isn't hard to figure out."

Esmerelda shook her head at the backhanded compliment— *I'm getting smaller?*—and realized that her muumuu had been a bit drafty lately, her shoes a little loose, her thirty-two-stair-and-eight-dip commute slightly less taxing. Maybe she had lost a few. Anyway, her children were growing quickly, that was undeniable, and the two of them did combine for an awful lot of weight and surface area.

She relented, with the caveat that the playpen could not be placed anywhere near the window and had to be accompanied by a DO NOT FEED CHILDREN sign. Within the first week the secretaries were making the pilgrimage to CopySmart three or four times a day, noting the children's food intake, observing their naptimes, floating theories about their life callings. A pot of coffee was installed, and the CopySmart flagship store became a break destination, with support staff overflowing onto the sidewalk and jostling for the best kiddie view, often running off a few hundred unnecessary copies to justify their loitering. Business,

Slippy Sanders reported, was booming, and Esmerelda's wages soared too.

Jasper Winslow tried to take advantage of the captive audience. "Free food! Who wants it?" he called, waving bunches of coupons at the secretaries. "Discounts here, pizza and beer. Why roll the dice with full price? You're better off with half off." Though most of the secretaries were on permanent dieting kicks or apprehensive of street promotions, some accepted his coupons, and a few even used them. Even so, Jasper's cash cow was shrinking to naught amid a flurry of efficiently processed photocopy transactions.

"Mama," he told Karen Winslow over morning grilled-onion-and-cheese sandwiches at the Tip Top Diner, "I'm losing it. No more 10 percent, barely even 5. Esmerelda's eating less, though I can't blame her. I sure did like having the money though."

"Wake up, son. The woman's playing you like a harpsichord. Doesn't pay rent and gets the kids all day. Before you know it, she'll get child support too. Better lock her up before she does you in. You gonna eat that?" Jasper passed over his crusts. "I'll take them home for your sister, God bless her. Now why couldn't you find yourself a nice girl like her to knock up, someone who wouldn't ever string you along like this?"

The seeds were planted for a horrible misinterpretation, an error that Karen Winslow never would have made when she was younger, but her children were all grown up, and she sometimes made the mistake of treating them their age. Still, the relevant bit got through too, and that night, after Marat and Robespierre fell asleep curled against Esmerelda's belly, Jasper came out from the bedroom and took a seat on the sofa, much closer to her than permitted when she was fully awake, nearly touching.

"Baby, marry me."

Esmerelda turned her head toward the weight on the couch. Jasper wore a yolk-yellow tie and powder-blue jacket with his overalls; his face was clamped shut, hands clasped and hanging between his shivering legs. Her eyes burned from a pungent cologne—paprika and formaldehyde teased with sweat. "You're a sweetheart, Jasper," she murmured, "really, you are. But I'm just not the marrying type. Come on, you don't want me around, ruining your life."

"Honey, you've been living here for two years now, and my life's better than ever." He almost mentioned the exception of the recent drop in coupon usage but managed to stifle it.

"Come on man, don't fool with me. You don't even have a ring."

"That's not true either." He reached into his front overall pocket and took out a ring with a shiny diamond in it, biggest one he could find at the pawnshop.

Esmerelda fell blue-faced and quiet, then touched a chubby finger to the stone's tip and ran it down the gold band's cool contours, circling over the sticky patch where the price tag had been recently peeled off. "Jasper. I never—"

"There's a lot you haven't expected from me. Food, shelter, and love, for starters, and I got all that in boxes. Now what's it going to be? Marry me, and I'll make all your days bright as this here ring." He wagged the prize in front of her, scattering the spectrum over Esmerelda's nose.

Esmerelda felt something hard form in her intestines and imagined how much her day-to-day life would change if she signed on, hardly anything, it was just a piece of paper for legal affairs and inheritances, an outdated convention, didn't matter to her. Jasper worked hard and took care of her, he was great with the kids, he cooked or provided heavily discounted food, washed the clothes and ironed them, even did windows; it was like getting a babysitter and butler for free. She imagined the glitter rock installed on her hand, filtering white light, a movie theater marquee announcing her preciousness. Right here in front of her, worth a couple grand easy.

To her surprise, the ring even fit her finger.

The wedding was held at City Hall during lunch, the groom's side consisting of Karen Winslow; Jasper's handicapped sister,

Tina; and Sven Johanssen straight from the wharves, his hair heavy with salty Bay winds and impregnating the clerk's office with the smell of burned oil. As for the bride's side, Esmerelda's mother hadn't answered her calls, so Lakshmi handled the flowers and Slippy Sanders gave her away and three of the regular CopySmart baby-oglers/coffee-guzzlers provided tear-drenched anecdotes afterward. Marat was well behaved in the presence of awe-inspiring police officers, while Robespierre wandered off after the ceremony to be located, after a harried address over the PA, trying to sneak into the mayor's office. This first-ever bout of misbehavior even made the paper, a whimsical story in the *Examiner* published largely because of Robespierre's newsworthy name.

"A toast!" Slippy lifted his glass at the postceremony luncheon at the Market Street Grill. "To Ezzie and Jasper, Robespierre and Marat! May your shared lives bring you happiness and prosperity!"

"A lifetime of love," Karen Winslow added. Again she looked shorter, Esmerelda realized, stunted by at least an inch, her newly acquired daughter-in-law surely having something to do with it. "An eternity of joy. God bless."

Lost in the aftermath of handshakes and marital aphorisms, way more wine than usual, a disappointingly Zoog-less dessert cart, the newlyweds slipped out to the sidewalk for a couple minutes of air. Standing ten feet apart and stupefied by the speed of improbable events, Jasper gazed back through the window at his younger sister's neckline as Esmerelda leaned against a parking meter and computed the temporal implications of a lifetime living with and fucking this guy. Jasper was sixteen years older than she and could easily die off in the next couple of decades; standing in the street and touching strangers all day wasn't the healthiest line of work. But she hadn't been doing herself any favors, even if she was down to 350—all that weight dragged on her heart. All told, she realized, her sentence ranged somewhere from ten to life.

Not even the sparkle of compressed carbon could assuage the pain induced by those overdue calculations, and by the time she returned to work she was sour and beat.

"Why the long face?" asked Slippy. "This is the happiest day of your life, Esmerelda. You've got your soul mate and father of your kids locked up, a stone on your finger."

"It's just a lot to . . . get used to."

"Overwhelmed, eh? Never thought I'd see the day."

A rap at the window: Jasper waving, blowing kisses. Esmerelda nodded, dumb.

"There he goes," Slippy observed. "A good man, a decent man. A bit silly in that outfit, I've always felt. But your man. Celebrate him." He handed her an envelope. "Happy wedding day."

Years later, when pressed, Esmerelda agreed it was conceivable that Slippy's unbalanced wedding gift had been an honest mistake, thrown off by an urgent phone call or a pressing personal problem that had forced him to make out the check under duress. But her far more favored theory held that the omission was intentional; a reprimand of Marat's occasional tantrums, rudeness, and standard little-boy behavior that was occasionally frowned upon by their customer base of nitpicking mothers; an imbecile bachelor businessman figuring that financial punishment could make a little kid grow up. Either way, the "Pay to the Order of" line of the CopySmart corporate check inside the flimsy unsigned card contained the name of just one of Esmerelda's offspring, and it was with confused celebration that Esmerelda trudged over to the bank, opened a money market account in Robespierre's name, and deposited the sum. She unveiled her hypothesis to Jasper after work.

"What's he got against Matt?" Jasper asked distractedly. "He's just a kid. Rough around the edges, sure, but he's kinda cute and making money for him besides."

"I know it, Jasper, but what are we going to do, complain? It's a very generous gift."

Agitation crept into his voice: "The nurse said he's got karma, got it in loads. Well that's fine and good, but I bet the boy would take ten thousand bucks over karma any day. Wouldn't you?"

Esmerelda refrained from discussing the intricacies of karma, as her matrimonial sellout didn't bode well in terms of just deserts. During the ensuing silence she smoothed over her muumuu and cleared wax from her ear, trying to remember the words to a punk song stuck in her head, when she noticed Jasper smiling oddly at her, an eerie absence. "Where are the kids?"

"At my mother's house."

"And Sven?" Alarms went off.

"Out. All night."

"It's quiet here. I've never heard it so quiet."

They listened to the surf roll at Baker Beach, wind easing through brush, puttering car engines. Jasper could almost hear his cock harden, bristling against his underpants, stretching out the elastic waistband.

He slipped his arm around his new wife.

"What do you think you're doing, Jasper?"

"It's our wedding night, baby. I'm about to make me some love."

He said it staunchly, no room for equivocation. "How about a shot of vodka or something," Esmerelda stalled.

"I'll do you one better." He produced the same cardboard box from their critical encounter thirty-four months earlier and popped it open, revealing two-thirds of the Zoogman's Zoog. Even freezer burned and stale, Zoog sent Esmerelda's pulse into overdrive on sight.

She ate the rest with her hands, breathing through her nose. She fell through the floor into lakes of warm milk and Mozart, while in a parallel galaxy Jasper shredded her muumuu and ripped off her panties with his teeth. She laughed when his penis was unsheathed, but fell mute as he felt out the right crevice and proceeded to pound. Practice made for significant improvement, she noted, and spirited moaning commenced in earnest.

"That's right, baby. That's how daddy does ya. My girl. My baby." Jasper was rotating his hips, hitting all her spots.

"Have you been watching porn or something? I didn't know you could do it like this. That info—unh—might have changed the equation." She reached to squeeze his ass but settled for a tired wave instead.

"Naw, baby, just finding my groove." A crooked smile spread over Jasper's mouth, his snaggletooth incisors jutting out preposterously.

Minutes of floor-thumping passed, sweat slicking the linoleum, dishes clattering in kitchen cabinets. Esmerelda was upgrading her karmic balance sheet and considering moving into an advanced, nonmissionary receiving position, when a possible coital consequence ambled out from her brain. "Jasper," she mumbled, "don't let it fly down there. Two's already more than we can handle."

"Unh-huh," he said, quickening his pace, his face a stack of hard lines and concentration.

"You hear me, bud? Don't bring your magic potion into my house."

"I gotcha," he said, and broke out wild, screwing in spin cycle, whirling with animal noises, way more motion than she'd thought possible. Not a bad ravishing, Esmerelda thought; she even felt somewhat sexy. She listened to his grunts accelerate, watched his brown neck sprout veins. It was hard to move.

"You like that shit? Aw, yeah. Eraser dick, nothing, this the hog for you!"

Jasper's frame shook; his neck craned back; his eyes fluttered; his lips wrenched open. She heard the mush of his grinding teeth, forced air blasting from his mouth and nose, involuntary ecstasy. It was too much, much too much; she could accept Jasper as a husband and father but not love, not yet, and she wasn't real comfortable with sex either. And she definitely didn't want more kids. She kicked out reflexively, her feet meeting his thin chest and cracking through.

"Yaaaaa!"

She pushed on. Pain hammered Jasper's middle. He gasped. He slipped out.

He spurted.

"You fucking retard!" Esmerelda hollered. "What the fuck were you trying to do? Ever heard of a jimmy hat? Cause I don't have the funds or the patience to deal with more of your hell spawn."

Jasper opened his eyes and saw semen curdling on the floor. Confused, disgusted, in pain, and still a little turned on, the path of least resistance won out: he stopped breathing.

"Seriously, is your brain installed? Do you own stock in abortion clinics? Christ almighty, that was a close shave. Dumbass." She pushed him away and rolled onto her side. "I'm hitting the showers."

It took Esmerelda a few minutes to work her way to her knees. From her elevated vantage point she had a direct view of Jasper's ashen face, his still chest, his bones piled lifelessly like discarded coat hangers. She heard Jasper's body thud to the ground and looked over to find his face ashen and still, his bones in a messy pile like discarded coat hangers.

"Oh no. Hell no." Propelling herself forward with her toes, she slid on her belly to Jasper's broken, nude body. "I'm not raising these kids by myself, bud," she whispered, "not a chance." She rolled him onto his back with a few rams of her offensive-lineman shoulders, propped back his head, pinched his nose, put her mouth onto his, and blew into her husband's trachea and jumbo lungs.

It was the first time Ezzie's lips had ever made good contact with Jasper's, the first time he'd breathed her air and tasted her tongue. There had been other kisses, or attempts at them, the latest of which had occurred at City Hall just ten hours earlier and came off to their witnesses as more of an accidental near-brush, not even touching—but this was different; this was life.

Jasper would never forget how a first kiss, even at the age of forty-eight, could shock the life back into a body.

A trembling man came back to Stillwell Road. "Jasper, what happened?" Esmerelda asked, her voice tremulous, her concern genuine. She could tell he needed a calm word, an act of love, something to mollify the worm of disgust burrowing through him. But Esmerelda had done a lot of work putting out, then crawling over and saving his life, and she felt she'd earned a jab or two.

"That's some lethal stuff, your devil juice," she squawked. "Do us all a favor and try not to ruin the universe with more from where that shit came from."

Jasper did not release another syllable, but his eyeballs spoke encyclopedias, palpitating, flooded with ferocious blood. Gone was the whiff of respectability he'd felt that afternoon while filling out the paperwork to marry the mother of his children, the calm solidness of marble pillars and laws, the comfort of establishment. Ten hours was all he got, enough time for a big lunch, a half-drunk afternoon at work, and one lonesome kiss before this inexorable torching, the scourge of her lips leaving busted ribs, a battered ego, uproarious anger, an unprecedented urge to skin kittens and sell minors into slavery.

He grabbed at his earlobes, then walked to the door and kicked it down. "What's the big deal? Your eyes are gonna blow," she ventured, but by then he was gone, naked, broken breastbone and all, hobbling down the steps and into the woods, and then Esmerelda's ears picked up the splashing sea and the undulating foghorn, and she stopped to savor the quiet.

No children, no husband, no roommate, no kids. A girl could get used to this.

Then she heard two small cries, pins sticking thumbs. An extreme suck of air. Shadows spiking through the woods, deleting colors and shapes. Alone in the apartment, Esmerelda washed off in the shower and sat on the couch in the dark, squeezing a blanket in her hands, knees hopping, watching for purple pits of rage embedded somewhere amid the Presidio flora.

Her state of karma, she realized, was exactly as deserved.

Then the special services van was honking, Karen Winslow was hauling in the kids, and teachers and CEOs were lining up for copies and binding.

"I'm going for a croissant," Lakshmi said at 7:30. "Jasper around? He had a 50 percent-off coupon yesterday."

"Not sure. You know where he should be." Esmerelda's face was frozen solid.

Lakshmi was back in ten minutes, mildly annoyed at paying full price. "I walked up and down the street looking for him. The guys at the bus stop haven't seen him. Everything cool?"

Esmerelda scanned the empty store, wishing for a customer, a sudden electrical fire, a mild earthquake.

"Esmerelda?"

Lakshmi took in Esmerelda's empty face, ice-white, motionless but for a flashing eyelid. She recalled it was the morning after her wedding night and walked quickly back to the workroom, inquiring no more.

That night the sheets on Jasper's bed lay empty. Esmerelda whispered invented prayers to the kids perched on her belly, running out of words after three or four lines, running from please and forgiveness to Christ fuckall and goddammit to hell and back, the curses sticking to her tongue like salt. In the morning she was up off the couch an hour early, and, with a quick-fire feeding and dressing, she managed to get to work on time. "BA-WAH!" Marat demanded as she settled in at her desk. He slipped on a discarded donut box on the floor behind the cash register and began to cry.

"I've got some water right here, Marat. Hang on."

"BA-WAH BA-WAH BA-WAH!" The punches landed on her kneecap, but with Esmerelda's protective flesh-jelly, they barely registered.

"Wheelbarrow," Robespierre explained.

Spirals of wheelbarrows bombinated through Esmerelda's head, spinning in paired trails like DNA helixes and awash in a blizzard of coupon confetti. A ticker-tape memorial parade; her marriage laid in state. Then two bangs in her head and she slumped, pissed, and exited the room for a few hours.

When she woke up in the back office—these short bouts with unconsciousness were a semiregular thing now, and Slippy Sanders knew better than to slap his prime producer off to the hospital again: "Stick her in the recovery room and have candy ready," he'd ordered, "she'll be a mess after missing lunch"— Marat and Robespierre climbed onto her with hot kisses, leaping onto her moonbounce belly and papering her body with their American-cheese-and-apple-juice stink. They asked long-winded questions about the nature of birds and told pointless jokes about peanuts and sang incoherent songs over terrible, rambling melodies. The wheelbarrow appeared completely forgotten.

Maybe everything would turn out OK, she hoped.

Beneath the Golden Gate Bridge, a man fell into a hole a decade deep.

Sven Johanssen, Jasper's crane-operating roommate, celebrated his wedding night exile with a case of Nordsjö Gårdsbryggeri beer on a bench by the beach. He went straight to work, endured nine hours flouncing inside a metal can, made his weekly rounds of the strip clubs, passed out in an alley for a few hours, and headed back to the docks for another shift. Reeking of cat piss and yeast, he was downright asinine by the time he got home.

"Jasper's gone, yah? Save deh suitcases for later," he told Esmerelda while he hacked at a tuna with a Chinese cleaver. "Too-night is a part-y."

Stuffing pizza in her mouth, Esmerelda grumbled her preference for a quiet evening alone.

"Gurl, hate to break it, but yer not on the lease. Yer vote's not counted, and we guhn have fun. Join up, if deh spirits allow." He salted the tuna and shoved it into the oven. "Heck if I'm not goin-a need more fishes."

Twenty minutes later, four lasses from Linköping rang up, bearing jars of herring and plates of butter cookies. Johan from Jönköping arrived with a tub of head cheese, then "Shark Bait" Ingemar with his left arm chewed off waded in and challenged the four lasses to an arm wrestling match, which he lost intentionally but not before cupping some premium Swedish boobs. They were followed by a parade of Malmöans and Göteborgians and Stockholmians and even a few Finns mixed in, swilling liquor and recounting recent fights and packing into the empty space created by a man lost in a hole. They downed grog, roast korv, and all kinds of large-headed fish, throwing scraps out the window for a couple of roaming dogs. Esmerelda watched wearily from the couch, a forlorn lump smothered by Roxette's *Joyride* album.

When the children were tucked away in Jasper's old bedroom and Esmerelda appeared to be asleep, a Viking hat materialized, bottles of Svedka, Sven's collection of Madonna-themed shot glasses. Someone suggested they all get naked. "Gustavus Adolphus commands you to consume!" cried a tall redheaded man, who, between his hair color and leadership qualities, resembled the Swedish king enough to invoke his authority. Through a newspaper bullhorn he ordered the first round of shots and disrobement, creating a heap of socks in the center of the living room. A fuzzy hour transpired. The pile of clothes rose steadily, absorbing caps, pants, socks, flannel shirts, undershirts, empty bottles, liquor-tinged pantyhose and brassieres and male thongs. A tannic glaze smelted over lips and skin, sloppy eyes reframed proportions, the feel of flesh grew significantly more scrumptious.

Esmerelda awoke to a shaking in her belly. She generally attributed such disruptions to hunger and reached for the carton of emergency malt balls she kept under the couch. Her hand brushed a sweaty foot, then a stiff nipple; she opened her eyes.

"Shark Bait" Ingemar was naked with three lasses and a lad; Johan was jamming it into what looked to be either a midget or a grossly underage girl; kitchen utensils were inserted into shaved orifices; fair hair and pale skin interlocked in a frighteningly Aryan human jungle gym. The sofa shook with their hectic movements.

"That explains the tummy trouble," she muttered. But somewhere south of her stomach a dime-shaped hub flickered to life.

Sven Johanssen tiptoed around the room, sipping vodka from a sealskin flask and coaching. "Knulla! Dat's a way to land a harpoon, yah. Open up, gurl, make it easy. De man bushed from work all day. Use deh hips, thrust forward, bang! Kjell, argh, no, no, no! No teeth, use tongue! Ay gurl, why no playfriend? Waiting for me? I finish deh bottle, I come see you. OK?"

After another circuit around the living room, he lowered himself onto the sofa and provided running commentary on an oscillating love triangle, three Swedes covered in raspberry jam and tongues. His stubbled cheekbones bit through the half-light of the dangling kitchen fixture, a hard gibbous moon that moved Esmerelda's clitoris a step closer to activation.

A minute later, Sven discovered a ham-bone forearm spider-climbing up his leg and let slip his first thought:

"Ya, big gurl, ready to play?"

Was she.

Her hand raced through its ascent and snatched Sven's harpoon. She took a long pull on his flask and bathed his rigid weaponry in a thorough vodka wash. After a few minutes of toothy lathering Johan got jealous from being left out of the fat-girl fun, so he raised her muumuu from behind, parted her whale cheeks, and dove in. The lasses wandered over intrigued, bringing their coterie of crotch-pumpers with them, and in a few minutes Esmerelda was completely covered in Swedish swingers. Somebody sliced off her muumuu with the blue-jeweled scissors from her great wool bag, and no sooner was Esmerelda's celestial nudity unveiled than it was consumed, entirely, exciting her sexual soul into a placid, perfect trance.

It was Marat's first night alone in bed, and he dreamed of cartoon devils dancing around him, poking his face with hot brands, spitting black lava. The door to the bedroom swung open, Hades light filtering around a one-armed monster.

"Alo? Helvete, this ain't the loo."

The monster left, the door was ajar, sugary pop music leaked in. Marat climbed to his feet and stepped through the vortex to another universe with

naked people lumped together in a pile

crazy mixed-up yelling

men thumping against women with their hips, spanking them

He ventured delicately into the room, staying in the shadows. The dream was so vivid it smelled. He saw his mother in the center, her head knocking about like when the Gargantuan hit a speed bump, her neck wild with sweat. Her mass of skin disruptively pink, outlining the moaning white-skinned ghosts in orbit around her.

Her eyes drifted over him, stopped, and blinked thirty times before Marat could move.

The monster grabbed him, hoisted him over his shoulder, threw him back in bed, and told him to stay put, buster, no sneaking out. Furniture scraped outside; the door wouldn't budge. For ten minutes he heard boots tromping and low gargled voices, the music cut, glass crashing, then quiet except for his mother's distinctive sobs, rumbling and endless, as if they'd run out of string cheese.

He woke up in his new bed to the staccato beeps of the special services van, the nightmare haze unforgettable in the back of his pixilated head.

THE TENNIS COURT OATH

On June 20, [the revolutionaries] took the famous "Tennis-Court" oath, "to come together wherever circumstances may dictate, until the constitution of the kingdom shall be established."

—JAMES HARVEY ROBINSON,
Medieval and Modern Times

The real event of the Tennis Court was to unite all parties against the crown, and to make them adopt the new policy of radical and indefinite change . . .

—JOHN EMERICH EDWARD DALBERG-ACTON,
Lectures on the French Revolution

On their third birthday, Esmerelda dressed the kids in matching Teenage Mutant Ninja Turtle sweat suits and took them to the zoo. Feeling optimistic after her recent slight but statistically significant weight loss and her relative success at single mother-hood, she left the Gargantuan at home. It was a mistake: the fog made her knees ache; her shin splints fired up on the hike from the bus stop to the ticket window; after a minute of sustained walking she barely had the strength to hang on to her walker, a loose knuckle away from a sidewalk sandwich. Robespierre and Marat ran ahead to look at the giraffes and great apes, climbing onto fences and digging half-eaten cookies out of garbage cans as Esmerelda gulped distilled water from her bag and humped over to the first-aid station. Fortunately, Esmerelda thought, as she announced their departure fifteen minutes later, they wouldn't remember a thing—a prediction that proved true with the exception of the roaring lion, which embedded itself in the bedwetting dreams of both twins for weeks to come. They took a cab across the street to the Carousel Restaurant, where a waiter planted candles in matching cheeseburgers and sang "Happy Birthday" in a faux French accent.

"This is why we live in San Francisco, kids," Esmerelda said. "Appreciation for the arts." But her children ignored her, lost in slurry tears from the cut of the waiter's soda jerk cap, which looked as if it had been stolen straight off the head of their father. The crying did not stop for hours.

After a few seasons in a nursery for abandoned infants, drinking formula overstock and wearing coarse municipal diapers, Murphy was placed with a Korean foster family in Wheaton, Maryland. It was a nondescript, two-story, off-the-rack home: three bedrooms but housing ten foster children, with two stacks of bunk beds in each kid's room plus a pull-out futon for the inhabitant with the most seniority. The Ahns aimed for full capacity to maximize their tax shelter, which translated into long lines at the bathroom, irregular feedings, plenty of name-calling, pinching, theft, brawls over the remote control, and whole meals stolen off plates, with close to zero in the way of basic supervision or instruction. Early on Murphy developed a system to keep himself fed, whereby he stuffed handfuls of rice from the cooker into his mouth until he spat up tapioca. After a series of blue-faced near-choking experiences, the Ahns figured out his racket and tried to scare him out of it, pointing out the health consequences in simple child language: stop breathe, no move, die, boom. But then the phone rang or a customer came to the register at the minimarket they owned, and as they slung him onto their shoulder and ran their business, his transgression forgotten, he watched the world watch him get away with whatever he wanted.

As the years passed, he graduated from rice to candy, consuming small hills of sugar that jolted him into hyperspeed and laid the foundation for a lifetime of skin problems. At least one body part was always jiggling, creating an aura of anxiety and shiftiness, his image less than trustworthy. He was unable to read anything for more than fifteen seconds, exploding with a combination of poorly executed gymnastics and undisciplined kung fu, rambling from the kitchen to the living room to the toilet, often extending out to the yard and into traffic. Chocolate captivated him; he blew his entire two-dollar allowance on Kit Kat bars and M&M's pounder bags that he hid from his foster siblings in the bottom of his bed, until his pediatrician told the Ahns to cut him off, at which point he resorted to stealing. On a Saturday morning in broad daylight, surveillance cameras at the Ahns' convenience store captured Murphy jamming Mounds bars down his pants from three different angles; he was apprehended on his way out of the bathroom, his lips smeared brown, wrapper shreds in his pocket. They questioned and requestioned him in the manager's office, and when he refused to confess, they showed him the incriminating footage in super-slow motion. "Not me," he repeated in a dour voice, "not me." When they eventually took him home, he ran straight to the kitchen and shoveled rice down his throat until it all came coursing back up.

Murphy was spanked, then grounded. But he held his position, repeating that it wasn't him, it was a case of mistaken identity, he'd been framed. He insisted so loudly and fervently that his foster parents, Marvin and June Ahn, started to wonder if there *had* been some kind of misunderstanding; maybe another kid in the store that afternoon had the same Washington Capitals T-shirt and buzz cut, the same addiction to sucrose. It wasn't impossible—the video was black and white and grainy, and Murphy was so vehement, his sense of injustice so furious, that Marvin and June, after dispensing tough love to dozens of misbehaving foster kids, ended the grounding after only two days.

The next afternoon Marvin found Murphy out behind the

dumpster with a carton of Reese's Pieces, his fingers stained with candy coloring, his breath sickly with corn syrup. Marvin was halfway through imposing a double grounding, with interest, when Murphy observed that he'd seen a big furry rat run along the grout. Maybe he should tell the health department— they could shut down the store, and that would really suck. Marvin grabbed the candy and shoved the kid into the office, amazed by the extent of the seven-year-old's ability to believe his own bullshit, his wanton dearth of innocence. In his years of foster parenting, he'd seen plenty of lying, name-calling, theft, and general loutishness, but blackmail was a first. And extra-alarming from a kid who could barely form complete sentences.

He put Murphy to work building a display out of expired soup cans and flipped open the Pepsi calendar on his desk. September. Maybe there was a way to get him in a football league. Not a team guy but hardheaded enough to be useful; open-field tackles and wind sprints were just the thing to burn off this edge. He checked in on the soup-can display, rising into two tall twisting staircases boxed in by Doric columns, a palatial grand foyer. Murphy lay on the floor working on stylized trim arrangements, gnawing on a pack of Rolos and working on his side kick. Martial arts could work, possibly boxing, and Marvin scanned the Yellow Pages for nearby training gyms until he heard a leaden collapse, dumbbells rolling off a sawhorse, soup cans rolling in eight directions, Murphy standing over the pile with chop-hands ready, favoring his left foot after what was likely a leaping roundhouse. Marvin threw the phonebook on the ground and watched the kid bounce out the door and across the parking lot, a whirling dervish yipping imitation Japanese, throwing Bruce Lee double jabs as candy corn spilled from his pockets. Last thing Murphy needed was mugger training, Marvin realized, and instead decided to tire him out the old-fashioned way: floor-scrubbing and shelf-stocking and all-purpose ass-licking; work him till his feet swelled up his sneakers.

❖

For four years Fanny lived alone in the modest banana-yellow house where Esmerelda had grown up, a block from the beach and within walking distance of the elementary school. The solitary space swelled with the morning of April 1, 1979: a bowl of oatmeal at 4 AM, an extra spoonful of brown sugar, a ham sandwich and an apple in a paper bag for lunch, a last scrape of her husband Harold's chapped lips against her forehead before the day's fishing expedition to the Farallones. The door shutting on a creaky hinge, which Fanny oiled immediately lest it wake up Esmerelda. Harold's truck coughing into the fog. A rainy day of soap operas, cleaning, grocery shopping, a hot bath. Dinner in the oven, Esmerelda doing homework in her room. The doorbell. A police officer describing squalls, dropped radio, Harold's skiff miles off course. The Coast Guard out in high seas, floodlights beaming over whitecaps. Two days later they found Harold's signature green net shredded by the sea.

The strike to her chest, her husband stolen away—part of her forever, a tattoo around a bullet hole. April 1, 1979, April Fool's Day, no joke.

Fanny wore the same clothing, ate the same food, lived in the same house, received the same amount of Social Security each month. Every election cycle she voted for the same presidential candidate, though Gerry Ford had been out of contention for some time. She drove the same Mustang convertible with the same expired registration, refusing to submit to a newfangled smog test. She hadn't approved when Esmerelda enrolled in the culinary academy, or landed the gig prepping pastries at the yuppie haven Incognito, or put on weight like a bear headed for hibernation, or started her worker drone job at the CopySmart flagship store, or showed up with her noisy pups and shipped out to Jasper's Presidio apartment. But after a few months Esmerelda's smell had wondrously evaporated along with her out-of-place clothing, modern music, perplexing street slang, and ineffective weight-management devices. Heavy ocean air and daughterless simplicity seeped into the house, cigarettes and gin propping Fanny aloft.

In the summer of 1994, she began receiving letters in Esmerelda's handwriting folded over photographs of brown children, a cute girl and a chubby boy smiling and scowling, both with Harold's bean-shaped eyes. In early August she received a phone call inviting her to supper at the Cliff House, and though she thought she knew better, when Esmerelda reported that her kids were getting into fishing, dropping poles at Lake Merced on weekends and digging for their own night crawlers before school, curiosity got the better of her. Esmerelda met her at the restaurant with a trembling hug and, after confirming Fanny had brought her checkbook, began narrating an eight-course eating extravaganza with tales of her missing husband, her monstrous credit balance, her years-overstayed guest status, the depravity of Little Stockholm hedonism. Her jaw-dropping grocery bill. The final decision of the city's eviction board, notice served by the sheriff's department. And the logical point that there were unused bedrooms in Fanny's house.

"I do not think so, dear," Fanny said, cooling her after-dinner tea with a nip of gin from her purse. "You are a big girl; you can take care of yourself."

Esmerelda softly gargled her water. She had forgotten her mother's snooty refusal to use contractions in speech, as if efficient diction was a mark of baseness.

"Ma, I need help." Slow, measured tea bag dips. "I do not think it would be a good decision. I do not like changes to my household, and the way things are suit me fine. Your tornado children would create a tremendous ruckus, and why should I put up with it? Besides, you left me in the first place. So."

Esmerelda dug her nails into her knees and waited for the urge to throw her silverware at her mother's face to peter out. Eventually: "I didn't want things to come to this, Ma. I know what you've been through, and believe me, I miss Dad too. But I gotta set things straight. First, I didn't leave home because I wanted to. I tried to bring the tots home, but you wouldn't have them—"

Fanny loudly tore open a sugar packet with her teeth and dumped it into her tea.

"—truth is, you're my only family. I'm in a bad place: my hubby up and vanished; my kids growing up in Orgyville, USA; work all day and kids all night and still not enough cash to cover expenses. And the sheriff's going to forcibly remove us tomorrow. So, Ma. Please. Let us stay with you."

Lumps of perspiration lazed on Esmerelda's brow. Fanny was perplexed—she couldn't remember the last time Esmerelda had said "please"—and somewhat swayed, her heart the tiniest bit thawed.

"You understand, Esmerelda, I am the boss. Things must remain the way they are. No changes whatsoever. That means you may not replace my classic furniture, or put your hideous modern music on the phonograph, or, heaven forbid, exchange my tasteful stores of clothing with the whoring outfits I see on the streets."

Ezzie nodded frantically, hair snakes snipping free from her bun.

"My word is final. If I ask you something, I expect it to be done right away. Not after you are done with your pizza or your gallon of ice cream or whatever it may be. Immediately."

Yes, said Esmerelda's shaking eyes, *I'll carry you on my back over continents and across solar systems if that's what it takes.*

Fanny extracted a ream of paper from her own massive wool bag and thumped it on the table. "I anticipated that you might want to move back in, and took the liberty of calling my attorney, to have my conditions written out."

The stack ran fifty pages deep, single spaced, a hard block of information and clauses. Esmerelda flipped through it, scanning first sentences and whistling appreciatively. Whereunto. Whereas. Be it agreed. Whatever. She dipped into her bag and groped for a writing implement.

Fanny swatted her elbows. "Read it first! I thought I drilled some sense into that noggin of yours."

"I'm moving in, not signing away my life. Ain't like I'm buying a house."

"Oh yes you are, dear." Fanny slipped a butter knife into the sheaf of paper and terraced off the top third. "That is part of the contract, section five. If you choose to relocate yourself and your offspring into my home, you must buy a house to leave. Not just any house either—a house in the city of San Francisco, with a bedroom for each inhabitant, and within three hundred feet of a park. A sound investment. I will not have you squander your money again."

Outside, a black Town Car glided into the parking lot, piping smooth jazz at a firm volume.

"A house? I work at a copy shop, Ma. Not really in the house-buying income bracket."

"It is high time for you to own something. This day-to-day nonsense, this absurd employment making photocopies, well, you are walking in place. You need a career, not a job. It is time to buy into something, to set goals and achieve them. The baking was a start, but you let yourself be pulled astray. Get it together, dear. It will make you a stronger, more focused woman. To achieve and accomplish, these are the traits missing from your constitution. Please, moving back in with your mother? It is the life goal of very few people."

Esmerelda clenched a smile. So many counterarguments burning: she'd just been promoted to assistant manager, what a lot of people called a career, thank you, even if it wasn't exactly the gig she'd always dreamed of; raising her kids right was a goal, a darn good one; and anyway, Fanny hadn't worked a day in her life, just scooted forward on the life insurance and government checks.

"I am sure that you are thinking about the many ways in which you benefit the world. You have two children, neither of whom appears to be deformed or unhealthy according to the photographs I received. To which I say: welcome to the club, dear. And what is more, your attitude toward the children appears to be that they are the ropes keeping you tied to the dock. But it is not apparent that you were going to leave the dock in the first place. You require motivation, a destination for your voyage. A house is a practical place to start."

Esmerelda placed her hand over her mouth and looked up at the ceiling. She counted the chandeliers, then the crystals in the chandeliers, the cuts in the crystals, the scratches in the cuts, most of this imagined, her eyesight not that good. She haronked into the tablecloth and began gathering her allotment of knives and forks for a direct facial attack.

Then the door chime jingled, footsteps cantered their way. A crash, a child's lethargic whine, and finally the appearance of a four-year-old black girl wearing a formal pink dress and a bow in her hair, carrying a carton of Parliament Menthols poorly wrapped in the newspaper funnies.

"Grandma!" Robespierre placed the cigs beside Fanny's tea-cup and hugged her leg, just like they'd practiced. "I'm so happy to meet you! You're even prettier than Mom said!" Robespierre's eyes fell shivery and teary, and she buried her nose in her grandmother's jeans. With song ringing in her chest, Fanny enacted a policy decision on the spot: she was done voting Republican down the line, so long as she could write in her granddaughter instead.

A yelp echoed from points unseen, and a boy dressed in corduroys and fire truck suspenders came tromping around the corner, gripping a handle of Beefeater with both hands.

"Gramma!" The Beefeater hit the floor and Marat plowed into Fanny's lap, his teeth sticking to her knotted sweater.

"And who is this?" Fanny asked, a bit shocked by the boy's sudden proximity to her skin but adequately charmed by the warmth of human contact.

"Marrraaaa," the boy blubbed.

"That's the team," Esmerelda summed up. "Good kids, obviously, and I'm on the comeback trail. Plus we brought presents.

C'mon, Ma, whaddya say?" She held out her hand like a dying flower.

Fanny slipped into analytic mode, tamping down the flight in her throat and the heat on her lap for a long-range assessment of the situation: the odds that Esmerelda would ever actually fulfill the real estate investment portion of her contract were a stretch; these children were initially quite attractive and friendly, but in the end they were children and would require decades of fussing and income and house policing to shove into adulthood.

A black tar oozed through her head, dropping her internal temperature, a sad and sticky weight. She closed her eyes and waited for the gloom to pass, creating a firm and stationary foundation which enabled the kid in her lap to squirm up into standing and wrap her wool sweater in a tight toddler embrace. She tried to ignore it, still aiming for a dispassionate decision, but then the kid kissed her heavy cheek and mumbled that he loved her and it was pretty much over. Fanny hugged back hard, both hands across his back and her mouth full of his hair, solid in knowing that despite all the uncomfortable parts of cohabitation these kids were here, alive, committed—hers.

The restaurant greeter slid into view, rustling his hands in his pockets. He was a skinny, olive-skinned kid, peach-fuzz mustache and eyes shaped like small envelopes. "How's your meal?" he asked.

"Fine," Robespierre said.

"Go away," added Esmerelda, igniting a fierce smile on Fanny's face.

"Good, good. Listen." His head cranking sideways, both hands up and out in a surrendering calm. "As a parent, you know, family, we have an obligation to tell you something." Two sniffs, then, gravely: "about your boy."

"What boy?" Fanny barked as Marat's legs flutter-kicked air.

With a nonchalant Latino nod he said: "We have reports your boy was consuming alcohol on the premises."

"Excuse me?" Esmerelda woofed, but Fanny had already scooped up a table knife and started hollering:

"What on earth do you think you are doing accusing my handsome grandson of such a thing? What a bunch of baloney—he is only a child! Cease these fabrications, and while you are at it, get your vision checked!" She dipped into her lap and yanked Marat free, then slammed a pile of cash on the table for a tip just north of thirty cents. "Come on, kids. We are going home."

Holding back giggles, the rest of the family followed Fanny through the main dining room and out the door to the idling Town Car.

"Ma, Slippy Sanders," Esmerelda peeped. "My boss."

"Hello." Slippy nodded warily, ticked he was missing his tee time, only doing this because Esmerelda had threatened to set up her traveling circus in the CopySmart lunchroom otherwise.

"Yes," Fanny agreed.

"Save the hugs and handshakes for later," Esmerelda said, flinging herself out of the wheelchair and waddling toward the car like a huge frightened penguin. "A little help?"

A blast of energy and they were all inside, Esmerelda splayed across the backseat and the Gargantuan strapped to the trunk, the doors slamming shut, the sedan gliding at low speed down the hill to Fanny's house, saccharin saxophone solos swimming out the windows. It wasn't until evening, after the children were settled in at Fanny's place and Slippy and Esmerelda had returned to the Presidio for the rest of their belongings, that Fanny broke open the Parliaments and Beefeater and found the seal on the gin broken and a gulp missing. Strange, she thought, casting a sideways glance at the children working on puzzles on the floor, Robespierre finishing up a two-hundred-piece jigsaw and Marat stumped on a puzzle of the fixed-edge board variety, taking more of an interest in rolling on the floor, singing an original tune about dentists and jelly beans, twirling his pinky in his ear, and drooling puddles.

Strange, but not impossible.

She told Esmerelda after they hauled Ezzie's steamer trunk into the house. "Unlikely," Esmerelda remarked. "With all the hubbub, there's probably a logical explanation. Maybe it broke. Maybe I took a swig and can't remember." She snorted. "Hell, so what if he did take a sip? He's feeling his way out in life. It's not a crime."

"Actually, it is." Fanny Wan Twinkle stirred her martini with a crooked fingernail and decided it was high time to invest in a secure home storage container.

Three generations of Van Twinkles under the same flat California roof, Fanny Van Twinkle the resident crackpot chieftain. She smoked two packs of menthols before lunch, watched eight hours of soap operas each day, chased her commercials with gin, and insisted on everything remaining exactly as she'd left it. She did not permit redecoration of Esmerelda's room, or the guest rooms, or any room; not one article of clothing could be removed, no stuffed animal discarded. Fanny said no to low-flow toilets, diet soda, computers, and cable television; the driveway asphalt was crumbly and decayed; the laurel tree on the sidewalk drooped with dead limbs; the medicine cabinet was packed with pills decades past expiration; everything in boiled suspension since the morning of April 1, 1979, when Harold Van Twinkle last set out for the Farallones in his thirty-two-foot trawler, trailing his green nets for albacore and rockfish.

Rooting through her mother's old bedroom, Robespierre discovered a broken Easy-Bake Oven, cardboard boxes filled with lace valentines and wilted homework assignments labeled with failing grades, a pile of singleton wide-heeled sandals, a bookshelf full of dog-eared typing manuals. She tabulated all the junk and substandard decorations with deep pride, because it was hers, finally, a room for herself and not her brother.

Esmerelda unpacked her muumuus in the den where she'd lived for six years up until her surprise pregnancy shook free the twins, where there was no staircase to the second floor to sweat over or shame her, no mirrors to reflect the unguent blob that constituted her body—just Esmerelda, a black-and-white television set from 1978, and the two king-sized mattresses jammed next to each other, covered by the most customer-friendly lifetime warranties Fanny Van Twinkle could find.

Marat lay on his bed in the dark as the world juddered around him, wishing that everything—the framed prints of floral still lifes, the rose-hued bedsheets, the closet full of leotards, a notebook full of boys' names and sausage drawings, the newly decapitated dolls stuffed underneath the bed—was a bad dream he'd been swirling in since he sampled the bottle of smelly water in the Cliff House lobby.

Upstairs, Fanny worked at the gin and watched tapes of soap operas in her bedroom, her saliva-soaked butts smoldering in a hula girl ashtray, her martini glass resting on the notarized contract in which Esmerelda agreed to: 1) change nothing in Fanny's home and 2) sleep in the house every single night unless she had Fanny's written permission, which would be granted in perpetuity upon the purchase of a home within San Francisco city limits with a separate bedroom for each inhabitant, located within walking distance of a park, and furnished exclusively with antiques manufactured no later than 1979.

Each child had a private bathroom, a personal closet filled with clothing, assigned seats on opposite ends of the dinner table and the slick vinyl sofa. The situation had a certain appeal, particularly for Robespierre, as her room was stocked with clothing from Esmerelda's childhood: baby-doll dresses and Minnie Mouse sweat suits and jelly shoes, vintage lunchboxes filled with mismatched barrettes and trippy bead necklaces and hundreds of hair bands in every imaginable shade of pink. The decorations were consistent with the general themes of fuchsia or doilies, with chintzy posters of kittens and kissing children and angels, a huge slice of sappy cheesecake, the former setting of dozens of annoying all-girl sleepover gossipfests.

Marat's bedroom was nearly identical, a guestroom designed to cater to Esmerelda's all-female cousins, with fewer angel paintings and a subtler tone of pink on the sheets, but mostly the same stuff. His dresser held the less girly items from young Esmerelda's wardrobe: no dresses or skirts, but the full allotment of frilly blouses and candy-cane sneakers, a drawer packed with rolled pink tights, an old Wonder Woman Halloween costume, a musty training bra. He found a couple of adult-sized San Francisco Giants replica jerseys balled up in the corner of the closet and wore them to pieces, but on wash day he had to slip on something purple or pink and wait next to the dryer for his shirts to finish up. The underwear selection consisted of thirty-seven panties stenciled with cartoon seahorses and blooming daisies and two pairs of aging long underwear. So Marat wore the long johns, every single day, wearing a pair the usual way, then inside-out, then taking care to launder them before the other pair was soiled. He cut a pathetic profile— large faded jersey hanging over him like a nightgown; thick, hardy legs; natty yellowed fabric peeking out from under his cuffs. On the ten truly hot days of summer and on excursions inland or to the beach, the weird sight of shorts over long underwear, mummy legs trapped in parchment, knees and shins darned with scrap fabric. Attached to those Egyptian legs: obsidian eyes sagging with sadness.

And always, between brother and sister, the smell of mothballs.

⚜

Though Fanny never volunteered for babysitting, hadn't the slightest desire to do it, was over and done with minding children, after Esmerelda caught the van to work in the morning it was just her and the two kids running their mouths and vandalizing priceless pre-1979 furniture unless she figured out something to do with them. Before school they walked over the Great Highway to the beach, where the children kicked up sea foam and ran at flocks of birds and hypothesized about the origins of waves. Fanny monitored them from atop a dune, chain-smoking and spitting. For lunches Fanny worked off her old stores of macaroni and cheese, which she made every night and packaged in ancient semifunctional Tupperware containers that she sealed with duct tape, forcing the kids to borrow the lunch lady's scissors to access their meal. Sometimes when they got home from school Fanny took them on a walk around the block to pick up candy bars and a bottle of discount-bin booze from the corner store, but usually the kids were quarantined in the backyard, flopping in overgrown grass while Fanny snoozed inside. She was usually up and moving by the time Esmerelda got home, but her hangover was at its worst, a radon steam bath, and the stress came through in her indelicate dinners.

This stasis held for years, unbroken circular motion, a pacing path three feet deep. Fanny fell dull and dazed, beaten back by centripetal force; the kids sensed her resentment and responded in kind. Windows for détente opened rarely and closed quickly: the positive feelings of breakfast in bed erased by dropping the hot frying pan on Fanny's lap; Fanny's attempt at making brownies for a school bake sale engendering a month-long stomach virus shootout across the school district. Still, in her sober moments Fanny recognized that these kids were all that was left of her family, and—this admission came only after the most moving soap opera episodes, featuring devastated marriages and operating-room accidents—the only hope she had to feel loved again.

On Sunday mornings, after nobody took her up on her invitation to go to church or head out for a relaxing walk down the beach or—and this one hurt like a hammer on an exposed toenail—accompany her on an all-expenses-paid visit to the brunch eatery of their choice, topped off with a trip to the movies, she sometimes took the Muni train down to Union Square. The department stores pulled her in with their glamorous displays, a wonder of color and luxury that she knew she could never attain:

skirts cut well above the knees and blouses fashioned from silk and lace like the Queen's wardrobe and shiny leather pocketbooks that cost a month's worth of Social Security. Staff in formal uniforms upgraded her measure of America with tasteful overpoliteness and hair gel, patiently explaining the variations between perfume samples and offering directions to the ladies' room and tactfully slipping her tissues when she broke down at the discount suit rack, the simple gray polyester outfits requiring only a beaten silver bolo tie and homemade fish-hook cuff links to be exact replicas of Harold's wedding day ensemble.

Later, when she dribbled back to the Muni station, harelipped teenagers accosted her at intersections, asking for change and twitching erratically and keenly eyeing her great wool bag. She pushed out her elbows and flapped past their grimy roadblocks, noting their smell of overflowing toilets and recording their wheezy grunts like a dying Volkswagen and, from the farthest corner of her peripheral vision, spotting their haunting appearances—shoes stapled together; frayed, threadbare hoodies; mud-streaked sweatpants riddled with holes from crotch to ankle—that appeared alarmingly close to her own grandson's daily dress.

"Marat," she announced at dinner after returning from Union Square ten days before the twins' eighth Christmas, "how is everything going at school?"

"Fine," he shoved out through four scoops of green beans.

"I've been selected for gifted and talented classes," Robespierre chimed in. "We're dissecting a cow's heart next week."

"We are well aware of your success," Fanny interjected, "this question was in regard to your brother. It can be quite a challenge to succeed in your shadow."

"Actually, I try to help him with his homework every day," Robespierre pointed out. "But he doesn't really care."

Marat dropped his fork on his plate and wiped his mouth with his sleeve, a hideous piss-and-shit stained brown fabric that was once, allegedly, the top half of a long underwear set. "Has there been a problem with the washing machine?" Fanny wondered.

"All the appliances suck," Esmerelda griped, "they're about a thousand years old and haven't been repaired ever. Our clothes are turning yellow."

"They are classic machines paired with vintage clothing," Fanny clarified, "which I allow you to use free of charge. Now, are there any problems with that arrangement?"

"Yeah, lots," Esmerelda said. "We look retarded with a side of pigsty."

"I like all the clothes," Robespierre smiled broadly, her teeth appearing to Fanny like perfect rows of chipped ice. "I have a new outfit every day!"

The admission is wonderful, roaring crowds beneath the palace window, a regal vindication. "Well then. And you, Marat? How does your wardrobe make you feel?"

Marat lifts his shirt over his nose for a bank-robber look, two bleak eyes topping off a gray-fuzzed and splitting San Francisco Giants jersey. "Fine," he mumbled.

"Fine," Fanny repeated, wanting to believe it but not quite able to. "Would you perhaps be interested in a wider array of clothing, perhaps for the holidays?"

"Sure," he said from beneath his gunslinger mask, and along the rim of his weighty eye sockets she thought she caught the slight uptick of a grin.

A week later, Fanny was unpacking a dusty box of Christmas decorations from the hall closet when a police cruiser rolled onto the sidewalk in front of the house. "Excuse me!" she called from the door. "Plenty of street parking around here, officer. Consider my azaleas."

"Ma'am," the officer said. "Got a boy who belongs to you. Says his name's Marat."

"What about him? He is at school."

"We had a call from a dollar store this morning. Nabbed him stealing a package of tighty whiteys."

"Impossible—I escorted him to school this morning myself. He has always been perfectly behaved, and besides, committing a crime at his age is unthinkable—" and Fanny remembered how Harold had been out on the fishing boats a lifetime's worth, and still the one squall had ushered in the impossible, transubstantiating his body into green nets and freezing her in the 4 AM black. Severity paled her face.

"The video camera doesn't lie. I can show you if you want, but they're not pressing charges. Though I'd recommend some corrective action." The cop opened the back door of the cruiser, and Marat darted out. "Merry Christmas, Mrs. Van Twinkle."

She nodded and he left. But there it was again: the word "missus," the word that went with Harold and his torn hands and his arthritic back and the songs he sang for her and Esmerelda at night when he fried up his catch of the day, fishermen ditties about mermaids and wind gods and bathtubs and liquor that never had much direction or rhythm. She looked at Marat, vacant as usual, kicking a plastic bag and mashing his nose with his palm.

"Go to your room," she ordered. He walked past her obediently, his face devoid of thought.

After a liquid afternoon of coffee and gin, she went to see Esmerelda. She was cranked back on her double-king bed, watching a game show and munching a plateful of gingerbread cookies. "Ma," Esmerelda said, her eyes locked on the television, "wanted to run something by you. I'm not going heavy on gifts this year, since I'm saving for the down payment and all. Was hoping you'd pick up some slack in the stocking-stuffer department."

"That boy, Marat. Trouble."

"Well, they're both a little troubled. Dad's gone, you know?"

"Not troubled. Trouble. A policeman just dropped him off. They claim he stole from a dollar store."

Esmerelda flopped onto her side like a sunning sea lion. "That so? Huh. What'd he take?"

"Underwear," Fanny admitted, the word tasting of copper and failure and dirt singed to toxic gas.

"Ha!" Esmerelda's face blasted into pink, her chest bouncing long and slow like a backyard trampoline. "Can't blame the guy, really."

"Of course we can. It is theft. Illegal. We cannot condone that behavior."

On television the game show host suddenly doubled the prize money, and Esmerelda upped the volume accordingly. "He's got no money and wearing shit-stained clothes from a lifetime ago. I can understand."

"Those are Harold's clothes," Fanny insisted, feeling herself fall into a deep sludge, decades boiled down into gooey bad memories.

"Yeah, well. Harold's gone, mom. Times have changed." Esmerelda looked up from her show and over at her mother, who was kneeling on the floor, forehead against the carpeting, back trembling, her braided hair switching like a happy dog's tail, the exact same position in which Esmerelda had found her on the morning of April 2, 1979, and April 3, 1979, and clear through the rest of the month and most of May until Memorial Day, when Fanny had gone to march in the parade down Market Street on Harold's behalf, falling in with the Vietnam vets with his service picture pinned to her blouse. "Ma," Esmerelda blubbed, "come on."

"The boy must be disciplined," Fanny coughed, "he will not disgrace the Van Twinkle good name."

"What good name?" Esmerelda asked. "We got a lard-ass and a do-nothing and a couple kids you tell what to do all day. Not a whole lot worth defending, in my opinion."

Fanny got up quietly and walked out of the room. She left the door wide open intentionally, which she knew would force Esmerelda to roll on her side and throw cookies at it until it closed enough to give her some privacy. Both spited, they didn't speak for the next two days, until Christmas morning dropped and the kids were leaping on Fanny's bed, singing Christmas jingles and tickling her toes. Slowly they splashed her awake, creaked her upright and walking, still quarter drunk, her hangover not fully formed, an act of Jurassic reanimation. After a pit stop for her morning menthol, they pulled her down the stairs and into the living room, where Esmerelda was sleeping on the floor as a Christmas present to herself, so she wouldn't have to clomp over from her room in the morning.

"Hiya, kids. Know what? It's 3 AM. Wanna give this another shot in, say, four hours?"

"Mom!"

"Esmerelda, I could tell some stories about Christmas morning if you like," Fanny said. They both thought back to how Esmerelda had pulled some extreme early-morning stocking raids in her day, many of which had technically gone down on Christmas Eve.

"Let's make this quick," Esmerelda huffed.

The boughs of the slanted fir, overloaded with decades-old dime-store tinsel, creaked perilously. A pyramid of presents covered in rosy snowman designs served as support, half the gifts wrapped professionally, with sharp corners and smooth edges and crimson high-weight paper, the other half covered in reddish tissue paper scraps, hastily patched, entire sides of gifts left uncovered. Next to the hill of presents were a couple of CopySmart plastic bags taped shut and a pair of Harold's old tube socks.

Fanny nodded and the kids pounced. Robespierre unpeeled her bulging sock and dumped out an hourglass filled with perfume, a slim bottle of cologne, two bags of miniature chocolates, a rolled-up Raiders T-shirt, and a set of gilded barrettes. Marat's stocking was limp aside from the knot in the toe, which he clenched with both hands and shook like he was mixing margaritas.

"Santa forgot me," he observed in a watery, doleful voice.

"That is not quite true, Marat," Fanny said. "I think there is something in that toe."

Nodding, Marat loosened his grip on the ball in the corner and started worrying the hulk downstream with his thumbs. Two minutes later his prize rolled out, hitting the carpet with a sooty thunk.

"No, you didn't," Esmerelda growled.

"What's this?" Marat asked. "Chocolate?" He lifted the lump to his nose and sniffed.

"There better be a barbecue grill to go with that," said Esmerelda. "Or a miner's helmet."

"Here, Marat," Robespierre said, "have some of my candy." But her run across the room bearing Hershey's kisses was blocked by Fanny's monolithic profile.

"Santa left that candy for you, Robespierre. Good children receive presents, and bad children receive coal. And stealing means you are a bad boy."

"Well, it's my present to my brother." Robespierre stutter-stepped, head-faked, and spun past Fanny to hand the kisses to her brother, who instantly threw the candies in his mouth and swallowed, foil wrapping and Hershey's flags included.

"Ma, I can't believe you. For crying out loud, it's Christmas!" Esmerelda said. She turned onto her side and tried to make her face angry, hard glass eyes and a treacherous mouth seconds away from spewing flames, but in practice she reminded everyone of an overinflated sheep's head, not intimidating anyone.

Robespierre went to Fanny and hugged her hip. She'd noticed how Gramma'd been cursing dollar stores and Marat's criminal tendencies the past few nights while making dinner, observed how the poison baked into her flavorless roasts and burned holiday gingersnaps, a failing government ripe for overthrow. "Marat's a good brother, Gramma," she said. "He's nice to me."

Fanny shook the girl off. "Santa told me that all the gifts in red wrapping paper are for Robespierre," she announced. "You may open those, dear."

Years later, what they remembered was the time involved. Even working at a speedy clip, Robespierre needed the entire predawn to tear through the gift wrap, untie ribbons, do away with puffy bows, pry open boxes, dig through foam peanuts, and unpack newspaper lining to get the end gift in her hands, at which point she beamed and hooted thanks, commented on the thoughtfulness of the item, its perfect color and size, imagined its many useful applications in her daily life, then bundled the wrapping into a garbage bag and moved on to the next package. Fanny didn't try to pretend the gift-giving was even, as pacing the disrobement of Robespierre's mountain of presents to match the lone plastic bag with Marat's name scrawled across it in his mother's hand was blatantly absurd. So the rest of the family waited while Robespierre peeled open gifts of boys' sweaters and khaki pants that were too big for her and polo shirts of assorted sleeve lengths, and then she found the microscope she really wanted and got quiet and delirious and hugged her mother and her grandmother and her brother, despite his position lying face-down on the floor in cryptic silence. The first hour elapsed with the pyramid only half deconstructed, vertically speaking, meaning that the voluminous base still awaited Robespierre's tiring hands—not that she wasn't thankful, but a lot of the haul wasn't really her speed (boxer shorts, moccasins, tank top undershirts, even a gray polyester suit matched with a silver sailboat bolo tie). The relationship between shoddy wrapping and boy-appropriate gifts sailed over the children's heads, but Esmerelda saw ample evidence of hasty regifting: smatterings of non-red wrapping paper stuck to 49ers-themed pajamas and belt buckles, the off-white of corrective fluid over gift labels, the queer smile from her mother each time Robespierre reached for one of those redirected presents, like she was trying to force her teeth through sealed lips.

Marat remained on his stomach, motionless as a truck-rammed deer with the exception of a ten-minute interlude filled with screaming of such tempestuousness that three neighbors called over to check if everything was groovy. Fanny cooked up excuses of nightmares and food poisoning, then settled in on the couch and watched Marat blub incomprehensibly as rug burns developed on his pounding knees and forearms. Even as his thrashing lapsed into eerie stillness, she did not change the flow of gifts from the dwindling pyramid beside the tree nor alter her pinched smile, which seemed more appropriate on a semiconscious patient enduring exploratory surgery than on a grandmother with her family on Christmas morning.

"Here, Marat," Robespierre said after opening what felt like her ten-millionth present and thanking her grandmother with another tired embrace and cheek peck, "you can have this." She tossed over a green turtleneck in Marat's size.

"Fanks," Marat said hoarsely. He wiped his face with the sleeve of his faded Giants jersey and rose to his knees.

"I am sorry, dear." Fanny scooped the shirt off the floor and stowed it in her considerable cleavage. "These presents are for you, not for your brother. That is how Santa wants it, and he told me to make sure that each child got the correct gifts."

"But I'm allowed to give my own presents, right? So I'm giving this to Marat. Actually, he can have this other stuff too," Robespierre pointed to a sweatshirt covered in race cars, two pairs of boys' blue jeans, a navy blazer, one-pocket T-shirts in all the primary colors.

"No." Fanny stood above her granddaughter, her silhouette deranged by blinking strings of Christmas lights. "Marat is not to receive those gifts."

Robespierre turned to her mother, who was snacking on a package of beef jerky the grandkids had chipped in for. Esmerelda chewed for a few seconds, then said, "Oh, lighten up, Ma! Is this helpful? Let him have some new clothes for crying out loud. You've made your point, whatever it is."

Marat touched Fanny's shin, his mouth knotted and grim. "Gramma, I'm sorry for taking the underpants," he said.

"No!" Fanny cried. "And that's final!"

Cracks of morning light struck from the east, refracting through the kitchen window and across the dining room in brilliant lines of orange. The moment caught: Robespierre's calculated grimace; Fanny's faded nightgown more than two decades old, her bosom plumped with the rangy olive turtleneck; a cigarette of beef jerky hanging from Esmerelda's cud; Marat a hunched iceberg on the horizon, his face cratered and purple. The sun rose another centimeter, and the portrait was obliterated by Marat's tattered San Francisco Giants jersey streaking toward the base of Robespierre's present pile like a wrecking ball at a dilapidated building, although in this instance the dilapidated building was responsible for propping up the Christmas tree, seeing as the tree stand dated from 1978, was missing a lug nut, and was coming apart at several joints.

He blasted through, scattering the presents across the living room like unpredictable atomic particles. Immediately the tree plummeted, whistling speed, a tipped tombstone caroming directly into, as karma would have it, Fanny Van Twinkle's head.

The blow knocked Fanny into her daughter's belly padding and sent Esmerelda's beef jerky flying. Dozens of antique Christmas ornaments fractured on impact: San Francisco–themed cable cars and Spode sourdough loaves, a collection of miniature trawlers, tugs, fishing rods, bait, even a few actual fish that Harold had captured in his green nets and stuffed for the holidays. The decorative light strings, fragile from more than thirty-five years of use, shattered decisively against the floor. Marat wailed in the corner, his invective against his evil grandmother obfuscated by an unintelligible, sob-drenched throat blockage.

Robespierre climbed over the fallen tree and bent over Fanny as she woozily worked herself upright. "That was wrong, Gramma," she declared, and ran up to her room to examine toilet water under her new microscope. Marat followed her upstairs carrying a personalized notepad from his mother, his only gift aside from the coal.

The room fell quiet with the sunlight, absence illuminated.

Esmerelda broke the emptiness with a slap against her thigh. "We gotta get out of this place," she declared. "Robespierre's right. This is no way to raise kids, with a nutjob at the helm. I need a new job, something challenging and high paying like the good ol' days. Gotta swim with the sharks if you wanna catch fish." She lifted her belly between her palms, let it bounce into her lap. "For Chrisssakes, look at me, big as a walrus. This eating's got to stop. And exercising, that's part of the equation too." She concluded the rally with a firm double clap, then spat out her beef jerky and spent the next half hour performing three slipshod holiday sit-ups and coughing up green brine.

Fanny went to the kitchen and whipped up her special Christmas morning breakfast, biscuits and gravy and omelets, listening to hymns on the radio and trying to forget the ugly rebellion her grandkids had fomented. But nobody responded to her singsong call for omelet orders; there was no movement when she announced breakfast was ready and on the table; quiet whooshes of notepad scribbling and microscope adjusting greeted her when she rapped her wedding band on the doors to bedrooms and warned she would throw out their meals if they didn't come to the table. Even her daughter, a human garbage disposal, refused to eat a single slice of glazed ham that Fanny fried up special just for her.

"Nah, already had me some jerky. I'm gonna see about losing a few. Call it a New Year's resolution a week early." Esmerelda pawed against an armchair, threw up an elbow, and leveraged herself up and standing within minutes. "C'mon kids! Christmas walk!"

The kids skittered down the staircase and into threadbare purple jackets from Esmerelda's childhood. "Way to go, mom!" Robespierre called.

"Yeah, mom! Ba-wah!"

Esmerelda turned her head at Marat's odd cheer, thinking for a second that he wanted a drink or something until Robespierre translated: "wheelbarrow." Then Jasper Winslow was everywhere: in Robespierre's big feet, Marat's crooked grin, Robespierre's resolve and cheerful outlook, Marat's gutsiness and enormous lung capacity. And even when Esmerelda was so out of breath she had to take five at the end of the driveway, catch a standing catnap at the next house, and demand in uncompromising terms to be taken home upon reaching the corner, she couldn't help but see Jasper Winslow's kindness blossoming in her children as they guided her over unevenly laid blocks of sidewalk and clumps of litter, down the narrow walk and up the five bowed steps leading to the front door and through the house back to her double-king bed, where they lay for hours updating her résumé and watching holiday specials on television while Fanny drank gin at the kitchen table and relived the great family Christmases of the 1970s in her head.

COMMITTEE
OF PUBLIC SAFETY

[T]he Convention nominated that first "Committee of Public Safety," which . . . was henceforth the true despotic and military centre of revolutionary government.

—HILAIRE BELLOC,
The French Revolution

The Committee of Public Safety . . . did not much care who were executed as long as a considerable number went to the scaffold every day.

—HENRY MORSE STEPHENS,
Revolutionary Europe, 1789–1815

At the millennium two-digit computer clocks threatened to crash airplanes, freeze elevators, shut down hospitals, put traffic signals on the fritz. Rioting was anticipated, and the cops were on full alert, supplemented by vigilante security teams formed by antsy shopkeepers. Marvin Ahn led the defense effort at his strip mall on Georgia Avenue, recruiting a mall militia to defend their eight-store complex and negotiating with the army surplus store for a donation of batons and dud grenades. They distributed walkie-talkies for the likely event of telecommunications failure, stockpiled spring water, topped off lawnmower gas cans, swapped out flashlight batteries, stashed canned food and dried fruit. On New Year's Eve, Marvin filled the station wagon with supplies and went upstairs to grab his eldest foster son.

"HELLS no!" Murphy yelled through the bedroom door from the unfolded futon, his foster siblings ringing him like a tribal council. "I'm watching Michael Jackson!" MTV was playing the top 100 music videos of all time, he screamed, and there was Dick Clark and the Three Stooges marathon too. Besides, what use was his runty ass in fending off crack-crazed looters?

Marvin chuckled. "Murph—think of it as an adventure. You like cop movies, right? The cop TV shows?"

That was well documented. Murphy watched every police reality show on television, had memorized all five *Dirty Harry* films, the four *Lethal Weapons*, the three *Beverly Hills Cops*, *Robo-Cop*, *Bullitt*, even the *Police Academy* series, often quoting entire multipart scenes verbatim at the dinner table—though the boy's underlying motives for watching police-oriented programming (to study their methods, learn their tricks, and one day beat them at their own game) weren't even evident to Murphy himself.

"You gonna let us put up a tree house?" Murphy asked, winking to the other boys huddled round.

"We can talk about that later."

"How about some candy? For dessert? For everyone?"

Marvin huffed at this, the nagging that never ended, how somebody had wanted something from him every two minutes for the past ten years. "Not now!" he shouted.

"I wanna see Michael Jackson!" Murphy threw back. He kept *Thriller* on his Discman at all hours, bonded to the star by irregular childhoods and insecurity about their appearance. The all-time music video countdown was a critical bellwether for the new century, he informed Marvin; if the King of Pop didn't win, the conspiracy was on, no one could be trusted, and he'd be forced to take it out on the furniture.

"We'll tape it. C'mon, this'll be fun. I'll give you your own walkie-talkie, and a billy club if you're good."

"Michael Jackson!"

After a few minutes of repeating the arguments to each other, Marvin Ahn shouldered open the door and hauled Murphy down to the car. They drove three blocks to the store, where Murphy soon lost walkie-talkie and billy club privileges for screaming the lyrics to "Beat It" while parading up and down the parking lot like a mad ghost, his ultrashort haircut appearing unsettlingly close to premature baldness in the mystical, century-changing gloom, his off-key falsetto haunting shoppers and employees alike. The platoon of shop owners yelled at him to pipe down, stuff his ugly-ass piehole, go back to the carnie camp he came from, but Marvin stepped in and sensibly explained:

"Think of it this way, gentlemen—he's a walking alarm. Nobody's going to mess with our stores with him out there rousing the dead."

The boy's head popped in the doorway, shouted out the opening lines to "Billie Jean," and vanished.

"Bullshit excuse," replied Tasos Mitrakos, who was Greek, rude, and an excellent barber when sober. "You couldn't control him even if you knew how."

"Patience," Marvin insisted, but a fuse activated in his liver and he begrudgingly recognized that Tasos was right.

Midnight slipped away without mayhem or looting bandits, all glass plating intact and free from graffiti, electricity still functioning, siren free. Murphy sang "Thriller" twenty-one times from when they started keeping track at 10:30, giving comic-store owner Ben Marg the betting pool win. Graciously he plowed his winnings right back into their New Year's celebration, sparkling cider and packaged cakes from Marvin's store, pickles and sandwiches from the deli, tambourines from the Music Emporium, toothbrushes from the commuter dental office. After sitting on the curb for a while and listening to the festivities, even Murphy came in for a Dr. Pepper, whereupon he stumbled on pile of hangers from the dry cleaners which he used to sculpt wire figurines of cops and robbers and guns of all sizes.

The car worked on the first try, the ride home was uneventful, and the immediate perusal of the videotaped countdown confirmed that "Thriller" had been selected as the number-one music video of all time. June Ahn, who'd moved most of her vintage tables into storage but ran out of time for her Pembroke set, shook like a set of maracas when the announcement came on.

The next morning at 7 AM, Marvin Ahn drove to the store and parked in a field of shredded candy wrappers. Black spray paint scarred the sign for Ahn Minimarket: a loopy FUCK, a meandering YOU, a bulging AHN. The window frames were ruptured and glass shards mined the floor. A flock of pigeons clumped in the doorway, pecking on burst packages of chips. Kalamakis' barber pole stuck out of a soda cooler. Lumps of gum were nailed to the ceiling and the candy aisle was empty. Marvin Ahn tiptoed into the punctured storefront and past ransacked shelves, leaking refrigerators, a smashed hot-dog-warming machine. The cash register was gone and the safe sprung, the only clean spots in the place. Along the inside walls, more graffiti spooled from the floor to just about the height where an eight-year-old boy could reach.

LIVE! LIVE! LIVE! LIVE! LIVE! LIVE! LIVE! LIVE!

The effect upon Marvin Ahn was oddly uplifting. A believer in the power of positive thinking, he found himself nodding to the affirmative message for a few seconds until he went behind the counter and saw the framed photographs of his parents back in Korea rubbed out with spray paint. He called the cops—"How did you guys miss this mess? You blind or something?"—and briefly wondered if the "Live" message could implicate some kind of left-wing health food movement, his fat- and cholesterol-heavy snacks scapegoats for the entire fast-food industry.

Investigator Rodriguez and Officer Bindle came by the house in the afternoon. June made coffee and warmed up some muffins.

"We think it's an inside job." Rodriguez peeled off a muffin top and nibbled the perimeter. "That safe was opened—nothing broken at all. All the pins are intact, meaning somebody knew the combination. They also knew how to disarm the security system, climb up to the surveillance cameras, and spray-paint them without getting caught on tape. But getting into the safe so easy—that's the clincher."

"All the employees got alibis," Bindle said. He was shaped like a surfboard, lean and tall with coarse features that suggested regular childhood beatings. "No witnesses neither."

Marvin silently thanked his insurance broker for convincing him to up the coverage the previous fall. "No leads at all?"

"One thing. We figure you're coming out pretty good on insurance. And not much in the way of alibi for the middle of the night."

"Please," Marvin whined. "Tell me you're not doing this."

"Let's have a talk at the station."

"Can it wait? The repairmen are coming in half an hour and—"

He felt Bindle behind him, six foot eight, 240, clipped mustache and pebble eyes, no capacity for sarcasm. A regular at the Ahn Minimart, his proclivity for Hostess products had earned him the nickname "Cop Cakes" among the night-shift guys. "Let's go."

At the station Marvin talked fast and passionately, detailing his commitment to rapid-sale merchandising, the recent renovations at the shop, his charitable donations, his work as a foster parent. Rodriguez bought it hard, and even Bindle started coming around when Marvin mentioned the ruined photographs of his recently deceased parents. The report from the county treasurer's office came in as they were standing up to leave.

"Everything kosher?" Marvin asked, anxious to check on his repairmen before they ate his remaining inventory.

"Could be," Rodriguez says. "Your tax records got flagged."

"What?"

"Nineteen ninety-eight payroll. Know a Su-Jung Kim?"

"Yeah, she works for me."

"You didn't pay her payroll taxes. Same for Diane Wing, Jao Park, five or six others."

"Let me see that." Rodriguez slid over the papers, the names and numbers circled in red. "I'll have to check with my accountant."

"Not a big deal," Rodriguez said. "You're free to go."

A month later, 80 percent of the store's staff was laid off to free up cash for back taxes and penalties. Marvin and June retained only a heavyset brother-sister duo from Kensington who accepted minimum wage, a pair so emboldened by their scarcity that they treated the minimarket as their personal buffet, snarfing chips and hot dogs and ice-cream treats whenever they liked, often clocking out with a bag of free victuals to last them until next shift. Hiring trustworthy employees wasn't easy in the minimarket cash game, where profit margins closely tracked the amount of time owners were on the premises; without loyalists manning the registers, Marvin and June spent nearly all their conscious hours sleepwalking around the shop.

No one objected when Murphy loaded up on candy and set to work on the tree house the boys had always wanted in the towering oak out back, lugging home overstock from the lumberyard and reusing nails from neighbors' fences while Michael Jackson moonwalked in his Discman. He was handy and patient when it came to making things, able to wait for weeks as projects formed from pieces. At night he snacked on a feedbag of mini chocolate bars and watched *COPS* and *LAPD: Life on the Beat*, documentaries on famous criminals, heist flicks, drug-bust exposés, police procedurals. Within weeks an extensive library of law-enforcement-oriented media accumulated in Murphy's bedroom, their retail value far exceeding his allowance.

After making a series of court appearances, negotiating a repayment plan, and settling a good chunk of their debt, the Ahns hired back two cashiers and took a day off to decompress. On their first day home, they didn't find Murphy's videos, stowed beneath a pile of shoes in his closet, but the big-screen television in the boys' bedroom was hard to miss. "Wow," said June, her matchstick hips curving onto Murphy's futon, which had been widened and repositioned alone beside the window, made up in satin police-blue sheets and four fluffy pillows and a much thicker mattress than June remembered. "Nice TV."

"Yeah," Murphy said, slumped on his bed and sipping Pellegrino through a curly straw. Two of the younger boys watched carefully from the top bunks, suited up in tight haircuts and authentic Redskins jerseys like real, if miniature, gangsters.

"Thirty-two inches?"

"Forty-two."

"Hmm." She nodded. "Pretty big."

"Bigger than the one downstairs."

"You know, I think you're right."

They watched a minute of music video, Michael Jackson yelling and playing racquetball on a spaceship. "Did you win a sweepstakes?"

"Nope."

"Murphy." Her pigeon hand locked onto his shoulder. "Where did you get this?"

"My real family sent me some money, and I bought a TV with it. OK?"

In the distance a cellphone rang, a MIDI version of a semi-popular R&B song. "I've been a foster parent for fourteen years," June began, "so don't think you can—"

Murphy pulled a black plastic log from his pocket. "Yeah? Cool. Be right down." The phone beeped off. "Gotta go."

"Hold on. We need to talk about where you got this television. And the cellphone."

"Circuit City. But I gotta go, my uncle's outside."

"Your uncle."

"My real uncle. He called a couple weeks ago, while you guys were working."

"I see. I need to meet this uncle."

"Fine."

One of the boys helped Murphy into a puffy Knicks jacket June had never seen before while the other held open the door.

Out in the driveway, a scuffed-up '82 Chevy Caprice grumbled and popped. A scrappy rat-tailed alcoholic-type leaned out the window, his smile a slice of rotten melon, his eyes bulbous and untrustworthy, his skin the color of Gouda cheese, wearing a denim tuxedo with cigarette packs loaded in every visible pocket. He laboriously pushed open the door, releasing the stench of water rot.

"Hey there, Murph!" The man got out, shut an eye, and shot a finger gun at Murphy. "Ma'am," he nodded.

"Who are you?" June asked.

The man chewed his cheek and spat brown saliva onto the road. "Name's Russell Taylor."

"My uncle," Murphy announced.

"Nice to see you," June said, wondering how Murphy'd put the poor schmuck up to it. "You're about a decade late."

"Huh," Russ Taylor said, not a fan of her tone. He was about to reach back to his junior boxing days to educate her about proper manners, when the kid got his attention with furious arm-waving and he decided the heck with it, mulligan. "My sister was Marisa Taylor, Murphy's mom. I was in jail when Murph popped out, couldn't take him in. Tell you the truth, finances what they are, can't do it now neither. But I did give him some money the other day, help out a little."

"Really."

"We're going to catch a flick and a milkshake. Care to join?"

"Uncle Russ!" Murphy kicked a stick and cracked it with his heel.

June laughed. "I need to see some identification."

"You bet. Wouldn't want you to think I'm part of some kiddie sex ring or nothin." He took a plastic wallet from his jeans jacket and pulled out a Maryland driver's license, peeling at the corners. Russell Taylor, Rockville, Maryland.

"I'm going to copy down your license number and address," June said, "and run it with the police. That OK?"

Russell Taylor grabbed at his ID and missed badly, falling back on his heels with an arrhythmic bob. "Hang on a second," he spluttered, "I ain't done nothing wrong."

"If you haven't done anything wrong, you have nothing to worry about."

"Chill, Uncle Russ," Murphy said. He'd circled behind the stranger, June realized, and was holding him by his belt.

"Shoot, taking my nephew out for a flick's tougher than busting out of prison. Not that I know anything 'bout that." Russ chuckled and spat on the sidewalk, then came inside for a diet soda while June went to the den and called the station. Ex-con was right, battery and domestic abuse, but he'd been out and clean for five years. Looked like Murphy too, the same dermatology problems, chronic impetigo and acne. Unbelievable, but the story held up. She reminded Murphy to take his skin medication, nothing rated R, home by seven. They piled in, the Chevy chucked alive, and Russ Taylor rounded the corner in the direction of the Cineplex.

He pulled over three blocks later. "Here's your money," Murphy said, and dropped a ball of twenties in Russell's lap. Russell scooped up the roll, tested its thickness with a quick squeeze, and began peeling off bills and piling them on his knee. He was three hundred in when Murphy swung open the door and eased out.

"Hang on," Russell said. "What if it's not all there?"

"What?"

"I said, what if it's—"

"I heard you." Murphy fronted his waxy smile. "What are you gonna do about it?"

Russell's shoulders sharpened; his cheeks went dark. "Rip your faggot face off, you little twerp," he hissed.

"Whatever," Murphy said, "that's the easiest grand you'll ever make." He hopped over to the sidewalk and set a course for the mall. At the next intersection he called up the Florida bank on his cell to check if the rest of the money had arrived, cash shipped certified mail, not the traditional way to make deposits but a quirk this financial institution had been willing to accommodate. Then a burger, a couple movies, a cab ride home. Maybe he'd pick up a can of paint for the tree house.

As he crossed the street to the mall he felt a flash of liquid against the back of his head, then a soft, metallic knock. He turned and saw the diet soda can on the ground, the Chevy peeling off toward the Metro station. "Two hundred short, assface!" Russell yelled out the window. "I'm coming back for it!"

Murphy walked to the median strip and sat down against a lamppost. Violence was the only response that came to him, violence against violence, violence against idiocy, clubs and kicks and immobilizing headlocks, like the cops on TV with heavy boots and backup. But Murphy knew he didn't have backup; he was a troublemaking bastard orphan, and no adult would side with him against the out-of-work mechanic he'd found in the phonebook, the only person with the same last name dumb enough to take the gig. They wouldn't even listen. Just another punk-ass kid.

He'd been on the cusp of insignificance ever since he was born.

He slapped the lamppost, swinging with open hands, the doggy paddle on land. He galloped over to the sidewalk and pulled down a NO PARKING sign, threw somebody's rake into the street, knocked down a mailbox. He found a tricycle and slammed it against a driveway until he got kind of ashamed for fucking up a kid's toy, threw it aside and took on a trash can across six front yards, head stomps and jawbreakers and bionic pile drivers and top-rope clotheslines and all the other wrestling moves he could remember, the one-sided smackdown slowly disemboweling his rage. As his body slowed, he realized this was the worst he'd felt since missing the top video spot live, the shit that started it all, his swan song repeated twenty-one times in the parking lot while the outside world fell lost in the synthesizer beats, the monster creep, the werewolf preening, the deranged cackles. He was capable of anything, and he stabbed an SUV's tires with a garden trowel to prove it.

Live! Live! Live! Live! Live! Live! Live! Live!

All Murphy had wanted was to see the fucking video live.

LET THEM EAT CAKE

The time had arrived when the abuses of the old *régime* could no longer be tolerated, and sweeping reforms were demanded . . . The nation, hitherto politically a nullity, had awakened to a sense of its rights; while absolute sovereignty, with its arbitrary dictum, *"L'état c'est moi,"* and its right divine to govern wrong, had lost its prestige, and had apparently no prospect of regaining it.
—LADY CATHERINE CHARLOTTE JACKSON,
The French Court and Society: Reign of Louis XVI and First Empire

If the people have no bread, let them eat cake.
—MARIE ANTOINETTE,
archduchess of Austria and queen of France during
the Revolution, executed by the Revolution in 1793

Until the age of twenty-two, Esmerelda Van Twinkle was a regular-sized person, even on the skinny side during summers. She enjoyed bikinis and Spandex and salads, jogged three times a week before breakfast, and often went on bike rides over the Golden Gate Bridge and through the Marin Headlands, once all the way up Mount Tamalpais. She was the sprightliest of the chefs at Incognito, the only one without a bowling-ball belly, the lone woman, the pastry chef. Her pretty picture appeared regularly in food sections nationwide, the accompanying articles discussing the finer points of piecrust preparation and dishing on the culinary dating scene, her bashful smile not hurting business one bit.

Incognito was a California fusion restaurant, steaks and sweet potatoes cooked with expensive wine and Asian seasonings, so pretty much anything flew for dessert. Upon landing the job, Esmerelda introduced a menu of fried green tea ice cream, eggplant tiramisu, papaya gelatin, Japanese plum cakes, cardamom shrikhand, and, on Sundays, raspberry fortune cookies with home-cooked haikus rolled up inside. Her profiteroles were made of thousands of choux pastry strips woven together, layered squirts of Swiss chocolate cream oozing within; her handmade ice cream was cool on the spoon and warm in the mouth, thick as mashed potatoes; her apple pie cracked with ripe fruit and fresh cinnamon, a dash of saffron spicing the crust.

But the showstoppers were the oatmeal raisin cookies, outrageously lush and creamy, always fresh from the oven and tongue-latheringly soft. Shaped in trapezoids and accompanied by scoops of vanilla ice cream, the cookies were light and rich, complex but simple, sweet yet savory, contradictions that tickled the palate so imaginatively that many diners broke out laughing for sheer joy. The perfume of fresh-baked goods meandered down the alley in which Incognito was housed, the thick, wholesome aroma giving the upscale neighborhood a downright homey feel, grandma's secret recipe and natural goodness twined up in a perfect, pure dessert.

Her secret was simple: butter and lots of it, the high-fat unsalted stuff from Jamison's Milk & Dairy up in Cotati, where three Jerseys worked exclusively for her in a barn she paid for out of her own pocket, eating vitamin-infused feed, drinking purified water, getting daily rubdowns and baths twice a week, and milked solely by hand while manager, lead milker, and deliveryman Camden Jamison played country tunes on his harmonica and listened to baseball on the radio. The butter arrived in San Francisco in a shade of light blue with the consistency of wet clay, until you warmed it up or used it for baking.

Then—zap! Within months of Esmerelda's hiring, Incognito was swarmed. Most diners skipped dinner entirely and ordered three or four twenty-dollar desserts with accompanying elaborate specialty coffees, lounging for hours amid politicos, socialites, and awestruck out-of-towners while the butterfat absorbed in their bloodstream. Incognito raised prices, expanded the seating area, paved a new patio with heat lamps and abstract sculptures, but it was still impossible to secure a reservation with less than three months' notice. Movie stars got turned down at the door, a cabal of reservation specialists was dismissed for accepting bribes—even the president was forced to wait without calling ahead, though he was thrilled with the cookies speed-delivered to him at the bar. The place was burning hot, a national keepsake, a pastry Mecca and investor cash cow, and Esmerelda received a correspondingly ludicrous raise.

She was apotheosized in *Gourmet, Bon Appétit, The New Yorker, The New York Times,* the fawning articles accompanied by large photographs of Esmerelda in the kitchen modeling evocative silk blouses and short skirts without pantyhose, chestnut hair strewn lazily over her apron like unraveled extension cords, seductive flour splashes on her cheeks. For a six-month period she was a mainstay of second-tier tabloid features, her string of flings with reality-show contestants and pro hockey players raised to sizzle level by a trail of trashed hotel rooms. Proposals flooded in to launch her own restaurant, join a national morning show, license her desserts to a prominent grocery chain, even go on a world tour. And the three Jerseys in Cotati barreled ahead with the world's most sublime butter, the exact location of Esmerelda's barn a secret to everyone except Camden Jamison, who was paid handsomely and was incomparable in his ability to ditch jealous rival restaurateur tails on his ride back to the farm on Highway 101, that hefty milk truck of his surprisingly nimble on the open road.

Esmerelda, at the age of twenty-two, was an enormous star.

She mulled her options, met with handlers, consulted astrologers, flipped coins. After eight nickels in a row rolled off the table and bounced off her sneakers, she decided to go for a run to clear her head. Outfitted in a plum-colored Lycra bodysuit and matching sneakers, she sneaked out the restaurant's back door and cut west through the tree-lined lanes of Jackson Square, up the hill through a warren of Chinatown alleys, hooking left for the Stockton Street tunnel straight to Union Square. She swept past the towering department stores and swung onto Market, cantering over the even terrain and through the city's needle-ridden gut, coasting past the homeless festival permanently parked outside the library, eluding the shaky stream of a man urinating into a trash can, and speeding up significantly when a pair of swarthy pantsless banditos gave floppy chase for half a block. She accelerated through dead blocks and slight rises, drove through the Castro's bobbing gay boogie. When she saw Twin Peaks Boulevard she turned onto it, why not, she was on top of the world and had earned a spectacular view; there was metaphysical poetry here. Halfway up she thought she heard a quiet clinking noise behind her, but her sideways glance detected only the typical line of turista rental cars puttering uphill at half the speed limit.

She ascended through the residential area and beyond the tree line, the road breaking out into a spectacular view of San Francisco and all the Bay Area, bleached buildings and fairyland-green crags and iron cruxes across the bay connecting kingdoms, the panorama held to just less than perfect by the bracing gale pounding in from the sea. Needling through a few final turns, she fired out into the flat summit, the planet hanging on either side of her, the wind wild across the city's canopy. As she sped into the overlook she heard the noise again, a series of clicks and a light hiss, and found a lithe little cyclist pulling in behind her outfitted in a spotless banker-white uniform complete with a long teardrop-shaped helmet and aerodynamic shoe covers, his bicycle shaped like an intergalactic phaser.

He gave her a rectangular smile framed by a ferrety Fu Manchu mustache. "Good evening," he said, his eyes basting her with cool blue.

Esmerelda spat viciously in his direction, then headed over to the water fountain for a long gulp.

The cyclist climbed atop the rock wall surrounding the over-look and waved his pinched fingers over the view like a symphony conductor. "Do you hear it?" he called, swaying on his toes. "Nature's music! The wind, the sun, the streets, the cars, even the fog out over the ocean. All unified, working as one."

He smiled victoriously at the sun, then turned back to find Esmerelda sprinting out of the parking lot, heading downhill.

The clinking followed her descent, accompanied by a faint whiff of confectioner's sugar. The cyclist raised a finger to his helmet, bounced his butt on the saddle. "Madam, I must know: who is your chemist?"

"My what now?" she coughed, eyes fixed to the road and scan-ning for sticks, scraps of paper, anything to throw in this nin-compoop's gears.

"Your laboratory, I must know. Also, your spiritual advisor: what is her name? Superlative work from top to bottom. Conti-nuity, synergy, strength." His white-gloved finger drew a circle in the air. "In my younger days I would have guessed Taoism, but I have learned not to presume when it comes to matters of the soul."

Esmerelda broke stride and stopped, then doled out the most intimidating hot-bitch glare in her repertoire. "Look, I don't care where you get your kicks, so long as it's not me. I'm trying to work some stuff out here, so why don't you take your psycho-babble sweet talk to someone who might fall for it and leave me the hell alone?"

The cyclist swung off his fiberglass weapon, undid the buckles and snaps on his helmet. "Madam, apologies, please. These days I do not approach strangers frequently. My conduct may not fit proper decorum." He tucked his helmet under his arm and offered a Gore-Tex-wrapped hand. "Bruce Zoogman, cakemaker."

"Bruce Zoogman? Like Zoogman's Zoog?" Blackness encompassed her, prompting heavy breathing and paralysis and a quantum dose of nausea. From the leaky boat of memory sprang her culinary school professor and his access to the most famous cake in California, one bite of which had slam-dunked her into incoherency for just over three months while he fucked her like a warthog and her grades flatlined and her personal relationships soiled and all she could think about was another bite of that ambrosial meal-ender, Zoogman's Zoog.

"Yes," he said flatly, straight factual acknowledgment.

"I heard you lived in a bunker and never came out," Esmerelda spouted. "And that you're retired, out of the game."

"With baking in your blood, can you ever truly quit?" Seriousness stiffened his face, the hard humorless sheen of the devout, the crazy. "I seek perfection. Harmony. Wonderment. The exact blend of ingredients and emotion and craftsmanship that changes the course of lives."

Esmerelda stared and marveled, love lighting behind her eyes, realizing this was the culinary equivalent of finding Christ under her pillow.

"I have sampled your desserts. You have promise." He paused to blot a lone drop of perspiration hanging on his temple. "I ask for your help."

"My help?" she burped, the vista of San Francisco spinning between pink and yellow.

"Be my disciple. Carry my teachings. Add and elaborate, contribute your knowledge. I have only one goal," he said, elevating a rubberized finger: "To seek the divine."

System chatter overwhelmed her, nervous flashes and respiratory schisms and digestive crunches, a scathing case of heartburn, her internal temperature fluctuating like the Dow Jones industrials. "Where do I sign up?" Esmerelda stammered, her lunch leaping up her throat.

"Meet me at sunrise at the summit of Mt. Tamalpais. You may bring one bag. Tell no one."

"Tell no one what?"

"Precisely." With an understanding eyebrow hitch, Bruce swung onto his bicycle and glided down the hill, a sleek, colorless missile diving straight into the city center.

Esmerelda took off after him, speeding down hump after hump until the view was erased by houses and trees, cars pulling up hills, the usual jangly crowd, none of which she noticed through her mescaline trance. She bottomed out in Cole Valley and caught the bus home, poured her favorite aprons and underwear into her great wool bag, slipped a toothbrush in her pocket, and knocked on her mother's bedroom door.

"Ma, I need a ride."

"Esmerelda? Why are you not at work?"

"Can you drive me to Marin? Early?"

"What for?"

"Camping trip."

"Since when have you ever gone camping?"

Busted. "Thought I'd try it. You know, get back with nature, clean out the head."

"Then you can start out with a hike from here."

A minute later Esmerelda slammed the front door so hard that four paintings fell to the floor, a hinge popped loose, and a tiny but menacing crack appeared in a stucco wall.

Up to something, Fanny Van Twinkle thought as she dug out her tool kit from the utility closet. She knew that behind her daughter's hard legs and outwardly sunny disposition was the girl who'd grown up in her home, the pushy, bossy kid who ignored rules and curfews, who ordered her mother around as if she were a paid servant, who never did dishes (despised getting her hands wet, actually), and only took over the cooking when her father's disappearance into the sea locked Fanny in her bedroom for an entire year. Even in those days Esmerelda got by with the minimum at work, never cross-pollinated with other top chefs, gave up on new recipes if they failed the first time, took several coffee breaks each day even though caffeine gave her hives, and liked to spend her days off dozing on the sofa. Everything was way too easy.

But at least she seemed happy, Fanny realized, and celebrated her small parenting victory with a triple-snifter of the finest New Jersey gin she could find in the cupboard. The taxi dropped Esmerelda at the Mt. Tam visitor center as a soft purple glow swept the horizon. She slung her bag over her shoulder and bumbled up the spiraling narrow path, clanging against boulders and stumps, stubbing both big toes and bruising a shin. When she limped out at the summit a cool ocean blue shimmered off the eastern mountains, the rippled landscapes emerging with vicious clarity. Wind slashed through her apron— she had come dressed to work—and her bones ached with the beauty of it.

After a few minutes gaping at the new day, her zeroed sensors detected a shift. There was no sound other than rustling wind, no visible motion besides the rising sun, no new smell in the vicinity. Instead she felt a minute change in barometric pressure, a slight drop in humidity, spotted some twigs a few inches out of place, the clues pulled into conclusion by an innate sense of phase completion—take the papaya pie out of the oven, enough blowtorch on the buttercup crème brûlée—fully developed among only the best of chefs.

"Bruce?" she queried.

"Shh!" She followed the noise to a massive stalagmite, jutting from the earth like a dinosaur incisor. On top Bruce sat Indian-style dressed in simple white pajamas, his eyes heavy-lidded in concentration. "Silence," he hissed.

"Nice morning for a séance," she joked. He noiselessly bared a set of lupine teeth, nostrils darting in precise angles. She wondered if this was Tai Chi or yoga, possibly a pagan ritual, then settled on a cult, as it also explained his permanent hermitizing, the secrecy, the devotion to perfection, the unreal ultraclean getups, everything about the guy pretty freaky. She was about to vamoose when the sun exploded into the sky, a miraculous supernova haloed with fire, the intensity and scale combining for a grand, triumphant vision that reminded Esmerelda of Apocalypse and Revelation, the end of the beginning—not a bad way to start.

"Wow," she said when Bruce climbed down, "color me inspired."

"Stop right there," he replied. "The first thing you must learn is how to keep your enormous fucking mouth shut." A pilot light flared, nuclei fused. Bruce held out his open hand, intimating violence, but already Esmerelda was launched and roaring, leveling her shoulder into his chest and slamming him into a boulder.

"My way of saying I ain't going," she shouted, raining saliva into his eyes. "Go find another protégé to pick on. Just know I'll be right behind you with a megaphone and baseball bat."

With an abundantly insincere smile Bruce wound himself upright, brushed dirt off his pajama tops, and limped back to his precipice. Suspecting a counterattack, Esmerelda made use of the interlude to compile an arsenal of rocks, dozens of light stones fingered for long- and mid-range attacks and a pile of big boys in reserve to finish the job. She loaded the ammunition into her apron pockets, then scooped up a discarded Snapple bottle and a handful of gravel and moved carefully toward the path back down.

She heard the rasp of scissors. A box flexing open. A meaty swish, a sponge adjusting to altitude. Distant internal noises: liquids resettling, gases finding equilibrium, sinuses breaking impasse. A smell like Sunday morning and fresh apples and a day at the beach. Professional curiosity got the better of her, and she double-timed it back to the peak.

He was flat on his stomach, facing her, a crimson-frosted pyramid on a gold plate by his head. Cult for sure, Esmerelda decided, and reached into her apron for a heavy-stone head cruncher. "My deepest, deepest apologies," Bruce mewed. "I have been out of the company of people for many years. It is a skill I must rebuild. How can I cook without appreciating the harmony of humans?"

"The real question is, how'd a rad chef like you turn into a total dickweed?" She lobbed a pebble across his bow and cleared her throat menacingly.

He lifted his face and stared at her, his gaze even steel, cheeks constructed from sheet metal. "This is my latest cake," he announced, his voice a clarion bell. "It is blessed with the peace of the rising sun; now, it is for you."

Pricks and bubbles ran across Esmerelda's back. She shuffled toward the slice, sidestepping matador-like, the Snapple bottle raised to defend against sneak attacks. When she reached the plate, she slowly descended into a catcher's stance and examined his offering. A marvelous mixture of scents blitzed her cells— fresh fruit mixed with the first day of vacation—shifting atomic structures and mushing her heart into a wispy, delighted haze.

"I am infinitely sorry," he remarked, his voice peppy and devoid of remorse.

"Better be." She scooped a hunk of icing with her pinky and held it under her nose. Majestic. "See you on the other side."

She entered an airport whirring with song. Passengers with formless faces danced across a capacious sun-streaked terminal, scatting and swinging to big band tunes. Ivory golf carts zoomed in synchronized routes, carrying cages filled with melodious songbirds and doubling as launchpads for cartwheels and som- ersaults and advanced tap-dancing combinations. Along the ceiling maroon fluid pumped through plastic tubes, sparkling with injections of glitter. Esmerelda pranced through the action, whirling and singing along in perfect pitch, conducting chug- ging flap heels and sugar brushes and rapid-fire quadruple spin moves alongside blazer-clad customer service agents, until she eventually found a diamond-shaped glass elevator with her name stenciled across the front. She pressed a large red button and the doors opened immediately. Inside, her pastry instructor from the culinary academy sat on a stool with a hand on a lever, portly and yellow skinned, his chin twitching as if poorly animated.

"God, you again," she said. "Haven't you had enough?"

"Don't blame me," he said, "I just drive." He threw the lever and the doors screamed shut, iron bars slammed over the windows, the elevator catapulted upwards. Sensations of heaviness and weightlessness battled in her torso; her head soared like a kite, her spine drilled into the earth's mantle. The elevator accelerated, smashing her into the floor and breaking her teeth and shaving off her apron, her body turning to oatmeal, then liquefying, a widening puddle across the elevator floor, licking her professor's shoes. A minute later he pulled back the lever, the elevator froze, and Esmerelda was pulled from her flatland into the glorious sun.

"How is it?" Bruce asked.

"Trippy," she drooled, "like a dream."

"A nightmare?"

"Not really a good dream or a bad dream. A weird dream."

"Not acceptable." His neck twitched three times. "I'll reduce the argon ratio."

"Know what it was like? Like your dreams after late-night Indian food. You sure you didn't put any curry in there?"

"What?" A metal splinter rose in the center of Bruce's forehead.

"Kidding, kiddo." She raised the gold plate and pawed another hunk. "Take the stick out of your ass and we might get on OK. Now if you'll excuse me, I'm going to finish my breakfast." The rest of the slice went down easy as wine, and within seconds she was overcome by jazz orchestras and soft-shoe acts circling on baggage carousels.

She awoke on a cot in a dark room, her lips caulked with sugar. "Ma?" she whined, wiping the scab from her mouth. She waited as no one rolled out of bed grousing about the electric company, no one dug out flashlights and old camping torches from the garage, no one clomped into her room suggesting it was time Esmerelda learned her own sweet way to the emergency locker or else she would be ten miles up shit creek in the event of a major shaker. Kind of nice, actually.

"Hey!" she yelled. "Power's out!" Dank air weighted her lungs. She sat up, felt woozy, flexed her toes, lay back down.

Next time she came to, a green light bathed her small chamber, emanating from a narrow hallway. She swung out of bed and discovered that she was wearing a set of white pajamas similar to Bruce's; her shoes and socks were missing; her hair was wrenched back in a bun. Her great wool bag rested on a bench on the far side of the room, and she rifled through it until she found a pair of flip-flops and her cake knife.

She crept down the hall toward the light, fixing an overhand grip on the cake knife for maximum-power downward stabs. A green lamp was posted beside a door, which she yanked open with her free hand and charged through into a sheer white electrified den. A series of huge red-lettered signs screamed to shower and suit up, complete with directions to changing facilities, but those were obvious red herrings; her chef sense was tingling, and she knew her creep captor was dead ahead through the big steel door marked DO NOT ENTER, though it didn't budge until she'd gone through a few hundred numerical combinations on the keypad, fast typing having always been one of her strengths.

She leaned into a gray bunker lined with a row of hoop-ring cabinets, a wall of refrigerators to the left, an enormous iron range heating eight pans of odorless goop to the right, the cumulative soul of a dentist's office. In the middle, a moon suit turned away from a long banquet table covered in blinking green computer screens and shuffled her way.

"Nice place you got here," Esmerelda quipped, easily dodging the moon suit's lethargic advance and skipping out to the perimeter. "What do they call this? Industrial chic? Bet it impresses the Eastern Bloc girls."

The moon suit jammed a glove to its neck. "You are in serious danger," Bruce's voice crackled. "Please, return to the clean room."

Esmerelda pulled open a drawer, lifted out a steel brick. "Whatcha got in here, building supplies?"

"Tellurium," the glove buzzed. "Radioactive."

"Eww!" Esmerelda threw the brick back in and wiped her hands on her apron. "What's in the other cubbies?"

"Most of the items on the periodic table. Plus essences. Scents. New strains from the lab arrive every day."

The muscles in her face released in a quick and surly sag. "Whatever happened to fruits and veggies, wheat flour, plenty of good butter, and a hearty helping of creativity?"

The moon suit stopped a few feet away, the gold face mask contorting her tall face and voluptuous apron-draped chest into a convex funhouse hologram. "Dairy's produced daily at the barn complex. We grow local fruits and vegetables at the farm and the greenhouse, with nonnative greens arriving on daily shipments at the landing strip. I haven't used wheat flour for years."

Liquid gushed into her mouth, building ravenous hunger. "Weird," she mumbled.

"I've been working on devising more sophisticated flour blends, improving the flavor complexity and mouthfeel. A creamy pistachio flour for summertime wedding cakes, for example; a coconut-and-gum-tree flour that will revolutionize hot cross buns. Recently I've been tinkering with a blend of acacia, kudzu, and field grass that makes for an unbeatable loaf of country bread. But if you prefer wheat flour, that's easy—we'll have it here tonight."

"Who's we?" Esmerelda asked, heavens streaming into her skull.

"Yakob, the caretaker, planter, milker, feeder, dishwasher, choremaster, all-around handyman. Won't see him much, but he's around."

She posted a hand on a table and felt sparks fly inside her head, the imagination engine room firing up to speed. "Can I see the dairy barn?" she asked.

"Tomorrow. First you need a laser bath, some injections. Then a welcome salad. Here, start with water," he ordered, pulling a retractable tube from the ceiling. "You'll need more sleep too—zazen starts at 4:30 AM."

At his command she stripped, let the white flashes kill her coating of skin cells, and accepted a procession of colorful vials into her forearm. She ate his plain salad as instructed: each forkful a quarter leaf of lettuce with three shreds of cucumber, chewing fifty times and circulating the vegetable mess counter-clockwise in her mouth, fifty milliliters of lemon water after every five cycles. By the end of it she felt fresh as a doe on a morning trot through the woods, nibbling dewdropped greens with the freedom of open land throbbing in her neck, though partially that was due to all the munching she had to do—which also explained why Bruce's jaw was built like a boxer's fist and probably just as dangerous.

"Enough of the salad bar," she pronounced, "let's get our bake on. Where do you keep the Cuisinart?"

"Patience," Bruce murmured, moving his fingers against her temples in a reassuring progression.

"Not really my strong suit—" Esmerelda admitted, where-upon Bruce's hands found their mark and she keeled over the table in a deep and dreamless slumber.

A soaring symphony roused her on her cot. She followed the music to a small chapel covered in miniature paintings, elephant men with eight heads bashing swords and blowing flames, hordes of winged monkeys attacking island goblins, giants hurl-ing mountains into seas. Following Bruce's lead she kneeled over a pillow and balanced on her haunches and attempted to throw memory to the clouds, forgetting where she was and what couldn't be, relying on the low oval "Om" word to carry her to a clearing in the wilderness, the purr of controlled agony, a trail of bread crumbs leading home.

When the droning was over, she stood and tied an apron tight round her torso. She felt cleansed, hands ripe and ready to make and bake, an even hunger stretched through her stomach. They funneled down another tunnel toward what was certainly the kitchen, the same green glow in the distance, her chef senses picking up massive stores of ingredients, the microscopic crumbs and fibers that eluded Yakob's intensive nightly scrubdown and bleach. "Glad to be getting down to business," she chirped. "Zen stuff's nice, but it ain't paying the bills. Now how's about you show me the tricks to your cake baking and I'll put you in touch with the best cowman this side of Cheyenne."

"This morning you will wash the measuring cups," Bruce announced. "When you're done, read the first five chapters of this." He handed her a textbook the size of a suitcase. "I'll collect you for lunch."

Esmerelda let the book slam to the floor, its thunderous *thomp* somewhat deadened by the humid cave stones but still a significant disruption to the tranquil morning of whispers and natural calm. "First thing's first. You ain't Kemo Sabe and I ain't Tonto. Get Yakoff Smirnoff to do the dishes, because I'm too good at what I do to put up with the wax-on wax-off circle jerk. As for your homework assignment, I did my time in the education system already, and now I'm done." She kicked the book against the wall, the spine slap accentuating her point: "Your move, Kasparov. Either suit me up and put me in the game or get me the hell home."

Nothing moved on Bruce's steely face, his lips flat ingots, eyes sturdy bolts, nose a metallic shark fin. A minute of robotic silence geared by, the green light steady as a sun. Then his parts mobilized, joints compressed and flexed, his face lit with the first snatch of warmth she'd seen in her stay. "Come along," he said brightly, "let's make some music."

"Dairy barn first," she insisted.

"Don't push it," he retorted, and instead helped her into her own moon suit and spent the next eight hours leading her around the kitchen on his quest to manufacture a frosting that tasted of berry fields without a powdery aftertaste. For dinner Bruce smoked a half lamb and Esmerelda boiled up a wild-raisin-and-boar risotto, and they chattered on about chemical formulations and ideal boysenberry planting conditions into the wee hours. In the morning Esmerelda skipped the meditation routine to fry up a pan of honey bacon and eggs, which they ate quietly over copies of Cook's Illustrated. After a tour of the dairy barn— identical in most ways to Jamison's, the biggest difference being the music, exclusively classical strings rather than the mix of honky-tonk harmonica and sports radio Camden preferred— they returned to the kitchen with a bucket of silky butter, which they used to bake a guava flan pie paired with spearmint ice cream and topped with chorizo brisket. "Holy hacksaw, we got ourselves a hit," Esmerelda declared three bites in. "What do you say we go to Vegas, put our names in lights?"

"Not so fast," Bruce said, jotting down a list of unwelcome supplementary flavors he noticed after chasing his sampling with cheap red wine. "Doesn't work with young merlots."

"Who eats guava flan pie with wine?"

"The French."

"Obviously," she said, and plunged into a round of merry guffaws until she saw he really meant it.

"Additionally, if you let the pie settle in an environment warmer than seventy-nine degrees, the guava tastes off, almost rotten. The chorizo's smokiness feels congested and slightly unnatural, like car camping as opposed to a backcountry hike. For people drinking gin cocktails, the pie will sometimes have a bitter aftertaste."

"Yeah, well, they'll live. And love." She licked her fork clean, felt the warmth in her chest settle and spread. "C'mon, Brucey boy—this pie's the bomb. It slices, it dices, it'll do your laundry and mow the lawn. Hell, you could sell it for brunch since it's got fruit and sausage, perfect for him and her. Let's put it out and get rich."

Bruce completed his notes and took another swig of merlot, his eyes misting and contorting. Sweat beaded to his forehead like lunar modules; he moved his head plaintively, a slow bob-blehead roll. "It's not perfect," he informed her.

"It's pretty darn close," she responded. "What are you, chicken?"

Bruce splashed down another hit of wine and explained in a low voice that as a young pastry chef known as Herman Sprutz he'd worked at Vida Vida, an ultra-hip experimental restaurant in an unmarked warehouse lost in the thick of the Dogpatch, where he put together several of the most decadent dessert offerings ever known to mankind, one of which had been dressed with a synthetic compound not far off from heroin that had indirectly resulted in the deaths of multiple dinner guests—primarily Japanese tourists, but a few Americans, and, toward the end, one local, a reliable and simpleminded mail carrier celebrating his sixtieth birthday with a rare night out. Court proceedings had absolved Herman of all liability, but the mail carrier's family and dinner companions had raised a stink in the local media, with all the families on his daily route piling on, so that the name Herman Sprutz, while beloved by serious gourmands across the globe, had been effectively turned to mush in Northern California and most of the world as well. No eatery would let him in the door, investors shunned his new restaurant pitches—he couldn't even get a job sacking groceries—so he'd gone the name-changing-and-plastic-surgery route, emphasizing squares and hard corners, projecting strength through his face. After a lengthy recovery on a remote Thai island he'd launched his comeback running a low-budget churro stand in the Mission called Zoog's Chocolate Fugue, a clever bit of assonance backed up by a sensational chocolate dipping sauce that attracted a huge number of intoxicated San Franciscans after bars closed and generated more than enough buzz to open the mind-shattering North Beach cake shop he'd always dreamed of. From whence came the fame, the money, the freedom to seek perfection in his own personal underground lair.

"I often invoke the metaphor of music," he concluded. "A conductor strives to intertwine the talents of excellent individual musicians to produce impeccable orchestral experiences, a universe of sound. With all the variables cross-tabulated and accounted for, can we create a masterful experience every time? Can perfection be sustained? Will the concerto linger in the blood for the rest of the listener's life?"

"Probably not," Esmerelda drawled, helping herself to another plate of pie. "People got too much to remember."

"No. Superior experiences always are so. Think back to your most electrifying life events." Esmerelda dug back in the mud, came up with high school graduation and gossip magazines, a lot of time on the couch, hours of television and dozing and solitaire and snacks. "These are immortal sources of joy. The brasserie in Paris. The café in Rome. The funnel cake at the county fair. The stuff of memories and deathbed reminiscing. These are the moments that make life worth living. This is the food I must make."

Esmerelda gave the thought a couple of nods, then polished off her slice and picked her teeth clean with a fingernail. "Spend your life chasing perfect and you'll probably never get it. So I say you get pretty close and drink up. Like this pie"— she knifed off a little sliver, last piece, that was it, to prove her point only—"damn good so long as you don't drown it in shit French wine."

Bruce untucked his napkin, rose, and poured the remainder of his wine over the pie plate. "Good night," he said leadenly, and left, leaving Esmerelda to fully explore the chemical interactions between merlot, guava, flan, and chorizo. She forced down the rest of the prototype in the noble name of research.

The next day they worked on a barley wine pudding that literally simmered on the tongue, evaporating into a spray that coated teeth and needed a slice or two of olive-cherry bread to level out, ideal for rustic retreats and destination restaurants and even gourmet camping trips. Bruce found it overpowering when consumed with a half bottle of fino sherry, but Esmerelda managed to push down all of her portion as well as Bruce's leftovers, then finished the other half of the Sandeman bottle for the sake of completeness. Next night was a cottage cheese–stuffed pork roast slathered with hickory and lime—a couple flecks too dry for Bruce, impeccable according to Esmerelda; all it needed was a six-pack of Hefeweizen to flush out the juices. On it went, a vat of crawfish jambalaya, squid truffle paste, cherry-apple-pork-chop marmalade, gooseneck onion goulash brewed with platinum flakes, emu casserole slow-cooked with periwinkle nutmeg and served with gingerbread pretzels, candy-cane venison stew, armadillo caper soup. Each dish loaded with otherworldly flavor sensations, titillating textures and exquisite composition, an overarching sense of painting on a bigger canvas, the sweep of history—and that was before they got to the desserts. Cookies, brownies, puff pastries, pies, ice cream, sherbets, puddings, all exquisite and headline-worthy, but the cakes dwarfed everything else, towering leviathans, slice after slice liquefying in Esmerelda's mouth, alighting the dim portions of her brain and helping her see across continents, into the future, through the webbing of souls. Though Esmerelda was firmly agnostic, and knew the cakes were born of trial and error, centuries of scientific research, and a generous dose of luck, she couldn't eat a slice of Bruce's cake without feeling the warm breath of God upon her.

Days and weeks melted by, hours bunched up and collided, a string of unfocused photographs drying on the line, sorcery in the kitchen, hours of eating and notation, Bruce ticking off shortcomings, then back to her room and the green glowing bulb. Sleeping more and more, breath coming harder, no life in her legs. Bigger pants, shirts, and aprons waiting under her pillow. Jerry-rigged bricks and two-by-fours buttressing her cot; a second bed added alongside to accommodate her growing girth. Internal cycles slowing down. Bathroom breaks an inhumane ordeal. Mild narcolepsy setting in, first sudden naps in the kitchen, then clocking out at meals, later falling asleep willy-nilly, night and day meaningless conceptual exercises, a life of black and white and the green glowing bulb. She developed the unfortunate habit of passing out face-first into her fourth or fifth dessert of the evening, a potentially life-snuffing series of collapses that tested Bruce's footwork, bench press capacity, and emergency medical training as he diligently cleared out her air passages and hurled her back into life.

One morning, following a top-dollar dinner of catfish quiche and pear-shiitake upside-down cake, Esmerelda was hauling herself off her cot combo when she caught a new aroma in the air: grease and perspiration with a bitter, lonely bite. "Who's there?" she murmured, settling onto her back with a manic grin, unable to disguise how glad she was to justify a break with the threat of home invasion.

"Yakob, miss." A small man glided out of a corner, his face covered in fur, a felt cap pulled low over his eyes.

"You! Glad to make the acquaintance. Doing a bang-up job keeping us running and all. Even baked you a cake a few weeks back, left it out with a note."

"My day off, miss."

"You can take my word that it was a good one. Braised vanilla asparagus cake, I believe. I'll make you another tonight."

"Probably shouldn't, miss." He grabbed his hat and stuffed it into his pocket, revealing a field of wire hair sprigs lining a smooth bald crown.

"Why not?"

He rubbed his head with his knuckles. "You should go, miss."

She floundered through her new waterlogged laugh, deeper and more authoritative thanks to enhanced vocal insulation. "Go where? Got about the best gig you can think of. The stuff we're making here? I love it. The best. Strike that"—she launched a baggy arm in the air—"the best of the best. We're a crack team, the kitchen Green Berets. Once we go public, the world won't know what hit it."

Yakob moved toward the exit, the comforting silence of solitude. "Better go," he mumbled, "this place is killing you."

"All we're killing is bad taste," Esmerelda shouted back, but Yakob was already gone.

She prowled through the day feeling nasty, grumbling expletives every minute or so, dropping pans and scalding her stir fry, the evening's marzipan malt-ball cake so badly undercooked even she had to admit it was a loser, though she did eat the whole thing just to be sure. Back on her cot early, she listened to her heart throb, felt her flesh squirm, tracked her shuddering lungs, her skin dead to the world, from every angle fulfilling the role of immovable object, a jackknifed tractor trailer paralyzing freeway traffic.

She was ready when Yakob arrived in the dead of night, her wool bag packed and slung over her shoulder, her fat feet packed into sensible walking shoes, a long pizza-oven poker serving as a hiking staff. But even appropriately appointed she needed a solid hour to putter down the couple-hundred-yards-long tunnel to the road, still plenty of time before Bruce finished his early-morning Buddhist chanting but putting Yakob well behind on his nightly schedule, a concern manifested in watch-checking every three minutes, the regular refolding of his cap in his pocket, the grind of his knuckles into his bald spot. Eventually she made it outside and, rejuvenated by the clean air and natural lighting, posted herself on the shoulder with her thumb out after a mere ten minutes. A cattle trucker pulled over a half hour later, thinking one of his stock might've somehow gotten into a clothesline, and graciously loaded her into the back, where she nested on hay and dozed amid tail swats for the drive back to the city.

He dropped her at the Transbay Terminal with a quarter for a phone call. Her mother needed two laps through the premises and a PA announcement before finding Esmerelda sacked out under a bench, unrecognizable, stinking of sugar and shaking like a massage chair. "Look what they have done to you!" Fanny exclaimed. "My baby, my baby! I lose your father to the seas and you to food, and what have I got left? We must go home and put you back together again." Fortunately Fanny had taken Harold's old truck, as her around-town Mustang was getting a new set of brakes in the shop, so she helped her daughter into the flatbed, told her to hang on, and drove well below the speed limit all the way home to the dismay of motorists behind her.

The months in Bruce's fortress had rendered Esmerelda 150 pounds overweight, incoherent, and sapped. She passed out on the living room couch for two days straight, until the new manager down at Incognito, Michael "Slippy" Sanders, made a swim move past Fanny's hip block at the door and slapped Esmerelda across the face with his briefcase.

"Worse than I thought," he said as Esmerelda drifted back to sleep. "Though it could have been horrendous. Took four men and a tractor to wheel out Zoogman's last lab partner, if you can believe that. Anyhow, we got her back, that's all that counts; she can get back in shape in no time. We'll give her a raise too—sales have been sliding without her, something's missing from the sweets, the girl's in demand. Think she can be back on the job tomorrow?"

"Asshole!" Fanny cried, breaking an antique serving plate over Slippy's head. He came to on his stomach positioned diagonally down the front steps, his briefcase in the middle of the street and badly bashed from passing vehicles, a bill for the serving plate in his breast pocket. He limped to his car and drove off without further argument.

For the next half hour Fanny sat on the edge of the sofa and watched her daughter sleep. New deposits undid her once-alluring figure; her limbs were reformed with impossible diameters; her hands and feet looked like inflatable toys. Conclusive proof of a spiritual shellacking. She pulled off Esmerelda's shoes and socks and rocked her slowly on her spine. "Esmerelda, dear, come, get up," she prodded. "The sun is shining; you are alive and free. You need a shower, fresh clothes, a walk around the block. And beyond that, Mr. Sanders has a point. You have a job and should do it. Who knows, perhaps the familiar environment will help snap you from this torpor."

The lollipop head lolled and blinked. "Ma?" it asked in a new, beefier timbre, "have you got any cake?"

"Only veggies for you," she declared. "Now quiet."

It took a week-long fast and detox program to shake the spell from Esmerelda's bloodstream, a series of enemas to wash out her intestines, and tanks upon tanks of drinking water to flush her body clean. Over the course of a month she became lucid again, walking without the use of crutches and preparing her own salads and using the bathroom by herself. Eventually she noticed the mountain of mail piled next to her bed and started to go through it. Sprinkled among the catalogs and fan mail she found legal notices from Incognito threatening dismissal, an assortment of overdue credit card bills, demand letters from collection agencies, liens imposed on her Ferrari. She reported for work the next day.

Silence descended as Esmerelda nudged aside the kitchen's swinging metal doors and waddled to her station. Her gait was new and dispiritingly ducklike; her frame appeared hugely oversized; her friendly face was lost in a bog of fat; her eyes emitted fewer lumens; her fresh-out-of-school bod was blitzkrieged and gone. Her hair was less lustrous and locked away in a Puritanical, sexless, librarian-style bun. She wore a dress-slash-hospital-gown thing instead of an apron, covering her whole body except her hands and head. The staff stopped preparing dinner and whispered to one another, wondering what the hell happened to the sweet, perky pastry phenom that had been such hot stuff just eight months before, until Esmerelda leaned against the counter and whaled two Bundt pans together.

"Things haven't gone so smooth for me lately. Plain bad, in fact. I'm fat, tired, and hungry all the time. My temper sucks too, so approach with caution. But I still want to kick ass, and I got some ideas on how to do it. So here I am. I figure we stay out of each other's way and keep the food coming, we're back on the map in no time. That's best."

The staff nodded and smiled quietly, excitement welling in their joints. An hour later a delivery boy out on a drop told a receptionist about Esmerelda's return, the CEO was informed, the country club was notified, the foodies alerted, and then the media caught wind of it, and before Esmerelda could preheat the oven Incognito was swarmed by journalists scuffling for a glimpse. It hit the six o'clock news, and then the phone system broke down; a line formed six blocks long; reservations were auctioned off for five-digit sums. After surveying the madness, Slippy Sanders ducked into the kitchen and found Esmerelda digging through the refrigerator previously reserved for butter.

"Nuts," she was saying, "this butter's old and cheap, and there's other stuff in here poisoning the pool. Look at this crap." She tossed a rotting butternut squash over her head.

"Maybe we slipped a bit while you were gone," Slippy said, invoking the sobriquet he'd earned in his lady-killing days. "What do you need to get back on track? Cheese from China, zucchini from Zimbabwe, hamburger from Hamburg, it's yours."

"Well, we could start with some decent butter. Where's my guy with the stuff?"

"Who?" Slippy thought for a moment. "There was a guy up north who kept billing us for butter, but nobody ever used it, and it was overpriced. Fuel costs alone were more than what we pay now." He watched deep crevices form in Esmerelda's face. "But you want him, no problemo," he added, jogging toward the phone. "I'll set it up right now."

Esmerelda waded through the kitchen, counting problems on her fingers. The pans had been swapped out, the seasonings reorganized, the ovens coated with a thick coat of grime. "Hey, guys," she called, wiping flour on her hands, "somebody get in there and scrub. You've been serving dirt, not sweets. Now who took my All-Clads?"

The kitchen staff stared at her, wistfully recalling the slender semi-sexpot hidden beneath her flesh overcoat. "Quit staring!" she called. "Chop chop!"

Her staff moved slowly, unmoored by her snappishness and resentful of her abdication, exasperating Esmerelda with their seeming disinterest in producing world-class desserts. They baked angrily, for too long and too rough, not adhering to recipes, forgetting key ingredients, plating sloppily, sometimes spitting in the batter. Even so, their creations marked a tremendous improvement over Incognito's recent end-of-meal fare, not quite all the way beyond divinity, diners agreed, but good, damn good, the woman was clearly a difference maker, if a bit rusty. Orders hailed down on the kitchen like hail and, when the oatmeal cookie crumbs had settled and the last of the hangers-on were forced out at 2 AM, the cash register had banked a record haul.

Slippy found Esmerelda in the kitchen, resting on a stool with a glass of skim milk. "Nice day, kid," Slippy said. "We needed you."

"My butter," Esmerelda growled, "what's the deal?"

Slippy hopped up to sit on the counter, an approachable managerial move calibrated to lessen the blow of bad news. "Jamison won't answer the phone, and his neighbors say he's been out of town. I sent a guy up to find him and he said the lights were off, the barn was empty, the mailbox was full. Hell, Esmerelda, I think your man's done up and skipped town."

"Fudge," Esmerelda said, "that guy's the best. We'd better find him."

"Or somebody just as good," Slippy said enthusiastically. "How hard is it to make first-rate butter anyhow?"

The next morning, when Esmerelda and Slippy drove up Highway 101 to Sonoma County and began knocking on doors of prominent dairy farmers, their offers of incentive-laden and unusually producer-friendly distribution agreements were steadily dismissed. The star power and well-tabulated rise in business that came with supplying a celebrity chef could not arouse interest, and, despite Slippy's most charming cajoles, not a single dairyman considered making a deal. "Shit," Slippy said under his breath, "it'd be easier to get our own cows." Which is precisely what they decided to do after a week of doors slammed in their faces, San Francisco being an ideal climate for bovine residents, and from a marketing perspective a glass-enclosed cow-grazing pasture in the middle of the restaurant would be a compelling attraction for diners. But the cow breeders wouldn't have anything to do with them either, preferring to ignore calls or pretend to be out or fake violent illnesses or in some cases actually retire at the door rather than turn down Slippy's request for cattle and face the antidiscrimination lawsuit he was itching to smack them with.

"What gives?" asked Esmerelda after a week of failed cowmen recruitment. "We've been blacklisted!"

"Probably your boyfriend Zoogman," Slippy responded.

"He is *not* my boyfriend," Esmerelda snapped.

"Well, one way or another he's screwing us over. I'll get to the bottom of this, and then we'll see what's what." Slippy headed for his office to type up a cease-and-desist letter while he was worked up, his legal prose spigot open wide. He found a gleaming white device blocking his doorway, skinny and long and outfitted with what looked like finely tuned aeronautics components, poten-tially a high-tech bomb. After close examination he wheeled the contraption out of the way and flipped on the lights to find Bruce Zoogman sitting in his chair and working on a bottle of Incog-nito's most exclusive white wine, an Alsatian Pinot Blanc from the late '40s, the last of three known bottles ever to grace the earth.

"You!" Slippy exclaimed, hurling the bicycle at Bruce and tak-ing out a desk lamp, a notebook computer, and his collection of classic snow globes in the process. "Away from my pastry chef!"

Bruce picked the bike off the floor, removed a few glass shards, and leaned it against the wall. "I dropped by to tell you that you can have all the butter you need, the embargo is off. You can even put in your little zoo."

"Why this crap?" Slippy demanded. "What has she done to you, other than sacrifice the prime of her career and her physical well-being in the name of culinary excellence?"

"She's done more than that. Thanks to Esmerelda's pep talks, I'm opening a new restaurant to complement my bakery. And, given the strength of the competition, I thought a supply-chain advantage could be beneficial. But it felt slimy and unharmonious, and my karma suffered—as it should. Also, chemical analysis shows my desserts are measurably superior. We'll let the public decide."

The air in Slippy's lungs fractured into rock-hard rage, barely bottled. "When she gets her butter, my girl will run circles around your kidnapper's club," he screamed. "And I'll get the FTC on you for the pleasure. You think you can collude against tax-paying Americans without a little federal interdiction? Think again, amigo." Slippy slammed his briefcase across his visitor's face and shoved him out of his office, through the front door of the restaurant, to the curb. "Sayonara, fuckface," he spat, his loafers connecting with Bruce's kneecaps. "I'll see you in chocolate-covered hell!"

With Esmerelda's hands on high-density butter, Incognito's desserts leapt back to presabbatical levels, the apple pie rich and savory once more, the profiteroles reclaiming their decadence, the oatmeal cookies again spurring faintness of breath, with a daily rotation of Zoogman-inspired cakes—polka-dot pineapple gumdrop cake, chunky peanut-butter fudgesicle whip cake, avocado horchata Guadalajara cake—that were unveiled each evening on a platinum platter to uproarious applause from diners. But while the overall quality of Esmerelda's concoctions was superlative, the regulars sometimes noticed tiny chinks in the armor that hadn't been there before: an oatmeal cookie without its sprinkle of Kerala cinnamon, the occasional hard scoop of ice cream that needed a minute or two to melt, slices of cake served without the secret apricot chutney layer that added the dynamite finish. The joie de vivre was lagging, the foodies mumbled amongst themselves, standards slipping by a hair.

And then Element opened six blocks away and everybody forgot about Esmerelda Van Twinkle altogether.

Element was an instant legend, enshrined in the culinary hall of fame before the first week was out. Bruce had wisely eliminated his cakes' occasional peyote-like side effects and focused his creativity on a single, unparalleled, easy-to-remember dessert called Mandibles of Chocolate, a luxurious conflagration of chocolate perfection. Not a single person who sampled the dish failed to fall deeply in love with it—even those who didn't care for chocolate, even those who were allergic and ate the dish anyway, so as they flailed in the throes of cardiac failure, a miniature dessert fork poking from their mouths, they released soft, moving moans of gastronomic nirvana. Critics raved, patrons formed lines around the block, diets were busted left and right. And, thanks to regular exposure to natural light and contact with multiple human beings per day, Bruce was looking pretty good himself, his confidence-inspiring hard features chatting away on the international talk show circuit, his murderous past buried deep beneath his bankrolls.

As Element flew to the top of visitor guides and dessert lore, the bakeries, ice cream parlors, confectioners, chocolate shops, and fine-dessert vendors of San Francisco took a beating. Scores of pastry wizards were let go because people simply weren't buying. If the sweets weren't from Element, the thinking ran, they couldn't hope to hit the expectations set by the reclusive kitchen magician.

Esmerelda did her best to beat the trend. She devised a luxuriously multifaceted frozen yogurt that was indistinguishable from her heavenly ice cream, but with half the calories; she crossbred bees to create a distinctively complex honey hinting of ginger and lemon; she paid international cooking gurus to teach her their secrets. She worked twenty-hour days with an unnaturally energetic, positive outlook and posted motivational sayings in the employee bathroom. The cracks in her technique were cemented over and repainted, and her desserts again left the kitchen at the consistent level of perfection that had announced her name to the world in the first place. But nobody cared: only Element mattered, Bruce Zoogman done and deified. Incognito chugged along with the customers who couldn't get in at Element, but they were usually irritated and tipped poorly and badmouthed Esmerelda's baking because it wasn't from Zoogman's oven.

Esmerelda plowed on with her flawless final courses, incorporating effervescent neon fluids into cake batter, chattering blithely about genus and species, installing an electron microscope by the baking prep station and tying a copy of the periodic table to her waist. After a few months in second place her face turned sodden, she began ignoring all conversation aimed at her, a smell of sour peaches and decomposing tires installed itself in her armpits. Her staff assumed she'd started drinking, maybe cocaine, but that couldn't account for all the food she was eating, two or three entrées per hour, trays of appetizers, at least 10 percent of the pastries she made. She ballooned and lost mobility, she tired easily, the mistakes flamed up, her work regressed, her spirit was crushed like a beer can. Six months later, when she was still kind of hanging in there, Bruce ran wild on her at a citywide bake-off, the Mandibles stampeding her once-beloved oatmeal cookies by unanimous decision.

Incognito soon shut its doors, dethroning the pastry queen and exiling her to her mother's house to eat and expand. Esmerelda's first estate continued to grow fat and loathsome, first feasting on unemployment checks and bulk cartons of ramen noodles and, years later, on coupon-discounted snacks funded by Slippy Sanders's venture into the world of discount copying. Yet the history remained, intractable, and close observers like Slippy and Fanny could see that the fundamentals of her empire were intact, its traditions of passion, imagination, and hard work still functioning, and that maybe, with a major upheaval, the situation was salvageable.

The spirit of insurrection infiltrated her days. It wasn't obvi-ous—Esmerelda fell mired in loneliness, her waistband expanded steadily, her disposition hit bottom. But this has always been intrinsic to the cycle of revolution, to fall so far that plodding on is nonsensical, better to burn the fields and reseed. Desperation sets in; turmoil is inevitable. And as hindsight crystallizes, it becomes evident that cosmic karma played a major role here too, the bedevilments of her painful journey cycling through in the brutal, necessary acts to follow.

REIGN OF TERROR

The period from the 31st of May, 1792, to the *9th Thermidor*, 27th of July, 1794, when Robespierre and Marat usurped more than sovereign power, was very aptly designated THE REIGN OF TERROR. At that period, virtue and nobility were certain ties to proscription or the guillotine; debtors paid their debts by renouncing their creditors; criminals punished by the law denounced their prosecutors and judges; those who had not places denounced those who had; heirs denounced those whose fortunes would descend to them; husbands found it a commodious way of getting rid of their wives; and children denounced their parents.

> —*The Reign of Terror: A Collection of Authentic Narratives*
> *of the Horrors Committed by the Revolutionary*
> *Government of France Under Marat and Robespierre,*
> *Written by Eye-Witnesses of the Scenes*

Terror is nothing other than prompt, severe, inflexible justice.

> —Maximilien Robespierre

On the afternoon of September 11, 2001, after a day of sitting around while frightened teachers whispered into cellphones in the hall, a day in which mysterious televisions materialized from closets and broadcasted the same catastrophic images and humbled voices over and over, an absentee day of independent textbook review and worksheets and extended recess, Marat set off a pile of M-80s in the boys' room and a smoke bomb in the teachers' lounge and ran down the hallway screaming like a freshly scalped prairie woman until an assistant principal took him out with a shoestring tackle.

Two weeks later, upon completion of a wriggling, energy-blasted, house-wrecking suspension, Fanny informed him that he was no longer permitted to leave the house without first performing one hundred sit-ups and one hundred push-ups, in front of the fireplace, naked. "Marat, I am sorry that it has come to this," she explained in a judicious voice. "But how else are we to get through to you that this is unacceptable? We are fortunate you were not shot on the spot. Exercise and shame are required to put you back in line."

Marat smirked and shrugged. "I was just trying to, you know, make a joke."

"You have grown too chubby and yet retain too much pointless energy. An exercise regimen will take the edge off and trim off that fat," Fanny explained. "And the nudity will serve as motivation to end your shaming and behave better."

"What if I don't do it?" he barked.

"You will experience a pain you have never known," Fanny said sweetly, receding into the hallway, the divot in her forehead deep enough to hide a quarter.

The next morning, Marat and Robespierre crammed toast into their mouths, kissed Esmerelda goodbye, and made a coordinated break for the door while Fanny was in the bathroom with her third cigarette of the morning. As they grappled with the complex array of locks, Fanny strolled toward them laughing. "Children," she wheezed, "I may have been born at night, but not last night. Now Marat, strip!"

"Hold the phone, Ma," Esmerelda piped up, unaware of her son's new exercise requirements. "Not cool."

"Silence, dear. Would you prefer to sleep on the street? Marat, please, get to it."

"I ain't kidding, Ma!" Esmerelda rattled her cereal spoon menacingly. "Lay off the kid!"

"Esmerelda Van Twinkle, I have had enough out of you. The

boy committed a terrorist act. He does not respond to grounding. He does not respond to child psychologists. He does not respond to the rescinding of television privileges. Perhaps he will respond to physical exertion and embarrassment. Enough squabbling, Marat, drop them!"

Fanny jerked down Marat's sagging jeans to reveal his bare, fleshy bottom, and spanked him with her open palm. "Hit the deck," Fanny ordered, "now!"

Marat aimed his decimated pupils at his grandmother and inched open his lips. Quietly but clearly he hissed:

"Fuck.

"You."

The ensuing blast took him to the ground and into a nap. He woke up in bed, pants refastened around his waist, a drag race roaring in his head. And for the rest of his life, through his adolescent revenge and adult regret, he always believed that it was his grandmother who'd laid the haymaker on him. She was the offended party, already steamed up, well within striking distance, with a track record of screwing him over. Even though Robespierre insisted that it was their mother who'd risen from her chair like a viper and hurled her breakfast plate across the room at him, eggs and bacon splattering across walls as the porcelain pigeon clocked him in the forehead, he refused to accept it—it didn't make sense. For he had divined, correctly, that Fanny Van Twinkle had cracked.

Even with a daughter and two grandchildren at home, Fanny felt a dearth of love so penetrating that she found her only moments of warmth from her daily slate of soap operas. They provided her with reliable attention, featuring juicy love triangles with handsome men who commanded large fortunes and cogently discussed world events, scripted into trustworthy hour-long blocks and timed for predictable commercial breaks. Whereas her home life had descended into Hobbesian chaos: Marat, the nasty one, Esmerelda brutish; and Robespierre—her one hope, the girl—unbearably short.

What went wrong with Robespierre? Already she had taken to issuing orders and ignoring advice, a subtle dictatorship, her understated disgust at Fanny's copious and free home cooking ticking Fanny off in a major way; and she was condescending, with an enormous vocabulary Fanny couldn't decode. "That meal was really dyspeptic," she announced after Fanny prepared her classic fava bean casserole. "Thank you," Fanny replied, thrilled to have earned such an unusual compliment. A stupid, elated grin stuck to her face for the next few hours, until Esmerelda asked what was making her so freakin' silly, and Fanny told her, and Esmerelda provided the definition. "Damn," Fanny growled, her smile vaporized, "that girl has too much peacock in her strut."

Fanny cleaned, she cooked, she shopped, she mended. She tried to help with homework and occasionally took a shot at physical contact: a handshake, a high-five, dipping in for a hug once a year. But her daughter was sullen, Marat cold, and Robespierre a goody two-shoes too calculating to be seen sucking up. The isolation was total. And yet despite the complaints, the animosity, and the resultant marginalization, Fanny never seriously considered that she might have been too rigid in her contract enforcement, too persnickety about the little things, particularly with regard to the boy's clothing options, and that the girl was only doing what she could to increase her general popularity among the household, to build her political capital.

And Harold wasn't coming back. She knew this. There was no secret rescue mission or mystery vortex or explanation for his absence other than a boiling sea, swirling rain, nautical collisions, gale winds, and bone-crushing waves. At least he had gone with the ocean. It was where he belonged, she thought, and when it stormed against her bedroom window she imagined his body banded with water and drizzling back to her as rain. Her love, trickling through her flowerpots; her love, leaking between her shingles. Her love filling her stomach when she drank from the tap. As the younger generations quickly figured out, Fanny fell apart during storms.

She was lonely. She heard the rain but could not kiss it. She drank her husband's love but could not feel it.

Her mind was melting with love.

"Gramma?" Robespierre was at her knee.

"Wha?"

"You were yelling in your sleep."

"I was?"

"Yes."

"What was I saying?"

"'Batten down the hatches! Storm coming!' You said that over and over again. And you yelled a bunch too."

"Well. Too much pizza before naptime I suppose."

"Really?"

"No." Her face flinched, nearly a laugh, and she privately reveled in her superior handle on sarcasm.

"This naked exercise thing, Gramma. It's stupid," Robespierre declared. "And wrong."

Fanny's sinuses churned. "It is my house, dear. And in my house, you must obey my rules."

"Your rules are stupid," Robespierre said simply. "They're just getting everybody mad at you."

"And how do you expect me to react, Robespierre?" Fanny's skin was orange, her hands shivering crabs. "You helped your brother disobey my rules; you are no better than him."

Robespierre glided back toward her room, soundlessly unpacking comebacks. Already she knew she was far better than her brother in nearly everything. "Cool it, Gramma," she said as she climbed the stairs. "We're all you have left, and you should treat us better."

Fanny sat back in her husband's recliner and did not move. She did not chide the children to turn off the cartoons they watched on the wood-paneled television set that sat on the living room floor; she did not return her daughter's perfunctory "Hey, Ma," when she came home at 5:30. She did not make dinner. She did not react to Esmerelda's queries as to what in the heck was shaking, how was the boob tube treating her, was there any chance she'd be cooking up some food in the near future or what. The sun set, and she sat alone in the dark while they ordered Chinese, the kids trundled up to bed, Esmerelda took her nightly shower and plunked onto her double-king mattress. Fanny sat with her eyes open and watched the wall, watched the window, watched the shadows droop across the street, watched the past fade into oblivion.

At 5 AM she rose from her chair, went to the kitchen, and warmed herself some mu shu pork. Then she drank a beer and went to sleep, leaving the dishes dirty, lunches unpacked, the kids sleeping through their alarm clocks, her daughter without someone to pull her muumuu over her mountainous body and help her out the door. In early afternoon she got up and walked to the beach, through the fog, to the sea. She took off her clothes and waded into the water. Harold's cold wet kiss lapped at her ankles, her knees, her thighs. He wrapped his arms around her waist and pulled her toward him, his stubble against her cheeks, his breath on her neck. She longed to be touched, to be his wife, and she let him run his hands through her hair and rub her back and blow bubbles in her ear. They made love softly, rolling in the waves, until she fell asleep.

She awoke on the beach, fists pounding her chest. "She's up, dudes!" a voice called.

Salt water spilled from her mouth. "Fuck-a-doodle-doo," the voice said. "Hang on, lady, ambulance on the way."

Ice locked up her muscles. She had lost him.

She pushed herself up and walked silently through the pack of surfers, dog walkers, dogs, joggers, and kite flyers, over the dunes and back across the Great Highway to her house. She sat naked in the kitchen drinking gin until the liquor was gone and Harold was gone and there was nothing to do but lie down and die.

But in the morning she found herself in her own bed, dressed in a nightgown and covered in quilts, both grandchildren hud-dled beside her. "Is this hell?" she screamed. Marat opened an eye and shook his head. "Is there a reason you people refuse to let me die and be done with it? Why the tricks? Save yourself the time and trouble; please, let me go!"

Robespierre crawled up the bed and pushed her lips against Fanny's ear. "I love you, Gramma. I don't want you to go." And then she began to cry.

For the rest of her bewildered life, Fanny Van Twinkle spent her days uncoiled across Harold's old leather armchair, watching her soaps, offering unsolicited negative opinions, never leaving the house, transmitting devil rays across the universe. She brushed her teeth with gin and spat blood on the carpet, murmuring her wedding vows over and over again.

Yet before she descended into the lair of madness where she would reside the rest of her days—so Robespierre's attorneys argued—Fanny revised her last will and testament. She transferred assignments, swapped out names; the total text was shortened considerably. After the executors compared drafts and the legal battles wound themselves out, the list of losers ran as long as Esmerelda's beefy arm, superseded by a lone winner atop the pile, the last words of love Fanny Van Twinkle ever heard reverberating as far into the future as she could make them.

Until then: anger, brutality, callousness. Shallow tirades and vituperation, frequently matched by howling. More than anything, insults—ad hominem, abstract, accurate, fantastic. The invective exploded from Fanny's lips.

"Get off me, you brazen twat," she said to her sobbing granddaughter. "Expect me to believe your bullshit? I have seen enough to know the games you play. Go find another fool to swindle, and take that criminal down there with you." She kneed Marat in the chest. "Move it, leave. You have done enough, now give me my quiet." She rolled onto her side. "That is all I have to say."

The children ran to their mother's bed and jumped on her mattress, trilling wretched screams. They'd seen the glint in Fanny's eye and knew something was big-time wrong, sensed it like dogs sense narcotics and women sense fertilization. Employing a mix of snack incentives and hysterical pleading, they got Esmerelda vertical and up the stairs, entering the bedroom as Fanny hung up the phone with her lawyer, Robespierre's words melting like snowflakes but lingering just long enough for the changes to go through.

Esmerelda's heaves filled the room. "Kids, get me some water! And a towel, while you're at it." She wiped sweat off her face with her nightgown and took three uneasy steps toward the bed. "Ma, what gives? The naked push-ups crap, all the lying around nude. For Chrissakes, 'twat'? How'm I supposed to define that one, huh? HA-RONK! So much gin, Ma, that ain't healthy. And our contract—shite, it's not workin' out for nobody. I can't afford a three-bedroom house with Slippy's money, you've seen the prices. What's the point anyway? Our contract probably ain't legal, and anyhow we're gonna keep on changing, like it or not. Kids do nothin' but change. At first I thought it might be nice, all of us holed up together, the kids getting to know their Gramma, and us, maybe, getting to know each other too, as adults. But it's more like prison, and you're the warden. Can't you ratchet down the crazy bit and let life move along?"

Fanny propped herself up on her pillows and took a look at her daughter. They had the same upturned nose, and those were Harold's bean eyes, but the rest of her was a big hill of horse manure that she wanted nothing to do with ever again. "Listen to me, fat ass. I can't deal with your shit. You're obese and lazy and underachieving. You've ruined yourself with that dead-end job, and now you're ruining the children. And all you do is waddle around and stuff your face and blame it on your cake holiday ten years ago." A chemical extract pooled in her mouth, and she wiped her tongue with the hem of her quilt. "Every couple years you say you're gonna slim down, and then you backslide. Remember that Christmas you took a walk with the kids and told everyone you were gonna be a size 6 in two years? Remember how the next day you ate half a ham by yourself? Grow up, Esmerelda. And get the hell out of my room."

For a minute no one moved. Partially because Esmerelda was exhausted, but mostly it was the unexpected venom, the rampant use of contractions, the frontal attack on Esmerelda's constitution. How Fanny spoke the truth, a meadow tipped with frozen dew. Robespierre brought her mother a plastic cup of water and Esmerelda drained it with her eyes fixed on Fanny's face, her slow eyes, her brindled hair, her assured chin. Then she hobbled to the door and left, the kids followed her, and Fanny was finally alone.

Marat broke into his mother's ledger, a dusty cloth-covered tome lined with miniscule figures. Assorted accounts contained just enough to put a down payment on a three-bedroom house out in the Excelsior, not the nicest part of town but starting to gentrify, within city limits and close enough to McLaren Park to fulfill the contract requirements, with a little left over for furnishings, a housewarming party, maybe a used vehicle. "And that's thinking conservatively, a standard thirty-year mortgage with 20 percent down," he groused to his sister as they strategized in her room. "So many other options these days; she's not even trying. What's the deal?"

"Grandma's all she's got left that's familiar. It's hard to get past her."

"Grandma's bad."

"Grandma's a problem," Robespierre decided. "She hates all this anyway. We gotta do something." And like that it was settled that Fanny Van Twinkle's vestigial presence would be removed like an orange highway cone, picked off the asphalt and tossed into the back of the truck. As time dripped by, the idea gestated from vague concept to firm belief to actionable plan with a timeline and budget and elaborate web of deniability, all the anticipated variables plotted out, horoscopes and travel schedules taken into consideration, crafted with elegance and care. The only thing missing was the courage to execute, the shove over the mountaintop and into the irreversible wild, which eventually came along in the form of one of Marat's fellow detention-goers, a spoiled Vietnamese kid named Duc who gave Marat his first dime bag and Marley's *Legend* CD and put the kid in a place of peace.

On a midsummer afternoon in 2004, Marat took three rips from a pocket bong and tiptoed toward Fanny's recliner. She was snoring heavily over soap opera dialogue, her face undulating with the flow of oxygen, rising and falling, a rippling circus tent, until he touched her slipper and she gurgled awake. She frowned, unaccustomed to personal contact and suspecting chicanery. "Whatcha got there, swamp water? Where's Ezzie?"

He handed her a glass filled with brackish liquid. "Iced tea," he said. "I made it. Robespierre took mom out shopping. Now drink up. I've got a surprise."

Fanny glared at the glass shaking in her hand, growing increasingly leery of her first grandchild-delivered beverage in years. "What is it?"

"I was thinking we could go out," Marat suggested. "Do a little sightseeing."

"Really," she said. "What do you have in mind?"

"I don't know. Where would you like to go?"

Her first time out of the house in years. An opening. She thanked him with a slight softening of her eyes. "The Golden Gate Bridge?" she suggested. "Is it a nice day for a walk?"

"Not really," Marat said. "It's pretty gloomy out. The view would stink."

"That's too bad," Fanny said, her words lugubrious, her fantasy exit crushed.

"But the zoo's open today," he said. "I haven't been in years. Let's do that. The zoo."

She wanted to hate him for the brief remainder of her life. She hated him as he helped her into her overcoat and walked her down the street to the bus stop; she hated him as he paid her fare and collected her transfer, as he smiled and talked about how in history class they were studying the French Revolution, the Jacobins and Napoleon, his namesake Jean-Paul Marat, distracting external wars, some stupid pendulum swinging back and forth between right wing and left. She hated that although it was foggy the zoo was not wet, it was not nautical, it was not architectural brilliance spanning churning teal seawater blocked off by a puny four-foot fence.

He paid her entrance fee at the zoo and took her by the hand. She hated him and recalled how Esmerelda had taken the children to the zoo many years ago on their birthday, a disaster of an outing, Esmerelda unsuited to chaperone in her hugeness, the incident at the diner across the street that they cried about for weeks. Little kids had long memories, she thought, like wives and husbands.

He took her to the monkey house. The primates sat on poles and branches, picking their teeth and sleeping. They were stocky animals, bordering on chubby, and their ridiculous hairless rumps made her feel uneasy. Marat spoke softly to her, pointing out a little guy in a tree hanging by one leg, waving at her, it looked like, when it pooped on the floor. Marat laughed and she laughed too, an unfamiliar feeling, laughter, her last laugh. She didn't hate her grandson so much anymore. She realized she didn't mind the monkey house smell either, no worse than a fisherman's socks.

They looked at flightless birds, foxes, a bear, otters. A herpetologist was giving a talk by the turtle garden and they stopped to listen, the woman serious and straining when she smiled. Though her delivery was muted, it could not hide the love that coated her recitations of genus and species, the specifics of the turtle lifecycles and details about rare breeds she'd tracked in the field; her sincere affection held Fanny rapt, unanchored, almost happy. She was focused on the herpetologist's inert description of the Aldabra giant tortoise's mating rituals when Marat touched her arm and they walked on.

Marat didn't say goodbye. He walked her to the edge of the

open-air lion sanctuary and said he was going to go to the bathroom, did she need anything? Some popcorn or maybe a cotton candy? She said no, thank you, she would be fine, go on ahead, she'd wait right there. He left and she turned toward the animal prowling the perimeter, humped back the color of fire, two globes of translucent jade for eyes. A vital, baronial beast. The drop from the wall to the moat surrounding the lion's habitat was about thirty feet, and she watched the lion pad back and forth along the edge of the protective waterway, an incorruptible sentry, soundless but for a quiet and terrible purr.

This was the place. In the open air near the sea, alone, going with pure nature instead of manufactured solutions like sleeping pills or nooses or ovens. Briefly she wished for a rain shower, but when nothing materialized she took the shallow moat for good enough.

She fell with her mouth open and sucking air. There was time to watch the lion react, hurtling toward her and widening its jaws, animal instinct in all its beauty. Shrieks from other visitors, the piss-stained air stale around her head. *Why so long, Harold?* she thought. *Why so long?* And then she kissed the shallow moat and drew a lungful of water, Marat's love and the herpetologist's love and the lion's primal love melting into her at once, and finally she was returned to the sky.

The cops pulled Murphy Ahn over for a broken taillight, but soon identified his driver's license as a Chinatown knockoff, recorded the vodka spewing from his pores, found the Beretta under the driver's seat, a half kilo of cocaine in the tire well. Fourteen years old, his very first arrest. *About time*, he thought as they threw him over the hood and clipped his hands behind his back. He needed a kick in the ass, a jump-start, a mental and physical challenge. If you weren't rising you were stuck, he thought, and gambled his one phone call on Château Versailles.

He knew he'd made a mistake when Allen answered. Problem

was, Allen was usually high and forgot stuff, basics like the way to the bathroom and his middle name. Most nights he played board games against himself and listened to funk in the living room while the rest of the crew partied downstairs.

"H'yo?"

"Allen, it's Murph."

"Downtown Murphy Brown. 'Sup! 'Sup!" A slap bass solo cranked over the line.

"Cool, cool. Listen, I got pulled in by the cops an' I need some help."

"The cops? Shit, what they get you for?"

"Bunch of things. I only got five minutes."

"Yeah, man, got it."

"'S cool. Look, I need you to tell D that I'm down at Rudolph Youth Center."

"Hold on, lemme find a pen." Murphy watched the guard at the end of the hall scratch his balls as Allen snorted into the phone, punctuating a horn-section vamp in the background.

"What was that again? Dude somethin?"

"Rudolph. R-U-D-O-L-P-H. Like the reindeer."

"Shit, this pen don't work. Call back later."

"I can't call back. Tell Big D."

"Tell him what, you're at the North Pole?"

"Nah, man, *Rudolph*."

The line cut out. "I get another call?" he asked the guard.

"One call, five minutes."

"C'mon, I got hung up on. That don't count."

The guard took a step toward him, observing his ragged hair, pustule-ridden face, yellow and red eyes like the Spanish flag, the bad-milk stink of small-time failure. "You suck my dick, you get another call."

"What the fuck?" Murphy reacted.

"You heard me."

"What, like now?" Not that he was into that faggot-ass shit, but he was used to leading people on until they fucked up, and it felt like the right thing to say. He looked around and tried to look paranoid and desperate, like he might actually dish out a tax-free hummer. It wasn't hard to fake it with all the coke still in him.

The guard curled his lips into a thick pink rosebud.

"Fuck, man," Murphy acceded, "just lemme use the phone."

Big D's cell went straight to voicemail. The clock on the wall said 12:37, prime party time.

"Big D, yo, this Murph. I'm down at Rudolph Youth Center in DC an' I need somebody to come down here soon as you can, get me out. Cool? Aight."

He put the phone down and took a long look at the guard. He was wide-waisted and black, with a rectangular Brillo-pad haircut and a sloped forehead like a pitcher's mound. He moved leisurely, nothing in the world to worry about, his back tilted back five degrees and straight as a prairie road. His hands stuck deep in his olive pants pockets, slowly working his crotch.

"Let's go," the guard said, and pulled open the door.

They tooled down the green-tiled hall, Murphy in front, the guard a step behind him and playing an extended game of pocket pool. They walked past the infirmary and the mess and the shaded director's office, and then the guard told him to stop. He picked a key from the chain tied to his belt loop and opened a door and told him to get in.

Plastic trash cans on wheels filled the room, brooms and mops against the wall, jugs of bleach and boxes of garbage bags stacked on shelves. The guard came in after him and shut the door. Murphy squinted into the darkness and found the guard's legs moving toward him. He traced the line of his pants, pinpointed his utility belt, his pistol.

"You done this before, boy?"

Murphy wasn't about to say shit to that.

"Don't use your damn teeth. The rest come natural."

He heard the run of a zipper, the clack of a belt. Fluids plunged in his throat. "Got some weed or somethin?" he asked. "Shit."

The guard laughed. "I got something that might help," he said.

There was a rustle and an unclipping sound and the top of Murphy's head buzzed black. He fell to the ground and stayed there until a hand grabbed the back of his shirt and dragged him to his knees.

The guard's dick was out, celery-thin and curving toward him in the shape of a bass clef. "Don't be afraid use your hands, your neck get tired. Get this right, I can gitcha all the phone calls you want." The guard chuckled and pulled the boy by his hair into a musk of piss and baby powder. Murphy held in his breath as the guard craned back his head and stared at the ceiling, held it while his fingers danced and the ghosts of his hands unsnapped the holster and pulled out the gun. The guard's hand came down too late; Murphy had the gun and fell back into the dark grappling with the safety. The guard kicked at him but he felt nothing and then the safety was off and the bullet was loaded and he told the guard that he was getting the fuck out of there now.

They walked back down the hall with the formation flipped, the guard a step out in front, Murphy rolling along behind, the gun bulging in his pants. The guard led him through the mess to a room filled with canisters of cereal and oatmeal, where he opened a locked door with another key from his chain. They pushed out onto a loading dock, jumped down onto asphalt. The night was cold, and Murphy wished he had his sweatshirt from the car, fuck how was he gonna get the car back, all that coke, the gun? They walked across a parking lot that smelled of dead fish until the guard took out his keys and unclipped one.

"That's mine," the guard said, pointing to an old Dodge sedan with a felt-covered roof that almost fooled Murphy for a convertible.

"I need my car," Murphy said.

"Impounded," he said. "Booted in a lot under the highway."

"How do I get it back?"

"That's hard. Gotta get releases, and they ain't gonna give it back in the middle of the night to an underage delinquent busted outta jail, I'll tell you that for free."

"Fuck." Murphy pounded his knees and was halfway through spitting a consolation loogie through a steam grate when the guard threw the key at Murphy's face and charged him. Murphy rolled, righted, and fired, basic police evasion. A poof of blood and sour smoke. The gunshot echoed off car hoods, converting Murphy's legs into uncontrollable rubber stems. The bullet hit the guard in the head, creating a small slit in his cheek and a large wet hole in the back of his skull. A blood-letting vacuum silence, his body folding onto the ground. Murphy's mind went to God, God this was wrong, God took away life, and now he had too. God would condemn him. God it was easy. A bubbly sound came from the guard's chest, and Murphy leaned over and put his frenetic fingers against the guard's neck until he realized how dumb that was, the guy was clearly dead, and besides he didn't know shit about taking pulses or what to do afterward, just saw it on cop shows. He sat on the ground beside the guard, hands in his in his armpits, gun on his thigh, panic bludgeoning his innards. His eyes went flat, wan sorry wormholes. Aircraft throttled noisily through the sky. He realized this translated into serious jail time, probably forever, the privilege of killing not worth it unless he managed to get away. Then he worked the guard's wallet and ID out of his pocket, crawled around on the ground until he found the car key thrown at him, and got in the Dodge.

He didn't think about the parking lot gate until he was there. He waved the ID at the uniformed Chinese lady watching TV in a little hut, but she looked at him closely, then put on her glasses and waved for him to roll down the window. He complied, and then it was obvious this was not Henry O'Dwyer driving Henry O'Dwyer's car, this was not Henry O'Dwyer waving Henry O'Dwyer's identification card. When the woman reached for the phone Murphy shot her in the head. This time he was ready for the crackback and smell, the ease of murder, a bloody eraser scrub, and he crashed through the gate and onto the street like he'd done it a million times.

He got rid of the car in Tenleytown and stole a dented Mercedes hardtop. He turned it to the classical music station and drove the speed limit on local roads until he got to Potomac and parked at the high school, his mind a big blank brick. The rest of the way he ran on foot, cutting through backyards and parks and baseball fields, darting across intersections. He was rocket-ship awake and happy for the exercise, time and space to let thoughts coagulate, burn off the excess jet fuel. He was aware of his guilt but registered no emotional anguish; no brutal images flickered through his head; his appetite was at full strength and his head was clear; overall he felt terrific. The guard was a kiddie rapist but still he was a human being, and the parking woman was just doing her crappy job, and he'd killed them both like that. Weird to realize he was such a cold motherfucker, but truth was all he felt was fear of getting caught and some jogging endorphins, not a drop of sorrow. The gun was crammed in his front pocket, weighing down his pants, so he had to hold up his jeans with his hand, but his legs burned cool and he ran fast.

The lights at Château Versailles were all on. He rolled over the low stone wall around the property and greeted the snarling Dobermans with his wrists bared. The blood and sweat made them a little unhinged, a little more slobbery, and they swirled around his legs like a dust cloud as he trotted over the uncut grass and past the fish pond and around the tennis courts to the garage. All the cars were in but his, he counted, nobody heading to bail him out.

Allen was sprawled on a sofa in the den, staring at a rack of Connect Four and bouncing his chin in time with a feisty ska guitar riff. "Seen Big D?" Murphy asked.

Allen looked up from the game. "Yo man, how was Santa's workshop? Shit, musta done something right. Put some color in your face. Don't even look that whack for once." He inserted a red chip into the Connect Four set and picked up a black one.

"I need to talk to Big D."

The black chip fell in, cutting off a red three in a row. "You

know where D's at, man. Down in the lounge, entertaining!"
Allen's ruby eyes slipped from Murphy's face. "That a gun?
Lemme see."

But Murphy was already racing down the hallway lined with
moose heads, through the cavernous kitchen where the late-
night sous-chef spiced curly fries, past the movie room and the
gym and behind the grand staircase to the small elevator beside
the coat closet. So far as Murphy knew the lounge could be
accessed only by a rickety metal cage the size of a phone booth,
a controlled-access security measure that sometimes backed up
lines ten minutes.

He'd never been all the way down to the lounge before, though
he'd heard stories about sex parties, boxing matches, week-long
poker games, once a half hour concert by Mariah Carey. The
elevator ticked as it dropped past the basement, the subbasement, the arsenal, the vault, the measuring room. It slowed,
sped up, slowed, slowed, crunched to a stop. Murphy dragged
aside the chain-link divider and found his path blocked by a
thick armored wall.

He examined the barricade. It was solid and unblemished
with no visible hinges. Thumping against it produced no sound.
A smudged screen glowed blue, a biometric scanner. He wiped
his thumb against his T-shirt and realized his shirt was stained
with grass and dirt and blood, he stank of excrement and entrails,
he was all alone in this.

He took the gun out and pointed it at the screen. He thumbed
back the safety and heard a quiet snipping sound, a petite blond
woman dressed in a genie costume pulling back the door.

"Keep it in your pants, sheriff," she said, taking his arm. She
led him into a dark room set up like a nightclub, blistered with
heat, deep mauve carpeting, cloying cigar smoke. "Old West
rules in this town," she said. "Check your guns at the door." The
pistol floated from his hand and he drifted into the scene.

It took a minute for his eyes to adjust. Dim light flashed on a
pair of bartenders mixing drinks behind a glass bar, their legs

distorted and knobby through the beveled lens. White fire snapped in a marble hearth. Clustered around red velvet sofas on the far end of the room he spotted a horde of blond women covered in sequins—sequined headbands and veils, plunging sequined blouses and form-fitting sequin-laced sheer pants, haunches lined in sequined thong underwear peeking above their waistlines. They wore pink sequined slippers and sat twittering in the laps of men dressed in basketball uniforms and drinking straight from champagne bottles. Murphy knew some of the guys from the car wash—Eli the accountant, McKenzie the payroll manager, Mike in security—but most he'd never seen before, probably dudes from the office, the back-room cage where they kept the drugs. He was the only one from the line itself, where they scrubbed and hosed and vacuumed and sometimes, if the license plate numbers matched up, stuck a potting-soil bag packed with cocaine in the trunk.

He went to the bar and ordered a double scotch neat. Every last woman was blond, he realized, including the Asian women, the black women, the Filipina women. "Wild, huh?" The bartender slid over his drink. "D wanted blond harem night, so they gave him blond harem night. Cost a fortune in wigs."

Murphy nodded and downed his drink in ten seconds. "Another," he said, then stood up and ambled toward a rowdy group in the corner by the fireplace. Men were shouting, pounding a table and knocking over drinks, their attending women looking on three feet behind, a cautious row of fake hair. He smelled the women as he got closer, their strata of designer lotions and body oils, and then he saw the masterpiece on the table, coke doughed into clay and used to construct a magnificent Arabian palace, minarets stippled with rimy granules and snot streaks, ornate sandblasted terraces, broad ramshackle swaths where the cocaine cement had been scraped loose and ingested, ringed by the men's runny noses and runny eyes and runny minds. In the corner Big D sat with his arms crossed, eyes blocked by gold slitted sunglasses. He wore the black turtleneck he always wore, black jeans, black socks, black sneakers. He looked skinnier, his bones more fragile than usual inside his loose skin, his long brown hair scraggly and thin. Like a budget Johnny Depp, without all his teeth.

"Murphy," Big D rasped. "Come here." He tapped the shoulder of the man sitting next to him, Deva the sourcing director, who plucked a cocaine palm tree from the palace grounds and left without speaking. Murphy claimed the open chair tentatively, nervous but deeply tired, an ache building around his brain. Across the table Martin the assistant manager crouched on top of his chair, his Afro headdress flopping over his languorous red-stained eyes.

" . . . so I says, kill 'em. Kill 'em! Cuz if that gets acceptable, standards start tumblin' and people turn wild like tigers, see? An' we got plenty a Dumpsters ain't nobody look inside of, plenty a folks wantin' to make the hit. Even little Frankenstein here, he beat like a pit bull, but look at dem eyes. Ferocious. We send kids out do the killin', ain't nobody git us."

"Funny you should mention that," Big D responded. "Murphy's done some killing. Tonight." The men around the table grunted. "Broke out of juvie hall too."

Murphy stared at Big D. What a competitive advantage, he realized, D's network of knowledge powering lethal-quick undercuts, insider information feeding a furnace of fear. And a bigtime asshole for leaving him on his lonesome, not just mean but stupid too—that kind of shit comes back around when you least expect it, in nursing homes or on cruise ships or in a Chinese prostitute parlor having dreams come true.

Big D reached for Murphy's hand, pulled him into a highly untrustworthy oil-soaked grip. "What we concernin' ourselves with is this Octavius Maximus shit. The Octopus. You seen him. With the rims."

Murphy knew the Octopus, a big tipper. He drove Lexus vehicles only, with razor-edged hubcaps that never stopped spinning, not when idling, not when parked, not when being washed. A couple of guys on the line had lost fingertips scraping for tire sludge; Murphy always used a hose.

"Octopus wants credit," Martin spat. "We don't do that shit. Heard of the slippery slope, yo? Cause dis is like a ski jump ice skating wax job off a cliff. We bend, we break. Simple's zat."

Big D lifted a cigar to his mouth and breathed in an impossibly long time, the ash tip turning red and purple and, briefly, hot pink. "Maximus want to make a large purchase," he said at last. "Price is good. But he don't have all the money together just yet."

Murphy nodded. He heard chimes in the distance, flies hovering by his ears.

"Tell him 'bout the collateral, D."

Clouds of smoke stormed from Big D's nose. "Deeds to houses. Jewelry. Sports cars. Fancy wines. More nice shit I can't remember, but overall pretty good. Thing is, I gotta ask myself if this the kind of work we wan' get into. I really gotta ponder that, reflect on that. 'Cause once we in, whole business changes. Gotta get some enforcers, no-bullshit guys. And eventually somebody gonna default."

The scotch in Murphy's veins slowed and sank, half-dollars hanging on his eyelids.

"What you think, killa? I a loan shark or what?"

Murphy lifted his head into the haze-red light. "I wash cars, man. Do some drops at night."

"You a killer twice over, Murph. This your night at my table, best tell me what you think."

He watched the sequins dance in the dark, little caterpillars crawling up walls. "Well," he said, leaning his elbow against one of the blow palace's supporting walls, "how much we talking about?"

"Hoo! Gettin specific on you, D!" Martin cackled giddily, then screamed over his shoulder for a Jack and Coke.

"Ten million from him, ten million I front. Interest a million every three days."

"What's that outta your bottom line," Murphy drawled. "You got ten mil to lose?"

Big D put his hands on his stomach and gasped laughter. "We can handle it."

"Worth a try then. Don't work out, don't do it no more." Murphy fell back into the chair and bit his lip, the ropes around his skull loosening.

"Your boy bleeding," Martin reported, accepting a tumbler from a blond Latina genie.

"Can we stop though, in actuality? That the thing, Murph. We get walked on, we pull out—then who we?"

"Fucked on both ends," Martin said. "'Pushover' stamped on your forehead."

Murphy pressed his tongue over the wound in his mouth. Tufts of cotton packed his brain. His skin felt chapped and grated, his body a slab of rancid meat. "Kill the guys that do you wrong," he said, "and that's that."

"What I was sayin'!" Martin yelled. "Kid ain't so stupid after all."

Big D pounded down an auxiliary palace tower and chopped the rubble with a Chinese cleaver, then pressed his face into the dust and sucked. Dirty white wrinkles stretched across his cheek. "I need somebody to call this in. A headhunter, right? Shit goes wrong, take care of bidness, hunt some heads. I'll toss you 10 percent of the interest, killer. You in?"

But night had caught up with Murphy Ahn, a sledgehammer of murder, narcotics, booze, and prison break, and he did not remember his *levée en masse* into the band of *énrages*, how he was handed a guillotine and a tumbrel and the backing of angry extremists. He yelled and slumped forward face-first Tony Montana–style into the cocaine palazzo, squirting a mist of drugs into the room and inciting hideous laughter from Big D, tweaked hacking sounds that made the women shiver and the security detail brace, because there was one exception to the Old West rule concerning firearms, and Big D was it. But weapons remained holstered and Murphy Ahn remained gone to the world and the processed coca remained suspended in air, flitting through the nightclub like snow. A generous tablespoon of cocaine squeezed up Murphy Ahn's nose—no avoiding it where he was positioned—knocking him into an eighteen-hour epileptic fury with a side of extreme dehydration. And though he didn't remember agreeing to go along with it, all the witnesses did, and the surveillance video showed him moving his lips for what was likely the howl of affirmation everybody said he delivered, a wholesome "Hell yeah!" that had reduced the women to giggles before the face-plant, when thousands of dollars of drugs wafted through the room and the ramifications scared everyone.

"What a kid," Big D said as the ladies carted him off. "Hide him somewhere good—cops'll be here first thing. Get him plenty of water, and food. Pizza. Gonna be a space cadet when he lands back on Earth." Big D lifted a highball glass to his lips, set it back down. "And strip the vacuums and air filters. Somebody always wants the schwag."

Two weeks after they did the deal with Octavius Maximus, a Mercedes convertible exploded in the driveway of Château Versailles. No one was hurt—all Big D's vehicles were equipped with remote ignitions—but the car was just three weeks old, with customized hydraulics newly installed and Big D's favorite golf clubs in the trunk. After a thorough, wordless inspection of the chilly November morning's carnage, Big D returned to the mansion and took the elevator to the subbasement apartment where Murphy was stashed. He sat down beside Murphy on his twin bed and turned off the television with one pull of his pistol.

"There's a principle here. One thing not to pay. But bombs? Imprecise. Inhumane. Collateral damage galore. Nasty, nasty shit." He thought about smacking the kid in the face, wake his bitch ass up. "What the fuck is that?"

A replica of Château Versailles covered a small desk tucked in the corner, an exact copy down to the satellite dishes and topless women in the Jacuzzi.

"I made it."

"Out of what?" Big D spotted the model of himself playing tennis and smiled.

"Pizza boxes."

Big D reached down and felt the thing, cardboard and latex paint, some ornate work around the windows he hadn't thought cardboard was capable of. Kid could probably break open a safe in under a minute. "How long you been here?" he wondered.

"What?"

"In my house. How long."

"Six years."

"Six years? Shit." Big D wound back and pictured the affiliate who'd offered him up, some crackerjack on the junk himself. Taylor. Three weeks later he'd gotten himself sliced into strips and shipped to the coroner in ski bags. "You been to school?"

"Allen used to take me couple times a week."

"Unh-huh. You like it?"

"It's alright," Murphy said. "I liked playin' football."

Big D chortled loudly, pounded his fist on Murphy's knee. "Shit, we got football here! Ain't you seen us out on the front lawn?"

Murphy nodded, the games were hard to miss with all the yelling and gambling, but he was intimidated by the size, the speed, the lack of officiating, the random gunplay.

"Forget school, kid. You about to get all the education you need with Octavius a week late and blowin' up cars. Go get him."

"What?"

"Kill his ass. Armen'll fix you up. I ain't forget what I promised, 10 percent of the late fee. Right now, that's two hunned K. You wrap this up tonight, I'll throw in another five hunge."

Murphy considered the cash he picked up on his night runs, the envelopes brimming with hundreds, the plastic blocks of powder. He considered life imprisonment. His fourth-grade education and current house arrest. His moniker in local media: Baby Cop Killer. No workable exit strategy, his future soaked in shit and loss if he didn't do something soon.

"Aight."

"Yeah." Big D punched his shoulder, pinched his nose. "Good."

Armen took him to the armory and fitted him with Kevlar, guns, bullets, grenades, maps and surveillance records, keys to a Hummer. "Big night, Murph," Armen said as Murphy pulled on his boots. "This your chance to get that seat next to D pinned down." Armen looked him in the eye and winked, then swallowed hard.

"What?"

"Put on some makeup. Blend in a little."

"Yeah," Murphy said. His ugliness was so old, he'd basically forgotten about it.

In the afternoon Armen's girlfriend, Raquel, came over with a shopping bag full of cosmetics. He sat on the toilet and closed his eyes as she brushed, padded, penciled, dabbed, hummed. A second skin firmed over him, toxic smells mingling with Raquel's gentle lavender perfume. She drew under his eyes and across his forehead with firm brushstrokes, then spread colored creams across his cheeks with her thumbs. Murphy swiftly determined that she was not only hugely attractive, with a deft rock-band pixie cut and big hawk eyes and a pert prim parabolic butt that could crack open pistachios, but also good, the type of authentic nice person he rarely saw in person but knew about from TV, who donated money to public radio and cleaned up her local park and gave restaurant leftovers to homeless people. After an hour in the bathroom she pointed him to the mirror, and he twisted at the sight of a strange face cringing. He almost, almost looked normal.

She crouched beside him, her V-neck ribbing his shoulders, her fingertips spider-tapping over his buzz cut. "You're kind of a cutie all dolled up," she said. "Like a marine out on leave. I always had a thing for military guys." She kissed him on the lips right before Armen came back in with beers from the kitchen, Murphy's blush blocked off from view by layer upon layer of life-saving foundation.

The Octopus was expected in Georgetown that evening, Armen explained. He had a fetish for teenagers and sat in a corner booth at a bar called the Tombs and bought drinks for college girls until one of them agreed to go for a stroll, grab some food, check out a band, put quarters in the meter. They inevitably wound up at the Octopus's apartment around the corner, a leather-covered pad stocked with Rohypnol and Barry White records. On the walk back he was consumed with charming the girl, Armen said, and thus vulnerable. "Course he knows Big D's mad at him, knows about you too, whole world knows about the Baby Cop Killer. But he won't expect you there, 'specially not in makeup. Unless we got a snitch. Which is possible." Armen resaddled his oval glasses. "Just get out fast, security's gonna be everywhere. Questions?"

"Why's he called the Octopus?"

"Hell if I know. Got his hands in a lot of shit or something? Who cares; just kill him."

For nearly an hour Murphy circled Georgetown streets hunting for a parking spot. The jarring bloops of radio pop songs combined with the endless red lights and the omnipresent double parking and the uneven cobblestones that kept pulling the Hummer off course to unravel his assassin's calm, but just as he was on the verge of ditching the operation he spotted a limo pulling out and hit the blinkers. It took fifteen approaches before sticking it, and at that a solid three feet from the curb, but he headed to a liquor store to celebrate anyway. The cheap metal shelving conjured up memories of Marvin Ahn's shop in Silver Spring, the same flickering mini TV behind the counter, the same overpriced Ho Hos, and he drank in the strange feeling of home until the manager asked him if he was going to buy something or what. He picked up a soda and went back outside.

Soupy light from streetlamps fell on students in fleece vests and khakis, miniskirts and leather jackets, loud and oozing alcohol. Sound cracked off the ground, a bright chill ripped through his clothes. He was underdressed—T-shirt, jeans,

Orioles cap—and thought about going back to the Hummer to get his sweatshirt, pick up the body armor and the grenades. But the extra gear made him feel slow and bulky, unmanageable, unbelievable. Instead he sipped on his soda and followed the students to a basement door with an oar stuck to a sign, a line thirty deep and growing. The Tombs. A stout bouncer stuffed into a polo shirt ran driver's licenses through a computer and peered down girls' shirts while dissecting the Hoyas' Big East schedule on his cellphone.

Every one of these kids was loaded. It was obvious from their catalog-fresh clothes, high-carat jewelry, abundance of handheld electronics, extensive dental work. He watched as warm taxis pulled up and unloaded more of them, blabbing about television programming and sporting events and dormitory liaisons. His bladder squeezed up, he pulled his chilled hands into his sleeves. Decidedly cantankerous, he looked down the line, scouting somebody to beat up.

A few hard shoves to pretty boys and their dates generated mumbled apologies and beleaguered grimaces, typical rich-kid pussies. The mercury cranked up inside him, his ears boiled, he charged to the front of the line and pushed in. The bouncer told him to get the fuck out and turned back to a group of freshman girls who were telling him about a slave-and-master party coming up, invitation only, feathers and handcuffs and jugs of chocolate sauce. Murphy grabbed his arm, fiercely, digging in his nails, and just before the bouncer slapped his head he saw the shadow in the boy's pants. Murphy was inside before the bouncer could hang up the phone.

The bar smelled of ATM-fresh cash. He tunneled through sweaty denim to the bathroom, kicked open a stall, hosed the toilet bowl. Two minutes later he farted, flushed, tucked the pistol under his shirt, and walked out of the stall and into a man running a comb through his hair in front of the mirror.

Murphy froze. Sorrel hair slicked back, scalene Roman nose,

aloha shirt, corduroy pants, dirty sneakers. Murphy imagined octagonal sunglasses and motoring gloves on him and knew it was the Octopus, the rims on his Lexuses spinning like a meat slicer.

"You the kid just came in here?" the Octopus asked.

Murphy made for the exit like his pants were on fire.

"They called the cops on ya. Like you a coldhearted killer or something."

"Nah," Murphy heard his voice peep, "I just jumped the line."

"Ho! Tell that to Johnny Law, sonny! Line jumpers do not require police action, normally, now."

Forward motion eluded Murphy at the door. "Cops?" he mused, feeling tingly and excited and yet deeply disappointed by his inability to take action, how he couldn't get out a complete sentence much less mow this guy down, the utter lack of luster in his style.

"Very very really yeah. Now where you going to hide with a mug like that? I like your look, kid, the movie-star makeup thing. But here's a news flash: it's dripping off ya, and you still need plastic surgery and a trip to the salon. Fake as a snake, di-rect from central casting. You are painted into a corner, buddy boy ol' pal." The Octopus smiled glazed manila teeth. "Lucky you, I run this place. Way out, hear? Follow me, through the kitchen, down the rabbit hole, here we go. And pull down that cap low, try 'n' block out your mug. That ash can's a lotta unwanted attention, homeslice."

The Octopus wrapped his tentacles around Murphy's wrist and they swam out of the bathroom into a sea of body parts and perspiration, police radios hissing close by. The bar brimmed with chatter and sloppy kisses, budget beer, the pall of forced happiness. Murphy floated through a swinging door into a hectic kitchen. "Hey, José," the Octopus quipped, removing bills from his pocket "taking the back way, ¿vale? Don't like the fuzz buzz." José nodded and led them to a skinny rusted door and they were out in the cold, Murphy Ahn, the Baby Cop Killer, and Octavius Maximus, the Octopus Beat Poet.

They shivered across the street and around the corner and up a flight of shag-carpeted stairs. The Octopus relaxed his suction cups, and Murphy fell into a cavernous room, maple floored, marble rimmed, chandelier topped. Leather sofas, leather chairs, leather-padded walls, an Impressionist over the fireplace, a sterile well-founded smell like the lobby of a sports club for elderly plutocrats. The Octopus disappeared into the kitchen and returned with a glass of soda and a bottle of beer, just as "What Am I Gonna Do With You" came on the stereo.

"Now, which one you want, dig? You read *Hamlet*? The death scene, switched cups and all? Probably not, huh. Not a reader."

He noticed the gun in Murphy's hands and smiled.

"Hey buddy, you took out your gun, whyzat? Bad news: I'm not into pervo swordfights. Leave that to the online bovines, man; I'm just helping a likeminded trouble-brother out of a jam." He held up the drinks in a two-fisted toast. "Truth is, I see you, I see a new recruit, officer corps. Market's always low on brass balls."

"I work for D," Murphy stated. Octopus was just another fast-talking felon with bad fashion sense, he realized, meaning not-awful odds of claiming self-defense if it came to that. "D says you're dead," he said louder.

"He said that? D did?" The Octopus sighed. "You know, I thought we had something, you and me. Couple of cool cucumbers, good rapport across topics. Already we've hit criminal justice. Fashion. English lit. But I guess once a Baby Cop Killer, always." He tilted his head sideways and slid toward the wall, the bookcase, the handgun he kept taped under the third shelf. "Tough nuts I can't help you through this awkward goofball stage. Fix the unslickness, put on the panache. Cuz I'll be toasted with a fork sticking outta me. From D."

"You owe him money," Murphy said and shot him in the chest.

The Octopus fell on his knees, his lips pursed and hard-swallowing air like sucking paste through a straw.

"You serious, huh?" he gasped. "How much he paying you?" Murphy counted in his head. "Seven hundred thousand dollars."

"Seven!" The Octopus winced. "I guess I gotta double it. One point four. And you actually get the cash, dig? Unmarked bills, et cetera, repeat." He rolled onto his side and coughed up brown phlegm, blood. "We cool?"

One point four million dollars. A preposterous sum, more than enough to melt down and recast and bounce back fresh. Wasn't like they'd miss him down at Château Versailles. It was a big country. "You gotta get me outta town, far away," he slished, "California or something."

"Look, man, one point four's some dough! Getcha a first-class bus ticket to the state of your dreams." The Octopus leaned onto an elbow, firmed up his head in his fingers. "You gotta make a call."

Murphy walked over to the Octopus and pressed the pistol into his crusted hair. "Sneak me out to California. Professionally."

The Octopus wheezed. "Fuckzit, fine. Make the call, kiddo, time's starting to drip-blip away. Speedy now, Gonzalez, kay?"

"How do I know you'll do it?"

"My word's straight shit now? Shoot me or pick up the phone, the deal's the deal, no welshing, get on with it! Scout's motherfucking honor." The Octopus sank into the wine-colored puddle forming at his thighs. "Puh-lease?"

Murphy dialed. A minute later a platoon of heavy boots pounded into the apartment. One of them connected with his forehead. He woke up in the same clothes, sprawled across the back row of a Greyhound bus. A highway scrolled past his window, slick with drizzle and dotted with orange construction barriers. He watched the rolling gray hills and the sifting gray air and the roaming gray cars, lazing through the day like lost clouds.

He was anywhere and nowhere, gorgeous anonymity. After a while he felt something move in his jeans pocket.

He discovered a cellphone, muted, the size of a dog bone. He opened it.

"Yeah?"

"Kiddo!" The Octopus was distant but peppy, clearly feeling better. "Got that bus ticket to the bank, didincha? Saved from shit by the one honest crook in all the land, believe dat. You are made, man. You're a made man, man. Man!"

"What?"

"There's a metal suitcase under yo seat. Combination's one-seven-nine-three. A lovely year for Bordeaux I hear."

"Uh . . . yeah."

"Seventeen ninety-three, kid, bank it. Or findjaself a blow-torch. It can be done. But your welder might get greedy, know-Imsayin? Also, ticket stub in your ass pocket takes you straight on to Sac-town, Cali. Didn't know where you wanted to go, L.A., San Dee-egg, Frisco, whatevadeva. So Sac-town's your hub. Play it like you see it."

Murphy listened to the drone of the bus and wondered if anyone else could hear.

"Thas it then! Bon vo-yage, fro-mage. What, you ain't got nothin to say?"

He gurgled: "Thanks."

"Thanks! Cranks!" The Octopus exhaled viciously. "Best thing coulda happened to you, skipping out on that faux French cess-pool. Too nice, boy. Too nice. They'd eat you like sautéed snails, watch that S-car go. Later, skater."

Octavius Maximus was an adroit businessman, a clever lin-guist, a strangely honorable crook, Murphy thought, but he was miles off on this one. Murphy wasn't tender like buttery pan-seared mollusks; he was short-tempered and ruthless with a long motherfucking memory. A bottomless motherfucking memory. A hard-ass non-snail short-tempered Baby Cop Killer with an endless motherfucking memory logging law-enforcement tactics from television and sound racketeering principles at the car wash.

A fourteen-year-old kid with 1.4 million dollars underneath his seat riding to Sacramento on Thanksgiving Day.

At the next rest stop, he took the metal suitcase into a handicapped stall and counted the banded packs of bills. A hundred bucks light, Murphy guessed for the bus ticket. He bought all the newspapers he could find and climbed back on the bus, looking for his picture in every section and even the ads but finding only the hand-painted mirror reflection, somebody handsome and mildly sexy, definitely not him.

Four days later he debussed in San Francisco. Downtown was cool but not cold, the people dressed casual, a policeman walked right by him drinking beer on a bench. He watched bike messengers slap fight in a plaza, then went to a bakery and paid two dollars for the best chocolate-chip cookie of his life. Nobody asked any questions at the banks, just ushered him into a private room, counted his money twice, and gave him pamphlets about financial advisors. He found a small creaky bookstore and bought a stack of guides to stocks and real estate development, the clerk taking his hundreds without blinking, a separate drawer in his register full of them.

That night he stayed up late reading and eating room service in a suite at the Fairmont. In the morning he'd buy new clothes and find a short-term rental, he decided, start scouting dumpy businesses to reinvent. He wanted to build a lasting place. He would leverage debt, hire a team of financial wunderkinds, and piggyback off profitable, no-lose trends. Thinking a focus on real estate, owning the earth and building it up into indestructible skyline empires. His 1.4 million dollars could do a lot better than interest, he knew this from Big D; it took some risk but not much. And his way it would all be double-insulated, audit-proof, invincible.

At four he forced himself to bed. So tired he was seeing

shapes, evolving phantom amoebas, he hadn't done more than doze for days. He looped the silk sheet tight around his body and under his back, over his head, binding his legs and feet, locked into physical calm. Still his mind exploded in blissful trajectories, cranes constructing cities, colors blowing out black, and he rocked softly in his sarcophagus until he heard the morning paper drop at the door and decided he might as well get back at it.

THERMIDORIAN REACTION

The fall of the dictator so emboldened that large number of
people who were determined to end [the Terror], that its
continuance proved impossible.

—HENRY PACKWOOD ADAMS,
The French Revolution

The Thermidorian Reaction, as the end of the Terror is
called, left the National Convention free to resume its task
of devising a permanent republican constitution for the
country.

—CARLTON J. H. HAYES,
A Political and Social History of Modern Europe

They put Fanny in the ground amid a full downpour, a ten-minute ceremony conducted in five by a Methodist priest for hire
who mispronounced Fanny's name. When he clamped shut his
Bible, they threw flowers on the anchor-adorned gravestone and
raced back to the office for a respectful few minutes of black coffee and drying off in the bathroom. They slipped into a taxi
before the manager could give Esmerelda the bill and rode home
in bumper-to-bumper traffic, an hour of painful proximity standing in for a funeral procession.

Released from the cab confines, Esmerelda heaved her great
wool bag to the floor and stomped enthusiastically to the kitchen
for her first-ever Fanny-free meal in the house. Unfortunately she
couldn't find any cookies in the cupboard, and they appeared to
be out of marshmallows, so she hit the fridge for a cheese sampler

or a side of bacon. The door snapped to a halt after an inch, and after giving it six more increasingly vigorous yanks she looked down to discover a thick metal chain snaking through the refrigerator and freezer door handles, padlocked shut by a Kryptonite bike lock. "Kids!" she called. "We're locked out of the fridge!"

The twins filed into the room staring at the floor so they wouldn't cry or laugh or sock a hole in the wall.

"Repo man, I bet. Somebody better check out Fanny's bills. I haven't been able to give it the proper study." She noticed the kids' downcast eyes and clucked her tongue. "Somebody lose a contact?"

"It's not the repo man, Ma," Robespierre said.

"Hang on, there's a hatchet in here somewhere." She grabbed the knife block out from the counter and pulled out a pack of rusted steak knives, serrated bread slicers with the teeth sawed flat, a dull-as-a-thumb sushi blade, a hybrid slice of metal that looked like a cross between a can opener and a barber's straight razor. "Raw deal," she mumbled. "Maybe we can do one of those urban bombs you make from the medicine cabinet. I know there's matches in the bathroom, lighter fluid in the garage. Marat, why don't you grab a few of your firecrackers?"

"Can't do it," he said.

"Come on, hup hup. Dinner bell's ringin."

"You're too big, Ma," he shot back.

"It's a medical condition," she clarified. "Metabolism and thyroid."

"You're overweight," Robespierre pressed.

"So are most people! It's like a national tradition!" She flung the knives at the fridge lock, watched them clatter to the ground.

"Not this bad," Robespierre said. "You have to lose it."

"I'm trying, I'm trying," she sputtered. "Why are you picking on me, today of all days?"

"We're gonna do things differently," Marat told her. "We're starting a new way starting now."

"What's wrong with the way we got?" They let a minute of quiet answer that one for her—melodramatic soap opera dialogue running upstairs, the stench of gin-soaked carpeting, the oxidizing Harold Van Twinkle portraits patching the dining room walls from floor to ceiling, the phone ringing and the answer machine picking up and Slippy Sanders whining about where the hell was she, they had a line out the door and an overheated photocopier, they needed reinforcements on the double, drop everything, run.

"The contract's done now," Esmerelda went on. "All those rules are gone."

"The contract wasn't the problem, Ma," Robespierre said. "It was just another excuse. Point is, if you want to live past dessert, you've got to change."

"The real question is why you want me around that long," Esmerelda snickered. "The real question is why I wasn't invited on that trip to the zoo."

All they got from Marat was breathing, long scratchy draughts and endless exhalation, his chest bobbing like a squeezed bellows. He wiped a thumb beneath both eyes and stuck it in his ear. "We're gonna help you get better, Ma," he gasped, "if it kills us."

"Marat." Robespierre guided his hand to his side and gave him a quick sideways hug. That face, Esmerelda thought, they had the same conniving, Jasper-cursed face.

"Show's over," she blurted, "and I'm hungry. I'm ordering pizza. And buffalo wings. And a salad for the health nuts around here." She clicked her teeth and smiled wide. "You're welcome."

They parted as Esmerelda plodded to the phone.

"The funeral feast is on its way," she reported a minute later. "Forty-five minutes. I'm gonna slip out of my mortuary garb."

Marat and Robespierre sat at the kitchen table and went over Fanny's finances while Esmerelda tramped over to the bedroom and wrestled with her clothes, starting off a soundtrack of wall-to-wall yelling and overturned furniture; tearing fabric and paintings crashing to the floor; leftover snack plates and milkshake glasses shattering grotesquely. They listened as Esmerelda's epithets and hyena screams gave way to frustrated pillow tosses and whines for help, moving on to mumbling rambles and, eventually, quiet whimpering. They heard the doorbell ring, and Esmerelda's soft moan, and the follow-up doorbell ring, unanswered. A few minutes later came the phone call, the answering machine pickup, the angry message. All was quiet for the hour required to finish their review of Esmerelda's bills and receipts and update their plan for boosting household revenues, at which point Marat put away the files and set the table while Robespierre took a key from her shoe, opened the bike lock, and prepared a Caesar salad made of local organic vegetables and topped with fresh goat cheese and toasted sourdough cubes.

"Dinnertime!" she called. "You want some, Ma?"

A whinny like a sick horse came from her room.

"Well, another new rule is only eating at the table. We'll wait."

A half hour of crawling, complaining, and expletives brought Esmerelda into position. She was swaddled in the festive serape her father had picked up on a Baja fishing vacation thirty years ago, all she'd been able to dress herself in. "Water," she rasped.

"All you can drink," Robespierre said, and went to fix her a tall glass at the tap. When she returned, the salad bowl was empty, the tablecloth was marred with lettuce and loose croutons, and her mother had a dab more color in her cheeks, overall appearing a smidge revived.

"Now, let's get something straight," Esmerelda burped. "I work. I'm the mom. I make the money. I'm like a million years older than you. Which means I'm in charge, the boss, el presidente, the goddamn big cheese. Got it? My word's the law, whereas you're a couple of underage ambushing Indians. Now hand over the key to the fridge and I'll rustle up a round of hot-fudge sundaes."

"You don't get it, Ma!" Marat yelled. "Everything's changing. Drastically. Your hot-fudge sundae days are over."

"We're helping you," Robespierre said. "So you can earn more money. And feel better. And live longer. So you can get ahead, and we can too."

"Money's no concern," Esmerelda said, "I just inherited a house. I feel great."

"Actually, the American Merchant Marine Veterans get the house once we move out or die," Marat clarified. "Says so right here in the will. And Robespierre basically got the rest."

"Bull-monkey. Give me that." She scooped up the stack of papers, flipped and scanned. "She was a crazy old loon, and mostly drunk. This won't stand up for a second."

"Think of all your skills," Robespierre said. "You're smart. Fast. Ultraefficient. You keep that store afloat."

"You need a raise," Marat concluded. "*We* need a raise."

"For your information, I ask for one just about every day. Slippy plays hardball, you know that."

"Then go get more somewhere else."

"I can't do that. I can't leave Slippy."

"Sure you can."

She shook her head. All the years of steady work when she was a Zoog-smoked soul-blitzed faker, no good to nobody, a huge boil on society's shin. Slippy always spotting, with the steady hours and the paycheck and the health insurance, a fair retirement program, even good for short-distance emergency rides. "He's done a lot for me, and for you guys too. You can't even begin to know. One of the best friends I guess I've ever had." One of her only friends, too, and the realization hit her square between the eyebrows, the emptiest moment in a day already overdone with lows.

"Well, you can make him scared you might leave," Robespierre said. "That way he'll pay you more."

"We've got a plan," Marat added. He went on to explain that they had mapped out a physical and financial regimen that integrated seamlessly with her hectic life, that she'd find various bits of her day slightly out of skew, but that was intentional, and with a little imagination and energy she'd figure it out in no time flat, burning calories galore and firming up her earning potential, setting the stage for a major payday and whole-life reinvention, which in turn would pay for space and college camp and semesters abroad in ritzy European capitals.

"Whatever you say, Jenny Craig," Esmerelda yawned. "I'm hitting the hay." But without any help the undressing and bathing portion of her evening took a solid two hours, at which point she was far too pooped to dream of gulping down her typical bedtime serving of ice cream, much less trek to the kitchen to prepare the nightcap herself.

She awoke to a room glowing in light, the sun halfway across the sky, three hours late for work. Incredibly her walker had vanished from its parking spot beside her double-king bed, which meant that digging out clean clothes from her steamer trunk required an inefficient if vociferous search peppered with no fewer than fifteen rest breaks. Actually changing into her fresh muumuu was another hour-long production, with the side effect of whipping her stomach into side-shaking contractions. She limped over to the kitchen and applied tugs of increasing ferocity to the refrigerator door; when that failed to make headway, she wolfed down the assortment of apples and pears left on the counter and picked up the phone. "Slippy?"

"Ezzie! How's the vacation going?"

"What vacation?"

"Robespierre called this morning and explained everything. Don't worry, I get it. Frankly, I don't know why you've never taken a vacation day before. You must have a world of stress inside."

Slippy's description brought it to life, the planet of wind and fire lodged in her abdomen that blocked every smile and drained flavor from food and tinted the world with grays and blacks. "Never mind that," she said, sad as week-old gravy.

"Well, allow me to give you some day-off pointers. Number one, don't call the office. The rest mostly involve alcohol."

"Right. OK. Just making sure you got the message."

"Course I got the message. Your kids are more reliable than you are, and that's saying something. Now hit the tiki bar and don't bug me until tomorrow."

She threw the phone across the room and looked longingly at the refrigerator, her mother's fridge, the stubby rounded-corners kind from the mid-1970s. Fanny had stocked it with fairly priced vegetables, bulk packages of meat, pitchers of homemade iced tea, bowls of fresh guacamole, usually a chocolate cake or two, a peeled box of baking soda in the back that she replaced faithfully every New Year's Day. Fanny took care of the vacuuming, the dishes, clothes washing and dry cleaning, semimonthly dusting; she handled the personal valet services and Esmerelda's morning wakeup call, bathing assistance and spa treatments, mortgage payments and property taxes and year after year of all the insurance bills imaginable. Three badly cooked but edible squares a day, with packaged cakes and cinnamon buns left out for midnight snacks. A universe of responsibility and diligent execution fueled by something close to love but vividly different. Pride. Filial piety. Guilt. The absence of a better thing to do. All of it and none of it and everything in between.

Esmerelda could never cry for her mother's death. But she wound up weeping anyway, for something less definable, a vague sense of her life heading in a new and harder direction like all the rest of the fish. It was her first good bawl since Jasper's wretched face popped into her hospital room, way back on the day the kids were born. She cried silently, her hands in her lap, her shoulders hopping like a girl skipping rope.

Ten minutes later she was done. She placed a call to the local taqueria for lunch delivery and used the travel time to reposition herself in the foyer and undo the locks so she could open the front door mere minutes after the delivery guy rang the bell.

"I'll get my purse in a sec," she said, grabbing the delivery guy's bag and peeling the foil off the business end of a carne asada super burrito, which she polished off, with the accompanying handful of chips, in under a minute. "Want to make some extra money?"

She led the guy back to the kitchen. "You want me to cut the lock?" he asked.

"No point," she responded. "They'll just put in another one. What I could use, however, is my own stash." The sentiment required significant further discussion to translate effectively, but a combination of pantomime, napkin diagrams, and busboy Spanish got the point across: she wanted a battery-powered minifridge that fit in her closet, was camouflaged as a shoe rack, made as little noise as possible, and could store a side of ham in a pinch.

"OK," he agreed. "I need some money."

"Fair enough," she said, "let me check my purse." Unfortunately, poking around her room for fifteen minutes didn't uncover her great wool bag, and by the time she figured out the kids were probably holding the thing hostage upstairs the delivery guy was gone. She used the rest of the day to fold her clothes, set her alarm clock to an energetic-but-not-disorienting radio station, and work out a system involving preselected clothing and strategically placed rest stations to get dressed and out the door in under an hour. She was reviewing an Emily Post book left on her bedside table when the front door jangled, the kids filed in, and the house warmed with the smell of a supermarket roast chicken.

"Hey, Ma," Robespierre called. "How you feeling?"

"Hungry!" she croaked, though in truth she was unusually satiated and comfortable, her soul somewhat at rest.

"Well, we've got dinner. Come on, and we'll eat."

"Have a good day off?" Marat asked.

"Wise asses!" she shouted, shoving herself out of bed. "You know perfectly well what kind of day I had."

"It'll get harder before it gets easier," Marat warned.

"I'm sure it'll pay off in beach vacations and miniskirts and hunky boyfriends who wash my car in their undies. Now pass me some damn dinner and let me feast in peace." They sat back as Esmerelda ripped the bird apart, draining meat off each drumstick and wing, scooping handfuls of flesh from the breasts, gobbling glazed skin scraps, sucking on bones. For the first time in a while she noticed the grease coagulating on her throat, the chemical taste paving the roof of her mouth, the low-grade quality of the meat, the pizzazz of a truck-stop restroom. The familiar ritual of chewing and swallowing imparted some small joy, but overall she felt burned and nasty and hardheaded and dumb. To complete the Pyrrhic victory, she finished off the chicken by herself, then sat back and absorbed a surfing frenzy in her stomach—cutbacks and hard snaps and whistling tube shoots—while the kids mouthed off about taxes and accounting and other tedious financial terms that shut down every last functional cell in her brain. She just barely made it to the sofa before she was out hard as nightfall, sitting upright in a pose not unlike the nightly position she'd taken on Stillwell Road, nesting on the couch with the kids on her lap. She stayed down through after-dinner dishes and homework, Marat's bedtime toke and Robespierre's nightly self-assessment, clear on through the night until she awoke early to the upbeat tunes of classic soul squawking on her clock radio. With a thumping fearful focus, she raced into fresh clothes and saw to her personal toilet, then munched on the apple lying on the kitchen counter and read her Emily Post book by the front door until she heard the familiar double-honk of the special services van.

"Coming!" she called, and pushed out into the day. Without her walker she proceeded in a series of miniature shuffles, her hands held out like a sleepwalker for balance, her eyes firmly affixed to the six inches in front of her feet. By the time she made it to the street she was cooking, her head a puffy old tomato, her pits sopped with sweat, her toes crammed in painful bunches against the tips of her specialty-fit plastic shoes. She looked up to find her way onto the van's electric lift only to discover the street empty as the dark side of the moon.

Sobs contracted her lungs, and she was seriously considering plopping down on the spot for the rest of the day when another double-honk got her attention. The van was idling on the corner, four houses down. "Back up!" Esmerelda called weakly, flapping an arm. "Reverse!" But all she heard was the crank of the parking brake.

Hell if she was going to burn another vacation day for this bullshit.

She pushed into her shuffling routine but quickly lost patience with the careful steps and geared up into aggressive half-steps, even catching a glimpse of air between her soles and the ground. Not so bad when you get the hang of it, she thought, and loaded herself onto the electric lift in such good spirits that she let the driver off with a couple jibes about his clip-on tie and preference for glam pop rather than the red-carpet aerial assault she'd planned in response to his dastardly parking job.

She conked out for the ride downtown, but when the driver shook her awake she felt oddly refreshed, her legs burning comfortably, a small but righteous hunger in her belly. After descending on the lift, she strode out across the sidewalk at her new rambling gait, enjoying the feel of flexing more muscles, the slight decrease in nauseated stares she received without the use of her walker, a significant influx of pride. When Lakshmi arrived with the Gargantuan, she started to wave it off, until her knees started twisting inward and her vision blanked for a second and she realized that was enough freelancing for day one.

"You OK?" Lakshmi asked.

"Pushing it a little," she grunted.

"I could tell. I've never seen you walk around on your own power before."

And even kooky with a light-headed wonder-tipped sensation that bordered on happiness, Esmerelda remembered that Lakshmi's stint on the job was at least as long as she'd been there herself, seventeen years and counting. Enough time for her kids to grow up without ever seeing Esmerelda at a reasonable weight, or able to support herself without assistance, or being an independent person by any conceivable metric.

"Get used to it," she retorted. "The kids have me on some kind of plan."

"Oh, I know about the plan."

"You do?" Esmerelda pulled her head sideways and took another look at Lakshmi, her simple scrunched face, pellet eyes behind pint-sized wire-framed glasses, a forehead long enough to land planes on. Faint hairs on her upper lip. The long gray switching ponytail, the brown cotton skirt and cheese-colored blouse. It didn't take a lot of imagination to conjure up an image of vermin.

"Nothing," Lakshmi said, and Esmerelda could've sworn she saw her nose twitch.

She motored the Gargantuan to the cash register and turned to her prework snack. While she wasn't any hungrier than usual her muscles were on tape delay, her thoughts took two or three pings to process, her body temperature was sinking fast. Sugar withdrawal, she suspected, and plotted a course for packaged strudels, a liter of orange juice, maybe a fro-yo for dessert. She kind of expected that her usual store of treats under the desk would be missing and the staff room fridge cleaned out; far more impressive was how her great wool bag had been messed with, her emergency stores of hard candy, leftover pasta, ham, cheese strips, and breath mints replaced with a ten-pound bag of Valencia oranges.

Esmerelda fished out an orange and lobbed it across the room underhand, a high gentle arc that playfully smacked Lakshmi in the buttocks, dead center. "Need you to go on a quick breakfast run. Couple of Hostess pies and a peanut butter–based confection, whatever's on sale. You know what I like."

Lakshmi aimed the twin dots of her pupils back at Esmerelda and picked the orange off the ground. "Can't do it, Esmerelda."

"Bull-oney. Always have, always will. Now get going fast before I have to call Slippy."

Lakshmi looked away from Ezzie and turned on her toes, her left paw windmilling, a tiny kick from her furry legs, the orange released at the top of her rotation and zipping like a laser beam six inches above Esmerelda's head. A gory splatter moved the room to silence.

"Slipped," Lakshmi said, and flexed her bicep like a champion powerlifter.

Inside Esmerelda's head castles crumbled, palaces burned, royal rouge carpets rolled up, the imperial court dispersed. Nothing, she had nothing, she was a beggar headed for street crime, her kingdom a shopping cart loaded with stolen bottles.

She shot out of her cash register station and onto the street, the Gargantuan whizzing at top rpm, veering up the sidewalk until she saw the first store opening up, the corner deli accepting a pallet of Gatorades. She broke for it in a near-blind delirium, zipping within sight of pink-frosted cupcakes on the counter, then felt her spirits shrivel as the Gargantuan's engine-whir rose, the chair decelerated, puttered, stopped, and rolled backward until she yanked the emergency brake and swiveled around stupidly on a dew-slick manhole. The battery had been drained, clearly an act of sabotage. She heated the morning with scalding profanity and haltingly wheeled the Gargantuan back to the store.

Entrenched in her bunker she hit the phones, ordering delivery from her five most-frequented breakfast joints, all of which regretted to inform her that they'd redrawn their delivery zones such that her office was no longer within range. "Bullshit!" she screamed at the waitress of the pizza shop four doors up the street, "who's paying you off?" She got the dial tone back but did not mind it—the cool electronic ring provided a baseline of calm, a soothing psychic vanishing point that helped her concentration reset.

She hung up when distress beeps took over the line, putting her head down on her desk and falling into a devil-doused half-sleep fever. It took a line ten-deep of gym-goers, executives, students, and teachers to rouse her from this daze, caws and cackles slipping from her lips, her stomach squeaking like a chemistry experiment. "Yeah, sorry," she muttered, typing extra slow and making several uncharacteristic billing errors, drooling a little, her face albino-white, generally appearing as if she'd escaped from the morgue. Impatient from the backed-up line, customers challenged her mistakes, then grew ever more irritated as Esmerelda slogged through the intentionally convoluted refund process aimed at inducing customers into giving up: completing a double-sided form in triplicate and turning four sets of keys simultaneously and inputting a random twenty-digit code that changed on the hour. Ticked-off customers withheld their usual tips and seriously considered moving their work to CopyTown, a rival shop that had opened up down the street a few months back and already established a reputation for runny ink and improper collating and an exploitative billing system riddled with over-charges and hidden fees. But at least service was brisk, and the staff, a set of slim Vietnamese sisters, looked a lot less lame.

Slippy rolled in around eleven, using his briefcase to plow through the steamy line. "What's the holdup?" he barked. "Ezzie, you've got to get it moving. I don't keep you around because of your charm or good looks. And by the way, something blew up on the wall." He raised his head and sniffed the aging orange guts. "Have we switched away from Pine-Sol?"

"Give me a cookie," Esmerelda mewed, then remembering Emily Post added: "please."

Slippy set his briefcase on the counter, flicked open the latches, and withdrew a wide Tupperware bin. "How about a fruit salad," he offered.

"So you're in on it too," Esmerelda said, grabbing the Tupperware bin and digging in with the pair of serving spoons she kept under her desk. She cleared out the container in fifteen seconds flat, which had the dual effect of rousing her spirits—more from the spirit of victory than satiating her exercise-shrunken hunger—and ruining the appetite of every customer in line.

"Feel better?" Slippy asked.

"No," Esmerelda growled, though in truth she felt clear-eyed and morning-fresh and at least three months younger.

"You will," he said. "Come see me in my office in ten minutes."

Visions of a professional life beyond the cash register station flooded her skull: corner offices and honest-to-god lunch breaks, a bank-busting pay bump, even a shower-enabled bathroom. She went back to work with renewed vigor, and in ten minutes had the roomful of customers on their way with correct change and completed projects in hand, with time left over for a quick run of her industrial hairbrush through her bunned-up hair and a backup application of air freshener.

She made the walk across the office on her own two feet, an intentional display of her newfound independence. "You wanted to see me?" she puffed.

Slippy looked up from his newspaper, swirled the coffee in his silver mug. "Take a seat." Slippy's office was outfitted with two low-slung, impossible-to-climb-out-of armchairs and a pair of cheap metal stools set against a sideboard bar where Slippy took his 5 PM vodka. She leaned against the wall instead.

"Right. Well. Esmerelda. I got your packet." He pulled a manila envelope from the top drawer of his desk and extracted a pile of binder-clipped papers. He flipped through the pages nervously, revealing pie charts and 3-D graphs and inscrutable digits organized into tables. Esmerelda searched his off-brown eyes, newly dimmed and drained of confidence, rewired with a passionless, servile timidity. "Did you print this somewhere else?" he blurted.

She shook her head slowly, a speck of awareness in the swirling recesses of her mind advising her to leave the talking to him.

"Good. Well." He withdrew a balled handkerchief from his blazer's inside pocket and passed it over his reddening forehead. "I can't agree to this."

She shrugged, but even underinformed she didn't believe him. He looked like he'd agree to just about anything.

"That kind of money doesn't just fall into your lap. We'd have to drastically reconfigure our business model. And the milestones you set are extremely ambitious. I haven't seen anything that demonstrates you can accomplish even half of what you promise."

She met his grasping glance with malaise, dismissal, impatience.

"Now, I'm going along with the plan Robespierre laid out as a favor, to demonstrate my goodwill," he continued. "I do hope you take that into account. Along with our long history. How I've helped you out. Et cetera." He scanned her empty face for a response. "Well? Say something."

But she couldn't even bring herself to shrug.

The phone went off, and he scooped it up on the first ring. "Slippy. Yeah? No, she's right here. Unh-huh. No. Really. Huh. How much?" A nod too calm to trust. "I see. Yeah. Thanks."

His hand settling on the switch hook, pointing the handset at her like a gun: "Have you been talking to anyone?"

She walked out without answering, took a seat at her station, and worked the rest of the afternoon with her eyes shut. Even blind she processed orders and handled transactions as speedily as always, every penny and project accounted for, the entire experiment accomplished without a single junk food snack. When she arrived home—the special services van dropped her off at the corner again, now officially the new bus stop, the driver explained—Robespierre was putting the finishing touches on a dinner of broiled salmon and grilled vegetables, and Marat was setting the table. "Guys," she said calmly, eyeing their industrious behavior suspiciously, and with a heavy dose of regret. "Siddown."

They sat. "I get the diet and exercise thing," she said, "and while I don't like the sneak attack I appreciate the sentiment. It's not atrocious so far, actually doing it. I'm willing to stick it out for a while, see where it goes." She palmed her belly, rubbed her fingers over musty fabrics and the familiar scaly softness underneath, this mattress wrapped around her waist, the sheer surface area of it, how exposed she was. So much to manage, it made living so much work.

"The job's a different animal. There's stuff here from way before you were born. You don't know. And you cannot send me in there naked. I need to be ready, to know where I stand." She tickled her tummy fast, miming a saxophone scale. "What exactly did you give him? Some papers and charts?"

And something else: "Did you call him today?"

Robespierre got up and left the room, leaving Esmerelda and her son, her red-eyed son, her son who was developing poser dreadlock stubs and smelled like a marijuana dispensary. Taller than she ever was, a fake-feeling maturity forced onto his face. Adult features of bunched skin and trouble-ridden forehead and weak, distrusting eyes. Carrying water, carrying weight. "How's school?" she asked.

"Fine." Amazed she never read the mail, or listened to the messages, or showed up for the dozens of one-on-one meetings his guidance counselor claimed to have scheduled.

"You starting up a band?" Lately she'd been hearing a lot of music upstairs, mellow bass beats and men singing out poetry like they were within an inch of death. "Sweet tunes coming out of your room."

"No," he said softly, and then she was out of material; she didn't know what he liked to do or what he was good at, his aspirations and fears, his favorite sport, his can't-miss TV shows, any girls he was into. She reached for food, found her plate empty, and gnawed on her fingernails with maniacal focus until Robespierre returned with a packet just like the one she'd seen on Slippy's desk.

"We laid out the case for him," Robespierre said. "It's pretty simple. We ran some models projecting how much business you account for, combining your customer retention rate and word-of-mouth referrals. It's an amazing number, more than half their revenue." She pushed the packet in her lap. "Mom, you own that place."

It was a truth she'd always known but had never bothered crunching the numbers on: Slippy's lifetime of profits had been built on the back of her industry and talent. "Not technically," she said.

"You're the fastest cashier in California, no competition. You don't make mistakes. You're actually pretty polite to customers. They respect you. And the relationships you have go back decades. You are their one constant. The car that always starts. A problem they never have to think about. That's power."

Like being a great chef, Esmerelda thought—Bruce Zoogman's bankable premium experience. "What'd you ask for?" she wondered.

"Triple your salary and promotion to managing director. A significant equity stake. Rights to own and operate additional branches with the franchise fee waived. Basically, a cut of everything you do best."

"Enough cash to leave this shithole forever," Marat said, his breath fragrant with Mendocino kine bud.

"I used to be on top of the world, you know," she said. "You've seen the magazine covers. I could bake my way out of a war zone."

"Well right now you're a washed-up nobody with twenty years' experience in paper products," Marat responded. "I've never seen you so much as reheat a slice of pizza. Seriously, when's the last time you cooked anything?"

She thought on it hard, no specifics coming to mind. "I think I made some toast back in '98," she lied.

"We have to play to your market strengths, Ma," Robespierre interjected. "You can make a lot of money in copy shop management."

Esmerelda saw the road and where it went, formal clothes and uncomfortable shoes, long days at a boring manager job, permanent salad crankiness, bodily pains from building up her muscles again, finishing at the gates of a midlevel career she'd never wanted for a second.

Far and away the best option she'd had in her children's lifetime.

By Friday she'd only cheated on her diet four times—a pizza smuggled into work with a paper delivery, sushi dropped off via the special services van, miniature Butterfingers slipped over as a tip, mail-ordered smoked salmon. Even with those daily dalliances her caloric intake was chopped by 80 percent, translating into an unencumbered aura that sharpened her mind and boosted her spirits and accelerated her foot speed such that she had a statistically significant chance of actually winning a race with any hunchback over eighty. Over the weekend she went shopping with Robespierre, cleaning out all the designer clothes in plus-size clearance bins and picking up several sets of custom-made quintuple-wide heels. Monday she showed up for work styled out like a CEO, slate suit paired with a full-on round of makeup that made her face look serious and organized, even hinting at the remote possibility of sex. "Goddamn, my feet kill," she muttered, descending into the Gargantuan extra slowly so she wouldn't snag her new duds on any corners or hooks.

"Talk about extreme makeover," Lakshmi said, her face falling into surprised mousey piles. "Did you get promoted?"

"Soon," Esmerelda retorted. "Better keep the fastball on ice."

All of the early-morning customers noticed Esmerelda's new uniform, with the professors spouting compliments and the students whistling fatuous catcalls and the executives doling out a professional, curt nod of the head, with the cumulative effect of everyone unconsciously increasing their tips 300 percent. At nine the secretaries reacted with shouts and screams, many clambering around back to hug her and check out her labels, then settling in to discuss how much she'd paid, where she'd shopped, how nicely the colors accented her features and made her seem authoritative and sophisticated. Slippy Sanders nearly dropped his briefcase when he caught a glimpse of her boardroom regalia, and hustled straight to his office without so much as a wave.

He was fiddling with a calculator when Esmerelda barged in a minute later. "Too busy to say hi?" she said. "Well maybe this'll get your attention—I quit." Sunshine filled her head, grassy fields and cheesy pop tunes and the childhood she could barely remember.

"No," he said, serious as she'd ever seen him. "You can't."

"Sure I can. Bye." It was that easy.

She left, wading through the store and shaking hands with customers, many of whom had overheard her and were cheering—cheering?—and walking along with her, patting her on the back and saying it was about time, she was the heart and soul of this place, the best copy shop person they'd ever seen, they'd follow her anywhere. "Esmerelda!" called Slippy, hopping across the room. "Wait!"

"Yeah?" she said, watching him run after her as if in a dream, a craven web of fear stitched across his face.

"I'll sign," he sputtered. "I need you. Please stay."

"No," she said, delirious with renewed stardom, right here in front of her the whole time.

"Think about it," he warned. "Do you really want to set out on your own? All the start-up costs? Buying equipment? Hiring people? Lawsuits? Making sure the toner comes on time and that people show up for work and that the health benefits check doesn't bounce? Being friendly to every two-bit idiot you meet? Dealing with landlords and fixing problems and being on call every hour for the rest of your life?"

She saw it clearly enough, the piles of mail and forms, constant appointments and negotiations, phones ringing through the night. Her body twitching in physical repulsion, sweat flowing from all orifices.

"OK," she bobbed her head. "OK."

The escalators at Van Ness station deposited Robespierre in a bank of fog, desolate gray streets infested with chilly cobwebs.

She had matured into a sensationally average-looking young woman, bean-shaped brown eyes spaced far apart, skin the color of cheap chocolate milk, small breasts, frizzy hair, and a face that wasn't quite pretty and wasn't quite homely and was just kind of there. Over the course of her seventeen years she had identified a tendency to collect extra pounds in her rear and thus shared her mother's perpetual diet, further buttressed by long jogs along the beach and daily sets of crunches and biweekly workouts to a hippie-ish yoga DVD she'd picked up at a yard sale. She looked bland up close, but through a distinctive if conservative taste in clothes, a never-say-die stylist, and an industrial hairbrush pilfered from her mother's wool bag, she crafted a seductive, imperfect, can-do allure, a look that said she could leap over buildings—almost a star.

A three-minute charge through the meteorological smokescreen on Market Street and she was seated inside the CopySmart flagship store manager's office watching her mom work the phone.

" . . . not stupid. At that volume, we need a major discount, bucko. And we haven't been doing business long enough for me to give a goat's ass about your costs. Call back with a lower number or don't bother."

Her mother's new height continued to astonish her. Esmerelda had become an extremely vertical woman, five foot ten when totally unwound, with wall-straight posture imposed on her spine by the now-defunct Gargantuan. Watching her move around the room with the phone pinned to her shoulder, still thick and double-chinned but oddly mobile, Robespierre experienced a sense of out-of-place impropriety, as if intruding on an office blow job.

"Talk it over, be my guest. My kid's here. Gotta run." Esmerelda hung up the phone and booted a trash can across the room. "There was a time," she grunted, "when I could get rid of assholes like that with just a look." Through the corners of her rolling eyes she noticed Robespierre's tired face and uncharacteristically tight lips. "What's the scoop, sheriff?"

Robespierre repeated the speech she'd given that morning over breakfast, a brusque version of the gentle pleading she'd delivered twice the day before: "We got a notice about taxes that you'd better do something about. Also I need you to pay me back for the grocery shopping. And Marat and I need new clothes for school."

"Hello, nice to see you too! My day was fine, thanks. A shitty sales guy just now, but I'll manage." She chuckled and pulled Robespierre against her side, jamming her up against the skeins of skin beneath her blouse, cascading from throat to thighs like rubber waterfalls. "Will you take a personal check?"

"Cash."

Esmerelda bent open a paperclip. "Can it wait until payday?"

"Do I have a choice?" A line delivered so benignly it sneaked inside Esmerelda before exploding.

"Tell you what. I'll buy you dinner for free, call it interest."

"Not hungry." Also impatient, sick of the dumb dopey dance. Playing accountant, little miss do-it-all, and whip-cracking bitch had certain advantages—she who controls the pocketbook controls the city—but Robespierre's credit card was maxed out and her mother's excuses weren't remotely plausible, or even entertaining.

"Then squirrel it away in your cheeks! Haven't I taught you not to turn down a free meal?"

"But then I'd owe you something."

Esmerelda slobbed her with a gooey smooch. "And what's wrong with that?"

They decamped for the Tip Top Diner across the street, a throwback joint with vinyl booths and personal jukeboxes and a cook who sang old soul hits while he grilled. Esmerelda ordered salads for both of them, with a round of glass-bottle Diet Cokes to patch things up, then sat back and took it as Robespierre outlined their perilous financial situation, transferred balances and deferred payments, the series of false addresses she'd set up to waylay the collections agencies, Esmerelda's huge salary going entirely into debt servicing and late fees. Their portfolio had gone sour, their investment in quick-grow Central Valley real estate was tanking, Marat's collection of rare first-press reggae LPs had devalued to squat no thanks to rampant overplaying. She pulled out a notebook and drew a chart like a dive flag, along with percentage symbols and decimal points leading to huge negative grand totals. Esmerelda slurped on her beverage and absorbed the colossal failure—all the hot stock tips purchased from online gurus fizzling up, the elaborately leveraged mobile home–community management deals now worth pennies on the dollar, the investment in a start-up karaoke bar chain deep underwater. Everything so bad it ran right around to silly, and Esmerelda maintained a go-lucky nutball grin accordingly.

A shriveled black woman appeared alongside their booth. "Esmerelda? That you?"

Esmerelda set down her soda. She blinked; her chin jiggled; her fingers straightened like a pack of pencils. It was the closest thing to fear Robespierre had ever seen her mother display.

She nodded slowly.

The woman smiled. She was gnomish in appearance, well under five feet tall, with child-sized fingers and a tiny bird head, her hair clipped back with plastic blue barrettes. She wore a pink dress and purple pumps and a huge gold crucifix chained around her neck. "You look great, girl. Just great," she said. She examined Robespierre through grapeseed eyes. "You must be Robespierre. I haven't seen you in a long, long time."

Robespierre stood up and held out her hand. "Pleased to meet you. You must be a friend of my mother's."

"You could say that," the woman said. "I'm your grandmother. In fact, I gave you your name."

Robespierre sat down, still smiling. "You must be confused,"

she laughed. "My grandmother's dead!" She paused for her
mother to launch a cavalcade of insults at this strange shrunken
woman who'd just lied her ass off, but Esmerelda sat perfectly
still and breathed hyperactively through her mouth. "Mom?"
Robespierre reached for her mother's wrist. "Are you OK?"

The elderly woman smiled. There was something refreshingly
gentle about her and her pink dress, something toylike and joyful and recognizable in her eyes, which were spaced a little too
far apart and colored a turbid shade of brown Robespierre knew
well from the mirror, balanced nicely by the freakishly familiar
spherical rump plumping up the woman's dress like a spare
tire.

"It's true, dear," said Karen Winslow. "Mind if I join you?"

"Yes!" Heat broiled Robespierre's head. "How can you expect
to walk in off the street and make some ridiculous claim that
you're my grandmother and then eat dinner with us? What kind
of idiots do you take us for? If you want money, show some guts
and ask for it." Robespierre had been itching to tell somebody off
for years—every day kids at school directed nonsensical accusations at teachers and each other, but she couldn't bring herself to
do it, hurt feelings and perennial standing as class president to
consider—and she was starting to get the hang of it when she
felt her mother's hand on her forearm and understood that
everything the woman said was true.

"Please," Esmerelda said, sliding toward the wall. "Sit."

"Thank you, Esmerelda. I can't get over how good you look.
Spectacular. If Jasper were here to see you now."

Robespierre listened intently, as Jasper was a name she'd
heard around the house years ago, a cornerstone of Fanny's after-
dinner harangue. "Jasper," Esmerelda hiccupped.

"Do you remember the rides your father used to give you?"
Karen Winslow asked Robespierre, her smoky eyes glowing.
"He'd strap you in his wheelbarrow and run up and down Mar-
ket Street, leaning left and right and backwards and Lord knows

what. It was silly and dangerous, but you kids loved it. First thing in the morning, before you went in with your mother at the copy shop."

Robespierre remembered those mornings in blazing detail, the whirl of color and oncoming traffic and cold ocean wind key elements in a recurring dream that had penetrated her sleep every month of her life. She felt her chest prick and recalled an inane pride at being able to say the word *wheelbarrow* clearly, far better than her brother. "I thought that was the babysitter," Robespierre said.

"Never could afford one, I'm afraid. Though I pitched in when I could. We all did."

"So you're my grandmother? My father's mother?"

"That's right."

"Then where is he now? Can I meet him?" She looked over at her mother and found a strange woman crammed into the corner, stone-faced and silent, her skin turning blue.

"Jasper disappeared a long time ago, dear. I haven't seen him myself in thirteen years. I haven't seen you in about twelve years, Esmerelda, since they closed the investigation."

Esmerelda lifted her chin a micrometer.

"Did you know that you also have an aunt, Miss Robespierre? My daughter, Tina, lives with me. She's handicapped, but a lovely woman. Just adores watching quiz shows. You should come over for *Jeopardy!* sometime."

"But what about my father? What do you mean by disappeared?" Robespierre stared at her mother's barren face.

"We don't know, dear. He just went missing."

"Is he dead?" Robespierre reached across the table and clamped Karen Winslow's thin shoulders. "Grandma?"

Karen Winslow sighed and shook her head, then slid off the booth to the floor. "I should go," she said. "You two need to talk."

"Grandma?" Karen bent her head back toward the booth. "It was nice to meet you," Robespierre said. "I'll tell my brother all about you."

"Marat," Karen said, "send him my love." And then she was gone, her pink dress flapping through the diner's hot cheese smell like a slow ship's sail, their table upended in her wake. Robespierre watched her leave, then turned her sights on her mother and fired at will:

Why did you tell us you were artificially inseminated?
Why did you say the man in our memories was the worst
*   babysitter in world history?*
Why didn't you introduce me to my grandmother before?
Are you ashamed of us or something?
Don't you think that's wrong?
Where is my dad?
What did he do?
What did he look like?
What did he like to talk about?
Why did he go away?
Do you love him?
Do you love me and Marat?
Do you love anything?

Esmerelda did not speak for the duration of their meal, the train ride home, her evening slate of television, preparations for bed. Robespierre followed her to her bedroom, her questions landing hot as napalm while Esmerelda crawled into her recently downsized single-king bed and read her nightly gossip magazine, extinguished the light, fell asleep immediately, and rolled through a couple of sleep cycles, until the weight of the day wore Robespierre into submission and she passed out in a ball on the carpet.

At four in the morning, Esmerelda got up and walked across the bedroom to where Robespierre slept bunched up along the wall. Esmerelda nudged her with her foot, attempting a toe tickle.

"Hey, kiddo, time to head to bed, you know? School tomorrow, don't forget. Giddyup now, up and at 'em. I haven't been able to carry you in years."

Robespierre rolled onto her side. "What did you do to him, Mom?" she whispered.

"I'll explain everything after school," Esmerelda said. "Get some sleep, OK?"

Esmerelda spent the day creating flow charts and probability diagrams on the CopySmart computers, detailing Jasper's general idiocy, her exploitable position as a washed-up chef, her limited employment options. Testimonials from Slippy Sanders and a couple of her long-term secretary clients established that she'd needed help and Jasper had been there, promising stability and affection and sizable dining savings, even dug up a ring, but he'd run out on their wedding night and hadn't been back since. Color-coded lists illustrated how she'd pondered for years her decision to move back in with Grandma Fanny, how once all the variables were weighed it had been best for the children and their mother; the long-term drawbacks of Fanny's one-sided contract were still a statistical improvement over living in a Swedish orgy camp connected to a perilous flight of stairs, and it wasn't like she'd been able to cover the rent anyway—they'd been evicted for Chrissakes. As for writing Jasper out of the script, let's face it, he'd abandoned them; he hadn't truly loved them or he would have stayed, visited, written letters, hired a skywriter, dropped a fucking dime. Instead he'd flipped out over a garden-variety wedding-night crack and vanished, a chicken coward pansy child-support-avoiding wimp. Not worthy of mention. Period.

Robespierre cried through the whole presentation. Marat stood still as glass and didn't speak, a plaintive ganja-blessed cool, making his only movements with his eyes, zipping between his mother and her easel, assessing the amount and density of the bullshit she was shoveling.

" . . . and so to minimize the impact, so you weren't, you know, messed up because of all this, I fudged a few things." Esmerelda

rapped her pointer against her thigh and flipped to the last page
of her presentation: a recent photograph of the family enjoying
a ham dinner, Marat throwing peas at Esmerelda, Robespierre
curled in laughter. "So you guys would be OK. So we could be
together and not get stuck on all those bad things from earlier
on. I just wanted us to get on with life."

"Why?" Robespierre said.

"Why what?" Esmerelda asked.

"Why did you want us to get on with life? What bad things are
you talking about?"

"Oh, there were just some problems that were going on."

"What problems? What are you talking about?" Robespierre
asked.

"Was it monsters?" asked Marat.

"No," said Esmerelda, "you'll just have to believe me that it
was a bad situation, and I did what I had to do to protect my
children." But already Marat saw the one-armed monster barrel-
ing into his bedroom, the naked group wrestling match in the
living room. Saw it for what it was.

"It was wrong," Robespierre said. "We have a right to know
about our father."

"Robespierre, please," Esmerelda said, "you're missing the
point."

She looked up and saw them standing next to each other, fra-
ternal twins but still close in body type, a little misshapen, with
matching big butts and skin of an unclassified brownish-ocher
tint. Identical chubby lips planted on their faces, the same gnash-
ing teeth and irritated eyes and overheated foreheads flashing
purple. "Point is," she continued, "things happened and Jasper
was there, but it's not like he was my top choice or anything. Or
my second choice or thirtieth choice or whatever. Life, you
know, foists these things on you. One second you're on top of the
world, the next you're working in a copy shop."

Her children started backing away from her nice and easy,

like she smelled funny, like she was wearing a bomb, like she was the dirtiest scariest beast hell ever shat out. "It's not something I wanted," she added. "I'd take it all back if I could."

The children receded to the far end of her sight line, beyond the hallway and the front door and the short, weed-plugged driveway, hanging out past the swirling cold Pacific waters on the edge of the horizon. Where breaching whales collided with the setting sun; where her father departed the world. Esmerelda knew she was close to losing them for good, and she tried to capture the moment in her memory: hands flexing at their sides, slack cheeks and tough tomato noses, thick knees bent slightly, seething bodies primed for vengeance, smacked with adulthood but for a last moment still hers, unsmiling but hers, unbelieving but hers, irreparable but hers, two mirrored figures of flinty resolve that dipped down into night like burned-out stars.

Switched to snarls, attacks, spittle-soaked tongue-lashings, leaps and slashes like demonic monkeys, slanderous names and nauseating accusations and the deep-down brutal truth. Followed by pitiless distance, the silence that never heals.

"Mom," Robespierre rasped, "we want to meet our dad."

Esmerelda stirred her glass of water and sipped it until there was none left to sip. She yawned and stretched her arms and rearranged her presentation a few times on the easel.

"You heard her, mom," Marat said. "Where is he?"

Esmerelda shuffled her cue cards, then carefully rolled up her charts and graphs and slid them into cardboard tubes. She was far more attractive as a thin woman, with plush lips and a needle nose and even a bit of a figure, but tightness pulled long her wrinkles, deepened her forehead's perennial folds, clawed the corners of her eyes.

"Answer," Marat hissed.

Esmerelda rattled a spoon against her empty glass. "I don't know where he is," she stated.

"Where do you think he might be?" Robespierre asked. "Where would he work?"

Esmerelda closed her eyes and set her head solid, barely lifting her lips: "No idea, guys, honest. I was young, you know, puppy love and all that. My mind's kinda cloudy over the whole period; I wouldn't know where to start."

"Bullshit!" Marat exploded, green smoke streaming from his nose. "You knew exactly what you were doing! You always know!"

"Don't speak to me like that," Esmerelda simpered.

Robespierre slipped her palm on Esmerelda's head and laced her fingers through her hair; part reassuring human touch, part head-yanking threat. "Mom," she whispered slowly, unstoppable as the tides, "tell us about our dad."

Esmerelda sank into her chair as her body raced toward the sky in a glass elevator, the raging skyward thrusters pinning her flat against the floor. Her children waited in pressurized silence until the elevator braked at a penthouse suite and Esmerelda leapt back from the dead, broke her pointer over her knee, and charged out of the house in the wide-thighed fat-person duck walk she never could shake, bobbling around the corner and down two blocks to Joel's Ale House, a brand-new dive bar housed in an old mechanic shop. She chugged three shots of vodka and put some Willie Nelson on the juke, then put her head on the bar and started to moan. A minute later, an ugly kid with a fiendishly bad haircut slid onto the stool next to her and dropped his hand on her thigh.

The ugly kid bumped into Marat as he brewed coffee in the kitchen the next morning. "Morning," he offered.

Marat was a pudgy little dweeb, the ugly kid noted, one of those mixed-race Tiger Woods types, with a wide forehead that made him look stupid and the tropical tang of wake-and-bake pot-puffing. "Who are you?" Marat mumbled.

"Joel Lumpkin. Friend of your mom's," the kid said. Robespierre bustled into the kitchen lugging a backpack suitable for a month-long mountaineering voyage, her blue skirt riding up over her paunchy butt as she reached for a cereal bowl and poured her cornflakes. Not hot but not bad, Joel thought; she had a look. With any luck she didn't talk as much as her mom. Or suck dick as poorly. "You guys need a ride?" he asked.

"How old are you?" asked Robespierre.

"Old enough to drive."

"Let's see a license."

"Left it at home."

"I don't think so," she said, pouring herself a mug of coffee. "I'm not retarded."

Marat played with the radio for most of the ride in Joel's Mercedes, switching from commercial to commercial as fast as he could and lip-synching the words. "How about a CD," Joel asked as he turned off of Sunset.

"Where do you go to school?" Marat retorted.

"I run a bar, Joel's Ale House. It's a couple blocks from your house." Making for a magnificent tax hideout, heavy cash transactions in an inconvenient location, too small to be a problem, the perfect place to start.

"What about school?"

"Not for me," Joel said, distracted by the lingering stench of bowling alley and old pudding, a blanket of biological secretions from his night in Esmerelda Van Twinkle's bed.

"Cool, a dropout," Marat noted, possibly sarcastic but probably not.

Joel raced through a yellow light, then stomped the brakes and swerved to the curb. He needed a long shower, a couple of Bloody Marys, never to see this idiot again. "End of the line," he said. "Bye."

"You know, I'm glad you did it to my mom," Marat said as he pushed open the door and spun out onto the sidewalk. "She's going through a rough spot and needed the pick-me-up. But technically she's still married, and one day you're gonna get it."

But Joel was speeding off in search of his morning shower, Marat's bogus threat lost to engine noise. Joel didn't think about Marat again, or his saggy-titted mom, or his mule-assed sister, until a week later, just before closing, when Marat walked into Joel's Ale House and ordered a Captain Morgan's and Coke loaded with maraschino cherries.

"Out late for a school night," Joel remarked, turning up the stereo so the bass line from Michael Jackson's "Black or White" made beer pulse in bar glasses.

"What's up with the Lego igloo?" Marat thumbed over at a five-foot purple hut, complete with icicles and a chimney and little Eskimo children making snowmen out front.

"Something I do for fun," Joel said. He poured a Shirley Temple and pushed it across the bar. "That'll be ten dollars."

Even in the bar's leveling dreariness Marat appeared exceptionally mediocre, tubby with a boilerplate face, his clothes decades out of fashion, dipped in a second skin of soot and redolent of pine-tar shampoo and ash. Too exhausted to bathe, or brush his teeth, or give a shit beyond attaining a slight evening of the score, a starter base of wealth, and freedom. "You hiring?" he muttered, all the charm of a dead rat.

"For what?" Joel asked, though he could read the code clear as mineral water, just felt like giving the kid shit.

"Don't know. Anything." Money, Marat needed money, piles of it, the liberty that cash built. Joel Lumpkin was the richest person he'd met since Slippy Sanders, and even more alone than he was.

"You scrub toilets?"

"Yeah," he said, stifling a burp, then scratching himself and breathing too loud and looking very much the dumb little stoner that he was. Belonged sneaking into movie theaters and trading comic books with computer friends and whacking off into tube socks, an average adolescent loser, the least suspicious guy on the block. Could do a lot of damage if applied correctly, another faceless face in the crowd.

"What are your salary requirements?" he asked.

"Hundred bucks an hour. Twice a week, after school." A pittance, a fortune; a place to start.

"Sounds pretty good," Joel responded, a few hundred dollars a week a small price to pay for a semiambitious junior associate. Aware of the prevailing wage, clever enough to discern that running a hole of a bar won't buy a luxury German vehicle, that there had to be well-compensated criminal behavior involved. And Joel's operation could always use a good street-runner, a client contact guy who didn't take too much off the top, easy enough to mail in as a patsy.

Marat oozed over the bar, a giant tube of toothpaste squeezed. "I need a dime bag."

"Say what?"

"You heard me." Another stalling, lying fuckwad like his mother. "Give it or don't."

Not that Joel was one to roll out the free-pot welcome wagon, but Marat was crying, right there, an ugly steady stream. The kid needed it, needed something. Joel went to the storeroom and plucked a pillbox out of the fridge. "Clean yourself up," he said, rolling it across the bar, "and get out."

"Fucking give me a minute. Douche bag." Matting his eyes with a napkin, the waterworks slowing down and replaced by a slow, sodden disgust.

Muscles wriggled in Joel's stomach, the situation spindling away, this kid smarter than he looked by a couple hundred laps and pulling away. "Come back Tuesday," he said, "and bring your bus pass."

Marat took a long sniff, mummbled, then ran out the door helter-skelter, arms wagging, bowlegs swiveling, tummy flab bouncing, so not cool. Clearly the kid was unpolished, Joel thought, but there was a fat bud of potential. Be nice to have a buddy to get rich and chase tail with, blaze up and watch the Giants game at the bar, all the beer you can drink. Worse ways to go through life, he thought, and started drawing up a list of surfers and trust fund kids for Marat's inaugural reefer run, low margins but huge networks, the fastest way to get big.

FOREIGN WARS

England, Austria, Piedmont, and the lesser German states were still in arms against the Republic. The first duty of the Directory [Revolutionary French government] was, therefore, to continue the war with them and to defeat them.

—CHARLES HAZEN,
The French Revolution and Napoleon

The external policy of the Directory soon evinced that passion for foreign conquest which is the unhappy characteristic of Democratic states, especially in periods of unusual fervor, and forms the true vindication of the obstinate war which was maintained against them by the European monarchs. "The [opposing] coalition," they contended, "was less formed against France than against the principles of the Revolution."

—ARCHIBALD ALISON,
History of Europe

Robespierre decided on her life's plan shortly after seeing *Cool Hand Luke* on public television. It wasn't so much the film itself, though she found it quite good, as her mother's swoon over Paul Newman, her inability to answer the phone or prevent the popcorn from burning while the movie was on, her repeated mentions of his handsome haircut while absentmindedly tracing of the inseam of her slacks. The next day Esmerelda filled up the shopping cart with Newman-brand salad dressing and cookies and tomato sauce at a 50 percent markup, a love-shot bloom in her eyes.

Belt and suspenders, Robespierre realized. Acting, spun off into high-profit gourmet foods, publicized by acting, made more interesting by high-profit gourmet foods. Diversification to ward off age or several bombs in a row or even a mass recall: in short, the perfect career model.

She had starred in school theatrical productions for the past several years, though it was getting harder to deliver the saccharine performances demanded of her, she no longer had the patience. But she recognized that audiences flocked to perceived likeability and sexually suggestive ass swings, so she focused on delivering jokes and small gestures of compassion—a glance, a touch, a cold word that implied more—and pestered her guidance counselor with daily visits until she made a few calls and secured an internship at the American Conservatory Theater. For her first food-service venture, she picked smoothies because they were easy to eat on the go, tied in with the health-food trend, and projected an appealing sense of California and slenderness. When she couldn't find any smoothie stands to manage nearby, she borrowed five grand from Slippy Sanders and started up her own.

The smoothie stand was wedged in a quarter slot between Mama's Sushi and Java Explosion at the Metreon food court, three feet of counter space, two blenders, and a chalkboard listing specials. The store was nameless until mid-June, when she decided on "BlastOff"—memorable, mildly suggestive, and amenable to a kitschy outer-space theme. Aside from optional vitamin additives, the smoothies contained only milk, fruit, and ice, providing an honest, frothy taste that turned out maddeningly inconsistent. Robespierre made drinks herself the first few weeks, smiling full strength for the benefit of her dopey customers while mismeasuring ingredients and blending for the wrong duration and often running out of the daily special a half hour in. Starting a business had its moments of neck-tingling thrills, but the actual work itself was repetitive as all hell, a moron could do it—which was usually the case, she soon found out, at other mall food outlets—so to entertain herself she picked great stage characters and acted them out: Shakespeare's Juliet rapturously mixing Banana Satellite smoothies, Albee's Martha shooting down hoary invitations to screw in the bathroom, the Wicked Witch of the West cackling into the cash register. She knew no smoothie ever tasted the same twice, her suppliers were unreliable, the fruit often bad, the pricing inflated, she didn't even have a logo, but she smiled and blended and practiced her lines. Eventually the customers showed, handing over money with huge corny smiles and odd timidity, teens elbowing each other, women hesitant, everyone a little uncomfortable, until one day she overheard a little girl ask her mom why the crazy lady was so quiet and she realized they were there to see her shtick. From then on she worked on her lines at full volume, reciting ballads to lonely old women and honing her stand-up comedy lines for the spiritually depressed and entertaining children with the best of Lewis Carroll, rolling her tongue over every made-up word until she was an "only in San Francisco" institution, like the World Famous Bushman and the Tamale Lady, the gibberish-gabbing smoothie loony featured in guidebooks and travel features, the only blended beverage in town worth going out of your way for.

After an early supper at a competitor's quick-service stand, she walked through Union Square to the theater, where she passed out programs and updated membership lists and watched the nightly performance from the orchestra pit. She stood up for the whole show to train her legs for the stage and paid close attention to actors' small muscle movements, vocal inflections, body position, breathing. Afterward she went to the dressing rooms to deliver positive feedback and her firecracker smile, feeling out insider information about who'd sandbagged whom, who was getting coked out and half-assing it, who was smacking it out of the park and why, until they all went out drinking and she caught the last bus home. It wasn't long until she talked a director into giving her a script.

"I'm in a play," she announced at a Tuesday chicken burger dinner just after Independence Day, her one night a week off from the theater.

"Which play?" Esmerelda asked, chewing a forkful of mango salad. Marat worked silently on his second burger, viciously hungry between growth spurts and all the weed.

"It's a debut drama called *Slopeside*." She touched her right hand to her left elbow, a new mannerism she was working on to insinuate vulnerability. "I play a ski lodge bartender. It's only thirty lines, but there's lots of room to show what I can do. If I nail it, I think I'll get talked about for some leads next season."

"How much they paying?" Esmerelda asked, eyeing the stack of overdue bills on the counter.

"Zero," she lied. "Just a résumé builder."

"Sounds like slave labor to me," Esmerelda noted. "Dead wrong and unfair and exploitative. Tell you what, I'll print up some pamphlets and we'll shellac the place, protest, start a movement: 'Pay child workers!' Can you see it?" She framed her hands into a chubby square. "They'll eat that stuff up around here."

"I'll go," Marat mumbled through a mouthful of meat. He was listening to fifteen reggae albums a day holed up in his room, sucking on spliffs and staring blank-eyed at the heavy shadows traipsing across the wall while the ocean of noise floated around him. It was a schedule, he sometimes noted, which alarmingly mirrored his grandmother's diet of gin and soap operas.

Robespierre reached into her purse. "Thursday matinee. I got you front-row seats," she said and pushed an envelope across the table.

Esmerelda pulled out the tickets and ran her fingers over the particulars, 1 PM on a nonholiday. "During work? Crap, honey, I'm the boss. You know how Slippy is with punctuality and everything, that leading-by-example stuff."

"I'll go," Marat repeated, stuffing fries in his mouth like he was packing a bowl.

"Could you throw in some free smoothies?" Esmerelda whined. "That way I can write it off as a business lunch."

But the last time Esmerelda came by BlastOff, she'd demanded free samples of all fifteen varieties, then listed the failings of each flavor at top volume, laughing so hard at the amateurish Carrot-Coconut Moonshot smoothie's ridiculous cinnamon overtones that she sprayed snot-foam out her nose and onto a team of undercover food critics. "I really can't, mom."

"I'll buy them for you," Marat said, just to shut her up.

"Well, at least one of you turned out polite," Esmerelda retorted, crumpling her chicken burger bun into a gelatinous ball and chomping off an edge. "It will be my pleasure."

They arrived after the play started, noisily filing into the front row, Esmerelda slurping on her smoothie sampler and Marat grooving with the last remnants of bud warming his lungs. It took a little while for them to place Robespierre working behind the bar; she seemed lankier and older, empowered and alone. She nailed the constant motion of service industry jobs, Esmerelda observed, changing the channel on the TV and running off to answer the phone, pawing change from the register, slicing lemons, greeting newcomers, whipping out the rag tied to her belt to mop up spillage and polish highball glasses, astonishingly deft with alcohol. About time she picked up a few shifts at CopySmart, Esmerelda decided, help pay down the family deficit while permitting Esmerelda to expand her social calendar with more cultured long lunches like this one.

Marat observed as close as he could through throbbing, arid eyeballs. He could pull off the role better, he thought; Robespierre had all the right ingredients but lacked honesty, the depth that pulled it all together. Artless, pinched; she behaved as if she didn't know drugs, as if she could never understand how they made you into someone sloppy and different and beautifully bad. Even surrounded by people, with all her smiling spasms and hitting off the checklist of poses and giggles and dangerous little mouth moves, she looked distanced up there. False. As if this didn't matter. Which it didn't.

"That's not what happened! I swear to God!" a skier exclaimed, half frightened and half excited, making the least of a juicy adulterer role.

Robespierre slapped him, openhanded. "Fucker," she hocked, and let him have another one with the backside.

"Hey," the actor squealed, shying back a half step and hiding behind stick forearms.

"Nice one!" Esmerelda hooted.

"You pathetic leech!" Robespierre vented, her sultry barmaid voice frazzled with static. "Take your little ding-dong and get out of here!"

"Damn!" Esmerelda called, clapping her hands over her head.

"I'm sorry," the actor shuddered, an amateur half smile forming on his mouth.

"Go!" Robespierre shouted, and threw a plastic cup full of beer into the audience on a trajectory dead set for Esmerelda's nose, dousing her eyes and screwing with her breathing and forcing out seven or eight mucus loads onto the floor in front of her.

Marat laughed more deeply than he had in forever, long irrepressible strokes that lasted well past the moment and on into the next scene, past where Robespierre stormed off the stage at the end of a decidedly noncomedic sequence, past anything remotely resembling reasonable. The delight of fucked-up justice, the absurdity of a world that rewarded childishness and good aim and doing the wrong thing. How amazing this public shaming was, even better than smoking up to mind-crushing bass lines and pissing out the window and never leaving his room. His mother glared at the stage with openmouthed hatred, a hideous deceptive head made for mounting over an alpine fireplace. How easy it would be to punch her out, whack her with a pool cue, shove her down some stairs. He wanted to try it, was winding up the courage, when he felt a troubled silence, the show out of sync, the house lights coming up, the shushes hitting him from twenty directions.

"OK!" he said, rising to leave. "I'll go!" But he hyucked it up the whole way out, faster and louder, a thousand monkeys yeeping for their lives.

When he fell out into the street he was laughing his hardest, his pitch climbing and tapering, his lungs bleeding vapors. Yet beneath the outward manisfestation of cheer he recognized that somehow his sister had made this happen. He'd been discredited in some subtle way. She knew everything important and how to use it and win.

Ice coated his neck; he felt pickpocketed, exposed. She'd turned out to be a far better actor than he'd been led to believe, and at that realization the chortling finally rolled out and died, replaced by a mile-wide tidepool of seething coral-green jealousy.

When they got home, Marat was reclined in Fanny's old chair, his shirt a wet rag, his eyes salted and stained lime green. A thick gray haze hung at his ears, an ivory pipe carved with gargoyles balanced on his belt. "How'd the play end?" he asked.

"Like crap," Esmerelda said. "It finished with a stupid class reunion where everybody got in a fight and went home angry. No jokes and no sex. I've had more fun at the podiatrist's."

"Do they chuck beer in your face at the podiatrist's?" Marat asked.

"It was an accident," Robespierre interjected, "I apologized."

"You guys have always sucked at sports," Esmerelda confirmed. "I can't get mad when a throw goes off-base."

Marat's face was unresponsive, a stone wall with a loose brick in the corner, a vital step short of completion. "Marat," Robespierre said, "are you OK?"

"Blow off," he said, and lifted a Bic from his lap, set flame to his pipe, and sucked in nice and slow until Esmerelda's eight-ring keychain crashed against his knee. He dropped his pipe and wheeled up in a blue coughing fit.

"HEY!" Esmerelda shouted. "This may be San Francisco, but you're still my kid! No smoking, and definitely no drugs, capiche? Especially not in the goddamn living room!"

He cringed and curled up, a dog busted for chewing a shoe. "Sorry, Ma," he croaked.

"Clean it up!" Esmerelda shrieked back. "Last thing I want is to roll around in your spittle."

"I got it," Robespierre said, and soundlessly began picking marijuana off the carpet. He was her brother, her partner, with all the right tools, the wiring, the irreplaceable genetics, but something wasn't processing. How to read people, how to break through, to identify weaknesses and wedge them into opportunities, when to keep your mouth shut and when to charge ahead to the end zone like a turbocharged ICBM. Bad judgment calls and inattentive errors, tactless miscalibrations and a general naïveté, the kind of second-tier mediocrity that ruins premier organizations. The anchor to her accelerating rocket ship.

And the drugs, all day long. Black smoke on the rooftop, making him aloof, stupid and sluggish, addled and weird. Building a rap sheet, liability, incriminations and attacks. Unreliable from sunup to Taps, a minefield of mistakes.

"You've got to go," she said, instantly regretting it, an extraordinarily rare slipup of verbal control. His crap rubbing off on her.

"Go where?" he asked, flashing black evil eyes.

"Upstairs," she recovered, "so I can clean up the chair."

He sloshed out of the chair and trudged up to his room, taking with him a funk, a miasma, an ecosystem of decay. Filthy and fucked up, he should be so much better. She would make him that way.

But it would hurt.

❧

A February morning, the sky studded with rain. Marat walked through the hall to English class, the only class he attended regularly, because he liked the stories and how he only had to pick a side and sell it to be right. He kept a novel in his front pocket and read on the bus, over beers at Joel's Ale House, on his back in his redecorated bedroom while girls got dressed and left, crosslegged on the beach while he waited to do deals with the dope acquired by Joel's library of forged prescription cards. He skipped slow sections and quit whenever he wanted to, reread riveting passages over and over, savored the scenes on his schedule. Even as a time-agnostic pothead, he recognized this small freedom for the wonder that it was.

"Marat Van Twinkle?"

Principal Quince was next to him, flanked by Max and Darrell from security. The guards were grade-A guys, scrawny police force rejects thrilled to have summers off, both soca lovers who sometimes burned him mix CDs; two of Marat's best customers.

"Huh?" he responded, detached and dim as always, not about to deliver incriminating behavior until he saw some proof.

"Come with me, please."

"Why?" Marat looked around, other kids drifting along like they didn't see him, zoning and spacing and bored.

"I'll explain in a moment."

The security guards reluctantly took his backpack and escorted him in a floating triangle to Quince's office in the front of the school. A police officer stood by the door, thumbs hooked on his pockets and chatting up barbecue recipes with the school secretary.

Max unzipped his backpack. "What's going on?" Marat asked.

"Where's your locker?" asked Principal Quince.

"I don't use a locker." He watched Max gingerly excavate his scant collection of notebooks and folders. "Careful. I got homework in there."

"You're assigned locker 1-8-0-8," Quince said. "We found a quarter pound of marijuana inside this morning."

"Shit!" Marat laughed. Keeping pot in a locker was bush-league stupid, something any serious runner knew not to do from the earliest afterschool special. "Got any leads?"

"Clean," Max reported.

"Have a seat," Quince said icily. He walked behind his desk and gestured to a squat wooden chair. Marat kept an eye on the door, the cop leaning against the frame, wondering if an all-out sprint might do it.

"Have a seat," Quince repeated, and Marat obeyed.

The cop closed the door. "Dope's tagged from the Green Mountain Dispensary on Haight Street," he said. "They've confirmed selling it to a kid who matches your description. We also know you work with a guy who drives a very nice Mercedes that changes license plates every few days, and that you've supplied most of the football team. And the marching band. And the cheerleaders."

Marat's insides collapsed into green soup. He held his mind on staying in character, something his sister would do so well. Faces flew by him, crazy customers and prank-playing punks, the crazy girls, the quiet girls, the dumb girls, the meatheads. Every one of his customers a suspect, not to mention his boss.

Quince sat down and looked the kid over, in sweatpants and burned-out sneakers, his duct-taped backpack held shut with safety pins. Radiating anger, impossible to tell if he was lying or not. Sure didn't look like a drug dealer, or else the bling was in storage. "Robespierre's your sister?"

"Yep."

"Didn't she get into Stanford early?"

"Yep."

"Huh.' Quince scanned Marat's file, reports of suspensions and fighting, straight As in English, associations with known felons, tremendous truancy. "What are your plans for next year?"

"Finding the guy who planted drugs in my locker and turning him in." Marat smiled white slabs, and Quince couldn't help but like him a little.

"Besides that," Quince said.

"Haven't figured that out."

"I see." Quince made his back rigid and folded his hands, projecting sternness with a glimmer of sensibility. "I'm supposed to turn you over to the police. I can't say exactly what they'll do with you, but my guess is they'll take you down to the station and interrogate you. They might put you in jail for a few days, or even longer. I honestly don't know."

"All depends on you," the cop chimed in.

Marat shrugged and raised his voice, as expected of a cool customer done wrong. "I told you, I don't use my locker. Was there anything else in there that belonged to me? Fingerprints?" Marat eyed the security guards, who were rolling their tongues through their cheeks and looking away sheepishly, as if nabbed mooching apples from a neighbor's tree. "No. Because I don't even know where it is."

Quince waited. Few of the kids brought to his office knew when to shut up. Marat kept quiet and threw back a half-lidded stare, wary and coyote cool. "I could suspend you for five days and ask Officer Greeley not to take you in," Quince said finally. "No police record. He doesn't have to listen to me. But he might."

"For what?" Marat asked.

Greeley stood in front of him, an overweight man made normal-sized in his police uniform, the beneficiary of excessive pockets and flaps and badges. The double chin gave away his heft, the lower half of his face overflowing his collar like a calving glacier, left unbalanced by his pewter eyes and thumb nose. "Who do you work for?"

Marat dangled his head over the back of his chair. The four adults ringed him like moons, their gravitational fields shielding the snitches buried among the student body. "Nobody at the moment," he said, calibrating his response. "Your mom fired me for a cheaper fucktoy last week."

"That's it," the cop said, reaching for his handcuffs. "Let's go." He lunged for Marat's hand, but Marat was moving, spidering across the office, shoving the officer over the chair, ripping open the door.

"I came as soon as I heard!" Robespierre's eyes were pink and puffed, and she froze him just enough. "It's gotta be a setup. You don't even use your locker!"

Then the security guards had him, his chin hit the floor, arms and legs locked behind his back. "What the hell is going on?" Robespierre screamed. "That's my brother!"

"Get my shoes," he told her through the black in his mouth. "Under my bed."

"Shut up!" Greeley barked.

Marat woke up diagonal in the back of a squad car, his shirt torn at the neck. At the police station they put him in a room with a table and two men for three hours. He said nothing. He nodded once. His sister was waiting for him outside, doing her homework under a streetlight.

"It was either jail time or the army," he told her. He laughed quick skip-beats, nervous irritation. "So I enlisted."

She hugged him. Her seditious, amazing brother, too smart for getting stuck like this, his precise tactical execution crushed by grand strategies he never saw coming. "Thank you," she whispered, flush with shame. "For the shoes."

"It's for college. Don't tell mom."

"I won't." The police were behind him. "Be careful."

Thirty-six hours later he was doing push-ups in Texas, sweating through his hat.

When college started up, Robespierre hired away Jamba Juice's most colorful staff to uphold the smoothie stand's quirky reputation, then stocked her schedule with drama, psychology, accounting, and English, plus jazz history as an elective so she could better relate to intelligentsia theatergoers. She tried out for five plays in her first two weeks of school, nailing leading tragedians and acerbic sidekicks alike, drawing buckets of laughter and misty-eyed gulps, culminating in a Taser-like full-body shock at the depth and breadth of her abilities. Her unrivaled talent outweighed her middling looks; all the plays wanted her, piling on compliments and bumps up to bigger roles and even offering a cut of the gate. It came down to Lady Macbeth or a lesbian rodeo champ in a student-written comedy, classic vs. upstart, laughs or tears, the two faces of drama spinning toplike in her head. She headed out for a jog to clear her head and nearly collided with a wall of chirpy students milling about the Quad.

"What's going on?" she asked a heavily tanned surfer-type scratching his back with a guitar.

"Barack Obama, man!" He gave her an unfiltered smile and put out a gangly hand. "Join us!"

She hadn't ever paid much attention to politics, aside from Fanny's lusty jeremiads comparing San Francisco mayors to Soviet premiers and the politicians at the gay pride parade her mother liked to put on TV and snicker at. She had enough sense to know that most people were trained to hate politicians' guts no matter what, and considered elected office your classic no-win career with bad money. But here were the people, apparently in good spirits, wearing—she started to look around now—T-shirts and caps with Obama's picture on them, teaming up to wave huge banners. Outside together on a chilly school night, the feel of autumnal shifts and cycles and change. It was exciting, intoxicating, this power to shape behavior. "What's going on?"

"It's a Meetup."

"What for?"

"For Obama, man!" With a chin-twist at the end, happy fresh-faced certainty.

"And are you doing anything special? Is he coming to talk?"

"Obama? I wish. Dude's got California sewed up like a . . . a sweater. Nah, we're just here, you know, to support the cause. See how we can help and everything." Sounding hokey, back-of-the-cereal-box starry-eyed stupid, like a ranch hand describing investment strategy to Goldman Sachs' board of directors.

"Why do you like him so much?" So eager to know she nearly shouted it.

"Well, he's gonna be different, you know? Work with everybody across the aisle and stay positive and bring people together. Restore our national reputation. Because we really need some of that, you know? And he'll end the wars too." Something in his face ticking here, a valve releasing, his voice switching to heavy, sincere evaluation mode. "So much bad stuff. All those people dying for no reason. It has to stop."

"My brother's fighting in the Middle East," she said, a creeper of guilt winding round her neck. "And my dad," she lied.

"Really? Wow." Sweeping the sidewalk with the sole of his shoe. "Wow."

"They both hate it," she continued, inventing a sturdy foundation for antiwar credentials.

"Well yeah, right? We all hate war."

His words caught in her head, the simple surfer poetry of it. "We all hate war," she repeated, feeling how it dropped and held. Words to chew on and stretch out with her teeth, pack solid against her gums, snap through with her tongue. Words that could move feet.

"If you don't hate war, you're an asshole," he pointed out. "It's life and death."

Whereas acting was wasteful entertainment and a smoothie stand was a superfluous capitalist extravagance. "I want to help," she said. "What can I do?"

"Cool!" He fumbled in his backpack for some stickers and a sign-up sheet. Already she felt firmer and squared away, saturated with the focus of deep reading or making music alone in a soundproof studio. Trivialities gushed away through her feet, a sensei's mind controlling the room.

She stayed with the bronzed Obama ambassador, learned his name was Ryan, made up stories about working on Governor Schwarzenegger's task force for climate change and registering the homeless to vote, watched his eyes sharpen and stare down her shirt. Back in his room she let him fuck her twice with all the lights on while she slapped his cheeks, squeezed his nipples, pinched his ass, called him filthy names. He was crying when she left, she wasn't sure why, and by the time she made it back to her room, he'd sent three emails and left two voicemails begging her to return. She didn't.

The next day she prowled the Stanford Mall, introducing herself to makeup counter ladies as a *Palo Alto Daily* reporter seeking out cosmetic trends. She received exhaustive makeovers at three different department stores and took copious notes on the attendants' chatter on makeup pairings with outfit style, recent earth-tone trends, weight-concealing strategies, who looked good in what and when. They all said she needed concealer and foundation, something to mask the blemishes bubbling on her cheeks and also to pull her face together, to distract from her spaced-out alien eyes. Focus on those thick lips, they all said, boost your average-looking mouth up to phenomenal with gloss and lip liner, make the men pay attention to your mouth, the juicy possibility of your tongue and throat. Licking your words into being, a glandular promise of fornication and pure primal attraction. She walked out of each store with a shopping bag full of lipstick samples and a pledge to lick her lips saucily before making to any public statement.

The next week she went back to the ladies' clothes section, her cover a follow-up assignment on winter fashion styles. The gleeful attendants had her changing in and out of dresses and skirts the whole day, establishing that she needed color and flair, something to distract from her noticeable behind—not that it wasn't beautiful, they added quickly, it was just a detour from her face, her ideas, herself. Loose bottoms and attention-getting tops drew attention upward, they advised, diverting the eyes onto a collision course with that succulent mouth. Robespierre smiled with her lips turned out and thanked them for their help, then hung around alluding to possible photo spreads and fashion shoots, a chance for significant free advertising, maybe they could donate a few of the more outstanding ensembles for the project, it was fully tax-deductible—but the shopgirls blathered on about favorite brands and all that weight Jessica Simpson put on, and she left before her head exploded. She thought about sneaking out a few of the choice designer outfits underneath the dark and flowing oversized skirt and trench coat combo she'd worn for that very purpose, even made it halfway to the exit smuggling a Prada ensemble, when she spotted the security guy standing just outside the mall entrance slurping innocuously on a soda, everything in place for the easy bust. She snaked her tongue across her lips and went back to the changing room, tore off the Prada outfit, and stuffed it under the bench in angry balls. The security guard burped filthily as she strode by him on the way to the parking lot, and she decided to never again issue a lip lick in the mall so long as he stood a chance of seeing it.

She hit five thrift stores on the drive home and followed up with an evening on eBay, snatching up every ten-dollar designer suit and colorful attention-getting top that was remotely close to her size. Decked out in baggy if eye-jarringly effective outfits, she slathered on tubes of concealer, base, and lipstick, and set out in full costume for political union events, Democratic club meetings, bars at power-brokering restaurants, rallies and marches and coffee-shop bitchfests, the occasional park drum circle. She read up on the issues and called for decisive action, the need to get people back to work through investment, an end to the wars, wild hard belief set in her eyes like stones. With time she learned to sew, slicing and stitching her ragtag ward-robe into a bona fide power closet. She got noticed for eloquence and intelligence and her provocative looks, toeing the line of angry but not stepping over it; a committed front-line fighter who made her points stick, with the men drawn to her seductive lip puckers that came every twenty minutes on the dot.

She quit the plays and sold the smoothie stand and dove full-on into political science courses, investigating how to entice people to give her the power to control the course of history. All of acting's thrill of persuasion but with a much bigger payoff, the chance to direct human civilization, working the biggest stage there was. She studied Reagan's avuncular charisma, Clinton's ease and sax solos, Kennedy's huge eyes and knockout wife. Obama did it better than anybody: inspirational and cool but above all inviting, a guy you'd never dream of hanging with in high school but here he was sliding in next to you in the cafeteria with a free BLT and chocolate milk and an offer to do your homework before making long and groovy love on a candlelit waterbed over hectic jazz scats.

That was the style; she needed the substance. The topics du jour did not excite: the economic debate all went the same way, with everyone agreeing on the importance of growing wealth but no real idea how to pull it off; energy reform was too distant, average voters didn't understand power grids or what a carbon ton was; gay rights had slumped into a second-tier issue that didn't promise a whole lot of electoral upside; nobody liked homelessness; and the impossible, intangible frustration of health care was a monster she did not know how to slay. She took sides on these fights and supported them but still searched for something emotional and visceral, the blade cutting skin, the electrifying angle to make her a star.

Her first day in Washington was sloppy hot and depressing. A flat-faced butch chick named Sushi introduced herself as Speaker Pelosi's summer intern coordinator and led Robespierre and a paunchy Asian kid from Bernal Heights on a five-minute office tour before putting in coffee orders and handing her a twenty. Robespierre introduced herself to all the staff and the rest of the dork patrol interns, licking her lips and offering her services to help with speechwriting or strategizing; she could call around and broker bipartisan agreements, maybe take a stab at drafting some of the simpler legislation. Instead they gave her a few thousand copies to run off and asked her to keep an eye on the fax machine.

The legislative aides took note when she turned around the copy job in record time—her mother had kept her on top of the latest tricks for time-saving document reproduction—and rewarded her with the office lunch order. When those came back early and under budget, they knew she was a threat. They ignored her for the rest of the day, leaving her to putz around on the computer and fend off date requests from wonky geeks who tracked down her bobbing butt in the hallway.

Day Two was more of the same, the executive staff feigning preoccupation with reports and memos, the administrative support pool chatting endlessly on the phone, a couple of jerkier policy analysts simply turning their chairs around when she puffed her lips in their direction. They ignored her emails, failed to answer her calls, and rebuffed her in-person requests for expanded duties with long-winded nonanswer stalls. She let them have their kicks—sniffles in quick, laughlike succession, eyes wrought with impossible stained-glass disinterest while they overtly played Sudoku online—and told Sushi she was heading out to a doctor's appointment. Instead she wandered over to the House of Representatives and took a seat in the balcony.

Luxurious marble and crafted wood and the great American flag hoisted behind the Speaker's podium. The floor was empty, except for a representative from Colorado reading off the accomplishments of a recently deceased Steamboat Springs rancher, a man who'd helped slash the unemployment rate by half and made significant contributions to agricultural development and the science of animal husbandry. Intermittent votes took place on a giant scoreboard as old men banged gavels and read inscrutable texts. It was like watching a cafeteria swell and contract, a subway station at rush hour. Everyone passing through.

She went back to the office and headed for a cluster of cubicles and lower-level staff that Sushi had introduced with a finger down her gaping mouth. Shuttling keyboards and repetitive yawns, humming climate control, a large clock over the door where the minute hand glugged through the day like the passing sun. This was the government she'd feared, the dozing administrative guts, lifetimes of passionless execution and paper passing. She slipped into an empty desk and composed a snarkalicious insider essay for the biggest blog in the land, razing the Pelosi organization for its dopey management hierarchy; its inability to do more when the resources were there; the conservative, do-things-the-old-way philosophy that alienated bright-eyed and bushy-tailed supersmart plugged-in-to-the-realities-of-2009 summer interns. Three lines into her rousing conclusion the scent of paper and cherry perfume overwhelmed her, followed by the uncommon sensation of being found out.

She minimized the program on her screen. Too late. "Delete it," a voice said.

"What?" Stalling for an excuse, nerves jerking in her head, followed fast by a chasm of disappointment, how authority still froze her.

"You're a smart kid, so don't do something stupid."

"It's nothing," she mumbled, fumbling with the mouse and turning the screen away. It had been so long since she'd been busted at anything, she wasn't good at playing dumb.

"I know what it is. Used a computer before too." The woman pulled up a chair, crowded her into the cubicle. She was in her mid-sixties and Asian, gray hair wrapped tight around her head, Elvira-style reading glasses dangling around her neck on a shoelace. "Delete it."

Robespierre nodded mechanically and opened the blogging window, removed the post, signed out of the website, and shut down her browser.

"Good girl. Now why don't you make yourself useful?"

"I tried," she said, thinking of her perfect load of copies, coffee orders filled in record time, standing offers to do any and all bitch work lobbed in her direction.

"You made yourself annoying. You think we don't see this? Hotshot summer interns come in and think they're world-beaters?"

"I never said that," she mumbled.

"This is the major leagues," the woman said crisply. "We don't have time for that. Now, with this—" she tapped the computer monitor with her fingertips "—the real question is: why should I help you out, when you already tried to burn this place down?"

"I'm sorry," she said dourly, opting for the time-tested ass-kissing apology road. "I made a mistake. Please, let me make up for it."

The lady nodded. "Good. I'm Maeve. You are?"

"Robespierre."

"Unh-huh. Well listen up, Robes, this is the bullpen. Which I run. In essence we are the public engagement arm of the Speaker's office. We receive, on average, five thousand letters, emails, and calls per day. Depends on the day, the issue, election cycles. But call it five thousand. Probably the most in all of Congress, since she's been around a while and is the Speaker. As you might guess, Ms. Pelosi does not have time to personally respond to all five thousand pieces of correspondence, especially as a large percentage of them are form emails or prewritten postcards, impersonal prewritten communications that people sign up for via an email forward or at the grocery store. You follow?"

She did follow, the long webs of connection and the power of people and demagogues and grassroots organizations and polls. "You tally them up?" she asked.

"Correct. Issues with the most correspondence get nudged

toward the top of the Speaker's agenda. Naturally, that can be gamed. But we assume anybody who really wants something is gaming the system, so in essence it's a minimum threshold of legitimacy. In fact, if you're *not* gaming the system, you're really not on the radar. That said, we also get plenty of people who write in about anything and everything. 'I saw a fire truck run a red light without its siren on,' or 'where's my tax return,' or 'my pants are missing.' Any topic you can think of, and more."

Robespierre imagined the crazies of San Francisco, dancing naked in the Tenderloin and operating candle shops and replanting parks by hand and overall making the city the bewitching, iconoclastic place it was. "And you respond," she concluded.

"Got to. We need their vote. And we get free mail, franking privilege. Paper letters stand out from email. There's authority to it, finding you at a fixed address. And people appreciate the labor involved, that we took the time to print something and sign and mail it. Now, the overwhelming majority of correspondence covers the same twenty or thirty issues, for which we have regularly updated responses prepared. Basic structure's acknowledgement, explanation, and either agreement or call for understanding. Constituents write in on different sides of an issue, but we don't get too deep. Most people just want to know they've been heard."

Which fit in with everything Robespierre knew about ego massaging and flattery, the keys to psychic conquest. It was a beautiful bureaucracy—people-powered, scalable and systemic, timely, simple, embracing democratic ethos and capitalist gamesmanship, the full splendor of America. "Maybe I can help write response letters," she suggested, "for the new issues that come in."

Maeve wrinkled her upper lip in a smirk of semi-respect. "Do a good job and I'll see if they need help over in speechwriting. You can start with these." A mail bin loaded with paper landed on her desk like a Yule log. "Plenty more where that came from."

She pulled out the top envelope, unfolded a loose-leaf sheet out of eighths. Wild handwriting recommended repurposing mothballed antiaircraft weaponry to stop dangerous hurricanes, as fired bullets would disrupt hazardous wind patterns with counterattacking air currents and the sheer force of hot lead. The next letter was typed, all caps, and contained profanity of a class not observed since Sven's sailor mates swilled beer by the gallon on weekend nights back on Stillwell Road. Following that was a lengthy exposé on the devious connection between military officials and the Vatican, involving parallel universes and subatomic weaponry, all of it explained by invisible ink on the Dead Sea Scrolls. One treatise on spies dressed up as farmers and seeding fields with toxins; another pointing out the indefensible sluttiness of the Speaker's wardrobe, her leg flesh visible from five yards or closer. Rants against homeless people, corporations, governments, nonprofits, flaccid passive everymen who didn't ask questions, annoying liberal brats who wouldn't stop with the questions, right-wing hotheads who screamed too much, idiot activists, idiot cops, idiot criminals, intelligent criminals, tight-assed media dopes, scamming banks and fucked-up CEOs, dumbass Mexicans who tried to buy their houses on orange-picker salaries, xenophobic blowhards who conveniently ignored their own immigrant heritage, greedy real estate agents and exploitative mortgage brokers, preps and hipsters, yuppies and too-cools, environazis and polluters, single mothers, single dads, married losers, useless children and seniors, faggot-ass homos, scumbag gay bashers, trannies, anti-transsexuals, crackheads, squares, drunks, gangs of kids throwing trash in the street, sanitation companies and their unions, exploitative national chain stores forcing their way into local neighborhoods, moronic communists who blocked well-meaning businesses from opening up. The Speaker, the Speaker's parents and husband and children, anyone who'd ever met the Speaker, the Speaker's ancestors and descendants, every last one of them to burn in hell for eternity-plus.

That accounted for about half the letters. The rest drove down on the wars in epic poems of battle and freedom, recounting specific attacks and missions, names of dead men and women, requests for memorials and remembrance. Screeds against military contractors and America-hating camel fuckers and all the evil that built this into being. Flags to fly at half-mast until the guns were put away. Some demanded bigger deployments and hydrogen bombs—might as well throw the kitchen sink and get out, like Japan in World War II—but most were tired and sick of it and drained and far beyond done. Personal essays on selling their dead son's car and donating clothes and living in orphanages. Pictures of kids growing up parentless. Needing an explanation. Why was America fighting in these places, why people mixed with explosives, why high school kids flew ten thousand miles to absorb a car bomb outside a restaurant. How they loved the country lots but these questions required answers. Teardrops and grease stains, small careful signatures, respectful salutations and congenial farewells.

Robespierre took these war letters home with her, read them over dinner and through the night. They would not let her sleep. She drank a pot of coffee and beat everyone into the office, fired up her computer, and typed. No filters, no calculations—she mined honesty and truth, the rising fluid she felt between her lungs. Individual responses, with direct answers, apologies, and a plan, a policy enacted overnight: that the wars would end. Speaker Pelosi would not support the fighting, would not commit another dollar of taxpayer money to support it, would never let this happen again. These wars were wrong, they were lies, their children were dying for nothing, for less than nothing. Dying for losing. With judicious copying and pasting she was through the stack by noon, then printed off the responses, applied the Speaker's autopen signature, stuffed them and mailed them, then hit the cafeteria for a salad and Diet Coke.

Three days later she returned from her lunch break to find Maeve sitting at her desk, clicking through her computer. "Let's walk," Maeve stated, taking Robespierre's elbow and moving her through the stately hallways and down elaborate winding staircases and outside into the swamp-heat sun, a little park across the street.

"Are you trying to ruin us?" Maeve asked, her voice separating into a fusillade of razor-tipped spears. "Everything a Democratic Congress stands for can be ruined by this."

"By what?" Letting Maeve feel in control.

"Don't act stupid. The fucking letters." She held up one of Robespierre's better missives, a searing three-page discourse on the institutionalized hypocrisy wrought by the military-industrial complex. "The lies you spread."

"I didn't spread any lies."

"You impersonated Speaker Pelosi and made policy promises the Speaker never would or could enact. Lies."

"Everything you send out is an impersonation!" she burst out, silly stupid with the doublespeak and side lingo and made-up shit. "Pelosi doesn't do any of it herself!"

Maeve's face arranged like a keyboard, jaws out and teeth like yellow wood, hair stretching back like piano wire. "Approval. That's the difference. I never authorized any of these."

Pieces fit inside of her and she knew this was how it was done, a perfect political dumping. "I didn't do anything wrong," she said.

"I found the letters on your computer. And the print logs. And a roomful of witnesses who saw you working there during the hours in question. Overall, real sloppy work."

The high slipped from her head and she landed square in the center of the jungle heat; these points were too true, she was tostada with a side of eggs, exercises littered with rookie mistakes. The only alternative was to take down as much as she could with her, make herself too knowledgeable to turn in. "I never had any instructions," she claimed. "There were no approval processes in place. I just used common sense."

No movement in Maeve's face, eyes barely open, a death mask

before burial. "There are clear approval processes in place, posted on the wall of every cubicle. All communications from the Speaker of the House's office require review and approval from me."

Robespierre vaguely recalled a laminated form on the wall of her cubicle printed in attention-getting, eye-paining red type, over which she'd pinned several photos of President Obama playing basketball and a postcard of the Golden Gate Bridge drowning in fog. "You've been frank with me, so I'll be frank with you," Robespierre said. "You can either go down with me for not telling me about your approval process, or you can blame it on a computer problem. I want a transfer. Somewhere important." But what was more important than the Speaker's office? "The White House. And not the Old Executive Office Building either; I want the real deal, 1600 Pennsylvania and the Oval Office and little Obamas running around the White House lawn with Bo the dog."

"Can't do it." Unbelievable in every contour.

"Maybe not. But you better try."

The death mask fell away and Robespierre sat down on a bench, watching the pigeons peck at sandwich crusts and bike messengers slurp Gatorade under trees and pasty-faced suits racing back and forth across the sidewalk with their heads down, as if the fate of the world hinged on their attendance at meetings or project outlines or coauthored reports on fiduciary processes. She walked back to her rented dorm room and fell on her bed like a stone, sleeping straight though dinner and on through the night, until her cellphone rang in the morning with an official by-the-book secretarial voice informing her to report for work at the White House as soon as she could get there.

In the spring of 2012, still reeling from her failed bid for Stanford class president the previous year—she'd lost by five votes to a guy who'd literally handed out free beer—Robespierre put on her sexiest skirt and a double dose of lipstick and collected signatures to get on the ballot for San Francisco supervisor. She staked out parking lots and approached shoppers loading their cars, chatted up moms pushing strollers, trotted out the two lines of Mandarin she'd memorized the night before, flashed a laminated copy of her intern photo shaking hands with President Obama. To young men she blew slow, fat-lip kisses; when asked for her number, she gave out the campaign hotline, an answering service in Fremont. Incredibly, donations came in: friends' parents and Stanford alums and prominent city businesses looking to hedge their bets on the supervisor race while building a record of supporting minorities. She spent her funds on dinners out with potential endorsers, spa treatments and makeovers, pricey designer outfits to reel in the votes. On policy she was inconsistent, contradicting herself on a sales tax initiative within the space of two sentences, pulling a triple reverse on a transportation proposal, not having any position at all on homelessness, other than that she was against it. A disorganized campaigner, a knockout on television, her campaign gave great photos and vapid vibes, more L.A. than San Fran, culling no traction with voters.

Up late on a Tuesday night with her advisory committee, punchy student organizers and a couple of political science professors excited to test-drive some of their more radical thought experiments. Her first door-hanger order was due in four hours, with a round of final exams shortly after that. She needed more than a slogan, Robespierre observed; she needed a creed, a philosophy of courage and candor and just enough dreaminess, something San Francisco voters would love to love.

"But no rhyming," she decided. "It's a cheap trick. They'll see right through it."

"So what if it's a cheap trick?" countered David, a gay teaching assistant with perfect hands. "It's effective. Like a jingle on the radio."

"But everybody hates it when it gets stuck in their head."

"But it gets stuck in their head and they remember it and you win."

"Like McDonalds," chimed in Sheila, a pink-haired Asian chick.

"This campaign is not like McDonald's," Robespierre declared.

"Nobody's saying that," David said, "but you can't argue away their market dominance."

They paused to watch the Iranian War on the television she kept on the closet floor. Creaking tanks, men coated with dust, bombs breaking in lightning bolts. The Khorasan Offensive was overextended, a journalist reported by satellite videophone; attacks on supply lines disrupted the American advance from Turkmenistan. Women launched rockets at cooking fires; children hurled Molotov cocktails at medics. Somewhere in the background Marat humped on patrol, conducting strip searches and shooting first and learning bigger ways to hate. Her contribution to the problem.

"Nukes can't be far off," Robespierre muttered, citric acid mixing in her mouth.

"No way," said Jenny Prescott, a Barbara Boxer–styled Marin yuppie who was exploring the nuclear prospect thoroughly in her dissertation. "Not in an election year."

"Worked for Harry Truman," a young poli-sci professor pointed out.

Snapshots of KIAs scrolled onscreen, names and hometowns, scowling photos in uniform. A camera tottered through a village of amputees, victims of bombs from both sides sitting in wagons, leaning on crutches made from sticks, signing documents with pens between their teeth. Legless, armless, smiling people, overjoyed from living, ecstatic with life.

"This is what I care about," Robespierre said, feeling skin tighten over her arms, a buzz in the room building into live particles and energy waves. "We gotta stop the war."

"Jurisdictional issue," yawned one of the older professors, an emeritus chair-holder up way past his bedtime but enjoying his consulting role as a way to stay relevant. "As a San Francisco supervisor, that's significantly beyond the—"

"Wait, wait, wait. We go big. Real big. Ultra-fucking big." Robespierre was up and walking, a quick lap around the room. "Write this down. *Stop the war in District 4.*"

The room bobbed with heads, yes, no, maybe, tired. "People want comfort," retorted the emeritus professor. "They want politicians who can lead, who are like them, who reflect their values. Not to mention hitting the issues they can understand. Like the economy, or local services."

"But if there's any place you can get away with a bigger story, something more than taxes or trash delivery, it's San Francisco," the younger professor added.

"I'm not sure about the District 4 part," Robespierre said. She stopped in front of the television and watched the grainy images, chaotic images, undirected unspecified images, light and dark scored to the sounds of destruction. "It's misleading, like there's a war in District 4 that needs to be stopped. And there's something to be said for the blunt power of *Stop the War*. It's easier to remember. And grander. A grand vision. A grand unstoppable beautiful vision of what could be. What should be."

"I like it," murmured a dreadlocked freshman everybody thought was sleeping.

"It's not bad," assessed the younger professor.

"Stands out," the emeritus prof agreed.

"Whatever," David sniffed.

"It's right, isn't it? Doesn't it feel absolutely fucking honest?"

And though her advisory committee members were bushed and hungry and propagating an unpleasant communal odor, slightly delirious, too much time sitting in the same clothes, off-kilter from the circular arguments and extended brainstorming and concentrated mental focus, they felt it work on their spirits, sensed a little lift in the arches of their feet, detected a fresh-tasting smell perfuming the inside of their clothes.

Three days later, when they received their shipment of one

hundred thousand STOP THE WAR! door hangers, nobody remembered ordering the exclamation point. Energized by their powerfully punctuated policy position, the younger political science professor gushed to an alternative newspaper columnist over espressos that Robespierre would block city services to the federal government unless the troops came home, stop policing the Federal Building unless the troops came home, introduce legislation that called for reclaiming the Presidio from federal control unless the troops came home. The columnist pumped his fist three times when the professor left to canvas doorknobs, the headline ANARCHISTS OF THE WORLD, UNITE! bursting into his head in eighteen-point type.

That same morning, Robespierre told a columnist at the rival alternative newspaper that, if elected, she would travel on official city business to Iran to stop the war in any way she could. This columnist, an analytical journalist with daily news experience, who enjoyed teasing out offbeat ideas and either pinpointing the hidden sincerity or dissecting the ludicrousness, asked her with a straight face how exactly she would do that.

"Simple," Robespierre said, swabbing her lips with a circular tongue-mop, "I'll lie down in front of tanks."

"U.S. or Iranian?" the columnist asked.

"Both," she decided.

"What about body armor?" he asked. "Protection? An escort?"

"Not sure," Robespierre said. "Depends if the city will cover it."

The two columns hit newsstands the next Wednesday morning; by lunch, Robespierre's volunteer database had swollen from 9 to 418, her campaign website had crashed, and she'd been called by three national news programs. Her interviews were slapped on the end of nightly broadcasts, the "only in San Francisco" story intended to give viewers a break from gruesome war footage. "It's what I care about," she explained, her steadfast, serious face radiant on the television screen. "I'm fortunate enough to live in a rich city with nearly everything we could possibly need. Stopping the war is what matters. So let's stop it." The networks rolled back to smiling anchors, sitcom reruns and rumor-mongering entertainment news shows, millions of viewers disagreeing on what to think of her—naïve, prophetic, a traitor, a hero, your classic San Francisco wackjob—but registering her fortitude, the guts to take a stand.

J. Malcolm Fletcher, attorney at law, rang her doorbell at 7:30 the next morning. Having fallen asleep a few hours earlier following a rum-heavy orientation with the new batch of volunteers, Robespierre gingerly wheeled open the door, kicked pizza crusts out of the hall, and asked the guy in the trench coat if he'd like any coffee, because personally she needed a fucking vat of the stuff.

"That's fine," said Fletcher, removing his hat. "Thanks."

Robespierre took his response as a no and stuck a half-filled mug from the day before in the microwave. "So," she said, distracted by the electromagnetic hum, "what do you want?"

His flighty smile was lined with gray stubble. "A campaign donation," he said. "Thanks."

"I see." She checked her wrist where a watch would be. "Look, I gotta get going."

He shook his head. "A check," he said. "A client of mine asked me to deliver it to you. On his behalf."

A green-gray force field descended around her skull, teeming with alcohol and teslas. "Great," she managed. She noted how he held his hat upside-down with both hands, like a religious offering, perfect for catching puke if she couldn't make the trash can.

"Well," said Fletcher, his grin broadening. "That's wonderful."

Crappy luck, a roundabout talker. She couldn't put up with this for long. "I can take that for you," she offered, angling her shoulder toward the lawyer, who was antique and stooped and would be a cinch to force out the door if it came to that. "The check."

Fletcher reached into a scraped suitcase and removed a gold card the size of a lottery ticket. "For you," he announced. He held the card with both hands and presented it to Robespierre with a slight bow. There was a charm to the gesture that penetrated her defensive earthworks—the slight dip in his hips? the unwrinkling of his forehead? the lacquered fingernails?—and she took the card and returned his smile and handed him the mug of coffee from the microwave.

"Coffee," he said. "That's fine."

"Sure thing," she agreed.

He set the mug down on the counter, picked up his suitcase, and walked out the door. Robespierre followed him as far as the sofa, when her knees gave way and her head disintegrated into a billion bone fragments and she fell unconscious for seventy-six minutes, until she was awoken by hangover groans, toilets flushing, the suck of the fridge pulled open and shut. The gold card adhered to her sweaty hand, and she peeled it off and opened it:

Heard you making a stir. Long time, huh? Guess you're all grown now. Saw you're running for government, so I thought, why not win? I can always use a favor from the big cheese.

See you on the finish line,
Pop

Cavernous breathing took over her body; she pushed her back against a wall and sank. Then she found the check on the floor, all the decimal places crammed into one line.

Her phone rang, and she let it drone on until an intern picked up.

"It's for you," somebody said, and she shuffled over on her knees, receiving the handset as if it were an ancient talisman.

"What?" asked Robespierre, but the dial tone was all that was there. She stood up, suddenly white-faced and heavy, and staggered over to the kitchen.

"You OK?" asked the intern, who looked like a fifteen-year-old version of Salma Hayek.

"We got money," she drawled. "A lot."

"Cool! That's awesome!" But all Robespierre felt was emptiness and hopelessness, knowledge lost forever. "Do you want to, you know, put it in the bank?"

"Not that," she whispered. "My dad."

The intern pulled her into port, a total embrace, kneading her jerky shoulders through her sweater. "What about your dad?" the intern asked.

"Nothing," Robespierre said, and went down the hall and started the shower. She sat on the toilet with all her clothes on and dove into a stump speech practice session, reciting campaign promises mixed with out-of-tune humming, errant spray from the showerhead spritzing her face until her blouse was soaked and her hair hung like heavy rope and she finally felt the slightest bit clean.

The quiet house chipped away at her. Even with the television always on and the fresh bag of low-cal Jiffy Pop that Esmerelda heated in the microwave each night, the building felt ghostly without Marat's island rhythms, Robespierre clacking out communiqués on her computer, Esmerelda reporting on her weight loss with jubilant shouts from the bathroom scale. She screened Fanny's beloved soap operas but couldn't get past the low production values; she found reality television repulsive; athletics barbaric. She watched her collection of Paul Newman movies, but even those ran out of juice after the third or fourth screening, his gentleman's ease feeling old-fashioned and unrealistic, reminding her of her age. The phone didn't ring for months, not when Robespierre announced her run for supervisor, or when it became mathematically certain that Marat had a day or two on leave, or even when she finally paid off the last of the collections agencies, so she brought the handset down to Best Buy after work to have it tested. It went off on the first try, and she could only withstand two lonely rings before ripping the cord from the wall and charging out of the store.

In April of 2012, San Francisco unleashed a rare stretch of midsummer—dry air and fogless sun, the ocean breeze watered down to nil, Esmerelda's secretaries skipping into the shop in skirts and no jackets, prattling on about weekend trips to the beach and barbecues and baseball games. Esmerelda caught the roofless trolley down Market Street for a meeting with her bookkeeper, watching office workers dining al fresco along the sidewalk, extended loitering and stoop-sitting and milling about, bicycle traffic pouring out of the bike lanes and weaving in with top-down convertibles and open-sunroof hatchbacks. She took off her cloak for the ride back, the simple act of exposing her arms in public still a significant thrill.

The Caribbean conditions stayed high in her head for the rest of the day, nurtured by the delivery men dressed in shorts, the increased use of the vending machine by thirsty patrons, the sweat stains forming under customer armpits, the prevalence of sunglasses worn indoors, the searing glow illuminating the store's large plate glass window. "Hey, Lakshmi," she asked as closing time approached, "wanna grab a drink after quitting time? Maybe soak in a little sun?"

Lakshmi let out a shriek from the back of her throat and bolted for the bathroom.

"Worth a shot," Esmerelda muttered as electric points surged in her brain, pushing her outside into the weird heat, unable to think, falling in with the comforting flow of pedestrians down the elevator to Muni, stepping onto a hot crowded train and gripping a steel bar until they stopped moving and a conductor shooed her out, switching to BART with a team of middle-aged women through a factory line of escalators and plastic gates, teaming up to issue a semicircle of scolding glares at perfectly healthy teens who refused to give up their dirty fabric seats. She shot under the bay, through the gasp and pull of tunnel pressure changes, rattling along the faded East Bay haze amid ancient brick warehouses and the smell of rail grease until a big clump of people got off in Berkeley, leaving her and a platoon of end-of-the-line losers sleeping against the window and staring into blank space, nobody worth being around.

She got off at the next stop and stumbled into a vast parking lot, pavement the off-white of pine smoke, a fleet of bumbling cars and kids in khakis whacking their skateboards into benches. Hot wide space and distant buildings, a bland suburban stink-hole, more alone than ever.

"Help," she said to herself. She slowly sank onto her knees, but even the joy of flexing her muscles without toppling over couldn't overcome the seismic ache in her chest.

An old Chinese man hobbled beside her, carrying a pair of cigarette cartons. "You need ride?" he asked, releasing a stream of hot gasoline fumes, a couple bottles of rice wine plus whiskey.

An angel. "God yes."

"Where you go?"

"Home." But to say it hurt, there was nothing there anymore. "Scratch that. Take me somewhere close, somewhere fun. Outdoors." She checked the guy out, seven sprigs of hair twirling from the center of his grape-skin smooth brow, small pummeled eyes, a dirty tuxedo and gold pocket watch, three playing cards in his breast pocket.

"Got it!" he spurted, then pushed his hair sprigs into his pate and hustled into the parking lot, disappearing behind a row of aged minivans.

"Freak," she muttered, and headed over to the pay phone. All that remained of the phonebook was a gutted plastic casing, so she guessed on the easy-to-remember repeating digits she always associated with taxi services, 999-9999, seven squared, crazy eights, connecting with pizza delivery joints and used car dealer-ships until she ran out of quarters. Making a note to research cellphone plans, she headed back to the BART station to make herself some change when an *awooga* double-honk broke through, followed by the hard screech of metal on metal.

"Come!" the man screeched from a pop-top VW van, its front bumper freshly wrapped around a no parking sign.

"Hell no!" she called.

"I take you!" he yelled back, the exertion turning his face red and dialing up an extended watery cough that took a few moments to run out. He blinked and slapped his cheek, then kicked the van into reverse and knocked over a plastic blue Vespa, swung into drive, and zoomed over the curb and down the sidewalk. He stopped the van by bumping the pay phone, knocking the handset off the receiver and mashing the green glass into cobwebbed fragments.

"Come!" he said, pushing open the back door. Black dust sprinkled the sidewalk, followed by a hot smell of retirement home and road construction. The van was filled with piles of junk, cables and wires, screws, nails, bicycle spokes and a gold birdcage, mousetraps, a couple of rakes, what looked like an old stovepipe, a cluster of skeleton keys, light sockets and European electrical converters, a section of railroad track.

"Where'm I gonna sit?" she asked.

"Here!" He threw a tangle of extension cords to the back and pulled a flattened cardboard box onto the floor by the door, covering an explosion of silver brad fasteners. A long fall from the luxury automobiles she'd traveled in during her kitchen monarchy days, but here it was, functional transportation, eclectic if in need of cleaning, with a personable driver attached.

She slid inside. Hot as pouring tar and just as stinky. "Easy on the gas, leadfoot," she coughed as the man hopped into the driver's seat and shot out of the parking lot just as the BART police car sneaking up behind them disengaged its engine. They were three blocks away before she could blink.

"Where we headed?" she asked, deeply enjoying the opportunity for a little nonwork human conversation as well as the breeze blasting through the roof.

"Cigarette?" he responded, and she saw he was already working on three—one in the ashtray, one in the cup holder, a red quarter filter stubbed between his teeth.

"Where we headed?" she repeated.

"You feel lucky!" he deduced, his sawed-off eyes popping pink in the rearview.

"Maybe a little," she acknowledged, hard to ignore the terrific weather or the intimate enclosed quarters with another human being.

"Ah!" He jerked around an idling school bus, then zipped back three lanes for a right turn and jabbed his index finger in the air. "Must capitalize!" A chorus of honking consumed his skittish laughter, followed by the triple wail of en masse police pursuit.

"Stop the car," she decided. "Our luck's over with."

"Almost there!" he responded, and floored it, flying through intersections and converting impossible toe-twisting turns, speeding through alleys and parking garages and short patches of sidewalk, cavorting through a playground, then banking under the freeway and into open space, the purple bay and a field of kites silhouetted by the blasting sun, which hovered across the Golden Gate like an alien mothership. "Nice moves," she admitted. "Ever consider getting into the high-end butter delivery biz?"

"Here!" he shouted, then cranked the van into a donut, head-shattering squeaks and the smell of extreme friction and the uncertain lean unique to worn tire rubber. A hard knock and another quick spin and the car stopped, the brake crunched. The door slipped open and a punch of sunlight carried her free.

She looked around groggily. Men from another era loitered outside a white stadium entrance, decked out in tracksuits and hair grease and plain white T-shirts stained with unhealthy foods, quiet obsession hollowing their faces in what could only be mad-ness or addiction. "I guess I've seen worse," she shrugged. "How much do I owe you?"

"Hundred dollars!" he shouted, firing up a pair of cigarettes.

"Kinda steep," she observed, but the temperature scrambled it, it was pushing ninety out, unreal hot for the Bay Area, mer-cury boiling, the point where facts became irrelevant and

Esmerelda was unwilling to fight. She threw the cash at him as fast as she could dig it out.

"Lucky day!" he hollered after her. "Bet big!"

She limped ahead to a ticket window staffed by a wide-assed woman who smelled like old government buildings. "Where am I?" she pouted.

The woman pointed up to the sign over the ticket window, a horse in full gallop under drool-blue lettering: GOLDEN GATE FIELDS. "Five dollar general, ten dollar VIP."

"Horse racing," Esmerelda noted, feeling her day melt into nonsense like clocks on tree branches, half expecting to see juggling penguins and flying toasters and Jay Leno dressed in drag. It was more fun than she'd had in years.

"Five dollar general, ten dollar VIP," the woman repeated.

"What's the difference?"

"Better seating, better view, better luck."

"VIP," Esmerelda decided, five bucks extra, a small price to pay for an invaluable omen of fortune.

The VIP seats were nearly empty, a couple of blazered businessmen tipping silver flasks, an old bearded man puffing a pipe, a small group of slick-skinned teens decked out in Cal Swimming sweatshirts. She parked herself on the lowest row by the aisle, close enough to hear conversations without being too pushy, then unfolded her racing form and checked off her picks in the random scattershot manner that had characterized her standardized test-taking as a child.

She watched the jockeys ride their steeds to the track. Such small men, bird heads and long muscles crammed into gaudy skintight outfits, like bullfighters or Elvis Presley. They were wrangling their horses into the gates for the first heat when the driver wandered into the grandstands, took the seat beside her, and handed her a beer. "Bet yet?" he asked.

"Got my card filled out," she said. "How'd you get in here?"

He snatched the racing form from her lap and folded it into

thirds, then slipped the sheet neatly into his breast pocket. "How much you bet?"

"Oh, enough to make it interesting."

"Hundred dollars each bet," he suggested. A ridiculous sum, but she was in a new world in terms of debt-free income these days, a land of first-class jet travel and designer key chains and several rings of servants requiring a union steward and a dedicated parking lot, with no one worth spending it on. Here on a sunny pseudodate with a trustworthy and strangely perceptive man. Might as well live it up.

She paid a visit to the ATM and placed the wagers, returning with a stack of receipts and a tray of cocktails which they consumed in heavy silence as the horses began circling, toned animal bodies at the height of execution, extending their long brown beautiful muscles in rippling tides, jostling and repositioning and bobbing like perfectly balanced machines until the finish, when they came in all wrong, out of order and out of time, the atrocious results announced in incontrovertible digital numbers. Her new friend smiled, and she did too, slugging back her liquor and sighing delightedly.

Sunlight dimmed, the temperature dropped a few degrees. The liquor globbed in her; it had been so long since she'd gone out for a drink with someone, a wonderful feeling, fibers loosening behind a soft even heat. "How bad is it?" she asked her partner, who was starting to look like a young Paul Newman after a tray of whiskey sours.

"Very bad. Almost all gone."

"That's fine," she said, and it felt so good to say it, there was no price you could put on this.

They watched one last heat, a lap and a half packed with nine horses, the jockeys' neon jerseys scrumming through pitch like designer M&Ms. Whips slapped rhythmically against rumps, the chestnut animals packed and separated in soothing patterns, creating the classic, reassuring cadence of hooves pounding turf.

Colored shirts cycled through the pack, interior shuffles and position jostling broken up by exotic breakaways, a worst-to-first sprint, neck and neck and neck down the stretch, the hundred-odd hardcore gamblers in the grandstands actually making a little noise. A photo finish decided it, coming down to head bobs and flared nostrils for a thrilling if muddled Hollywood ending.

The last finger of pink left the sky, and she was ready. "OK, Mr. Magoo," Esmerelda announced. "Let's skedaddle."

He did not respond, instead running a pencil over a slip of paper and tugging at his seven hair sprigs, periodically slapping his cheek and snorting hard. "Hey!" she yelled. "Time to boogie!"

"Soup feathers," he murmured.

"Never was much into the Marx Brothers," she said, "but if you're inviting me for a double feature, the answer's yes."

He leaned forward and showed her the receipt, four numbers in a row checked off, her hundred-dollar bet. "Soup feathers," he repeated shakily, the red veins in his eyes running hot.

"I don't speak Chinese," she retorted.

He grabbed her arm and yanked her out of her seat, something which hadn't happened since elementary school and thus left her too floored to scream or fight back or do anything other than stumble along after his firm lead, up a short set of stairs to the ticket window, where he handed in the receipt.

A beehived woman ticked off the numbers with a blue pen and pressed a button on her desk. "This is yours?" she asked.

"Yes," Esmerelda confessed.

"You'll have to come up to the office," she said.

Two slovenly rent-a-cops took her through a series of locked doors and up an elevator to an ancient press room, which stank of smoke and perspiration and was populated by slack-jawed middle-aged broadcasters hop-talking into radio headsets. They sped her into a shag-carpeted lobby and then a tall, narrow office lined in hard plastic the same blue as the sign out front, a white-haired man in a plaid suit behind an empty desk, against the wall a young woman holding a camera and a burnt-eyed black man wearing a porkpie hat.

The white-haired man came out from behind the desk and shook her hand vigorously. "Congratulations, congratulations," he said.

"You're welcome," she responded. "So what's the story?"

"We want to hold a press conference," the man said. "In, say—" checking his Timex "—twenty minutes."

"What for?" she asked, trying to decode her buddy's code word, soup and feathers, stew and hair, chowder and fur, maybe horse names, until her eyes fixed on a Parimutuel Betting Instruction Handbook framed cover on the wall, a dirty rag-worn thing at least fifty years old, the words "exacta" and "daily double" and "superfecta" popping in cartoon thought balloons.

"Your superfecta payout," the black man said, and handed her a check from the land of make-believe.

"We'll use a larger check for the press conference, like golf tournaments," the white-haired man said. "The director of the board will be there. The jockeys, of course. We have calls into the mayor's office. Be sure to set your VCR!"

She felt the hammock of alcohol collapse and take trees down with it. More money, more questions, more reasons for her daughter to screw with her and her son to hate her, neither one taking her back on the merits. "No," she said, "I'm leaving." She folded the check and held it delicately in her hand, a nuclear grenade.

A clench came over the white-haired man, sudden simultaneous contractions, and then he frosted over, blue ice etching his eyes, a face riveted on survival. "We recommend that you speak with a financial advisor," he began. "I can put you in touch with—"

"Do you need me to sign something?" she asked, and the black man held out a clipboard and a pen.

"A photo for our Hall of Fame," the white-haired man pushed, waving the camerawoman into position. "Please."

"Blow off," Esmerelda retorted, then held the clipboard in front of her face and barreled past the clicking camera to the retro lobby, the press room sweatbox and the dying elevator and her escort's van parked right out front.

He drove her home carefully, stopping cleanly at all the lights and smoking slow, thoughtful puffs. "What do I owe you?" she asked when they arrived home.

"Already pay," he said with a triple-drag on his cigarette.

"Well, thanks," she said, running back over their evening together, witnessing simple physical grace and fresh air nicely blurred with booze. Only one thing missing. "You wanna come in?" she asked, slapping her hip for friskiness.

"Ha!" he said, and tooted the horn twice before slamming around the corner back at standard ball-shredding speed.

She thought about waving after him but decided against it, then went up to her room and unfolded the check in her hand. Locked alone in a vault with mountains of cash, the loneliness of it burying her alive.

She deposited the money in her checking account and went back to the track twice a week, set on losing and accomplishing it through impossible combinations, the longest, dumbest bets on the books, occasionally converting a wager or two but in general achieving a pleasant burn rate. A quiet, essential pain that started scraping toward atonement. Sitting in the first row in the VIP section, eavesdropping and sipping liquor, fog and sun slashing the sky. She made friends with the ticket ladies, got to know the bartender on a first-name basis, bought rounds for the hardcore regulars and complained about their bad luck together, even made nice with the track CEO and took in the occasional heat from his box. Far more welcoming than her house had ever been, the closest thing to home she'd known.

Peaceful, perfect afternoons flushing away a fortune while horses ran in circles, the music of their hoofbeats cleansing like cool summer showers.

❧

District 4 was a conservative district in the San Francisco political landscape, a fog-packed residential area with ample parking and quiet avenues, clean children, clean schools, clean parks. Violet Chin was the incumbent supervisor, a centrist, fond of power pantsuits and dangly earrings and a rapid arm-swinging walking pace, a mother and pet owner, formerly a competitive skier. She was a UC Berkeley graduate, a bit of a hippie philosophically, having gone to her share of Grateful Dead concerts back in the day, but above all a realist, a take-charge woman who appreciated that there were individuals in the world who would not snap to it and accede when a neutral third party politely requested they give up the nukes; who understood that some people were bad and needed to be spanked or at least scared to shape up; and in any event there was no reason to discuss national issues like military policy on the local level, because what the hell were they going to do about it, pass a meaningless resolution? She'd won the election four years ago on pledges to repave the potholes, improve bus service, and renovate the schools, and she'd delivered on most of her promises. Violet drove a purple Corvette, held a master's in botany, and owned a popular flower shop on the corner of 21st and Irving. A few years back friends had tried to pin her with the nickname "Chinese Lily," but it hadn't stuck.

"She's lame," Robespierre whined to her executive committee, this time gathering at one of the nicer downtown restaurants, both to be seen and because their recent fundraising spike permitted it.

"She's absolutely safe," declared the professor emeritus. "She's the establishment candidate. Which means you have to stand for change."

"She's kinda cool," remarked Kelly, a new intern who spent rush hours twirling a STOP THE WAR! sign along Lincoln Way. "I mean, she's amazing in a half-pipe."

"We have to do something," Robespierre said. All the options in the world in front of her, and the money made it real.

"It really depends what kind of leader you want to be," observed the emeritus professor, who was feeling at home between the fine wine and upscale environment, nearly as comfortable as the faculty club. "The conventional route is to come up through committees, earning your way to prized positions through seniority."

"I want to be the leader who stops the war," she said, watching the committee warm to this, their bodies shifting in her direction, somewhat incredulous but in love with the idea, the balls.

"Typically you'd start with a personal introduction," the younger professor said, "because people want to know who they're voting for. But you're weak there. So I think you dive right into the issue and overwhelm them with emotion."

"You have to provide the spiritual genesis for your journey," David continued, and she had it, the flash point, thousands of withered souls and a lifetime's supply of air strikes compressed into a dot on her forehead.

Their first mailers were composed of photos of dead and dying soldiers, charred corpses, leaking body bags. Pictures of funerals and memorial services, framed grade school portraits of the deceased, wives and children clutching hands, paltry floral arrangements. Blood figured everywhere, matted dirty burgundy blood, bloody clotted bandages, blood tarring hands and faces, blood seeping through uniforms, dripping from eyeballs, blood washing cavities where limbs should be. Body parts scattered across sand, wedding rings on severed fingers. Beaten helmets balanced on rifle tops. Flattened Iranian houses flying fresh American flags. Blood trickling from rippled, screaming mouths, missing teeth, missing flesh, high-resolution shots printed on glossy cardstock slipped into the daily mail haul.

And what happened when children came home from school and saw this carnage on the kitchen counter, when they asked their parents what was wrong with those men, why were they

bleeding, were they sad, did it hurt? Did parents shred the mailers and flush the scraps down the toilet where that crap belonged,
being totally inappropriate for kids and adults too, worse than an
R-rated movie, they didn't ask for this garbage, all they'd ever
done was pay their taxes and work hard and keep their nose clean
so why this in their mailbox? Did they place searing telephone
calls and send vitriolic emails to Robespierre Van Twinkle's campaign headquarters and ask what kind of made-up name was that
anyway, was this a joke? Did they rant online and demand apologies, inundating Violet Chin with cash? Or did they dig deeper
when their shock simmered down; did they reflect and metabo-
lize and explain to their kids that there was a war going on in the
Middle East, the United States had attacked a fundamentalist
regime that had fired missiles at Israel, denied the Holocaust,
threatened to turn North America into a quenchless fireball, and
gotten started by setting the podium at the United Nations
ablaze? That the Iranian people had revolted and hanged President Ghodrat Mohtashemi from the Azadi Tower, deposed the
rest of his regime, and apologized at length, but the boots were
already on the ground, the tank brigades rolling toward Tehran,
the emergency budget authorized, the oil fields within range?
How seven hundred thousand American soldiers were fighting a
war already won, and losing it, and dying?

Frozen over the kitchen table with a curious child nibbling
graham crackers beside them, these passions swirled raw.

Stop the War!

Robespierre's campaign email blasted a video the following
week: desert footage with no music, no voiceover, no intro slate,
tricking many viewers into thinking the wrong version was up,
they'd served up the nightly news by accident, the omnipresent
Iranian massacre splattering onscreen from different angles
until they realized it was a war footage compilation and that was
the point. The narration was edited out so the battlefield filled
their speakers and headphones, tracer fire zipping across living
rooms, detonations behind desks, distant screams in the center

of their brains. A bazooka connected with a helicopter, the rotor stripping off and shearing a platoon of infantrymen, clouds of sand scratching the screen. Bearded men dropped flaming soda bottles into tank hatches. The sky dark with metal. Panning through a hospital tent, armless Americans on thin mats on the ground, desiccated Americans twisted into mannequin poses, seemingly unhurt Americans drawing pained, broken breaths. Some ranting and muttering from the wounded came through, but most of the agony was muffled and internal, sundered American lives reaching for dignity in their most terrified moments.

Then Robespierre appeared in a somber charcoal suit, devoid of jewelry, minimal makeup, her widely spaced eyes imposing calm through the lens, shiny lips hanging a notch open, hair drawn back in a high ponytail. Lines etched into her forehead strained red.

"I'm Robespierre Van Twinkle, candidate for supervisor in District 4," she said flatly. "Join me to stop the war. Thank you." The slogan filled the screen and disappeared.

TO: vantwinklem@us.army.gov
FROM: robespierre@stopthewar!.org
SUBJECT: staying alive, campaign, etc
DATE: Monday, October 20, 2012 8:36 AM

hey, hope you're still alive & kickin. they showed footage from the raid on tabriz last night on the news. anderson cooper got killed there, you know the guy from cnn? shot through the head on camera. cripes. i couldn't find anything about fighting in qom on the news or the net, so i assume it's pretty calm & you're doing ok. but i can't shake the feeling you're on some supersecret commando raid & you're not allowed to talk about it, so whatever you do try to keep all your blood in your body ok?

the campaign's going pretty well. the videos and mailers are getting noticed, lots of controversy, but i have no idea if it's working. we're way behind in the polls but i'm not that worried. i think my candidacy needs to grow inside people for a while, to make them think about this war & what it's really about.

i opened up a brokerage account for you with some of dad's cash. risky & high-growth as requested. don't blow it all on strippers when you get back.

-R

TO: robespierre@stopthewar!.org
FROM: vantwinklem@us.army.gov
SUBJECT: RE: staying alive, campaign, etc
DATE: Monday, October 20, 2012 23:48:36

Reenactments. Hire some homeless people and stage skirmishes in the street. That'll get them talking. And thinking.

Fuck Anderson Cooper. What a dipshit.

Halloween morning was warm and breezy, the sky clear as a raindrop. At 10 AM a small fleet of motorboats bounced through the Ocean Beach surf. The transports rode over sliding waves and puttered into the shallows, then swung parallel to shore and held steady as best they could while ninety ragtag men splashed overboard. Holding toy guns over their heads, the men looked generally military but less professional, with most out of shape and wearing mismatched fatigues and certainly not charging ahead for a power landing in the proud tradition of the United States Armed Forces. Instead they trudged and twirled through hammering breakers, shrieking and coughing up seawater and mouthing off about how fucking cold it was. Several men launched into incoherent ranting accompanied by spitting; two emitted long brain-busting high-pitched whines. They were older than most active soldiers, but similarly unshaven and nervous, chemically dependent, battle-realistic tremors in their muscles. Eventually they made it to the beach, where several kissed the ground and a few began crying and one took a leak in the direction of a frolicking schnauzer. A bullhorn announcement interrupted, and the men assembled in three loose formations, shaking out their ill-fitting surplus-store boots and the plastic helmets bought in bulk from the costume shop on Haight Street, every one of them uncomfortable in wet underwear. They waited for a few minutes while a video team tested the live feed, trying to remember what came next.

"Move out!" the bullhorn crackled. Unsavory language ripped through the assembled forces and, after a few minutes of complaining, they began walking east. It was a grim start, their heavy heels dragging over seaside dunes, their pants accruing a dark mud liner, sand sneaking into their mouths and socks, the cold progressing from shock to body shivers, the total effect being to devastate élan and stoke hearty agreement that this was a ding-dong clusterfuck of epic proportions. Eventually they piddled over the Great Highway to Santiago Street, which was cordoned off with police barricades and made for an unimpeded if slightly uphill stroll. They stamped their boots and shook the grit off their clothes, rolling along in a disinterested mosey until another bullhorn transmission reminded them of their orders and they grudgingly peeled open their backpacks and lobbed flowers onto the sidewalks, planted flags on lawns and parked cars, pulled on bottles of whiskey hidden beneath their flak jackets. Passersby gathered and cheered sedately, assuming a costume parade, a war memorial, a movie filming, some weird combination. The troops perked up with the attention, picking up the pace and waving, tipping their helmets to ladies, whistling and passing out cigars. For a few blocks they marched with honor, long purposeful strides taking them in the direction of downtown.

Mothers pushing strollers, dog walkers, cyclists, repairmen, letter carriers, café dwellers, telecommuters—when they saw the street shut off, the rows of damp ragtag soldiers cracking jokes and carrying toy rifles, they came and watched and called their friends. Television crews jostled for position at intersections; Mexicans pushing ice cream trucks materialized and did some business. Police officers observed from the sidelines, reviewing the soldiers for familiar criminal faces.

The troops pushed past the swelling crowd, their shot of morale started to falter. They'd been drafted from a long-term hotel in the Tenderloin, enticed with cash money and new clothes, and most hadn't hiked this far in years without a break. They were not reinvigorated by the young women picking up the soldiers' flowers and tucking them behind their ears, and were flat-out annoyed by the kids from Lincoln High jumping the crowd-control gates and walking alongside them in mock military stride. The formations loosened as they lumbered into the sun, stragglers from the first group dropping into the second, some breaking ranks to find a liquor store, some stopping to sit on the curb and rest a while. Three caught a bus and went home. They'd already been paid half up front anyway, a solid day at the office.

Ninety mock soldiers dwindled to eighty, seventy-five, seventy-three.

The procession slowed to a country stroll where Santiago bent steeper at 40th Avenue. The men cursed and spat, spat and cursed, half-English rants buffeted with exhaustion. In the last platoon, a bottle broke against the pavement. This was far enough, they were out of juice; they hadn't been trained or built up or given decent supplies; and anyhow what was their objective, what the fuck was the point?

At 10:45 a trash can between the second and third units started steaming. A police officer was jogging toward it when a thunderclap boomed, men hit the deck, children cried out, and chaos arrived. In the smoke troops lit firecrackers as instructed and fired their fake weapons at each other, civilians, police officers, the skies. Noises churned together, crossfire pops from weapons, war cries, hissing steam, cops' emergency reaction shouts, the slaps of sprinting shoes. Mothers grabbed their children from strollers and pulled their shirts over their noses. Normally sedate spectators started flailing, shoving, and throwing elbows, trampling and kicking. Car windows shattered, sounding alarms. Mist billowed through the avenue, a tipped column of white smoke bleeding into alleys and cross streets. Some in the crowd gave up and lay on the ground, unable to react; some broke into homes and searched for knives, shovels, vases, heavy chairs. A plurality ran like hell, fingers firing across cellphone keypads. A news chopper dipped down for a closer look, cameras rolling, wind-whipping blades impressing the beat of war. Among the uniformed militants, a handful began to bawl—even though the attack had been detailed in their contract, the briefing, the reminder phone call, the predawn briefing, they'd forgotten about it, or it was worse than expected—while the real vets among them took cover behind parked cars and started planning exit strategies.

Then the liquid hit them. Some kind of magenta juice on their clothes and hair and skin, fired from invisible artillery, salt-flavored shrapnel dripping down their faces. It landed in lines, painless, easy, discoloring contact lenses and staining socks. The sounds of pumped water, hidden sprinklers shooting red tracer fire, painless bullets blanked by shock. The crowd ran calling for medical attention, shelter, a goddamn explanation, but instead found unrepentant Van Twinkle volunteers a block away handing out campaign literature and coupons for free dry cleaning.

On Santiago a cluster of troops fought through it, baring

shanks hidden in their socks, lengths of hard plastic pipe, a crowbar. Bottles flew through the air, at the smoke, at cops, and then the police backup units arrived and it ended. Cops flung soldiers' faces onto asphalt, clubbed necks, chained wrists, kicked knees, shoved punched disarmed, threw them in the paddy wagon and hauled them off to jail.

Five minutes later Robespierre's campaign released a statement and the city caught on fire.

Robespierre Van Twinkle was incarcerated in short order, fervently booed on her perp walk. Bail was not posted. Her money had run out.

She won no endorsements, a condemnation in the *Chronicle*, dismissive remarks from Violet Chin, an ocean of hate mail and scathing online chatter, rebukes from mothers and fathers who claimed to want her corrosive gimmicks gone—she didn't respect the law and had ruined a good outfit and scared the crap out of the kids and besides what could she do about that war anyway? When did lawlessness become a virtue? How's inciting a riot for bad judgment? Why give the conservatives more ammunition, a left-wing lunatic soiling the Progressive name?

But within many homes they thought it out, the tension turned, and they knew she was right, and they were ashamed for not having the courage to bring it home like she did.

The guards updated Robespierre with poll results every hour on Election Day, falsely reporting a blowout loss to fuck with the bitch. Her life took on apocalyptic qualities; she saw it in red and black insects that flashed on the insides of her eyes; all that money thrown away and nobody changed; a wasteful, painful exercise purely for her own entertainment. At least she'd grown as a person, she tried to console herself, but all that stuck with her was the futility of it all, the impossible planetary inertia, how little there was worth getting out of bed for.

She slept in angry bunches, wriggling through demented dreams involving blood-soaked Iranian battlefields and whirling red wheelbarrows and driving Violet Chin's Corvette off a pier into the sea. At some point the door to her cell clanged open, that lawyer guy was there, somebody was telling her something, whispers chewed her brain. "You again," Robespierre mumbled. "How bad was it?"

"Ma'am, it's a pleasure." J. Malcolm Fletcher removed his hat and handed her a bouquet of roses.

"This some kind of asshole joke?"

"They're for you." He gyrated his head and bunched up his lips, a look of conquered emotion, fighting back tears or pain or last night's undercooked chicken pesto. "Allow me to offer my congratulations," he allowed.

This set off laughter, loads of it, at the absurd situation and the preposterousness of the claim and this guy's asshole charm, not only dressed like a 1950s gumshoe but playing the part too. Briefly she admired his acting. "Blow off," she giggled.

"Certainly." Even as a cold glass of water. "May I buy you breakfast?"

"Go for it. Got a muffin with a file baked in?"

A guard appeared in her field of vision, microfiber mustache and shaved head. "Bail's posted," he reported, "you can go."

"What?"

"Correct," the lawyer said. "Additionally, I thought you would be interested in this morning's newspaper." He passed over the *Chronicle* late edition, a block of election results with one circled in marker.

VAN TWINKLE 47%—CHIN 44%

"No shit." Color vacated Robespierre's face as errata compiled in her head, to-do lists and program initiatives, applications of the unbelievable.

"All right, you won," the guard said. "Now get out."

"I won." This was the only fact that mattered, barred windows and jail jumpsuits nothing compared to the truth of victory. At age twenty-two, fresh out of college, she'd fucking won a city election.

She wanted to kiss J. Malcolm Fletcher more than anything on earth, and did with a full-tongue treatment that got the whole cellblock whooping.

The lawyer dabbed his face with a handkerchief and replaced his fedora on his head. "Shall we go?" he asked. He looked over his glasses at Robespierre and was struck silent by her slivered eyebrows, bleak mouth, pores clogged from nerves. She was shutting down, eyes sinking gumballs, cheeks the color of skim milk. He stepped over and caught her before she fell, then helped her hobble out with a hand from the guard, her jailhouse slippers dragging with a war's worth of fatigue.

NAPOLEON

He had no scruples and he had no manners. He was ill-bred, as was shown in his relations with women, of whom he had a low opinion. His language, whether Italian or French, lacked distinction, finish, correctness, but never lacked saliency or interest. The Graces had not presided over his birth, but the Fates had. He had a magnificent talent as stage manager and actor . . . He could cajole in the silkiest tones, could threaten in the iciest, could shed tears or burst into violence, smashing furniture and bric-a-brac when he felt such actions would produce the effect desired.

—CHARLES HAZEN,
The French Revolution and Napoleon

I found the crown of France lying on the ground, and I picked it up with my sword.

—NAPOLEON BONAPARTE

She say she love me, say she want me around
I put up my dukes
But that woman done break me down

Werewolf became famous in the months after Katrina, lying on a flooded-out Buick in St. Bernard Parish and singing to the sky. For months he was ignored, hollered to, shot at, and busted while he sang hymns and love songs, doo-wopped and bluesed.

His voice was reedy and soft with depression, a man with everything already lost but pushing on anyhow, not really sure why.

He appeared with a bottle of vodka when the moon lifted over the horizon at night. He wore pink plastic sunglasses, a red fez, a checked tie that barely reached his third rib, crusty overalls, an eggshell-blue velour jacket with yellow zebra stripes, cheap flip-flops. Spun out and wiry, he groped down a gravel driveway and eased onto the hood of an abandoned '96 Skylark. He waited until he felt the moonlight break on his brow, a slash of warmth across his forehead that unzipped his mouth and delivered his lyrics, holding notes for eons, music without breathing, the only slight breaks in sound coming on the quarter hour when he twisted sideways for a slug of vodka. By the time the moon went down he was wasted with tears, his voice strong and terrible. He always finished with "Amazing Grace," then rolled off the hood and passed out in the backseat.

He became an attraction when Tiny Jake Haddox started playing with him. Air-conditioning unit salesman by day and jazz drummer by night, Tiny Jake lost his house in the hurricane, then his job, then his band said they were moving to Houston and he wasn't invited. He started drinking all day and all night, until his wife took off for Canada and he moved on to drugs. A month later he was driving through the abandoned blocks of St. Bernard Parish, shooting out windows and smoking PCP-dipped cigs two at a time when he heard the lonesome call come to him from a driveway, the saddest, scrawniest thing he'd ever heard, bloated with grief, a dirge to bury them all.

He pulled over, sipped the froth off the man's vodka, and set up his drums.

When the people trickled back they didn't ask questions. *Ragtag bopop a boom ba husss* filled the driveway once the bulldozers quit for the day. *Poppoppoppalopppalop yah* they tore out dry rot, hauled scrap, painted, and upholstered. *Spewy de leelee shambam babababam* they drove home from night jobs working security and fast food, cat burglary, fucking. Occasional potshots whizzed

over the Buick's bow, intending to miss and accomplishing it as
the man in the blue jacket was thin as a twig and near impossible
to hit keeled on his back. His voice hung by a stitch, dry and
trebly and a little flat on the high notes, but his words came true
like bombs and bridges, the despair caught in his tremolo, and
people understood how it helped carve out their home. After a
few weeks they stopped messing with him altogether; the music
was part of the city's fabric, a train rolling through the night.

> *It ain't the rain 'pon my shoulders*
> *Or the world hangin' round my head*
> *But when she pushed me*
> *Out that window*
> *Ain't a thing she coulda said*

On the first anniversary of Katrina, a reporter found them
assembled in the driveway under a waxing crescent, the singer
splayed out and cornhole drunk, Tiny Jake using brushes on one
of their slower numbers, a melancholy tune that usually came
on late in the night when the man on the Buick was two-thirds
out and falling.

> *Hiss hiss*
> *That's what I get for a kiss?*
> *Why not slap my face?*
> *Why not split my lip?*
> *If you won't have me*
> *Stab me*
> *Because I ain't here no more*

Warbling and scattered, the words came like a sacred spell.
Then he launched into "Amazing Grace," slithered into the backseat, and punched down the locks. The reporter caught Tiny Jake
while he was packing up his cymbals, a doobie stuck in his lips.
   "Excuse me," the reporter said. "What was that?"

Tiny Jake glared at her. It was the first time anyone had spoken to him at the driveway.

"Can you tell me about the music? How long have you been playing here? And why?"

He loaded the rest of his drum set into the trunk as she repeated her questions. The presence of her voice felt profane. He climbed into his truck and started the engine, but she stood in his way with both hands up like a traffic cop, a pushy, bitchy move that kind of turned him on. He rolled down his window.

"It's jus' our thing. Ain't nothin to say. Come, play. Tha's it."

"How did you two start up?" she asked.

"Ask him," he said, nodding to the decrepit Skylark's backseat, the stench in the sealed chamber palpable a few yards away. "Werewolf here come out with the moon and sing to his woman. I jus' play drums."

When Tiny Jake came by the next night, he had to lay on the horn to part the crowd. The street was stopped up, the sidewalks overrun with folding chairs and blankets. People chugged cans of beer, tossed footballs, smoked cigarettes, laughed on cellphones, scratched dogs, threw garbage in the bushes, tickled kids. Combating subwoofers birthed wet, heavy bass lines. The aroma of fried chicken mingled with the night's mildewed heat. Some kind of fucking picnic, he thought, some kind of disrespect.

The driveway was lit up like a car dealership, stuffed with people and hot. Reporters encircled him as he stepped onto the street, capturing exclusive shots of his raised middle finger. "Shithogs," he whispered, then pulled his snare out of the truck bed and set it up on the driveway.

He started back to the truck, but the rest of his drums were already floating toward him, portaged by a band of twelve-year-old boys. Somebody handed him a Corona. He heard Teddy Pendergrass on the sound system, watched an acrobatic one-handed football reception. The journalists receded. He cracked open the beer and watched a Chinese girl in a tank top blow him a kiss.

Suddenly it was the best day he'd had in years.

A fat slit of moonlight washed in from the east, creeping over portable Dumpsters and decimated homes, water-sunk land. The crowd hushed. Ten minutes slugged by. Tiny Jake tightened his skins and finished his beer and wondered what his wife was doing. He'd last seen her three months ago from under a bar-stool, high heels kicking aside beer cans and stomping toward the exit, prattling on about Vancouver. He couldn't really remember, it might have been Montreal, he'd been in a bind then, eight sheets to the wind and then some, drowned in Jack Daniels, his rhythm off for weeks. He looked over at his truck, technically half of it still hers, insurance past due and a leaky transmission but there when you needed it worst. Kinda like Werewolf, he thought, sticking around.

The crowd murmured. Network engineers repositioned satellite uplinks. A girl ran up to the Skylark and tapped her finger on the windshield. Then a crash in the back, a woman's oof, Werewolf's fez bobbing over a field of craned heads.

"I smell Carnegie Hall tonight!" Werewolf called. "Where you kitty-cats been all my life?" He lurched down a rapidly opening corridor toward the car, postured like a crunched telephone pole and groping. When he got to the Skylark he pulled a bottle of Uncle Joe's vodka from his pants, uncapped it, and chugged. Then he sneezed into his hand and parked his caboose on the hood. "So many of you came out, shit. Feel like I should ask if you got any requests."

Utter silence. Responding felt wrong; they didn't know his repertoire, his range, how serious he was. The quiet held for a minute, until a sloshed insurance adjustor suggested "When the Levee Breaks," Led Zeppelin, in C minor.

"Gotta be an asshole to ask for that one," Werewolf said. "But a nice tune, used to hear it on the radio all the time out in San Fran. We'll lose the power chords. Maestro?"

Tiny Jake put drumstick to head in the approximate pace of the one Led Zeppelin song he knew from his wife playing it all the time, "Going to California," until he realized the song didn't have much if anything for a drumbeat and was too slow for Werewolf's vibe. He threw it all out and went free flow like usual, the line coming out cresting and punchy, with long gaps for improvisation. He worked the cymbals over easy, toe-tapped the kick, closed his eyes, and felt Werewolf sipping his vodka and unloading melody. The whole street cottoned to it, he realized later when he saw the video and the crowd sobbing to Werewolf's undone lyrics, the cameras flashing like a swarm of lightning bugs, the music holding over everything but a growling dog somewhere. Wolf hummed through the parts he didn't know, and the lyrics he remembered he didn't go buck nasty on, didn't push it down to empty. The song came together stark and broken, mucked up like a pigpen, fitting the souls of New Orleans snug as new socks.

Five months later they were the opening act at the Comeback Mardi Gras, crowds packed in like stock cattle and crying arduously when their encore ended. Over brunch the next morning they inked an eye-popping record contract, celebrating with Sazeracs and mimosas and a spontaneous jam session, beating forks and spoons on the table, the diners at Commander's Palace supplying lyrics Werewolf wouldn't sing during daytime. Videos of their driveway duets went viral, streamed across the planet, played as slow songs at proms and formals and later remixed into club dance numbers. Fan websites materialized; Led Zeppelin's lawyers sent menacing letters demanding royalties. Tiny Jake went whole days without thinking about his wife.

They didn't talk to each other, Werewolf and Tiny Jake. They made joint decisions on song selection, financial planning, tour dates, cover art, distribution strategies—but too much was caught in their deadeye feel, knowing the holes in each cadence, rim shots tied to huffed breaths, the serene emptiness that filled their music. It couldn't be wrecked with words. So Werewolf kept away from Jake's scent and Jake steered clear of the ratty fez, and it was only on stage that they came together, distant strangers partnered on a macadam driveway, their agents fighting over points in day-long meetings downtown.

On the Buick went platinum before the first week was out, in a year when industry analysts posited that there was no point to recording music anymore with all the piracy; artists should play live venues only, with jacked-up ticket prices and the full complement of overpriced band merchandise. The blind man and his sheep flew off record shop racks and into computers, the lowlight cover photo of them knocking out a tune on the abandoned city's driveway jacking into hearts, pity, wallets. The moon broke the sky like an eyelid, the vodka bottle digitally removed.

Word spread that Werewolf had made the entire album from the hood of the Skylark, he'd towed the vehicle to the Music Shed on Euterpe Street and recorded his vocals in the garage. He only sang when the moon was out, he could hold a note for ten minutes. He ate bats and pissed puss and drank vodka like water. He said he was blind but didn't carry a cane, didn't have a seeing-eye dog, walked straight down the street like the sun showed the way. The rumors crawled across radio shows and gossip columns, festered in internet chat rooms, selling magic and albums by the crate.

Werewolf moved out of the Buick and into Marriott hotels, top floor corner pocket, two adjoining rooms, the most space to himself he'd had in his life. Pay-per-view porn played all day while he slept, his dusk wakeup call consisting of fake orgasms and ass slaps. A stack of room service sandwiches passed for dinner, accompanied by the entire contents of the minibar taken straight, no ice. He wore the same wretched outfit, never washed, the desperate getup pilfered from a St. Vincent de Paul store after Katrina and still the only clothes to his name. Every few weeks he called a disconnected phone number and pulled on his earlobes, then fell onto one of his four beds like dirty laundry.

They toured for a year. Tiny Jake's agent wanted arenas but Werewolf's agent said clubs, so they settled on stages and charged ludicrously. They dubbed the tour Moonrise, with a great jelly orb of a satellite and a padded Buick for Werewolf to lie on and cases of cheap vodka, dump truckloads of gravel, as close as could be gotten to St. Bernard Parish without all the unprofitable downside. The tour was noted for Werewolf's mephitic smell, his extreme tardiness, the variability of the start time, the nights cancelled without explanation, building a reputation as the least reliable ticket in town. Because when Werewolf's agent had insisted that the shows correspond with the lunar calendar there had been big pushback, stage policies and union contracts and blue laws to consider, and he'd had to settle for a floating start time but the show ending by 2 AM no matter what. Tiny Jake could only riff a solo for so long before the crowd rumbled angry, streamed for the ticket booth, called for refunds, and booked.

Tiny Jake knew it wasn't star bullshit, a wacked-out trip or too few flowers in his trailer, his name not in big enough lights. Part of Werewolf was wrong, everyone knew that, but Jake guessed it was viler than they thought, something about a woman that gnawed tears from him and made him worship the moon like some alley cat or fucked-up Aztec. Bullets from his past ridged under those sunglasses, crooked his walk. That vanquished voice: the man was older than he let on, Tiny knew, at least sixty-five and not much more to it if he didn't cut out the liquor and start hitting the salad bar. But Tiny wasn't gonna rebuke him or lay down the law—no need to prime that bomb so long as the royalty checks kept rolling in. Wolf'd sing when he was ready, and that was it.

Tiny delivered his observations to his agent, who huddled with Werewolf's man and moved for Vegas. They set up at the Wynn for a trial stint in the fall of 2010, show start times ranging from 6:30 PM to 4:00 AM, drifting thirty-one, thirty-nine, forty-two minutes later each day, until the sun came up with the moon still out and the show went dark until the lunar calendar cycled through a couple weeks later.

"A floating craps game," Werewolf said after he crawled out of the Buick's backseat on their first night in the Full Moon Theatre.

"Nice job, you caught us. Let's play." He reached into the car and took out two martini glasses and a pair of dice. Opening the vodka bottle with his teeth, he filled both glasses and handed one to Tiny Jake. They looked at each other for a quick second, eyes shining loss and torched women, then drank it all down in one toss. Werewolf rolled the dice on the snare and Tiny Jake made them hop and shimmer until the drumroll peaked, the crowd was shouting, the ricochets filling the theater with the rap of cold rain. He batted the cubes into the lights with his drumsticks as Wolf fell back on the Buick and belted out "Luck Be a Lady" to a crush of lurid whoops. No schmaltzy Nathan Detroit greased handshake, this was the shook-down version, unwired. Straight like the morning mirror through a hangover, so true it bled.

The audience of celebrities and high rollers yawped and hooted. "Y'all happy?" Werewolf asked, his smile a drooping hot dog bun. "Hafta know pain to know what happy is. So let's ride." He sang "Black" by Pearl Jam, tearing through notes like loose flagstones; he sang Muddy Waters like the dead; he sang the Beach Boys and Al Green with love snatched from his chest; he sang his own blue, tortured concoctions while Tiny Jake whisked over cymbals. Laid back on the Buick's hood, his fez lodged between windshield wipers and his feet walling in the hood ornament; his sooty, stained outfit masking his features save the inside of his nostrils, his Adam's apple, the underside of his lips, occasionally a quick glimpse of his ears. A boom microphone draped over his face caught his heated lamentations, his delivery channeled by vodka and turning frustrated and vexing as the night moved on. There was no sign of him stopping and the crowd ate it up, so they let him go past the scheduled close and into the night, Tiny Jake aching but toughing it out, throwing in some Latin fusion he'd been working on to get people dancing, plumbing out Werewolf's pipes all over the contour map until daybreak hit like a slap shot and "Amazing Grace" lay in. The curtain crashed down, and the audience hobbled back to their rooms, their intestines laced with hemlock, their souls forever changed.

Two months later, the lifetime contract was signed and stamped home. Tiny Jake filed for divorce soon after, trying to cut out all the nights lost watching the audience for the peanut butter eyes he'd known his whole life, his wife lost to liquor and acts of God, floating free across the Great White North.

Who was this man?

No interviews, never sighted outside the casino, quickly becoming one of Vegas's richest and most reclusive residents. His televisions were always on, now playing news as well as porn, war footage, death lists, martyrs, elderly women strapping bombs under their abayas and blowing up food trucks, weather, motorsports. Small-cap funds and cellular implants. The first crop of cloned soldiers in accelerated development. Fun snacks to make with leftover party cheese. He paid the most attention to the crowd scenes, feeling out the dead space in the correspondents' reports, probing the chumming masses for some sound, some thing, someone.

He began to gamble large sums of money. He favored the slots, playing alone at a thousand dollars a shake, his fortunes announced by a roll of bleeps. It passed the time. He hired investigators to provide him with in-depth briefings, hi-res videos with interpolated audio, phone numbers, photographs, report cards, copies of deeds and tax returns, birth certificates and death certificates, all of which he kept in his room safe and never discussed with anyone else. Liquor filtrated through his mind.

At the encouragement of his marketing team he was coaxed out of his ragged attire and into an identical getup, different only in terms of cleanliness and number of Nike insignias. A sponsorship agreement, his agent informed him, had been reached. Something was done about his hair, crusted up into the fez for who knew how long, shaped like a thimble except harder, the sweat and filth of decades compressing it to stone. They hacked it all off and shaved him down to skin, then rubbed lotion onto his scalp and lined his neck with cologne. He liked how his new shiny skull felt in the shower, the texture of rain suddenly violent and striking, how the Marriott pillows nestled gently around his skull and comforted his anguished brain. Onstage he wore a black Nike toque to keep comfortable against the rusted car hood, the tight synthetic fibers making him feel catlike and sleek, finally worthy of the spotlight.

On the day of Robespierre's release, he waited in his uniform outside the Hall of Justice, leaning against a railing and smelling the sea air again. He sang her name across the morning, over camera crews taping her release, the press of microphones, supporters, curious bystanders, three rows of demonstrators. J. Malcolm Fletcher gave her a tap, then a nudge, then put his hands on her waist and swiveled her toward the face from lost photographs, the face on magazine covers, the face that surged from memory in the depths of her dreams.

Reason froze her; here was her absent, fair-weather father buying his way out. He didn't deserve instant affection, a spot on her victory platform—a rotary saw and a barrel of hydrochloric acid and three days in a Kansas basement felt far more appropriate—but she shoved the urge down a steep and rickety staircase, because she knew hokey make-up crap won votes, and she'd already bought in big herself.

When they collapsed into one space everything else fell away. Jasper sniffed the hair he'd always loved and hummed an old lullaby, cradling his daughter like a soft-boiled egg. The supervisor-elect clung to him, rubbing his shoulder blades with her fingers and head-butting his chest, gravity diving through her skin, foam rising in her chest.

"Werewolf?" Robespierre asked. "Dad?"

"Yeah," sniffed Jasper.

"I have all the songs on my iPod," she mumbled.

"He's quite popular," Fletcher concluded. He pushed back into the crowd and watched in respectful silence as Jasper and Robespierre held their hug in the November morning's dry light, a plank over an abyss twenty years deep, the restoration of history within shouting distance.

Four elected years of change. On the official trips to Iran, Robespierre toured devastated villages and squalid refugee camps, visited cheerless classes held in bombed-out buildings, slipped booze and cigarettes to wounded soldiers, penned sizzling editorials and endured nights of total black. Returned to San Francisco, she battled federal jurisdiction, tried to cut off U.S. government offices from city services, proposed boycotts of national holidays, passed strongly worded resolutions calling for cease-fires and withdrawals, whatever she could think of to somehow stop the war. When the 6.9 earthquake hit in November 2013, she was out in her pajamas with flashlights and crowbars, directing firefighters and passing out coffee. Nights wordsmithing legislation over takeout, reviewing the latest fashion and cosmetics catalogs for max appeal. She went for a public jog every morning at six, with a standing invite for constituents to come along and talk shop, so long as they could keep up on the hills.

Men came and went. A hippie investment banker, a nonprofit director, a local comedian, the Giants' utility infielder. Wonderful, well-meaning men who couldn't fill the empty white space that separated her cells. She tried sleeping with women, taking her Hayek-like former intern to a seven-course meal at Fleur De Lys and a suite at the Clift, then the peculiar fate of emotion fleeing her body when clothes came off. Not full or hungry—the absence of appetite entirely. She refrained from physical contact when she was out of the public eye, turning her shoulder into hugs with friends and serving up a limp-dick handshake to her board colleagues and, as much as possible, employing a quick finger wave by way of greeting. She didn't mind; she was mostly happy; her nonstop days were filled with productivity and piled-up accomplishments and satisfying career progress.

Sometimes she felt she was getting close, that her successes nearly outweighed how she'd expelled Marat onto his desolate path, the subversive infighting that nearly chopped off his head. She could almost believe the excuses: he'd deserved it; somebody else would've screwed him anyway; in the end he turned out loaded, so it didn't matter; the army was the best thing that ever happened to his delinquent future-felon butt.

Almost, but not quite.

The city lurched through recession and endless war, the sad cycle of layoffs and demonstrations. She watched the board pass regulations on leash laws and baked goods freshness and wave energy and congestion tolls and knew that the war was still what hit hardest. Her issue. The most penetrating cause that ever existed, the one that scooped outrage from quiet citizens, elicited tears and shouts and dumb quiet, imposed the bewildering feeling of powerlessness and claustrophobia and never-ending death. She saw the rambling public statements at board meetings, the prevalence of antiwar signs and bumper stickers, the massive turnout at demonstrations, how fundamental belief made people overly certain and scary and really fucking freaked. How they sought a superhero to mend the frayed ends of reason. Only in this city, where people thought beyond jobs and commutes and what to make for dinner, where idealism was a way of life. She opened every public conversation with a statement condemning the war, served up aggressive antiwar resolutions, formed political action committees and sponsored pacifist arts festivals and funded think tanks to come up with a way out. Every Sunday she brought donuts to the VA hospital and listened to the new arrivals' stories. It was the best available way to win.

So when she won reelection and the mayor's office was open three years later, the hell with youth, she would conquer and reign. The executive branch reached for her like a beaten nation, needing care and righteous direction. And Robespierre Van Twinkle was positioned as the only serious contender for the job, a courageous synthesis of leadership, imagination, and community values, her heart pumping life through San Francisco's veins.

✤

Esmerelda slept in her apartment with the television on mute, her graying hair circling her neck like a lagoon around an island. Outside, the night was clear and quiet except for the occasional owl bus, a rising breeze. She slept in the nude because after nearly fifteen years of working out and dieting, she finally could, undressed by her own hands, the sheets crisp against her skin, able to turn over without cracking a spring. At 1 AM Werewolf and Tiny Jake came on the television, an infomercial pushing a twelve-CD compilation set of All-Time American Hits. Jasper's stage name appeared on the screen for two seconds and fell away, a footnote to Americana, another detail missed.

She rose at two and pulled on her uniform: polo shirt, blue slacks, black shoes—basically a golf shop attendant. Looking out her bathroom window from a few choice positions she could make out lights from Oakland across the bay, winking promises of sunrise. She brushed her teeth and imagined a civilized schedule, not being dreary and tired eighteen hours a day, biorhythms aligned with her favorite television programming and breakfast in the morning and dinner in the evening, Wednesday and Sunday evenings cordoned off for her absolutely necessary missions to the track, picking losing ponies and pounding mint juleps with her pals the only form of therapy that'd ever worked.

Her alarm went off again, demonic angry chops. She pounded the clock backhanded and tore the plug from the wall, then doused her face with hot water, pulled on her purple polyester jacket, and stumbled down to the garage.

The streets in SOMA were lit with traffic and scraggly men rasping canes against the sidewalk. She drove west on Mission, bending south by the abandoned office buildings and sex clubs, then hung a right at the BART station and turned onto Valencia. It was the best time of night to find a parking spot, a half hour after closing time and bar-goers trickling into their cars and wobbling off, leaving whole sections of street open. Even so, it took Esmerelda three tries to parallel park, as years out of the driver's seat had left her tentative, the angles not intuitive. Basically she'd had to relearn how to drive, and she had always been a poor student.

"Hola," she called as she trudged into Bagel Stop. The store was loud with Spanish hip-hop and blitzed with light, enough wattage to illuminate a football stadium, and her body needed a few minutes to adjust.

"Buenos dias, señora," Carlos hollered from the center of the musical maelstrom.

"Coffee?" she squeaked.

"Tengo agua, gracias."

She slumped over behind the counter and crushed decaffeinated coffee beans, dumped them into the machine, and hit go. Edging onto a stool, she watched the coffeemaker *drip blip swish pop* until her eyes heaved shut, she sank into a heavy black goo. For three minutes she was blissfully lost to the world, whereupon Marat clapped his hands in front of her nose and smacked her back to reality.

"Morning, Ma!" he peeped belligerently.

"Marat," she yawned. "Hey."

"Interesting supervisory strategy, Ma. Did you learn that at business school?"

She came to like a kicked grizzly. "I know what I'm doing!" she shouted. "I used to be hot shit in the restaurant world, don't forget. Way bigger than all this."

"Once upon a time." He pulled a beer from his pocket with his good hand. "Hear about Robespierre?"

"Not lately." The girl never called, didn't ask advice, didn't take her to lunch on Mother's Day or send flowers on her birthday, all of which Marat knew well. She thought about spilling coffee on his pants accidentally on purpose.

His eyes refocused; noxious fumes hurried from his nose. "She's running for mayor."

Esmerelda tightened her face into her trademark bristle, inured against revealing an inch of pride. Her daughter opening freeway exits and community centers, officiating major weddings in City Hall's cupola, directing policies and barnstorming and bleeding empathy at police officers' funerals. Much as Esmerelda'd been maligned for cockiness, it was nice to see the management knack had turned out useful. "What's wrong with the guy we got now?" she asked.

"Term limits and a revealing IRS audit," Marat deadpanned.

Esmerelda mixed her decaf with a tablespoon of cream, a squeeze of honey, a slosh of Tabasco, and four packets of sugar, her morning depth charge. "Well, good for her," she said. "Got my vote."

Marat chuckled. "Does that mean you're actually going to vote?"

This bullshit she took. Every day with the digs and jabs and names and barbs, all of which were accurate and earned and she had to eat without complaint. "I better get moving," she said. "Me and Carlos gotta start the machines, get the bagels into the oven. Morning veggies are due in twenty minutes."

"You still swimming?"

"Three days a week, so long's I can keep my eyes open."

"It's working, Ma. You're looking good."

She looked over Marat for signs of deception. He was handsome in an angry sort of way, hair attractively shaggy in intimidating Afro curls, his face long and hard like his father's. The mangled arm from the war the one blot but still shading him with character, an honorable depth.

She decided he was being genuine and let him kiss her on the cheek. "I gotta roll," he said.

"OK," she whispered, and fell deluged with sadness.

He put his beer back into his pocket and slipped out the door. She heard his Porsche grumble awake and peel off into the night.

Her coffee was cold, so she threw it out and made another. Then she went to the back and helped Carlos move the bagels from the boilers to the oven, the hottest dance tracks from Ciudad Juárez unable to sweeten her mood. The door buzzed as the rest of the Sunday morning shift shrugged in: Maria the counter girl, Henry the egg man, Jacqueline the coffee lady, Geoffrey the janitor, some Chinese guy fresh off the boat Marat employed as the result of a poker night bet. They were all paid well but still moved lackadaisically, because it was agonizingly early; because the work was mind-draining and repetitive; because even being surly, slow assholes, they couldn't lose money at that place if they were only open an hour a day.

A typical weekend minute: three egg sausage bagels, a pint of veggie schmear, ten dozen plain to go, Asiago cheese with sides of lox and red peppers, Thai chicken sammy, three poppy seeds toasted, plus coffee, coffee, orange juice, coffee. There was no real seating in Bagel Stop, a couple of stools and a counter, a bus stop outside with some fold-down seats, but within ninety seconds of opening every linoleum inch of the place was jammed to the walls with East Coast ex-pats and hipsters and suburban folks making the pilgrimage to the city, tourists thumbing guidebooks, legions of ornery breakfasters dumping money on Esmerelda, wondering where the napkins were, asking if they catered, how many ounces in a medium, was there any soy-based creamer, which way to the restroom, millions of stupid questions clearly answered on the menu. As the lone cashier, she sat in an elevated platform by the door and took orders as customers inched in, accepting their soiled bills and credit cards, making change, inputting orders, passing over receipts, withstanding brain-dead musings and shouted cellphone conversations, not even trying to smile. The scene drove her brain back against her skull, the same mimicked excitement from customers that today was a day they were going to eat some real New York–style bagels, not that unboiled crap down at Noah's, this was real Manhattan hardware, ovens bought used from H&H. It was food, she wanted to scream, the same crap you had last time, the same thirty-seven menu options every day, pretty good stuff but nothing nearly as revolutionary as what she'd done at Incognito, and largely coasting on reputation. Generally speaking, the customers were pushy street scum compared to the ladies at CopySmart, never asking her how she was doing and rarely saying thanks, demanding dishes they didn't make, complaining about parking and the fog, dressing her down with cold civility, late for work, late for church, raging hungry, push, take, and leave. By noon Esmerelda was bitched up and sassy, and she yelled at Jacqueline to take over for the rest of the day so she could go lose some money with her buddies at the track.

"You sure 'bout dis?" Jacqueline asked. She was short and built like an icebox, naturally pushy, the kind of person who always captured a seat on the bus and wormed her way up to the front row at concerts. Fourteen years ago she'd emigrated from an unpronounceable island in the Pacific, possibly in the Philippines, and had been zealously working two or three service jobs at a time ever since.

"Course I'm sure. I can barely move, my arthritis acting up."

"Ho-kay, I go. But I got phone call. Rubbapear coming by soon."

"Robespierre?"

"Oh yeah! She come get some bagers, OK?"

"Weird. Real weird." Especially since Robespierre had never visited Bagel Stop before.

"Relax, Miss Ezzie! I not gon make up story! What da point of dat?" Her fervent smile reminded Esmerelda that Jacqueline's children were similarly grown up and more important than her, husband long out of the picture, her only friends a deaf aunt and her knitting group.

"How long til she gets here?"

"Dey say twelve firty. You know how supastars go. Whenever convenient."

Esmerelda put on some lipstick and a little mascara and dove back into work, filing streams of cash in the register, ripping receipts, punching orders into the computer, moving the ceaseless crowd along even faster than usual, so that the line backed up at the pickup counter and she received snotty sneers from the kitchen staff. She knew Robespierre was close when a photographer backed ass-first into the store. "Face front!" she cried, slapping her hand against the counter, "and order something or scram!"

"Hey, Ma," came Robespierre's voice as she strutted into the store in a night-black half-dress half-suit, a blazer with skirt and leggings, serious but kind of sexy, an emerald scarf tied to her neck, balmy lips swollen from her permanent bee sting. Her hair was an elaborate weave of highlights and styles, a fraud in Esmerelda's opinion, these were not her genes, but she smiled anyway, because votes mattered, this was her daughter, she owed her, she had no choice.

"Hello, hon!" she called, climbing off her perch for some half-assed hugging. "Can I get you the house special?"

"You got it," she said, her patronizing smile warming up. "Ma, I wanted to tell you something."

"I know," Esmerelda said, "you're making Bagel Stop the official breakfast restaurant of San Francisco." The reporter laughed. "Always had good taste," Esmerelda continued unconvincingly, not in the mood for palling around. "No wonder everybody loves her."

Robespierre took both of her mother's hands and spoke ultraslow, as if giving directions to a European tourist: "Mom, I wanted to tell you that today I'm formally announcing my candidacy for mayor."

Esmerelda reacted as she had to, flurried arms and squawking and a round of free bagels for everyone, then calling friends on

Robespierre's cellphone and kissing her daughter all over. And through the hullabaloo she despised—What kind of daughter informs her mother about an important life decision on television? Why is the hardscrabble mother brought front and center only at her shameful retail job? Was cheap manipulation what it took to get votes? What about the issues? Wasn't this against everything her bold, idealistic daughter held dear?—she knew she had to do it, and sell it.

She owed them. Childhoods penned in under Fanny's rule, recycled clothing, her own immobility and uselessness. Trading down kitchen stardom for the dumbest job in the world, missed sporting events and plays and back-to-school nights, helpless with homework, no mentorship or initiative, encouragement coming in derisive shots the kids couldn't understand. Letting Marat's dope-slanging fester in front of her, never laying down the law or highlighting applicable sentencing guidelines or offering replacement income in the form of a decent allowance. Life-long financial mismanagement and her newfound gambling habit, burning money everywhere. How they pried Fanny free when she couldn't, devising and executing a liability-proof suicide facilitation plan she hadn't had the creativity or stomach for, the gray mark on their souls more than worth it: the sham contract burned in the fireplace, the ceaseless bitching abuse finally silenced, the elephant in the parlor returned to the jungle in the sky. The years lost to hyperobesity and lack of will, only clawing out through kid-imposed boot camp and calorie control. But she owed them the most for Jasper. And so long as breath was in her, she'd work their shitty jobs and smile her shitty smile, so they knew how much she regretted everything. To see her eat it when she didn't have to, when the money was there. She'd volunteered to work at Marat's hag-faced boss's bagel venture because she was a world-class chef, a master of quality control and kitchen hygiene, she understood how to calm customers when tempers flared and had decades of management experience, and of course she could process data faster than anyone she'd ever met and might as well use the skills she had—but mostly she did it because of Jasper.

Haunting her sleep for decades. Capturing stardust on the stereo.

The impossible spiritual hero she never would have let him become.

A moon big as a basketball hung over the Bay Bridge. In the Fairmont hotel ballroom, a Buick with tinted windows puttered onstage, Tiny Jake driving. The stage clogged with smoke, the car eased to a stop, two toots on the horn and out from the passenger side rolled Jasper Winslow, Werewolf, shriveled like an old cat and decked out in blue basketball warm-ups. He smiled and tap-danced a little for the moshing crowd, slick socialites sloshing cocktails and shoving for position, already convinced their ten-thousand-dollar donations were worth it.

He hopped around the stage and went back to the car, pulled the seat back, and helped a woman climb out. She was dressed in an identical jumpsuit, thick round sunglasses, her hair pulled in a shiny ponytail, giant hoop earrings weighed down to her shoulders, a strained mouth-tucked smile. She walked stiffly, her swing a beat off, something phony about her style. Wasn't until she started giggling up tears that the crowd realized it was Candidate Robespierre, and detonated.

"Hello," Jasper said into the microphone, breathy and punchless over the din. "My daughter, Robespierre Van Twinkle. Next mayor of San Francisco." Robespierre pushed her smile wide, looking young and uncharacteristically hesitant, her father's arm a feather boa on her shoulders.

"Lots of you know my daughter and I were apart for a long time," he gasped. "So it's good to be here with her. Made so much out of herself without me helpin'. I couldn't be prouder." Beside him Robespierre's face retreated, she raised a hand over her eyes. The crowd burned with noise.

"Think about all this woman done. Leading the movement against the foulest war America ever fought. Taking a stand against what's wrong. Got the guts to go further than anybody says she should, take her Supervisor role to the federal government and raise the issue. Getting down in the trenches to make it better." He slid back a step, propped a fist under his chin. "Beautiful, ain't she?"

He picked the mic off the stand and started to sing. She slipped down to the floor, her head hanging over her lap. It was hard to hear or see her father's serenade over the crowd's shouting, but those up front could make out the faded lyrics, "Hello Again" by Neil Diamond. He sat down next to her spinning out long notes, hopscotching the circle of fifths, harmonizing with himself, Tiny Jake mashing the drums up-tempo. The song ended, and she stood up and hugged him so hard he burped. She wiped her sunglasses on her jacket and blinked butterfly wings into the stage lights. The microphone moved into her hand.

"My father. Jasper Winslow. Everyone . . . "

The applause defeated her. "A man . . . " she took two long breaths " . . . a man who exemplifies what this city is about. A city of compassion and opportunity. A great, majestic city that leads the country on the edge of the sea. My father."

In the back of the ballroom, Marat chewed gum a step or two in front of Joel Lumpkin, blocking him from the curious glances of donors who'd seen him around and wondered if he was a war victim here to raise awareness, deformed from uranium exposure, face melted from Iranian cluster bombs. A head arresting for its chemical odor, multiple layers of makeup topped with several unnecessary loads of hairspray plastering down his trademark buzz cut. The outlandish white suit Joel insisted on wearing attracted extra attention, white shoes white slacks white gloves white blazer white vest white top hat, accented with aviator sunglasses and a camel-bone cane. A porn-star circus ringmaster; even for San Francisco, a sight.

"All this self-love shit," Joel mumbled. "We're the best, pretty and expensive, rah rah. Like a goddamn pep rally."

"It is a rally," Marat reminded him, though in principle he agreed; the fawning oratory felt like overkill even for his finagling sis.

"We're a family here," Robespierre continued. "We take care of one another. That means boosting the minimum wage. Building homes people can afford. World-class health care for everybody, I don't care who."

From the crowd somewhere: *Stop the War!* They swelled around the call, sang it out like a hymn, in rounds.

Robespierre held her hand to the light. "That's my issue. You know that. There's no other public servant against the war more than me. It's getting our kids killed. It's encouraging terrorism. It's feeding extremism. It's built on a foundation of lies and oil-company shareholders. You know me and where I stand."

"In front of a tank!" a shout came, and they remembered her trip to Iran, her interviews with soldiers and Iranian peasants. Her good fortune sitting in the backseat when an IED exploded along the road to the Tehran airport, her escorts not as lucky, their brains piling in her lap.

Like banshees the crowd yipped and bucked.

As Marat brooded below the din, he noticed a pair of young women a few rows in front of him, Asian girls in black satin dresses and gold jewelry, touching each other's arms. Discreetly he tracked them through the rest of his sister's speech and his dad's next few songs, their slight hips swaying, their lean curved backs, knuckled spines. Hair long and glossy, the color of outer space. His prick tingled, he felt motion. God, it had been a long time.

When Werewolf launched into "We Built this City," Marat asked the woman closest to him to dance.

"I'm sorry," she said, wrapping her fingers around her purse defensively. "I'm married."

"Nothing to be sorry about," he said. "Maybe your friend then."

"That's my wife."

Marat gave silent thanks for the most erotic constitutional amendment ever. "Oh—thanks for coming," he backpedaled. "That's my dad and sister up there."

"Yeah, right," the first one said. "What's your name, King Louis? Richelieu?"

"Actually, it's Marat. No kidding." A slug of pride struck about how San Franciscans knew the history of their names, often going on to offer opinions about Republicanism and gluttonous monarchs, stringing connections between the Revolution and the Hegelian dialectic and the roots of French identity.

"Marat!" exclaimed the second one. "How'd you wind up with those wild names?"

"My parents wanted to make it easy for me to start conversations with women," he said, selecting one of the dozens of responses he'd come up with over the years. "What's your name?"

"I'm Marie Antoinette," said the first one. "And this is Cake."

"I have bad news," Marat said. "Things may end badly."

"Don't they always?" asked Cake.

"Let's dance," Marie Antoinette said, "just us." She took Cake's hand and led her to a patch of open space amid couples and canoodling hippies. They danced forgetfully, three feet apart, eyes flashing around the room in a slow undirected swirl, no mojo to speak of. After a few minutes of aimless bouncing, they were confronted by the pillar of marble known as Joel Lumpkin.

"I'll pay a hundred thousand dollars to watch you two get it on," he said through level lips.

"Ex*cuse* me," said Marie Antoinette. "Who are you?"

"I own the place," he whispered.

"Then you know where the free booze is," Cake suggested.

"What, the Fairmont? I thought the holding company was publicly traded," wondered Marie Antoinette, whose mother managed a boutique hotel in St. Helena and kept her relatively up to date on the Bay Area hospitality scene.

"Come with me," he said. "I'll explain."

They followed him cautiously to the bar, where he produced his business card and a round of champagne, then detailed the elaborate stock leverage plan he'd developed to wrest control of the hotel, listed the directors on his payroll. They listened intently. He offered them another hundred grand for video, with sound.

And before Werewolf could drool down to "Amazing Grace," Joel Lumpkin walked back to his private elevator with the wives on his arms, chatting about decorating themes for the grand entrance and the ideal rum for mai tais. A Twinkie, Joel later described it, pasty white cream surrounded by yellow fluff.

Back on the floor, Marat pulled out a joint and puffed it until the smoke beat back the fire ants scrambling under his skin, until people started pointing and coughing and he offered a toke to a chubby purple-haired lady who obviously blazed. She dismissed him with a double-chinned grimace.

"Why not?" he asked. Suddenly he wanted to fuck her, to see if he could fuck her or fuck anything, find out how to fuck again.

"Smoking inside's illegal," she said.

"And disgusting," somebody added.

"It's weed. We're at a concert." The pot sheared off the edges, put the knives away. "You wanna dance?"

He put the blunt to his mouth again and took in the heat. When the smoke floated away, he was alone on the floor, a ten-foot bubble around him. He danced by himself, slow shambles and arm wiggles and the rhythmic ingestion of spine-melting marijuana steam. Werewolf's voice was all jumpy though, singing new notes and swapping out words to songs Marat thought he knew, which fouled up his rhythm and betrayed the balance he was closing in on.

"Play some goddamn reggae!" he bellowed after his father wound down a Garth Brooks cover, filling a dead moment with a demand that was both unreasonably on point and heard by every last person in the auditorium. His father nodded a couple of times, stomped his heel, licked his thumb and traced it over his shiny head, walked ponderously left to right across the stage.

> *Running down deh alleyway*
> *Thieves and children coincide*
> *Daylight catching up to me*
> *Until I finally learn to fly*

By the time he hit the chorus the crowd owned the song. Arms hung over shoulders, illuminated cellphone screens flickering Rasta peace.

> *Come and soar past deh moon*
> *Round round deh sun*
> *And into Jah heart*
> *Into Jah heart*
> *Into Jah heart*

In the voices of millions. Marat sang clouds of smoke, wandering to the edge of his buffer zone and aiming to latch onto a comrade, the purple-haired chubby chick, any live human being. His good arm could not find purchase, each targeted cosinger slinking out of reach when he sidled in. What else to do but smoke and smoke until all he could hear or see were stars, the gold fragments glittering in his eyes, the spangled guards entering his private zone and lusciously asking him to come along. Played that game in high school, he laughed, got his arm smashed up for the pleasure. They smiled back with strong teeth and let him clutch onto their shoulders, towing him through heavy oak doors and columned foyers with tiered light fixtures, the fire in his blood devolving to chilled gas and the barest air as security ejected him into the cold.

⚜

Marat Van Twinkle's first act of the day was to take an atomic dump. He had developed this routine in the army, when mornings on base were the only time all day he'd been near running water with sports magazines on hand. His bathroom stop was brief, just long enough to speed-read a single article before using a modicum of toilet paper for wiping, lighting a match, and moving to the shower.

In Iran there hadn't been space for masturbation between the group showers, crowded latrines, days riding in Humvees taking potshots from Iranian civilians. This had resulted in a frothy temper, frazzled nerves. An urge to fire his weapon more frequently. So in the spacious shower in his Pacific Heights mansion, a dab of shampoo on his palm and two minutes later the violence was out for a few hours. His staff was aware of his friendlier disposition early in the day but had yet to figure out the reason.

Usually he played golf or tennis from 7:30 to 9:00. This depended on the size of his hangover. His biggest deals were conducted in this period, sucking down beers and spliffs, betting hundreds of dollars per point, his high-stakes partners appreciating his irascible edge. He was ineffective at golf and didn't like it, his bad arm only in the way, the minimal physical exertion and posthole celebratory pot smoking not enough to ward off the sense of imminent terror creeping back in. Tennis was more active, his one-handed backhand deadly accurate, all the sprinting and squeaking pleasurable to his drug-heightened senses. Somewhat spent, he was at his most agreeable during his morning tennis match, most flexible on his terms. Some of his business partners found a way to like him then.

Marat was kingfish at Lumpkin's associated offices, running the ad agency, the bagel shop, most of the real estate projects. They'd landed in Iran together courtesy of the SFPD and a mutually despised anonymous tipster, felony drug and assault charges dropped for the pleasure, and a couple of targeted bribes pushed them into the same unit for the duration of their prescribed five-year tours. Lumpkin hit sleaze bottom with his spying and extortion scheme, but he'd paid Marat extremely well for his help scouting and deflecting suspicion, managing the surveillance film library, building up his blackmail. And as with pot, Marat's lifestyle grew to require it. When they returned to San Francisco—Marat with his blown arm, Lumpkin with his boxes of video—Joel came through as promised: a mind-boggling salary, a choice job, an immaculate résumé that made Marat one of the most hirable executives in his age bracket. He'd thought he'd get out when there was a good opportunity, but when offers to run flashy startups and established powers came in, he turned them down. His work wasn't boring, he rationalized, he did a lot of critical thinking, mostly he was the boss, no complaints whatsoever on money, and when he didn't talk to Joel for a while he got to feeling OK.

It was only at night, enjoying the opulent view from his wraparound deck and absorbing Buju Banton playlists through a green fog, when the true state of the world sponged him. A family he couldn't trust, his only friends the ex-security guards from high school, a career that failed to improve the universe in any way, the gnawing certainty that everything he ever did was tainted. Fallout pulsated with the music's juicy bass lines: the death of his untreated grandmother, ruined soldiers, end runs around pot laws and supporting Colombian drug cartels and propelling the biggest asshole he'd ever met into unimaginable wealth. The humiliating attacks on his staff, just because he could. This was the world he'd made.

Upon arriving at work he showered again. The desert dust was always on him. The ad agency senior staff meeting was at 10:30, account directors and star creatives selling him their crap to sell crap, the irony seemingly lost on everyone but him. He listened as long as he could take it, asking clipped questions, ragging on his staff's cheap clothes, curtailing discussion with a gravelly throat clearing, answering his cellphone with exaggerated volume.

The morning after Robespierre's mayoral kick-off bash in February 2019, Marat endured a nine-hole ass-whupping at the hands of his real estate broker, his head shattered with alcohol. Getting outbid for Marie Antoinette and Cake rumbled in his stomach, along with four bong hits, two jelly donuts, and a quart of black coffee poached from the kitchen.

By the time the senior staff meeting rolled around, he was percolating.

"Levi's brand strength has always been tied to American roots and a sense of authenticity," Garrett began. He was lean and wore a Hawaiian shirt with teal sharks eating palm trees, Dickies painter pants, a straw hat with a beer logo, argyle socks with red sneakers, unflinchingly overcreative.

"Historically," Garrett continued, "Levi's has emphasized frontier, rural settings and urban America in their advertising. The cowboy. The hipster. Rough 'n' ready heterosexual icons. The American Dream."

A heavy gong shook in his skull; twists of stomach bile spouted up to his mouth. "Enough with the God-bless-America bull," he raged, "there's too much jingoist crap out there already."

"You're right." Garrett's green stoplight eyes bored in on him across the conference table. Marat hesitated. This reaction was precisely why he'd hired Garrett in the first place.

"Consumers are tired of the old stereotypes. We want to take this in a new direction. Suburbia." A row of identical aluminum-sided homes flashed onto a projection screen, mirrored yards and lawn equipment, the same forgettable cars in the driveways.

"Suburbs get a bad rap," said Maureen, the new creative director, tall and muscular with a wide round nose like a doorknob. "Boring, sterile, lots of driving. But people move to the suburbs for a sense of community. Family. To own a yard and deck and garage, paid for with the money they earned. It's the new authentic America."

"Bullshit," Marat declared, hating himself for saying it but feeling justified, something overly simplistic and goading about this presentation, the only hope that it was misdirection for a whiz-bang finale. Which he doubted.

"Friday morning, jeans day," Maureen pushed on. A grainy amateur video appeared on the wall, junior staff members strolling out of a small stucco home. "A family's leaving the house in Levi's, mom and dad on the way to work, kids going to school," Maureen narrated. "There's a big traffic jam on their little street, everybody trying to get out at once. Meanwhile, the Levi's family takes their time going into the garage, nice and easy. Suddenly dad roars out of the driveway on a motorcycle with a kid in the sidecar, zooming around traffic. Then mom and kid number two hit the street on horses, galloping around the snarled traffic and off to attack the day." In the film two giggly copywriters hopped broomstick ponies out of the garage.

"Gap did jeans day last year," Marat noted. "I guess they're smarter than us."

"Neighborhood kids are throwing around a football in the front yard," Maureen flipped to the next clip, "a boy and a girl in Levi's, everybody else in shorts. The boy hits the girl on a long bomb, she catches it, touchdown. A truck drives by." An animated truck puttered across the wall. "Now it's ten years later, and the guy's playing football with a bunch of friends. He's in Levi's, friends are in sweats and athletic pants. The girl, now a beauty, walks down the street in Levi's. He throws the ball up on a pass—and she runs onto the lawn to make the interception."

Marat closed his eyes and listened to his brain palpitate. "Have you ever seen Levi's do a sports commercial before?" he asked wearily. He waited while the table went dark, his staff braced for the predictable outburst he was doomed to deliver. "LeBron James doesn't wear Levi's when he's on the court. I don't wear Levi's when I play tennis. Can somebody explain to me why Levi's should try to be a sporting goods brand?"

The video on the wall sped through a high school basketball game and a street hockey shootout, settling on a shot of Garrett shoving a lawnmower. "A kid mowing lawns in Levi's," Maureen picked up. "It's tropically hot out, the kid's sweating buckets. He peels off his shirt—and notices a pretty girl in Levi's watching." Maureen swayed on screen, not bad looking at all with a supportive bra and some postproduction work. A couple of creatives along the wall whistled. "He throws his shirt in front of the lawnmower. Boom, lawnmower eats it. He smiles, keeps walking. Then, bang, the girl's right in front of him. She throws her blouse in front of the lawnmower."

Marat snorted. "I presume this spot will run exclusively on the Hustler channel?"

"She's wearing a tank top underneath." The videotaped Maureen had one on, pink and form-fitting and made of sensual high-end creative-director-salary material. "And it's more of a flannel shirt than a blouse. They lock eyes. He runs over the shirt." A thousand cotton balls blasted from Garrett's discharge pipe, and Marat felt the gathering steam of a midday erection.

Fine. Done. He stood, causing the rest of the room to rise too, a pseudo-respectful-sarcastic gesture they'd implemented over the past month. "Get me a script and budget by Tuesday. I'm meeting with Dirk on Thursday. Tomorrow's Tide. Something colorful, guys, I'm sick of whites all the time and so is the rest of the universe."

He sped back to his office and barricaded the door. He turned off the lights and sat down in his chair and took three blasts from the vaporizer he stored in a false compartment in the back of his filing cabinet. He stared at the ceiling, examined the holes punctured in the ceiling panels, wondered what they were there for, ventilation maybe, possibly to relieve structural pressure, exactly how he couldn't say. He gauged the color of the atmosphere in the room, not all the way to pitch black but darker than gray or slate, the color of early afternoon shadows, undiffused static, a windowless bar for night-shift workers. Twenty minutes slogged by. When the octane chortling in his forehead reduced to a simmer, he asked Joan to set up the call.

"It's Marat," he said into the phone.

"You gotta see the film we made," Joel Lumpkin said, female voices and clinking glassware in the background. "They turned out to be fucking dancers. San Francisco ballet, I shit you not."

"I'm here," said Ankra, Joel's accountant.

"Good fucking morning!" Joel said. "Pun intended!"

"We're working a Levi's pitch," Marat began. "A new angle of Americana. Playing the suburbs."

"I was playing Shanghai last night. And Bangkok. How's the tax shelter?"

"The foundation set a record for donations last quarter," Ankra reported. "Also, Marat's December billing just closed. Five percent growth over last year, also a record."

"Hey now! You really stuck it to inflation, kiddo."

"I moved all profits into the fund for mayor's race," said Ankra. "So far, twenty million dollars total."

Marat's stomach seized, his head pinched shut. "The mayor's race?" he asked. "For Robespierre?"

"For me."

The whir of Marat's computer rose to a furor; dueling tidal waves rushed through his ears. "Murphy, you're running for mayor?"

"Do not address me by that name."

"You motherfucker."

Fifteen years of leaden history summed up in a painfully accurate word. They gave the line a moment to freshen.

"I want you to work exclusively on my advertising campaign, starting now," Joel said. "Right after I announce my candidacy, we hit primetime."

"What are you talking about?"

"I'm advertising on television, Marat. Also on the Internet, cellphones, billboards, radio. The works."

Marat rolled off his chair and onto the floor, rocked fatalistically side to side like a beetle on his back. "I can't work on this," he said. "Not now."

"I thought you might quit outright. Not that I want you to—you're very talented and have a lot of damaging insider information. But I could see it."

Marat placed the phone on the hook and took another shot from the vaporizer, then called his sister. Voicemail. She never took his calls on the first try.

Marat explained that Joel Lumpkin was in for mayor, that he owned 247 coffee franchises, twenty-nine pornography websites, an island in Dubai, three office buildings in midtown Manhattan, half of the acreage abutting Yellowstone National Park, an chain of upscale assisted-living facilities, eight suburban office parks, a thriving international advertising agency, the largest foster care foundation in the country, a dive bar, the most profitable bagel shop west of the Rockies, and a banana-yellow house out by the ocean for which he'd fantastically overpaid. All this built in just over a decade, arranged out of the public eye to avoid scrutiny, and he was obsessed with construction so she could expect a lot more. The man was only twenty-seven. He did whatever he wanted. The auto-attendant overrode his soliloquy, and he hung up with a smash.

Motion overtook him, shuffling and clicking and resetting, the possibility of battle an enthralling option. He deleted files on his company laptop and took down the framed picture with his sister on his tank in Iran, his baseball autographed by the 2014 World Series champion Giants, and the photocopy of his first massive paycheck, packing them in a grocery bag along with the bandages and ointments for his arm. He loaded the bag in the trunk of his BMW and drove west into the Tenderloin. Grungy men leaning on shopping carts watched him park with great interest, offering advice and access to fabulously discounted prescription meds. Marat passed out dollar bills and asked them to watch the car, then walked uphill past dingy Indian restaurants and massage parlors and cigarette discounters. Robespierre's campaign headquarters was located between a pizza stand and a nonprofit arts agency in what used to be a neighborhood insurance office, bars on the windows and a huge green banner draped across the second story.

STOP THE WAR!

He said hello to the volunteer manning reception, a smiley college kid clearly relieved Marat wasn't a homeless acidhead. He looked around the empty open office, phones ringing, a platter of dissected Danishes beside a row of industrial coffeemakers, pizza boxes on the floor, piles of paper shoveled across desks.

"They're in the back," the receptionist called. "Weekly staff meeting."

He smelled the conference room before he saw it, grubby volunteers packed in too close, college kids, high school kids, old folks with time on their hands, thrilled just to be there, sweating their belief. Breathing through his mouth, Marat found a folding chair in the back and watched a Cal upperclasswoman in a stupendous purple skirt call out precinct assignments.

Robespierre slipped into a chair beside him. Her face was thicker than when he'd last seen her in person, though when that was he couldn't recall. She punched his solar plexus, hard.

"Go back to work," she whispered.

He doubled over until breath returned. "I can't work there anymore," he said.

"I need you to go back in there and do what you can." Her fingernails crimped hairs on his wrist. "For us."

"Let me buy you lunch," he insisted, discovering a deep thirst for company, loneliness lining his blood vessels.

"Go back to work. Go." And with one last pincer tug, finally her point got through.

He returned to his office, replaced his photographs and knickknacks, and got cracking on strategies for Joel's campaign, something that might seem like a good idea at first blush but would spoil soon enough. Not unlike the night in the Khorasan desert escorting Robespierre on her first official visit to the front, when he'd sat on a kitchen table smoking a hookah while two soldiers under his command tore apart an Iranian home searching for weapons, overturning the stove, slashing the mattresses, tearing off wallpaper and punching holes in the doors, kicking toilets off their settings, peeling the soles off shoes, ripping apart pants at the seams, hurling underwear into the street, then locking all the men in the closet and threatening to rip the clothes off their women unless they gave up five terrorist addresses, at which point Robespierre had asked him to stop. He'd continued smoking as she'd laid out her justification, as her arguments grew louder and more indignant, as the men began pounding and whining in the closet, as his soldiers tossed shredded medieval brassieres out the front door, as his tobacco burned down to gray pellets. He put down his hookah hose and told her that he'd pieced together the money trail—Slippy's uneven birthday donation, the rewrite job on Fanny's will, cash dug from his shoes. The unidentified snitch and her timely arrival at the principal's door, blocking his escape with convenient concern. This with the family bankrupt and Marat doing the dirty work, knocking off grandma and trafficking narcotics and eating shit in the army, a hellish hustle decade. How easy it was to slingshot ahead with all the money she ever needed, her competition hunting snipe in Iran.

A long suck on the hookah and the haze in his head told her how he'd dreamed of killing her, it would be a cinch to put a slug in her skull, there were millions of bullets lying around, she had to sleep some time.

She'd responded with noncommittal silence, her eyes constricting to brown pins, standing with her feet together and arms crossed, her tormented disapproval holding his complete attention while an Iranian civilian came up from behind and whacked his arm with a tire iron, fracturing his ulna and radius in two and four places respectively, never to fully heal. He was unable to fight back, the shock had him frozen, but his soldiers responded with massive force, fifteen rounds at close range, his attacker's face like a rifle-range tin can. Robespierre cried lavishly while they mopped up the blood, then sat on the floor holding hands with the women of the house while a medic escorted Marat back to camp.

A night he deeply regretted, and had to get past.

He called Joel at home. "I'm in," he said.

"Good," Joel said. "Maybe you'll land that rematch with your sister you always wanted. I'll put a hold on the defibrillator."

Marat's instinct was to get aggressively vocal, but he stopped himself before sound materialized and instead delivered a slow, droll joke about Joel's parentage he knew would hurt a lot more.

Joel laughed pleasantly, practicing the measured response behooving an imperturbable politician. "Forget Tide. I'll be in tomorrow, and I want ideas."

Marat hung up before another insult slipped out and set to work hungrily, developing banal creative briefs to soften things up artillery-style, crafting a cavalry charge of inefficient media-buying guidelines, diving into infantry combat with ad scripts loaded with incomprehensible, outdated street lingo. The pre-fight ritual comforted him—creating time-tested baseline documents and aligning with industry standards—and win or lose, he felt progress coming, the slight succor of hope.

On a Wednesday morning in early June Esmerelda noted an unusually large group of men huddled by the Bagel Stop entrance when she drove by on her nightly hunt for parking. Drunk bachelor party, she guessed, jonesing for late-night booze sopping carbs. She found a parking spot a half block away and nailed it on the first go, two good omens long overdue, this small spate of luck an odd feeling. By the time she hiked over to the store, the group had swelled to a couple busloads' worth of loud dressers, maybe a pro sports team or a fraternity event, except the men were older, forty and up, their heavy faces marked by unexpected sweet glances in her direction.

She was digging her keys out of her purse when music fell on her like rain, sliding down her hair and into the rivulets of her jacket.

And my lights are lit down this county backroad
And wheels are looking for some place to stay
And my engine's tickin' to some old love song
The radio don't know how to play

The voice moved toward her, an old black man wearing a purple Nike sweatsuit, purple Kangol cap, purple sunglasses, white sneakers, no socks. He walked with a jittery hop, a familiar creak in his step. His lungs squeaking like overdrawn balloons.

She was crying when he put his arms around her. She pushed her fingers through his knotted hair.

"Ezzie," Jasper said. "Hey."

She buried her face in his jacket and breathed in his soft wood chips smell. Felt his gnarled body, his thin, indestructible bones. He put his hand on the back of her neck while she held his lapels.

The block bulged with people, curious about the crowd, the flashy suits, the memorable vocals. Jasper's men cordoned off a patch of the sidewalk, dissuading intruders with hand claps. "I saw the show in Vegas," Esmerelda said when the tears ran out.

"I know."

"I've been seeing you around, helping Robespierre. Catching up with Marat. Hear you on the radio and see you on TV. I didn't know what to say."

"You don't need to say anything, Ezzie."

"Your singing's real nice."

He chuckled quietly. "I got good inspiration."

Esmerelda's chest cracked into fractions, small twitching shreds of meat cycloning in a swirl of color and lifting her off her feet and over the sidewalk to Jasper's limousine.

She saw Carlos accepting the day's egg shipment as Jasper

directed the driver to the hotel. Her last tether to earth. "My job," she muttered.

His mirrored sunglasses turned to her, reflected headlights winking miraculously. "Don't mind that," he said. "Unless you'd rather go."

She felt physically sick at the suggestion, her stomach rolling, a wooziness in her temples. She shook her head once.

"Good."

He laid his head on her shoulder and she put her hand on his cheek and they sat together in electric silence while the limousine slithered up the tipsy streets home.

Following Marat's advice, the Van Twinkle mayoral campaign went negative after Joel Lumpkin's first television ads aired. They put together an initiative based on the weirdest Joel Lumpkin photo they could dig up—on a farm spanking a goat in its pen, his lone venture into agriculture an uproarious bust—plus bullet points:

- Registered Republican
- Lives in San Francisco three months a year
- No political experience
- Made his fortune exploiting veterans
- Only publicly announced position: moving poor people out of San Francisco

The campaign rolled out on a dull July afternoon; within hours it was bursting through the blogosphere, radio talk show hosts screamed warfare, they even made the crawl on CNN. When Marat arrived at work the next morning, Joel Lumpkin was sitting in his chair, chewing on a bagel.

"What is this?" Joel held up the *Chronicle*, LUMPKIN LAMBASTED stenciled across the front page.

"Smart move," Marat said. "Gotta hand it to them."

"Did you know about this?" Joel retorted.

"No," Marat replied automatically, slipping into his hard army face, facts and data only.

Joel's jaw reset, eyes jerking in circles, indicating that he was well past enraged and pushing psychotic. "I want to triple our media buy. And we're going to do a new ad, something meaner."

"Hang on," Marat cautioned. "Don't stoop to her level."

Joel folded the newspaper into a taut rectangle and flung it at the window. "Tried that. Not working."

"It will," Marat said, his voice cold, omniscient truth.

Joel pounded Marat's keyboard with both hands. "Then it's on you, adman. Put together something that'll work." He tossed his bagel in the garbage. "Another thing: since your mom quit, something's wrong with the bagels. They're not New York; they're shit."

They filmed the new commercial on Fisherman's Wharf, Joel in a banker's suit and skinny black tie strolling past beggars and street performers, trinkets on blankets, spray-paint artists, ramshackle one-man bands. In the distance sea lions wrestled on wooden rafts. The sky smelled of diesel fuel and dirty salt.

"San Francisco is a city of experiences," Joel said to the camera as he walked along a dock. "I want to make the San Francisco experience better for our residents and businesses, to make important neighborhoods like Fisherman's Wharf thrive. Building one of the most successful companies in the state has given me unique perspective on how to build a winning organization." He stopped in front of a tourist shop, racks of cheap sweatshirts pulled onto the sidewalk. "As founder of Home Safe, a national nonprofit, I've helped thousands of foster kids grow up safe." The camera panned down the wharf, fat tourists and bad restaurants, the only Hooters in town. "Join me, Joel Lumpkin, to help San Francisco grow up safe."

"You've got my vote," Marat told him from off camera, still amazed that Joel didn't know Fisherman's Wharf was strictly for visitors, the black sheep of San Francisco, faker than a four-titted whore; not to mention the ad's tagline, implying childishness and frivolity, insulting as a comparison to San Diego.

"That was good," Joel admitted. He kicked a fluttering bus schedule off the dock into the bay and raised his arms in victory.

They played the shit out of the spot, five times during every local newscast for two months, during all the primetime sitcoms and NASCAR broadcasts, every ten minutes on the giant television screen on Market Street, right after the hourly station ID on the rap radio stations. They sponsored monster truck rallies and chili cook-offs, Joel outfitted in a silver-and-green vinyl jumpsuit and taking questions from a Harley sidecar; they sponsored a blimp to drift over the city with Joel's name in cloud-gray across its envelope. FOX signed on for a reality television show, *On the Trail with Joel Lumpkin*, which, despite the 1 AM timeslot, pulled decent ratings because Joel swore a lot, got around in a helicopter, and took the camera crew along on his paid dates with supermodels.

Gradually Joel Lumpkin, Independent candidate for mayor, crept up to 12 percent in the polls, in sole possession of third place.

"I did some math on the plane," Joel told Marat upon his return from a quick trip to Bahrain, where a subsidiary was constructing the tallest building in the world. "At twenty million dollars for approximately seventy thousand votes, that comes out to 285 dollars per vote. For the pleasure of getting my ass kicked."

"If you don't like my work, fire me," said Marat, his response prepared months ago. "I'm an ad guy, not a campaign manager. Your problem is the issues. You're an outsider, and you haven't told anybody where you stand. What do you expect?"

"For 285 dollars a vote, I expect to win."

"People want to know why you're putting so much effort in to this. Why do you want the job?"

"Isn't that obvious?"

Marat knew he was in it for uncreative reasons, wealth and

power on a colossal scale, his obsession with erecting huge buildings and lots of little ones too. Nouveau riche going for nouveau richer. "You need a real answer," he said. "Even the biggest ad campaign in city history isn't gonna win San Francisco by itself."

Silence over the phone line, Marat cocked up in his chair. "I want dirt," Joel huffed, trying to sound pissed but underneath pretty pleased he'd smashed an advertising record or two. "Info, skeletons, shit; everything she's fucked, I wanna know. Everything your parents fucked up on, that too. I'll pay you twenty million dollars."

The number bounced around Marat's head, the limitless untamed future of fortune. "Why should I believe you'll pay me?" he asked.

"I'll put it in escrow. Arrange it with Ankra."

Marat spun his chair toward his office window, the tinted light marking the edge of the day. "You know about the thing in Iran," he squeaked.

"Let me think about it. Army jack-off threatens to kill his pathetic, sloppy, communist sister in the middle of a war zone, proceeds to get his ass beat. Rewarded with cushy job by Mayoral Candidate Me. Not helpful."

Marat nodded to no one in particular. His parents had been pathetic and sloppy, his whole life had been pathetic and sloppy—and here, at last, was a way to get clean.

"I'll find something," he snapped, and hung up before Joel could change his mind.

She would be content just relaxing, she told him. Maybe she could garden, or learn Japanese. He kissed her and said he'd do anything for her, honest, so why waste her life on bullshit when her heart was firm on desserts? She was still good at it, her gorging instincts all burned off, the city tiring of Element's dominance and ready for a change of scenery. As for Zoogman, Jasper'd heard on the T.V. that he'd been thrown in the slammer for drunk driving and tax evasion, his mug shot described as a more metallic Frankenstein. If pastries were still her thing, Jasper'd fund it, do it right.

Esmerelda opened Luna in the Mission in the summer of 2019. Jasper arranged the financing, put his legal team on the contracts. He sang for opening night, the Buick towed in from Vegas, Tiny Jake slapping skins, unveiling a new album's worth of material as carts covered in grapefruit soufflés and marigold muffins trundled from table to table. The buzz was sensational, the crowds voracious and forgiving. The comeback of a culinary myth: from anonymous fall to magnificent resurrection, complete with Grammy-winning soundtrack.

Luna had misted glass walls, floors stained Israeli blue, the name scripted in pink neon and flickering softly onto 15th Street. Diners entered through a dome modeled on Casablanca's Grand Mosque, took drinks at a long maple bar salvaged from a Memphis truck stop, and rode a moving sidewalk past a graffiti remake of Guernica to their mod table constructed of industrial plastic. An open fire hissed in the center of the dining room; an old Victrola honked out jazz in the corner. Jasper's gold records hung from the ceiling, strung up with wire and twinkling.

Entrenched in the kitchen, Esmerelda crafted plates, bullied staff, enforced quality control, and badgered suppliers over the phone, breaking periodically to parade out to the dining room and defend her desserts from uninformed critiques. During the day she devised recipes, experimenting with beakers and Bunsen burners, sampling fruits flown in from Asia and Africa, building a comprehensive collection of the world's greatest chocolates. She planted an organic wheat field in drained marshland by the airport and turned the crop to flour in a mill she installed in the restaurant attic, then added yeast and desalinated ocean water, pumped in purified oxygen during the kneading process, and baked world-class bread over smoldering Scottish peat in a dedicated hillside kiln. Every day after the lunch rush she walked down to the Mission Pool and swam laps, the chlorinated stress burn she called it, coming back rambunctious and at her most creative, hitting her peak as the big spenders rolled in. During crunch time she was indefatigable, a finger in every mixing bowl, jotting down new ideas at a hundred miles a minute, taking no breaks and still outshining her younger, friskier, and narcotics-powered staff. She attributed her stamina to the exercise regimen, her sensible diet, and a delirious trepidation that had taken root in her head: she knew how good she had it and would never again piss it away.

She invented vanilla soup, jalapeño chutney pie, baked bananas infused with pineapple reduction sauce, Fluffernutter cake layered with raspberry jam. She torched ice cream and froze fondue into popsicles, coated oranges with anise and sprinkled with gummy bears, flambéed star fruit in grappa and served hot slices on graham crackers. Out in her wheat field she caught insects, mostly flies and ladybugs, which she roasted over a mesquite flame and encased in butterscotch fudge for a dish called Cretaceous Amber. Her desserts were Petri dishes of flavors, she explained, reminding anyone who asked about inspiration that when you work in a copy shop for twenty-five years, the ideas pile up. For the old-timers who remembered her glory days at Incognito she brought back the oatmeal cookies, still fabulous and trapezoidal and topped with luscious homemade ice cream, the only tradition she allowed was worth keeping.

It took her a few weeks to understand that she was cooking for Jasper. He put the show on hiatus and stayed with her, parking himself and his gang at a long table in the back corner, sampling the first batch of every dish and telling showtime stories and signing autographs for guests. A hot handspun swagger bolstered his speech, and he came off as more put-together than the peaky voice on the radio implied. Esmerelda tracked him on the security cameras as he swigged soda through a straw and hobbled to the people-mover for a smoke on the sidewalk, his face hidden behind sunglasses the size of DVDs. She watched him nod and smile at creaks and clanks from the kitchen, the possible sounds of his fan base rustling. Sniffing the air for her smell.

At work in the kitchen she finally fell in love with Jasper Winslow.

"Come with me," she said a month after opening, on a night he was tapping his fingers and toes in half-time from boredom, his spirit smothered by constant fan handshakes and empty greetings, more pastries than he could digest properly, not a drop of vodka. She led him upstairs to the washroom by the wheat mill and took off all her clothes. He sat on the toilet and pulled on his earlobes.

"I believe this belongs to you," she said, guiding a hand over her breasts.

"Well, huh, that's not bad," he admitted.

"This too," she said, placing his other hand inside her thighs.

"That ain't terrible neither."

"And this." She put her hand on his cheek and pressed her mouth on his rubberized lips, tasting burned firewood and aspartame. She kissed his chin and his nose, and reached for his sunglasses.

His head retreated, his hand had her wrist. "Don't do that," he said.

"It's me," she said, soft as cotton.

"Don't matter. That ain't for the lily-livered."

"I want to see you," she insisted. And by applying some elbow grease and using a toothbrush for leverage, she eventually pried the sunglasses out from behind his ears and off his head. His face was blanked with strips of scars where his eyes had been, discolored patches rolled together like overlapping coats of paint. She breathed in and kissed them like they were cool cream eggshells.

"I'm sorry," she said.

He shivered. "Me too."

"Well, no point sitting around feeling sorry for ourselves." She reached for his dick. "Might as well make the best of it."

Inside a week they were tossed into family, turning up aged wedding bands and dusty pictures, sharing coffee mugs and shampoo. She moved in with him at the hotel and sold her flat in SOMA for an outrageous celebrity-enhanced profit. He held court at the restaurant; she attended all his shows. They made love constantly, gently, affectionately. Bonded solid through history and habit.

SECOND CHANCES WORK, announced Robespierre's campaign literature as she called for providing the homeless with psychiatric help instead of bussing them to Modesto and Stockton, increasing police walking patrols in the Excelsior rather than razing crime hotbeds for strip malls. Her parents went to campaign events as often as she could rope them into it, Esmerelda tucked under Jasper's arm like a baseball in a glove. Sometimes they told their story of separation and reunion; mostly they stood offstage and clapped. Everyone who heard them speak felt inclined to vote for Robespierre just a little bit more.

Marat recognized his father's charm, his mother's verve, their poetry cooking within him. Hanging with them wasn't awful, they were polite and respectful now, even tried to pay for meals. He felt their reunion stemmed from easiness and desperation, which sickened him, but the part of him that crafted cheesy ads for Middle America knew they made a terrific story, a delicious pile of comeback and true love horseshit, ripe for a TV miniseries.

But the facts still seared: Jasper was a coward, Esmerelda a fuckup, his sister a manipulative thief who'd nearly let him die. This he could never ignore.

Twenty million simoleons hung in the air without a place to land. He took a Cohiba out of his office humidor, repacked it with bud, and puffed until the smoke detector went off.

The guys from his unit were in the right places. It took an hour of phone calls to get things moving: the guys in private security, the psychiatrists, the financial advisors, the cops, the lawyers, the computer guys, the high-clearance government staffers. All had seen Joel Lumpkin's footage from the Iranian plains, their permanent disgrace. Poking Iranian detainees' penises with sporks. Dog piss poured into soup. The Koran rolled and smoked in front of prisoners; hysterical, vengeful cries; boots dead on their ribcages. Spiked knuckles and lighter fluid. Blindfolds and pistol whips, involuntary evacuation. And the ugly kid with the hidden camera whirring away in his helmet the whole time. They hadn't known about the spy system until they came back stateside, when Joel showed up on their doorsteps and demanded the deeds to their homes.

Between friendly fire and munitions accidents, no chance that shit'd fly on the battlefield. But in tranquil Homeland America, Joel Lumpkin had more guys than they did, plus those incredible videos that they played on a portable TV right on the porch. So much blood, they hadn't remembered how much, pouring shame down their shirts, blackening names and faces, totaling hard time and probably worse. Even if they managed to find a legal loophole, these were obvious atrocities—what else could they do but sign? And when Marat went back to the well years later looking for dirt on Joel Lumpkin's behalf, they gave him what he wanted, ready to be done with it, no fight.

They packed her story into the American Dream template: local girl rises up from a dysfunctional family, overcomes poverty and bad parenting, excels at Stanford, gets her feet wet interning for Pelosi and Obama, wins election young, energizes the city, puts principles first. They leaked the *Examiner* clip of when she wandered into the mayor's office during her parents' wedding ceremony and it was everywhere—the featured story on gossip websites, batted around with coworkers over Friday beers, a punch line for area comics. It helped a lot that she was devastating through the lens, her pouty lips and spread-out eyes appearing mysterious and desirable through a judicious application of cosmetics, her hair vivacious and springy, her body contorted into attractiveness by her ultrastylish, form-sensitive wardrobe. She drove a 50 percent bump in traffic when pictured on news websites and spoke fluent sound bite:

"Joel and I are both young and energetic and running for mayor. The difference is I'm running on ideas, and he's running on greed."

"I've seen Joel's new commercial. Never have accident lawyer ads looked so professional."

"You may have noticed Joel's obsession with construction. He calls it visionary. I call it an edifice complex."

"Out of touch with San Francisco? I'd say by his social programs he's out of touch with the twenty-first century."

"That's not to say Joel Lumpkin's a bad guy. Bad guys pick on poor people. Joel won't even let poor people stay in the city."

But during commercial breaks Joel Lumpkin's face plowed down the screen on his overdressed walk along Fisherman's Wharf, swinging by a kitschy tourist shop blabbing something about business and a foundation, sea lions woofing in the background. Viewers complained about the frequency of the ads, the ridiculous market saturation, the indeterminate point, the obvious unfamiliarity with the city's values, but they grew to know them intimately. Joel Lumpkin was a guy they spent time with whether they liked it or not, and the stability of his routine implied some dedication, a guy willing to put in the time and money. Possibly this man was reliable. Feasibly someone to vote for.

And there was something about running as an Independent that stirred the latent nonconformist in all San Franciscans.

Phone calls from vets flooded Marat with tales, hearsay, conjecture, myth, the occasional factual nuggets mixed in. Names of every man his sister had kissed, credit card numbers and passwords, an itemized list of all the garments she'd had dry-cleaned in the past four years. Medical records since birth. Her favorite brand of soap. An inventory of her garbage. He confirmed that she was a compulsive liar, an adroit manipulator, a backstabber and an under-the-bus thrower, but by public official standards there was nothing particularly repulsive—her rap sheet was no worse than a frat boy's blog.

In the second week of September he met Joel for starchy bagels. "Inedible," Joel decided. "How much to hire your mom back?"

"I didn't find anything," Marat reported.

"Marat, come on." Joel telescoped his neck and puffed up his cheeks, an incredulous screwball-comedy smile. "You mean to tell me no blow jobs in the office john, no fast-tracking her friends' business permits, no girls-gone-wild trip to Cancún on the government dime?" He took another bite of his bagel sandwich and chewed in a flurry of angry contractions. "Everybody does it."

"She lies about things. Weird things."

"Go on."

"Her favorite food. The number of times she's visited Asia. How much her clothes cost. The time her next meeting starts. Her location. All this small stuff." Executed with a samurai's touch, he'd heard over and over again, these tidbits of misdirection cultivated fear and affection and huge respect, painting a portrait of power.

"What about money?"

"She keeps it clean there. Doesn't misuse city funds or embezzle. And nothing's on the record, either. It's all hearsay, small talk." Each button pushed just long enough to get what she wanted and leave. "That's all I've got."

Marat heard himself say it and knew it was false. He hadn't even started. It was hard to cut Robespierre out all at once.

Joel choked down a half glass of OJ. The pressure point was nearby, he knew; all Marat had to do was follow his nose to where the shit stank worst. "Get dirt on your parents," he directed. "Between the two of them, somebody's covered in it."

It took Marat two days to track down Sven Johanssen, teaching phys ed at a Fresno middle school, twice divorced and living with an auto shop manager. They got drunk at a bar that smelled like hay, domestic beer four bucks a pitcher. Raising his voice over a player piano in the corner, Sven explained the one-armed monster and mad Swedish bacchanalia, Esmerelda's sleeping spot on the couch, Jasper's huge snoring problem, the unpleasant but necessary hubbub with the eviction board due to Esmerelda's penchant for rent-ducking. "Nice voman, ya," he said, his face warming, "and ahl-vays ready to hahmp. Like bouncing on maarshmellows, sveet and soft. Oy, de gurl could eat!"

Marat sped back to San Francisco in a hot lager stink, smoking and repacking his pipe every five miles, his hotboxed BMW steamy as a rainforest at lunchtime. Even soaked in relaxants, the only thing on the planet that made any sense was going back to Fresno and beating Sven senseless with the tennis rackets he kept in the trunk. His angry hands scrolled through radio stations and briefly settled on loud church music, a roof-rattling hymnal that called up fractured memories of minivan rides, the fable about his grandmother at the diner, Jasper's mom, the one who'd cracked open the past and could probably do it again.

A few calls around the city got him an address in the worst part of Hunter's Point, no phone number. He went first thing in the morning. Fifteen gangsters monitored his parking job through red eyes, and he hustled up caved-in stairs and rapped the weak door as hard as he could, staying low and moving around to make for a difficult target, until an array of locks were slowly unwound and he fell inside.

A bare bulb illuminated junky furniture obviously excavated from trash piles, a trash-bag-covered loveseat, a green plastic lawn table balanced out with folded newspaper under the legs, a couple of folding chairs and a hot plate and two twin beds in the corner, a wheelchair parked in front of a black-and-white television featuring Alex Trebek sans mustache. An ancient midget in a bathrobe held a broomstick warily. "We won't have the rent until the Medicare check comes," the midget said slowly, her voice a dying frog. "I told the last three that."

"I'm Marat," he said.

"Marat?" She dropped the broom and took a step closer, eyes widening like blooming black flowers. "Got your father's eyes," she ribbited. "Can I fix you a drink?"

"I'll get it," he said, and picked two chipped mugs off the dish rack, scrubbed them with a filthy rag, and filled them up with lemon-colored water from the tap.

"Thank you," she said, easing into a folding chair. She held the mug under her nose. "I'm glad you came," she said, "and I'm sorry we haven't met sooner. I don't get around like I used to."

"You need help," he stated. "You gotta get out of here."

"Oh, I don't know." Her watery eyes circled the grim room. "Been home for a long time. We're used to it."

"You'll die in this room," he pointed out. "They might not find you for months."

Her face shuttered and reopened, fresh purple discoloring her irises. "That's your Aunt Tina, watching television," she said somberly.

"Jasper never gave you money?"

"He tried." Insinuating something deep and dirty, everything Marat needed.

"Ditch this hole," he said. "I'll get you into the Sequoias today. It's the nicest old-folks home in town. Gourmet meals, round-the-clock medical. They'll take care of Tina too, from here on out, I'll see to that."

"I don't know," she warbled.

"They'll be here at noon. Otherwise I'll get this place condemned. It should have been torn down years ago."

"Well." Dabbing her hand at her face like a moist towelette. "I guess we'll try it out."

"Good." He sniffed the tap water, detected chemicals and rust, then placed the mug on the table. "I need you to tell me about my father," he said.

"What is there to know? He's a big star now, up from the streets."

"He's had problems," Marat said. "Made a lot of mistakes."

"We all do," she nodded.

"I need to know what he did," he said. "He must have told you things. You must have seen things. I need to know where I come from, what's inside me, so I can stop it."

A long slow *pssh*, air leaving the tire. "He's my son and I love him," she said, "but part of him will never be right." In slow, dispassionate detail Karen described the swimming pool abduction, the impromptu stop at the gas station bathroom, the massive gravity of diamond rings. Jasper ducking prophylactics, Esmereda's judo press and cruel taunts setting off heartbroken thrashing, self-immolation, the darkness from which he could never dig out. A decade camping in the woods under the Golden Gate Bridge, his meals begged off the visitor center snack bar at closing time. Learning to climb hills sightless and fend off thugs with sweep kicks. Washing hollowed eye sockets with salt water, padding over excisions performed with a wheelbarrow wrench.

Nighttime trips to Tina's bed. Forced entries and hanger abortions. Then hitchhiking to Louisiana and years on the hot sidewalks, stealing vodka out of grocery stores and singing in the sewers.

Marat walked to Tina's wheelchair and stood behind her, placed his hands on the taped-up handlebars and watched half of *Jeopardy!* over the top of his aunt's gray hair bun while she gurgled and snored. All the details lining up, much too right to be wrong.

How everything hurt. He kissed his aunt and grandmother goodbye, then walked to the car and called Joel. "Schedule a debate."

"Not now. I got major cost overruns on the Manama project. They don't tax their own people in Bahrain, but apparently it's OK to tax me triple."

"Last chance. Do a debate."

"So I can get my ass waxed on live television? She has the training, the pedigree, the moves. I can't hang." Gobbling noises, the rapid and sloppy consumption of life force. "In other words, this dirt has to be mind-blowing. Sloppy pigpen election-winning stuff. And all truth too, or else—consequences."

Marat waited. Fading stars wavered like scattered plutonium seeds. Him and Joel Lumpkin, a couple of genuine bastards. A long suck on the porcelain potcooker he kept in the glove compartment, and he knew what he had to do. "I'll give it to you at the debate."

"There's not gonna be a debate."

"Then you've got nothing."

The phone breathed in Marat's hand. He thought about cutting free, clenching his palm and ending it with a clack.

But what else was there than this?

"I want the dirt before I go on that stage," said Joel.

"You will," Marat declared, letting the fumes lock him shut, suffocating saturnine smoke.

"All right."

The next night Marat stumbled out of a taxi in front of the Fillmore, six hours drunk, long sips from a gravity bong blipping in short-term memory banks. Brown and black spots flecked across his shirt, he couldn't remember from what. His crotch was oily and sore, his scalp itched like a horse's ass. His head filled with bus exhaust and honking and Robespierre's volunteers' voices urging pedestrians to join them, young women in designer outfits projecting cheer, men wearing limited-edition baseball caps cajoling quietly, understanding and unpushy, as if selling high-end small-room stereos, perfect for master bathrooms or pool houses or tucked away in the sailboat cabin. Their energy carried across the dirty boulevard, sweeping over the garbage pasted to the gutter with urine, freshening up the smell of burned grease wafting over from fast-food joints. Robespierre's campaign supporters streamed from buses and cabs, parroting smiles, their eyes snapped open and dashing sprightly across the evening streetscape, something musical in their faces.

The weight of pervasive optimism collapsed his chest like a dropped piano.

He paid the suggested campaign donation at the door and slinked upstairs to the ballroom. Gorgeous women roamed in packs, flexing wetsuit-tight pants, tits cinched into tank tops and necked with silk scarves, their smart eyes and sensual lipstick and hard cheeks creaseless in conversation. Crafted untidy outfits swelling with flesh, heaving in calculated disarray. He hadn't had the courage to date a woman in years, his only sexual encounters coming in quarterly smoke-stuffed overnights to Nevada cathouses. Starved so long he wasn't hungry anymore, his prick a forgotten wedge of cheese.

Werewolf was on stage already. Live at the Fillmore, like Jimi and the Stones. He'd developed a stalk lately, a tiger with a broken leg, marking the territory around Tiny Jake's drum set.

> *There's a hole where the sun once shined*
> *And I ain't satisfied*
> *No I ain't satisfied*

His voice sounded rich under the pink lights, helped by recent years of solid meals. Marat knew the vodka bottle was filled with water these days, part of Esmerelda's plan to wean him off the sauce for good. He talked to Jasper on the phone once a week, mostly about baseball and movies, the years lost to the wilderness pitting every interaction. A man he'd met seven years ago after a concert in Vegas, who'd tried to autograph his ticket stub until Robespierre knocked the pen out of his hand and squeezed them together in a weird chest bump.

He spotted Robespierre across the bar, dipping her fat lips into a beer glass and chatting with reporters about wage inequality and technology infrastructure, citing obscure Swedish ethnographers and reciting Beat poetry to drive home her more esoteric points. He punched out a finger wave and winked, but she looked past him, around him, through him, Jasper's eyes burning hypnotically on her face like little campfires.

Marat ordered a pint of cheap tequila at the bar and spied a dessert buffet ringed by two lines of people, paper plates piled with éclairs and fruit salad. Donations from his mother he guessed. His drink arrived, a tall glass of gasoline. Near the stage couples waltzed tentatively to "Blue Danube," most stubbing toes and backing into each other with gentle "oofs," with the exception of a couple sets of show-offs who'd taken lessons for their weddings. His father's voice waded across the ballroom, carrying a strange ether that detached Marat from the room of semi-wealthy urbanites and propelled him toward his future home with ridiculously wealthy urbanites, the ones who wouldn't risk being included in the Fillmore's psychedelic record books if their fully butlered vacation estates depended on it.

Through the effluvium a languid voice drifted to him: "What are you drinking?"

"Water," he said, staring into the scuffed bar counter.

"Make it your last one."

"Gonna hang around for 'Amazing Grace.'" The words came with great resistance, requiring focused chest compressions and a tremendous volume of oxygen. "Comes last," he managed.

His sister leaned against him, her lips flopping against his ears like overstuffed pillows: "Come on, Marat. Not here."

He turned and outlined his ongoing subversion on her behalf, all the wrong moves, meathead marketing to latte liberals, millions of dollars of misguided media buys, running the same crappy commercial over and over again, and whoever took Fisherman's Wharf as a credible San Francisco neighborhood would vote for a cow anyhow. He was on their team, their inside man, keeping the coast clear while Robespierre's ship set sail. She'd done a lot right in mobilizing all these people; getting rich, self-important, naïve idiots to think the job made a difference, to stop a stupid camel-fucking war in a stupid camel-fucking country with the only tangible results being a nationwide jump in funeral home business and jacked-up gas prices and deficits for decades. The most irrelevant city this side of Havana saving lives from stupidity. He'd seen men buried in blood and sand, he'd locked Iranian women in closets, he'd forfeited his arm, for all the worst reasons. He knew she was right.

And the best part? Lumpkin wanted a debate, mid-October, television and radio, the works.

First round knockout, bank it.

He awoke eating fried chicken behind a supermarket, crouching in a bus aisle, throwing his necktie off a pier. His head blinking with a billion buzzing bees. The sustained functionality of his legs was praiseworthy, maybe from his father he'd acquired this knack for survival. Sweating up stairs cut into sidewalks, a police officer herding him out from under a bush, unexplained nicks on his hands. Somewhere chasing a cat and laughing about it. Streaks of salt coating his upper lip.

Sunset stained his living room orange. Dried upchuck on his shirt, his head dumb as frozen beef. His shredded left arm stuck painlessly under his ass.

Fuzz. Drinking water from the kitchen tap, fisheye vision, objects moving with unpredictable speed. His phone dancing to a television theme song.

"Unh," he croaked.

"So. A debate." Wind whipped through the receiver, strummed guitars mewling in the background.

"Robethpierre?" His larynx a strip of salted fish, vacuum-packed.

"He's barely in third place. He's a joke."

"Can athk. Publicly. Whath his plan. Take him on."

"I don't see any benefit in debating the laziest, shittiest candidate for mayor in city history. What are you up to?"

This pain in his head, a police car screaming up his nose. "Nothing," he hocked. "Help. You. Win." He tumbled onto the couch and nearly fell asleep, heavy gel packs weighing on his face.

"Where?"

"Wherever."

"What about Han?" Leslie Han was in second place, a centrist Democrat from the school board who wore cheap brown suits and spoke exclusively in cliché.

"Him too."

Robespierre sliced through traffic, feeling a need to move quickly, to be decisive, to cut and kill. "What side are you on, Marat?"

"Alwayth. On. Thame. Thide."

"I guess that's true." Her brother. Her crazy fucking twin brother with the gangbuster moves, so smart but so dumb, her footprints scarring his back. Their shared childhoods cared for by a witch and a wildebeest. All she'd ever had. "OK."

WATERLOO

In 1815 the Emperor was no longer a lean, sinewy, tireless, eternally vigilant human tiger—the Napoleon of Rivoli and Marengo. He was no longer the consummate General-in-Chief of Austerlitz and Wagram. The mysterious lethargy which had overwhelmed him at the critical hour of Borodino . . . had been the first visit of the Evil Genius which was to come again.

—THOMAS WATSON,
Waterloo

The loss of the battle of Waterloo was the salvation of France.
—THOMAS JEFFERSON

The debate was to be held in Civic Center Plaza across the street from City Hall. Mid-October weather being traditionally superb, and the spirit of participation and inclusion a priority for all candidates, the event was open to the public. A local political editor, known for his aggressive questioning and rimless spectacles, agreed to moderate.

Saturday morning, the city leached with sun. Marat stumbled into Joel's limo, finding Joel tilted back on the long leather bench, his head on a pillow, eyes welded shut. A heavily tanned woman held a paintbrush to his cheek. His face was half normal, half apparition, a jumbie tribal mask. Thick guards crowded the seats beside him.

A joint from Marat's inside pocket found its way to his mouth. Two placid drags and Joel snorted: "Cut it. I gotta focus."

"Looks like you got surgery," he mumbled, stubbing out on the door ashtray.

"Running late on makeup, man. Building a better me."

Marat sprawled over the back bench and stared out the tinted windows. The frantic city sparkled by, double-parked Audis and lines outside brunch joints, joggers and cyclists slicing through well-dressed pedestrian traffic, windows crammed with political signs, VAN TWINKLE, VAN TWINKLE, VAN TWINKLE, HAN. "Now the dirt, please," Joel grunted.

The limo braked for a hill and the makeup lady clucked, her line of paint jumping onto her dress.

"I'll tell you during the first commercial break. Right before the section when you answer questions from the public. When the money's confirmed."

"Search him," Joel said. A minute later Marat sat in his boxer shorts and dress socks, the bodyguards squinting at crushed scribblings in his wallet.

"Nothing," one of them reported glumly, "not even a wire."

The makeup lady dipped her brush over the tips of Joel's hair, adding light highlights, a funky beachcomber streak. "I'm gonna need you to stay with the fellas during the show," Joel said, "keep you on hand."

"Quiet!" The makeup lady's head snapped up, prissy pride clotting her face. Marat wondered what other services Joel employed her for; his money was on masseuse and come receptacle at brain surgeon rates, another guest at Joel's lifelong money party.

Just like him.

He pulled on his pants and buttoned his shirt, fast, before the metallic taste in his mouth could spread. By the time he looped on his tie they'd turned onto Market Street, trailing a lemon-colored streetcar over slippery track. He felt the tires catch toward the curb as the first egg cracked against his window.

The street was crushed with people, kids waving signs and chanting, a sea of cameras and cellphones, helmeted policemen directing jammed-up motorists. Saucy girls licked ice cream cones outside a mediocre burrito joint. Escalators from the subway coughed up dweebs and suits, prepsters and families, freaks and crazies, confused tourists wondering what the heck was going on and searching for department stores amid the punk bands. The looks on people's faces looking at Joel's limo ranged from disinterest to revulsion, like he led a team of kitten-drowning nun-rapists, like he dined on human heads, like he was nothing and no one, a zero branded on his forehead. Speckled among them, a homeless element watched obliquely, interested for panhandling purposes, eyes peeled for loosely held handbags.

At a red light Marat saw his parents and sister disembark from the streetcar. Robespierre led the way through the UN Plaza with Jasper on her arm, his father broadcasting that humongous Stevie Fucking Wonder smile as if he should be happy he couldn't see, buying rounds and holding a motherfucking hugathon. Esmerelda was on his other side, their fingertips touching every few steps. She looked like cash these days: papered in svelte clothes and glittery rare stones; hair recently cut, dyed, and styled; the confident clean eyes of a highly productive person who'd kicked a lot of bad habits. An unlikely troika at peace with their lot, all the more aggravating when viewed from captivity with a modern-day plunderer, his moronic security detail, and five gallons of face paint.

He pushed open the limo door and sprinted after them.

In twenty seconds he was behind Esmerelda. He was about to slip her a surprise hug and tell her she was looking like her burning-hot daughter these days when Robespierre spun around and faced him, an iron sentry guarding a critical bridge.

"Hey," he said, feeling failure creep in, all the mistakes he'd made and would make again. His lungs contracted, in need of weed, a cigarette, a rolled sassafras leaf, fucking helium. "I'm sorry," he finished.

She pulled him into a hug. She smelled amazing, like friendship and warmth and that first beer after work, a place of sanctuary. "What?"

"That night in Iran," he gulped. "I'm sorry."

They hadn't talked about this ever. "Why?" she asked cheerfully, waving over his shoulder.

He'd thought about it at length and had never come up with a good answer. The boys hadn't been really hurting anybody, maybe it was insulting, there was minor property damage, but the civilians were all going to get out with only temporary discomfort, better than plenty of men in his unit. He'd been tired. The Iranians were faceless and foreign-speaking and very whiny. Whiny, sand coated his mouth and his nose and his ears and his brain. It had been the end of a long, dangerous day guarding her, Supervisor Van Twinkle, the most important person ever to visit Iranian soil under his watch, the one most likely to break off from her escort and trot over a mined road to talk to some kids, so many questions, so impatient, always up to something. A day trying to keep his family alive. A bit of rest and a stale cigarette.

Another order he didn't ask for. The sanctimonious onslaught that never seemed to end. How she'd screwed him every chance she'd had.

And still, here and now, the only person he had left.

"I don't know," he said, "but I'm sorry. About everything."

Robespierre looked out toward the stage and turned back to him, her face dried up and achingly professional. He watched the crowd, talking, singing, setting up lawn chairs, skimming newspapers and paperbacks, hugging and French kissing, passing around wine bottles and champagne and coffee. Across the plaza one of Joel's guards nodded at him, his hand inside his blazer, talking into his watch.

"I want you to know I'm with you," he said. He wasn't sure exactly what that meant, but it seemed to address the moral quicksand he was in, watching his clan move on without him, all the money, the mistakes, the shifting loyalties of rival factions.

"That's a nice thing to hear," Robespierre confided, "but maybe he's paying you off."

There it was. She knew him better than anyone else on earth.

He sat down on the pavement and put his head between his knees.

"Don't worry about me," she said, pulling him up by his collar. "C'mon, c'mon."

He couldn't say anything. She knew that was what happened when he got unbearably sad, like when Fanny's corpse was carried out from the lion habitat and he'd gone silent for weeks, a war-addled grimace hung on his face. Over the cliff and still falling, beyond the world of words. "I'm off," she said. "Wish me luck."

He waved until he felt a bodyguard's hand on his elbow.

Robespierre kissed her parents' cheeks and walked to the stage through ranks of her supporters, waving back at their exuberant cheers and catcalls. She felt savagely pretty, a movie star riding a box office hot streak, a supermodel eviscerating the catwalk. They chanted her name and gave her limitless money and recited odes to her movement, zealous declarations of allegiance and pride. From Vietnam on, wars brought out the love in people, and she knew why. With so much death, people loved all that was left.

Some irritations. The way they talked to her, like they were intimates. "How's the geezer?" a middle-aged man in a brown monastic robe asked her. "Love the cheesecake," said a young Asian woman with purple hair, "but tell your mom parking sucks." Comments on her figure, her wardrobe, what they'd like to cram between those life-preserver lips. But instead of sitting at home eating waffles and watching Saturday morning cooking shows they were with her, shooting the moon, insisting the world could be fixed and that she was the one to do it. Their strident conviction undergirded her days, and she felt her supporters' souls in the cadence of her speeches.

Her staff asked her how she was doing, refreshed her beverage, touched up her mascara. She lied that she was nervous and made a show of leafing through her briefing book, but she'd memorized the responses days ago: insightful, uncanned-sounding answers to every imaginable question. The day was turning hot and her armpits began to water. "Tell me a joke," she said, setting off her staff—a joke, to lighten up, genius!—and they cooked up something entirely inappropriate about Britney Spears and sanitarium conjugal visits and soon she was fake laughing so hard she swallowed her own snot.

When they called her backstage, she went alone. Lumpkin looked ill, contagion cracking his skin, his teeth radioactively clean. "Hello, Joel," she said, "find a place to park the helicopter?"

"We're on wheels today," he grunted back. "Easier on the stomach. Even the best of us can get a little jumpy." But that was complete bull, and both of them knew it; Joel Lumpkin was notorious for his titanium balls, swallowing unholy interest rates and shitting gold bars a month later. Even with his fakery of a campaign on display—no volunteers handed out fliers on his behalf or talked up his positions to undecideds waiting for the bus, his official campaign staff an ad agency with more money than seemed fair—the man was cockstrong and ready to knock heads, pretty good for a guy painted up like a doll.

Leslie Han walked over and said hello, great day for some baseball, his brown suit atoning for its off-the-rack monotony with a crisp press and a carnation pinned to the lapel.

"Ladies and gentlemen, the candidates for mayor of San Francisco," a voice rumbled, and they walked out to their assigned podiums. Over the open plaza San Franciscans squeezed together, screened guests for the first couple hundred folding chairs, reserved seats distributed evenly between candidates, beyond them a field of Robespierre's supporters singing love songs and blowing kisses and pumping placards emblazoned with STOP THE WAR!, noise booming from their mouths. Jasper and Esmerelda sat front-row center, the crooner megastar massaging the neck of the whirlwind superchef, ruffians to royalty in the blink of a decade.

"Good afternoon and welcome to the only debate between San Francisco mayoral candidates," read the political editor with the signature specs, a hardass when the cameras were rolling but one of the best bawdy joke-tellers in town, especially after a couple fingers of bourbon. "Mr. Han, we begin with you."

Robespierre smiled into the camera with all of her candle-power and let her tongue out for a microsecond, just enough to spark subconscious fantasies.

"First I would like to thank the city of San Francisco for coming to support our democracy in action," Leslie Han said. "It's time for a new beginning in San Francisco, and I can provide the leadership necessary to carry the mantle of this great city."

Han's slow-rolling and pinched explanation of generic policy positions filtered out as Robespierre scanned the swelling crowd, spotting staff, colleagues, friends, interns, advisers, classmates, volunteers, community activists, professors, donors, supporters whom she'd never been introduced to but recognized on sight, the citizens who stopped her in the street with intrusive questions. In Lumpkin's seating area, Marat sat between a couple of hired henchmen, behind them mostly vagrants paid to attend, some of them drinking, sleeping, crawling away.

Her cheeks throbbed from the extended display of positivity and she dialed it down from energized to respectful, always a statesman.

" . . . safety for all of our citizens. I ask for your vote." Leslie Han backed away from the microphone to polite clapping, his cheering section buoyed by old ladies and school principals, their applause unfailingly even.

"Mr. Lumpkin," the political editor announced. Joel hulked over the microphone, dominating it, his nostrils pulled back in long ovals, zombie eyes flickering over the crowd, streaks of olive peeking through holes in his face paint.

"Greetings, San Francisco!" he barked. "I won't insult your intelligence with platitudes or foreign policy solutions. I will say that I am uniquely qualified to make the changes this city needs to thrive."

Huge portions of the audience called bullshit, yapped witty

comebacks, waved dismissively, delivered old-fashioned silent-movie bad-guy hisses. The political editor cleared his throat like a power washer and popped the microphone with his fist.

"It's well publicized how I've become financially successful in a short period of time," Joel continued. "I worked hard, used my smarts, and got more than my share of lucky breaks. Don't hate me for it. I grew up a foster kid, fending for my own. I served my country in Iran—"

The noise rose from all corners, spearing toward the stage, generalized anger contorted into insistent respectful applause for the troops.

"—and when I got back, I had business opportunities and I took them. I give back to the community through my foundation, helping thousands of foster kids achieve better lives. I am relentless, and I don't stop fighting until I make things better. That's what I want for this city. No whining, no goddamn excuses—I will give you the city services you deserve while taking as little as possible from your paycheck."

To many of the twelve thousand in the plaza indoctrinated to despise and distrust this insincere corporate apologist, no response was possible other than predetermined derision, booing and jeering laughter and unflattering comparisons to animal excrement. But dead spots hovered over clumps of onlookers, voters equating Lumpkin's straight talk with the dedicated advertiser they knew so well, a guy who didn't seem scared to buck the city's ongoing flirtation with socialism and install some sound business practices. Also, cursing in a debate took balls, and there was never enough of that to go around.

"Supervisor Van Twinkle." The editor nodded at Robespierre. She tucked her shiny black hair behind her ears, curved her back slightly, angled up her face, bunched her lips in a playful pout. A few seconds as the surf of livid San Franciscans pounded in the backbeat, and she launched her fist in the air. "Stop the war!" she yelled.

Delirium. Raucous unchained madness popping out in watery eyes, a wall of sound. Even the viewers occupying dead spots felt their skin surge over their frames, synapses sparking, their rooted disappointment voiced in unanticipated calls of agreement. She spoke for the rest of her allotted time, the words coming but instantly forgotten as shared frustration metastasized across the plaza. Stuck on a dot lost in the west, envied for their hills and sunsets and gastronomy and creativity but ridiculed for their politics, they were tired of the nationwide running joke. For wanting more for themselves and their city, paradise propped up on a fault line. How was humanism such a bad thing? When did love of life turn into treason? Why couldn't imagination conquer the dead?

As they cut to the prearranged break, Joel Lumpkin observed the raw emotion and knew he was almost done for. He waved at Marat and skipped off the stage.

"My money's not there," Marat stated. "I called."

"Tell me," Joel said. One of the bodyguards inserted a gun into Marat's bellybutton.

"Check it out," Marat responded, and nodded at the Lumpkin seating section.

He was walking toward them from the back of the plaza, a tall, dark-haired man surrounded by a platoon of gangsters, flabbier since they'd last seen each other, his hair longer and locked into dreads, but his bratty face just the same and directing a madcap stare at Murphy Ahn, a starved animal locked on lunch.

Reaching into his pocket, Big D couldn't help uncorking a grin, gold-capped teeth wedged in his beak like dominos.

"Give me a fucking phone," Joel said, grabbing the first one presented and calling Switzerland. He whispered long series of numbers. When Big D broke into joyful song, he plugged the phone into Marat's hands.

"The confirmation number," he said. "Call him off."

"I don't have a pen," Marat said, enjoying this too much to end it.

"Fuck you."

"Fine then," Marat said, and hung up calmly, assured that whatever came next would be right.

Midday heavy under the bleeding sun; past, present, future wound into a fragment of space. Troops marched into the light, taking final sips of sweet California air as they dipped into their pants and under their shirts.

Joel Lumpkin knew things looked bad, but a drop of hope still vibrated, his invincibility cloak. He was smarter than all of them, and he'd beaten bloodbaths before.

The phone rang. Marat answered. An accented voice confirmed.

Marat was twenty million dollars richer.

"OK," Marat said, whipping his arms at Big D to stop. They kept coming, bleating screwy laughter, all these guys really wrong in the head and thirsting for Murphy Ahn's bountied skull. "Hey!" he yelled, "green poodle, green poodle!" but they stumbled through the abort code word, eyes yellowed and dim.

A producer hopped down the stairs and told them showtime in thirty seconds, move it.

"Get the helicopter ready," Joel Lumpkin growled. Sweat carved mud banks on his face. "The dirt. Now."

The information in Marat's head, hubris encased in sugar glass. He whispered ten seconds of terrible history into Joel Lumpkin's ear, because Robespierre would have done the same to him.

Then he ran.

"We're back," the political editor announced as Joel Lumpkin returned to his podium. "In this portion of the debate, the candidates will respond to questions submitted by San Francisco residents. Mr. Han, we'll begin with you." As the political editor posed a question comparing school system management to municipal government administration, Joel watched Marat press stacks of bills into the hands of Big D's posse, their gaits slowing, scarred hands jerking away the cash. Their deadened faces sneered at the stage, their bodies jerking erratically.

"—and at the end of the day, what matters is if I can get the job done, if I can make this city a lean, *friendly* machine. Based on my experience with the school system, I've demonstrated that I have the skills to pay the bills. And that's the bottom line."

Leslie Han nodded and drank from his water glass, ignoring the tepid applause. The political editor turned to Robespierre. "Supervisor Van Twinkle," he said, "Jessica Benson from Noe Valley asks: 'After serving on the Board of Supervisors for seven years, how can you continue to justify spending time and resources on international policies that the city isn't qualified to enact or enforce? We don't ask the federal government to pay for our local police force or firefighters, so why should our city government go barging into international affairs?'"

Robespierre turned to the camera, eyes wide open and dizzyingly brown, her mouth circular and hot like a steamed-up jacuzzi. "Excellent question, Jessica," she said, keeping her voice level, easy to trust. "The City of San Francisco has many connections to the federal government, which pays for a great deal of local services, sometimes by funding specific programs, but mostly through block grants to the state, which the state in turn distributes to us. Then they use our services while ignoring our rules. For example, the Presidio is considered federal land, so while they use city resources, our electrical grid, our sewer system, our gas lines, they don't abide by city ordinances and aren't held to the same local laws as the vast majority of San Franciscans who don't live in the Presidio.

"Now, the San Francisco Board of Supervisors isn't Congress. We don't reflect the country as a whole. But we still have a duty to act against things that are wrong. I'm proud to live in a place where hatred isn't tolerated, where the underprivileged are given the help and respect to get back on their feet, where art and music are treasured, where compassion is integral to our lives." She laughed lightly, conveying delight and wonder, presenting a portal to everlasting joy. "Come on," she sprayed, "where else could we have all this?"

Bedlam swarmed her, pandemonium crashing across the stage. "In San Francisco," her voice rose an octave, "when we see our soldiers dying in a war that should never have been started, that is worsening our national security, that is mortgaging our future, that is killing hundreds of thousands of innocent people and forcing good people to do evil things, we have a moral obligation to stand up and declare that it is unacceptable." She threw her arms skyward to evoke victory, her campaign's capstone within reach. "This tragedy has been playing out for over a decade, and it's as wrong now as it ever was. We must stop the war!"

Calls from the backs of throats, zinging whistles, beautiful back-breaking disorganized chaos. Esmerelda squeezed Jasper's hand in the front row; he came back with a dry kiss on her forehead. Onstage, Joel Lumpkin parsed the dirt in his head and Leslie Han clapped politely.

"Mr. Lumpkin," the political editor butted in when the clamor slipped a notch, "your question is from Randy Spiglowski in the Richmond. He asks: 'I've seen your advertisements many times, and I'm impressed by your attitude and appearance. But what do you stand for? Everything I've heard about your positions is rumor, secondhand, or vague. What, specifically, would you do for San Francisco?'"

Murphy Ahn looked over the crowd, gunning for a friendly face to start with but finding only hostility, disgust, in many cases clear-cut malice. "I'm going to make the city transportation system free," he began. "All buses, trains, and cable cars. I'll pay for it by selling ads. I'm going to cut business tax rates to attract the biggest companies from Silicon Valley, which will pay far more in cumulative revenue in the long run to offset the near-term losses. I'm going to knock down dilapidated buildings in Bayview and build state-of-the-art office complexes for these companies to set up shop and rejuvenate the neighborhoods. I'm going to build twenty job training facilities and after-school centers in my first year in office, and triple the police presence in known gang areas, so we can stop the killing and move forward.

I'm going to get the 2028 Summer Olympics in San Francisco so the rest of the world can experience our marvelous way of life. And, in a point very dear to my heart, I am going to create a sexual assault center staffed by the police department and medical professionals to help the victims and families of the most psychologically ravaging crimes." He paused to savor the freshly cut quiet, the slow accumulation of respect. He spotted Big D and Marat passing a pipe back and forth, then glanced over at Jasper Winslow, his marked head shaped like an anvil and oblivious.

"Of great concern to me is a rash of unsolved rapes that occurred in the mid-1990s here in San Francisco. I'll give you an example. Tina Winslow is a handicapped woman who lives in the Excelsior. For years she endured rape and incest from her brother, but was too intimidated to report it."

Esmerelda's felt her husband's hand fidget in her grip, his lungs pulling like a vacuum cleaner. "Honey?" she asked, and saw he was crying.

"These crimes have gone unpunished for decades. I've learned that the criminal is not only at-large, he is among us." He went quiet, foreboding, true: "The rapist is Jasper Winslow."

Voices real and imagined chopped across the plaza:
what?
did he really just say that?
how could he say that?
asshole
liar
fucknut
isn't that Van Twinkle's old man?
the singer, Wolfman or whatever?
heard they found him after Katrina drinking motor oil and snorting Vicodin, a world-class weirdo
damn . . .
. . . what about Robespierre? what did she know what did she do did she cover it up did she obfuscate not tell I can't believe Robespierre

Van Twinkle's remotely involved she's the best politician ever deeply decent strong-willed honest and good no chance she misbehaved but then again maybe maybe possibly can't rule it out you just don't know and it's her father her dad her dad

All eyes swept to Robespierre. Her throat clenched, and there was a pitter-patter in her forehead and some whine in her ears, and the worst thing in the world was happening, her life wrested away by her father, the long-lost pops, the dead man reborn as rock star; in the end he'd ruined her and Tina Winslow and everything but the stupid war in Iran, her only dad did all this.

Calmly she walked off the stage.

"Excuse me!" Leslie Han blurted. "I object! This is neither the time nor place for accusations out of left field! Let's get back on track with the debate!"

Esmerelda turned to her husband. His face was choked and runny, his hand retreated from hers. "Jasper," she said softly as he tugged on his earlobe. She pulled him close and kissed the tears on his sallow jowls, rubbed his bony shoulder.

"Ahhh," he murmured. "Ahhh."

The political editor was standing and saying something, but all eyes were fixated on Robespierre's rapid poker-faced exit. Leslie Han left his podium and put his arm over her shoulder, walking alongside her until they were both off in the wings.

Joel Lumpkin was alone on the stage. Last man standing. As usual. He allowed himself a smirk, close-lipped and masked by his wrenched nose and cosmetic wallpaper. He closed his eyes and listened to the shocked silence of an underdog victory, everyone unsure of what to believe; could this be true?

When he looked back down at the world, the old sow in the front row was up and sidearming objects from her purse: Tic-Tacs, a can of tuna fish, a roll of dimes, fancy-looking scissors, a calculator with oversized buttons, a heating pad, what looked like a light dumbbell. Landing close, around him, slamming against the podium, accompanied by Esmerelda's shouting: "YOU FUCKING DOUCHE BAG LIAR SCUM! YOU SOULLESS

LIFE-SUCKING PIECE OF SHIT! MY LAWYER IS GOING TO
TURN YOUR ASSHOLE INTO A PRISON PARKING LOT!"

Even though it was strategically enervating, Joel couldn't
resist a few small chuckles. Did the stupid ever learn? He smiled
broadly as a team of cops shoved past Big D on their way to
clamp down Esmerelda.

Then Big D putting a gun in a cop's face and pulling and
screaming white noise, a cacophonous rebel yell.

Offstage, Marat hugging his sister and whispering that everything was going to be all right, he was there for her, always, his
only sister, the only one who knew.

Big D and his boys pulling out guns and shooting at everything, cops and trees and TV cameras but mostly at Murphy
Ahn, the shitfucker Octopus traitor hogging the stage, so many
bullets they couldn't miss, a fire hose on a match.

Joel Lumpkin's bodyguards turning heel and skedaddling,
they weren't paid enough for that shit and the man was dead
anyhow, fuck if they were going down with the ship.

The audience racing and shoving and frozen solid, thinking
this is San Francisco this doesn't happen here this isn't real is
this death am I dead where am I?

Murphy Ahn's face an exploding jack-o'-lantern, black burgundy shrapnel over the San Francisco city seal backdrop. Screwed
landless veterans watching the broadcast and cheering it on.

Marat holding his sclerotic sister, absorbing her sobs on his
shoulder.

Leslie Han directing the police toward the shooters, identify-
ing Big D as the ringleader and hurling his cellphone at him,
nailing him in the eye and freezing him long enough for the cops
to get him five times in the gut, his gold-plated incisors catching
on the edge of a metal folding chair as he fell.

Jasper and Esmerelda on the ground, rolling through discarded programs and grass smelling of sulfur and spilled soda.

Police feeding bullets into Big D's crew, every man taken
down from seven angles, then kicked, cuffed, kicked again.

Errant bullets cutting common carotid arteries, lodging in legs, shattering shoulders.

Slicing screams into thick, wet wheezes.

In the back of Robespierre's seating section, Karen Winslow walking Tina's wheelchair carefully toward the subway, ninety-five years old and feeling it, lips buttoned in, barely able to see the sidewalk over Tina's hair bun, pangs of misery hitting like thrown bricks.

Billowing crowd noise when they realized the shooting was probably over and it was safe to make calls, 911 and their mothers and boyfriends to tell them they were safe, this shit was unbelievable, there was death everywhere, and blood, and everything all fucked up, but they were safe they were safe they were alive.

An off-duty radiologist cupping a Van Twinkle volunteer's head as she burbled on about Robespierre, how her heart belonged to Robespierre, flubbing her words with all the blood but still declaring her life for Robespierre's ideals through the heaves until she stopped.

On his knees Leslie Han performing CPR on Big D, his suit jacket stuffed in the gangster's side, pumping hard until Big D sputtered into consciousness, somehow.

Marat Van Twinkle carrying his sister to the paramedics, a scarlet curtain crashing down her face.

Twenty million dollars bubbling in the bank, ready to rebuild.

Esmerelda Van Twinkle crawling on top of her husband and kissing his lips, wiping his nose, telling him she was his forever, prison and Tina didn't matter, the restaurants and record deals didn't matter, he had so much more now, meat on the bones, depth and struggle, you could hear it in his voice, her champion, begging him to hold her while he sobbed apologies to his sister. A final shared moment before accusations and trial testimony tainted the rest of their lives.

Marat sprinting through the war zone, threading the advancing SWAT team to find his parents rolling on the ground; pulling them up and shouldering them through a field of abandoned chairs to huddle under blankets; the Van Twinkle family locked together; united and devastated; guilty and wronged; faces chiseled with the weight of hard-fought years; excruciatingly rich.

The national crucible cooling down, the Republic charred with glorious ideals, and faults.

LIBERTÉ   EGALITÉ   FRATERNITÉ

And with that, France was saved.

Acknowledgments

Thanks to Meredith Norton, Caroline Roberts, and Ben Lorr for their careful reads through early drafts. Their delicate, thorough comments helped deliver this book from screaming infancy into rambunctious semi-adulthood.

Thanks to JJ Schultz and Jamey Graham for their generous technical help, which has made this book so much more than a book.

Thanks to my grandmother Dorothy Stewart for helping me understand how fiction makes life better.

Thanks to my parents, David O. Stewart and Nancy Floreen, for inspiring a lifelong love of words and letting me run down this rabbit hole for years guilt-free.

Thanks to Carrie Dieringer, Anne Horowitz, Tiffany Lee, Charlie Winton, and the rest of the Soft Skull/Counterpoint crew for making this book real.

Thanks to my awesome editor Denise Oswald for her deft touch and immense patience and for generally being a badass motherfucker.

Thanks to my amazing agent Lisa Grubka for making this book so much better and green-lighting all my zany ideas and never giving up.

Thanks to my wife, Karla Zens, for comforting me when I'm high and low and all over the place in between, for her countless reads and brilliant feedback and permanent love. You will always be my first and last reader.